the
WAITING
HOURS

ALSO BY SHANDI MITCHELL

Under This Unbroken Sky

the WAITING HOURS

SHANDI MITCHELL

VIKING

VIKING
an imprint of Penguin Canada, a division of Penguin Random House Canada Limited

Canada • USA • UK • Ireland • Australia • New Zealand • India • South Africa • China

First published 2019

www.penguinrandomhouse.ca

LIBRARY AND ARCHIVES CANADA CATALOGUING IN PUBLICATION

Mitchell, Shandi, author
The waiting hours / Shandi Mitchell.

Issued in print and electronic formats.
ISBN 978-0-14-319900-7 (softcover).—ISBN 978-0-14-319901-4 (electronic)

I. Title.

PR9619.3.H564B66 2019 C813'.6 C2018-904287-7

Cover design: Jennifer Griffiths
Cover images: Jean Ladzinski / Trevillion Images;
Texture © Fox / Unsplash

Printed and bound in Canada

10 9 8 7 6 5 4 3 2 1

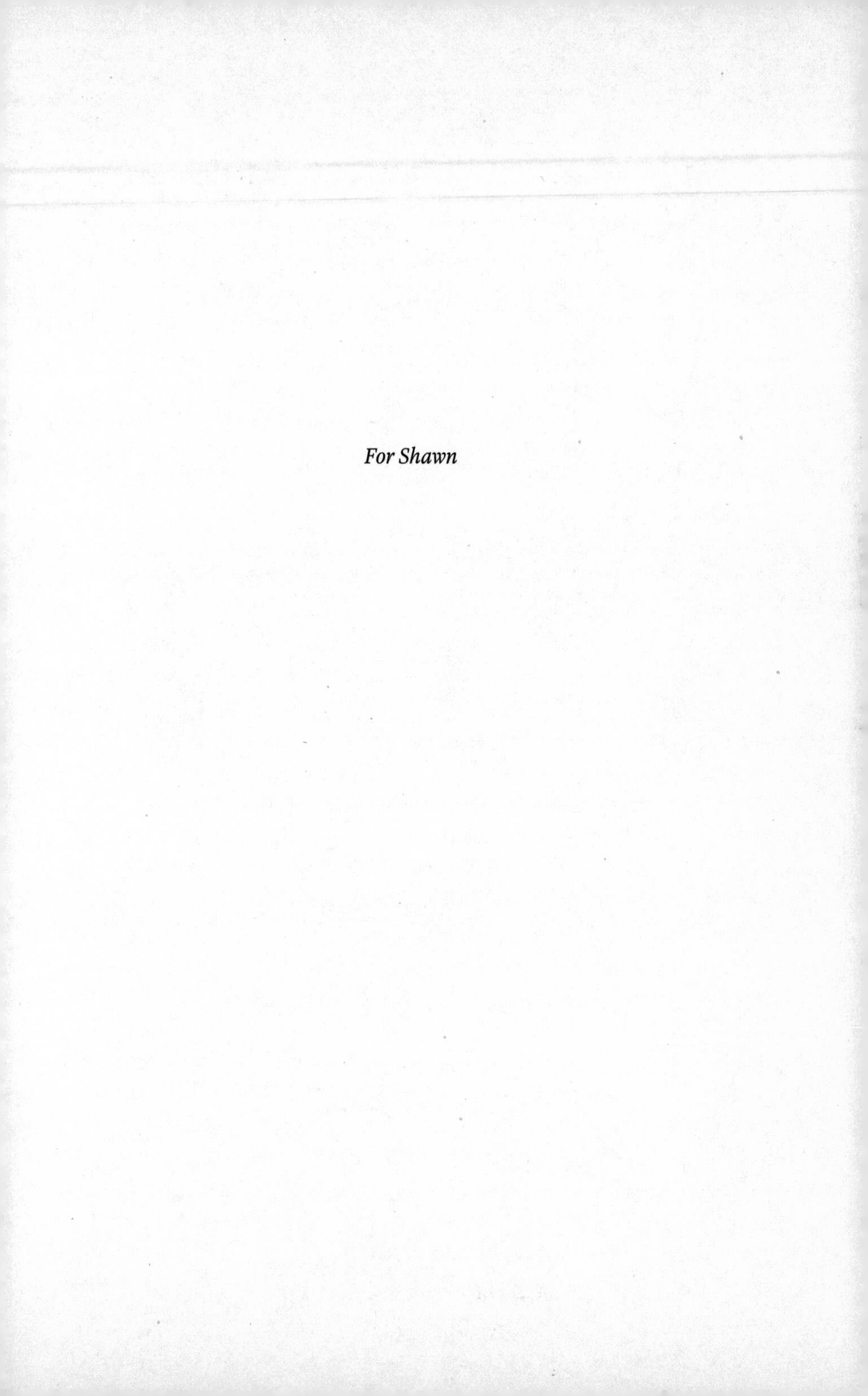

For Shawn

Fear has a smell, as love does.

Margaret Atwood, *Surfacing*

It was hot the day Ruth is said to have died. The kind of hot that makes babies cry, dogs lie belly up, and underwear cling to scrotums and breasts.

Ruth had just finished setting up her flea market table in its regular spot when she realized she had forgotten her patio umbrella. Her stall neighbour, Mr. Poranek, a widower and shameless flirt, hung a blanket to shield her from the searing rays. Several commented on how good she looked under its pink cast, and this pleased Ruth. At sixty-two years of age, she enjoyed being mistaken for a young fifty, and attributed her youthful looks to a regimen of Oil of Olay and Clairol auburn No. 5. She always said a world without hair dye would be a damn ugly world.

The prime selling hours were still ahead and she had already sold two sets of full-length curtains, three teacups, and a rusted bucket with a hole in the bottom for the grand total of fourteen dollars and fifty cents. It was shaping up to be a very good day.

Fellow vendors dropped by to complain about the heat, the cheap bastards haggling for something for nothing, the wholesale merchants undercutting prices, the crooks fencing hot goods giving everyone a bad name, and the *unbelievable* deals to be had at the virgin tables. As they griped and gossiped, they scanned her table for bargains to double their own profits. These were her friends. She couldn't imagine a Sunday without them.

Between the lull of church getting out and the influx of blessed Sunday shoppers, Ruth asked Mr. Poranek to watch her table. She gave him the rundown on her prices and made him repeat the numbers several times until she was confident he could differentiate between the five-dollar and ten-dollar items.

After buying an iced diet pop from the chip wagon, she took the long route back, hunting for deals to triple her profits. That's when she saw, perched on a hamper, the angel. It was the most beautiful angel she had ever seen. Its porcelain face was serene and loving, eyes lowered forgivingly, and arms raised, inviting embrace. Its purple dress shimmered with iridescent sequins. And its wings—its wings were *real* feathers. It must have been two feet tall, and by the looks of the cord draped over the hamper, it could light up. Or maybe, Ruth dared to hope, lift its radiant wings.

Not wanting to appear eager, she forced herself to browse the youthful clothing, DVDs, and candle holders. She sized up the girl with the money pouch and *please-talk-to-me* smile and correctly assessed she was a rookie.

"How much?" she asked.

"Five bucks?"

Ruth heard the question mark and knew she could get it for half the price, but she didn't haggle. She wouldn't tarnish its worth.

"I'll take it."

Setting her pop can on the edge of the table, she fished in her faux crocodile skin purse for a tightly folded bill. Her heart was beating fast. The girl asked if she wanted a bag, but Ruth had already picked up the angel by its slender, perfect waist and was walking away staring into its blue, expressive, hand-painted eyes.

The heat of the parking lot seeped through her thin-soled shoes and the sun burned her scalp and the tip of her nose. Her cheeks and neck flushed. She swayed. The wings *were* articulated, and miniature lights were stitched into the hem of the dress!

"You forgot your drink . . ." the girl called after her.

Ruth turned and the world tilted. The sequins on the angel's dress flashed and haloes bloomed from its magnificent wings and Ruth's fingers dissolved into light.

She thought, Oh my . . . , as the aneurysm on the right side of her temple burst.

Somewhere a man kicked off the bedsheets but did not wake; an infant suckled, a mother hummed; a girl looked up; a bird took flight; a dog caught a ball; a boy held a gun; a mosquito drew blood; a plane lifted off; a car stalled; a toilet flushed; someone laughed, someone wept, someone said hello; someone said goodbye; someone said I love you, je t'aime, 我爱你, Я тебе кохаю, jeg elsker dig, miluji tě, ich liebe dich, Любя те, Սիրում եմ քեզ, حبك, ᓇᒡᓕᒋᕙᒋᑦ, ti amo, I love you, I love you, I love you.

The rest did not.

At the Sunday morning flea market, a man administered CPR; a woman dialed 911; an angel's moulting wing snapped underfoot; and Mr. Poranek sold a pair of curtains for far less than Ruth would have wanted.

1

Kate swung open the jeep's rear gate and was greeted by Zeus's tail thumping against the wire crate. Eager to be released, he stretched and pawed the latch. She made a visual check of her search-and-rescue gear, first aid kits, rations, dog supplies, all-weather kit, boots, and backpack. All that was needed to sustain them for a couple of days. Nothing had shifted. She unhitched the crate door and Zeus waited for her to indicate work or play. She fastened a line to his collar, and his tail hoisted higher. It wasn't work yet.

"Ally-oop," she said.

He jumped from the hatch, his nose to the ground before his hindquarters landed.

"Do your business."

Trailing the line behind him, he headed around the SUV to check out the tires.

Kate scanned the debris field of twisted rebar, concrete slabs, mangled cars, and a collapsing barn. Flames and black smoke churned from a rusted oil drum. The team had done a good job mocking up the scene. It wouldn't be an easy test.

Zeus bumped her fist with his nose.

"Done already?"

He sat and looked up at her.

"You think you need a treat?"

She opened her hand. It was empty. He nudged the other hand. Nothing. He looked to her eyes and breathed her in. He liked this game. Snuffling over her jeans, he focused on her right pocket. His velvety snout brushed her wrists and palm. He was correct. A biscuit had been in that hand and that pocket.

He circled her legs. His nostrils flared, inhaling sharp breaths and snorting out short puffs. He was filtering all that was extraneous to extract the singular scent, separating the air he breathed and the cookie he wanted. He licked his nose, heightening the sensitivity of the million receptors that catalogued his world.

The conditions weren't ideal. In this heat, his nose would dry out quickly. She lightly tapped its wetness. He expelled her scent with a breath and zeroed in on her left ankle. His tail wagged faster. His tail was incapable of lying. His nose bumped her boot top and he sat expectantly, snorting one small woof. She hoisted her pant leg. Ever so gently, his lips tickling her shin, he extracted the biscuit protruding from her hiking boot's cuff. In one crunch, the biscuit was gone.

She looked to the assessment officer overseeing the exercise. It was Riley. Beside him, Heather was serving as designated note taker. His wife was still in basic training with a six-month-old Belgian Malinois that was far too much dog for her to handle. She wasn't a strong trainer. She flustered easily and talked too much. It definitely wasn't her calling. Unlike her husband, who was legendary in the search-and-rescue community.

Riley had a reputation for impossible finds, unwavering calm, and a relentless will. He had been a medic in Iraq until he took IED shrapnel in his chest. He had told Kate about the girl who rode on the back of her father's bicycle and her brother who sat on the handlebars. How he gave the boy a chocolate bar and the girl a pack of gum and how shyly the little girl took it. She wore a poppy-red dress and matching velvet shawl embossed with full-blown roses stitched with golden thread. He showed the little girl how to blow a bubble. It was large and pink, and her eyes widened when it popped.

In the camouflage of night, when she couldn't see his face, he had told her about the sound an IED makes five hundred feet away, detonating in the trunk of a car. How the pressure drops as the concussion kicks your chest, and the air is sucked from your lungs. And the silence. The depth of silence, right after, and the fall-on-your-knees beauty of white smoke against a robin's-egg sky. He told her how hot the parts of a bicycle get when it has been incinerated . . . and the weight of what remains of a poppy-red child. He told her this as her fingers traced rose-petal scars on his bare chest. Zeus looked up the leash. He felt her tension in the line. She smiled and loosened her hold. All's good.

She watched Riley and practised not caring. He was a good-looking man and tough. During SAR's brutal three-day winter survival certification, he broke his ankle less than half a mile from course completion. He wanted to keep going, and she didn't doubt he would have crawled to the finish line if they had let him. As it was, he had to run the course again the following winter. He set a new record.

Every team member was loyal to him, and every handler aspired to reach the mastery of Riley and his beloved Belgian, Annabelle. Despite the pressure to get another pup before she died, he refused. They say he was with her at the end. They don't know he injected the needle. Kate understood why he couldn't get another dog. He had been with Annabelle for ten years. Four years longer than his wife. She had never seen him interact with his wife's unruly pup. Kate looked to Zeus. She couldn't imagine bringing home another dog.

Riley's arm shot up in the air. It was time.

She grabbed Zeus's working vest from the truck and he fell in tight against her leg, assuming the heel position. She slipped the stiff Kevlar vest over his back and secured the straps across his belly and broad chest. She completed the task in under thirty seconds. No talking. No dallying. This was work. She strode to the edge of the field. She had trained Zeus for both tracking and air scent. He could alert for cadaver or survivor. It gave him versatility as a search-and-rescue dog. They had never failed a certification test.

Near the burn barrel, Chris and Jake were sitting at the pump truck monitoring the fire. It was twenty-eight Celsius and they were wearing black T-shirts, turnout pants, and boots. The fire boys could have been posing for a calendar. She wondered who the volunteer victim was this week. There were three other dogs running. A German shepherd had already failed with an off-course. She was the only civilian without military training attempting qualifications today. Riley nodded and his arm dropped.

She leaned over and patted Zeus's lean, muscular side.

"Find live," she said and unleashed his lead.

Zeus bolted forward. He huffed the air, making quick tight loops over the drought-stricken grass. He swept the open field in a grid pattern. In this stagnant heat, he would be working the updrafts. She kept pace behind him. He ignored the pumper truck crew, but she noticed the bob of his nose indicating their presence and his dismissal, as though he knew it was too easy. He kept course, not slowing or veering around the billowing smoke. She tasted gasoline and wood at the back of her throat.

His head swung back and forth, his body leaned in, and his ears perked forward. His nose popped up. He was on a scent and she jogged to keep up. Her muscles responded with the easy lope of her daily two-mile runs. It was more than a scent he was following. A scent was the past, a memory. He was gathering a story assembled through pheromones, skin cells, follicles, bruised grass, snapped twigs, and the molecular compositions of man-made scents—the traces left behind.

If he were trailing an animal, he would know the species, gender, and social order, alpha or follower. He'd be able to discern what paths it travelled, the food it ate, and whether it was friend, foe, or prey. Presumably, with a human he could smell the cheapness of their shoes, the sourness of their pants, the soap used, the scrape of a knee, nicotine on fingers, alcohol in pores, and the cancer in their bones. He could smell fear. And death. And weakness. He could smell narrative. She often wondered if he knew the outcome before he reached the ending.

His ears twitched and she noticed the slight rotation of his head, widening his peripheral scope. He was working the scent cone, intent on his directive to find "live." With a sharp bark, a thrust of his nose, and a sit, he indicated the objects on the ground as possible clues. She marked a sock, a glove, a ball—his eyes watched hers: *this might be something.* "Good boy," she said.

His path oscillated and the cone of his track narrowed. He zeroed in on the debris pile. Pacing the base of the massive, upturned cement blocks, he looked for a pathway up and leapt. His hind legs clawed, his hocks knocked concrete, and he scrambled up and over. Kate's knee clunked the ragged edge.

Zeus nimbly treaded the twisted rebar, tangled wires, and large rocks that had been heaved up onto the loose boards and plywood sheets. Kate noted the clothing strewn about to condition her emotional fortitude—a pink floral dress, a plaid shirt, and a baby's shoe. Zeus hopped over slabs driving upward to the ragged peak. The structure was more solid than it appeared.

Kate was huffing. Her trail pants were damp and her long-sleeved shirt stuck to her chest. Her feet were broiling in her boots. Slung at her waist, two water bottles slapped bruises on her thigh. She smelled suntan lotion and body odour. Her lips were already dry. Zeus poked his nose into a crevice and inhaled. She watched his ears and tail. There was nothing here.

The rescue organization she got him from had named him Zeus. He was from a litter of eleven found duct-taped in a box and left in a dumpster. Three had died. He had a border-collie brain and physique but his coat had the curl and wave of a spaniel's. He was all black. His sleek racing body and spindly legs culminated in powerful haunches and a plumed, ever-alert tail. A black dog in the afternoon sun. He was panting.

It had been her weekly routine to walk through the pens of quivering and yapping adoption candidates looking for something extraordinary in their eyes. Zeus was the most inquisitive, fearless, and confident of the litter. As the staff recounted the pups' brief, sad history, she had surreptitiously run her own tests. Tests that gauged fear, drive, aggression, intelligence, curiosity, frustration—all gently concealed in the guise of belly rubs, head pats, and her fingers dancing across the floor. Commands designed as play. When the other pups had tired of her, Zeus remained, wanting more. It had taken only three hand gestures to teach him to sit, before he offered the behaviour unasked.

That was five years ago. Together, they'd had four live finds and three cadavers. They were catching up to Riley and Annabelle's record. Kate stumbled and grabbed for a jutting metal rod. A cold-hot sliced through her leather glove. Zeus's head turned, but she kept moving forward.

Focus, she berated herself. Zeus trotted across a narrow plank, stopping at a fractured opening. His nostrils flared. He bowed and leaned into its space.

"Wait."

Kneeling, she shone her flashlight into the hollow, checking the ceiling and walls for stability, and gave the all-clear. He belly-crawled down the incline. She suppressed the urge to call him back to her safety. She had raised him to be tough physically and mentally, able to withstand gruelling conditions: heat, sound, and ever-varying stimuli. It was the handlers who were the most difficult to train. Choosing to trust their own meagre senses over their dog's acuity, thus missing obvious communications because of emotion, fear, ego, and fatigue. In the field, these mistakes could cost a life.

She kept her flashlight trained on Zeus. Several mattresses and pallets were propped against the low, bunkered walls. He paused, considering the cross breezes. Honing in on a mattress in the corner, he bowed and barked his deepest voice. Loud. Strong. Certain. A hand emerged. Zeus's backside swayed with joy. The mattress jostled aside, and seventeen-year-old Ben's grinning, sweat-drenched face appeared. Riley's son from his first marriage. He had his father's eyes. Kate raised her fist.

Found!

Zeus bounded up the makeshift ramp and slammed against her chest. He pranced on her lap, his hot tongue licking her cheeks. She rewarded him with his favourite toy, a ball with a tether rope. She tugged and the ball squeaked, squeaked, squeaked. She wrapped her arms around his squirming body and held on longer than he needed.

"Good boy," she said.

She pulled off her glove. Blood seeped from her palm and dripped down her fingers. She reached for his water bottle. Only then did she feel the pinch of pain.

In her pocket, her phone vibrated. She checked the number and wondered why the hospital was calling.

2

"911. What is your emergency?"

Tamara limbered her neck, rooted her feet, and settled into her ergonomic chair. Her hands hovered over the keyboard.

"Ma'am, you need to calm down. I can't understand you. 52 Sycamore Road. Are your doors locked?" Her fingers clattered across the keys, filling the requisite fields on the screen before her.

"Did you see the gun?"

She glanced at the monitor to her right. A map of the area and corresponding available units zoomed to the foreground. She tapped the screen and it telescoped closer. Her eyes mapped the route—left off Glendale, first right onto Maple, left onto Sycamore . . . the nearest car was three minutes away.

"Ma'am, what's your name? Denise what?"

She typed in the name. To her left, Denise's profile opened on the third monitor: seven domestic calls in twelve months; two children, aged five and eight; restraining order against the husband. The woman screamed at someone to shut off the TV.

"Denise, talk to me."

Tamara leaned forward and listened intently to the background noise. She could hear children crying. The caller's voice, nearing hysteria, cut in and out.

"Denise, are your children with you? Keep them away from the windows. Have them sit on the floor."

The woman yelled at the kids to SIT DOWN. Tamara nudged the headset from her ear, then slid it back.

"Denise, I need you to stay calm. Can you do that for me? Is he parked out front?"

She typed in the Who, What, When, Where, How. Never the Why. She wasn't interested in the Why. She nodded impatiently as the caller conveyed the Why.

"Denise, what's his name? Jamie."

She clicked the husband's link under Denise's profile and scanned the particulars as she typed.

> 1:35 a.m. Domestic in progress. Restraining order. 52 Sycamore Road. Suspect James (Jamie) McIntyre. 5'9" 140 lb. Blue pickup truck. Complainant ex-wife, Denise. Says he's been drinking. Possibly armed. Weapon registered. Semi-automatic Winchester .308. Children in house. Aged 8 and 5.

She pressed the Send button and craned to peer over her monitors to the adjacent cubicle. Colleen, on dispatch, sat up straighter. Message received. Tamara half listened to the relay: "All units in the vicinity of 52 Sycamore Road. Domestic in progress. Possibly armed . . ." This was the kind of call that could go bad fast.

Her intake file scrolled to the top of the screen, taking priority above other active calls-in-progress. With the push of a button, her words were now streaming on the sidebars of every call-taker, dispatcher, supervisor, and on-duty police vehicle. The markers for car 245 and car 322 attached to her file. She looked at the map. The corresponding GPS tracking blips were converging on her quadrant.

"Denise, the police are on the way. Is he still in the vehicle? Stay inside. No, I won't hang up. They'll be there soon. Tell me your children's names."

She tilted her head to better catch the woman's spilling words and visualized the unfolding scene. She imagined an anonymous suburban house tastefully decorated, betraying none of the chaos inside. The polished voice was strident and struggling to maintain composure, but still enunciating. The woman was educated and her job required manners. Retail or perhaps business. Appearances would matter. Blonde, shoulder-length hair. Professional but approachable. She would dress younger than her age, especially since the divorce. Crouched behind the sofa. Barefoot. Mascara running.

"Denise, the police will be there any moment."

Tamara's voice was calm, her register soothing. She coaxed the caller to stay with her. Stay connected. Stay alive.

She wasn't supposed to imagine the scene. She was supposed to keep the phone between her and the calls. Stay detached and unaffected. She had been extensively trained to remain objective, uninvolved, and efficient. She excelled at multi-tasking, crisis management, problem solving, communication, and risk assessment. With fourteen years on the job, she was considered a senior member. But there were others who had been there longer. Bob had twenty-three years and Wendy, twenty-one.

"Do you hear the sirens, Denise? They're just around the corner."

Car 322 would arrive first. It was making the turn at Maple. Soon, Tamara would no longer be part of this story. Taking a call was like reading the first chapter of a book and then having it snatched away. Occasionally, she would pull up the police reports to see how it ended, but not often. Most times it was better not to know. Sometimes, though, the story ended while the caller was still on the line.

No amount of experience or training could help on the bad days. When the worst happened, someone would be available to talk you down. Supervisors constantly checked in, and there were professional crisis teams trained to debrief and decompress emotional trauma. There was a quiet room where you could close the door, and on a table, beside a fake leather chair, was a full box of Kleenex.

"The police are going to help you now, Denise. Stay in the house until they come to get you, okay? Yes, you can hang up now if you want or I can stay with you."

The line went dead.

Tamara removed her headset and slung it onto her neck. She rolled back her chair, pivoted around, stretched her legs, and took stock of the snack carousel's inventory: jelly beans, chocolate bars, oranges, apples, chips—nothing that appealed to her. In five hours, her twelve-hour night shift would be over. Six p.m. to six a.m. Two days, two nights, three days off. It was a good schedule.

She yawned and isolated the room's one-sided conversations: the neutral reassurances of the call-takers, the staccato of police dispatch, and the silent waiting of fire. There were fifteen dispatchers and call-takers on shift tonight. The sounds lulled into a soft cooing.

She gazed at the grey concrete walls, security-coded steel doors, fluorescent lighting, and bowed heads of her co-workers communing with their monitors, and out to the triple-glazed windows that showed only that it was night. She rarely noticed the outside world, unless the weather pertained to the emergency. She gauged the passage of time more by the patterns and cycles of incoming calls.

Intake volumes increased with weekends, holidays, daylight savings, and the full moon. Day shift clocked morning rush-hour accidents, after-lunch DUIs, mid-afternoon B&Es, and after-school vandalism-shoplifting-nuisance complaints. Evening rush-hour accidents led into supper-hour domestics.

Night shift clocked drug busts, prostitution, robberies, public intoxication, mentally unstables, and the regulars, dubbed the Lonelies. Once the bars closed, assaults rose, followed by a sharp spike in domestics, and an hour after that, DUIs, these ones often the most lethal and catastrophic—yet rarely fatal for the drunk drivers. Midnight to three brought kitchen fires, overdoses, and the attempted and achieved suicides. And finally, between the twilight of three and six, came the Waiting Hours.

These were the longest hours when everyone hoped there wouldn't be a call, because a call then would mean something had gone very bad. If the phone didn't ring, it meant people were just living their lives.

The air conditioner droned. She wished someone would tell a joke, something particularly dark and inappropriate. Outsiders would call their humour ghoulish, but laughter kept them from being sucked into the other end of the line. They never joked about legitimate, life-altering calls. Their bile was reserved for drunk drivers, the stupid, and those who wasted their time.

She stood and stretched her back. No other call-takers were waiting. Waiting was a strange empty place. Plugged into the console, tethered by the headset's umbilical cord, active but standing by as emergencies whirled around you. She once thought of the act of waiting as passive, but she now knew it was active. She chose a bottle of water from the carousel. This was just a pause.

There were times when the calls unnaturally stopped and everyone was forced to wait. That's when the room's mood became brittle. People paced more and complained more. The coffee was bitter, the snack bar lacking, the chair too high, too low, the headset too tight, the room too cold, too warm . . . Some tried to read, but their pages didn't turn. Some fired emails to each other, though their stations were a mere arm's length apart. *Pizza?* Others stared at their monitors waiting for something, anything, to move. Inevitably, someone would say, *Are the phones working?*

You never commented on it being qu*et. Qu*et was a taboo word. You could say it was a good day or a good night. But to invoke the Q word guaranteed all hell breaking loose. Q periods always broke eventually, and when they did, the monitors would light up and it was always bad.

Tamara sat back down, flexed her ankles, and worked on lowering her shoulders. She wondered if Robert would call. Robert was a Lonely. He called in often to report his impending suicide. The frequency of his calls increased with bad weather. When someone like Robert's ID came up, the room groaned. Call-takers would ask to trade. They had all traded at one time or another.

Hello, Robert. How are you tonight?

I'm going to kill myself.

Where are you, Robert?

I've been waiting for my bus for over an hour and it's friggin' cold. I'm done. I'm doin' it this time.

Are you at the bus terminal, Robert?

That's what the GD lying sign says!

I'm going to send an officer to check on you. You'll be there?

Where the hell else am I . . . ? My bus is comin', gotta go—

Robert hadn't called in a long time, not since late last winter. She liked Robert. He kept his calls brief. She hoped he hadn't killed himself.

She put her headset on and swung her chair around. She couldn't actually say she had heard the atonal buzz of the incoming call. The sound was now as deeply a part of her unconscious as her own heart's murmur.

"911. What is your emergency?"

3

Mike was the first officer on the scene. He shut off his siren and lights on approach and parked tight to the curb, ten feet behind the blue half-ton. Licence plate MJD 4MB.

Car 245 lurched to an abrupt stop behind his cruiser and he signalled to shut off the lights sweeping the neighbourhood red and blue. He wanted stressors minimized. Constable Peterson assumed the right flank, passenger side, to cover him. Neither officer spoke. They knew the protocol. As lead officer, it was his walk to the vehicle.

He took inventory of the middle-class suburban houses. The street was empty and lights were on in the complainant's home. In the vehicle was a lone male. Mike unstrapped his gun and Taser holsters. Stay alert, stay alive.

His constricting bulletproof vest chafed his armpits. With each step in tight boots, his walkie slapped hard against his thigh, and his utility belt strained his back muscles. He should have hoisted it higher on his hips.

It was a routine check, but they all knew domestic disturbances were never routine. Domestics and mentally unstables could go bad fast. He slowed and raised his flashlight with his non-weapon hand. Light swept over the pickup's box. It was empty. Reflected in the side-view mirror, he could see the man. What was the name? James, Jamie. The man's head was down and his window was lowered.

Mike was sweating under his vest and shirt. It was the middle of the night and it was still too damn hot. He stopped short of the driver's door. He couldn't see the man's hands.

"Hi," he said. "Are you Jamie?"

The man's head barely turned. Stubble shadowed his cheek. Caucasian, brown hair, medium build, black T-shirt, tattoo on his left bicep, partially obscured by his short sleeve. It could be a portrait. The man bowed his head again. His shoulders hunched.

"I'm Officer Brandt," Mike said. "How're you doing tonight?"

"I just want to see my kids." Alcohol, sweet and sickly, seeped from the man's pores.

"It's pretty late to see your kids. They should be in bed by now."

The man's shoulder flinched.

"You been drinking, Jamie?" His tone shifted, requiring an answer. "Jamie, have you been drinking?"

"Had a few."

"That doesn't usually help things, does it?"

The man's head dropped lower.

"Jamie, I'd like to talk to you about what's been going on, see if we can get you some help. You haven't done anything wrong yet, so we can still sort this out." His voice was calm, friendly, and in charge. His fingers loosened and tightened around the flashlight flooding the truck's cab. "Jamie, I need you to put your hands on the steering wheel where I can see them."

The man remained motionless.

"Jamie, put your hands on the wheel."

He glanced to the rear of the truck. Peterson had his weapon drawn with both hands on the grip and the barrel pointed to the pavement in a low ready. Mike shook his head.

"I can't," the man slurred. He said something else.

"I didn't hear that, Jamie. You have to speak up."

"I got a gun."

He said "gun" as though it were a small child that he didn't want to wake. Mike leaned forward, and in the side mirror he could see the man's chin resting on the barrel.

"Okay," he said. "It's good you told me."

He leaned back, so he wouldn't be seen miming a gun under his chin. Peterson mouthed "fuck" and took a step out to widen his view of the cab.

Mike became calmer. His back pain disappeared. His feet didn't hurt. He wasn't hot. He unholstered his weapon and held it loose against his leg. The world sharpened to just him and the man. He stepped forward until he could see him in the mirror. The man's eyes were darting back and forth, looking for something to focus on, something on the dash that would make sense.

He spoke to the man as though he was a friend. "Jamie, you can put the gun down."

"I can't."

"You don't want to do this here. Your kids will never get over that. You don't want to do that to your kids, do you, Jamie?"

"No." The word was soaked in phlegm.

Mike took this as a good sign. The man was talking. He wasn't committed. He was still listening. "You love your kids, right?"

"Yes." The word squeezed from his guts and tore at his throat.

"I know that. You just want to see them and things haven't been good lately. But this isn't going to help."

The man's shoulders shuddered.

"This is just one bad day. You can have a thousand good ones once you get past this one."

The man was crying.

"So let's do the right thing here. All you have to do is set the gun down on the seat beside you. I'll talk you through it, so we all know what everybody's doing. Okay?" He didn't wait for agreement. "Take your left hand and slowly extend it out the window."

The man's breathing became more rapid. His forearm twitched.

"You can do this, Jamie." Don't lose him now. "You can do this for your kids. They need their father. I know you're a good man," he lied. "It's just a bad day."

"I'm a good man," he slurred. His thumb slid from the trigger and he stretched his arm out the window. Mike took half a step back. The arm was trembling. The fingers were stained with nicotine. He was still wearing his wedding ring. Tattooed on his bicep was a monochrome portrait of a baby and a little girl wrapped in thorny tendrils. *Ryan* and *Sofia*.

"That's good, Jamie. Now, I want you to lay the rifle on the seat beside you. Barrel towards the passenger side. Real slow. That's it."

He took a step forward. Booze and defeat wafted from the car. "Good. Set it down gently and let it go. Now bring your hand to the steering wheel. You're doing real good, Jamie."

This is when it could all go bad. That moment of choice when panic and despair could kick in. This was when Mike had to hold on tight and not let the man see the moment.

"Now I'm gonna open the door real slow and you're going to step out." He lifted the handle and the latch clicked. He eased the door open wide. He didn't want to startle the man. He was aware of the smooth quiet of his voice.

"Keep this hand up. Good. Now bring your other hand out and keep them both in front of you. Now you're going to step out of the truck. Go ahead."

The man stepped out of the truck and turned towards Mike. Blinking in the light, he had a face that looked like someone you'd want to have a beer with.

"For officer safety I'm going to ask you to put your hands behind your back."

The man complied, and Mike holstered his weapon and slipped the cuffs on his wrists. He nodded to Peterson, who opened the passenger door and retrieved the rifle and a box of ammo. He ejected two hollow-points. Son of a bitch had wanted maximum damage.

"You did the right thing, Jamie." He patted the man down, thoroughly and efficiently, not bothering to put on his gloves.

The man spoke to the pavement. "I just wanted her to see me. That's all I ever wanted."

"I know. But this didn't help things, did it? You've had too much to drink tonight, so we're going to take you in. Do you understand? We want everyone to be safe tonight."

He guided the man, the man whose name was—Mike searched for it—Jamie, to the car. It wasn't his place to judge. He didn't know their stories. He didn't know who they were outside of this moment. He saw people on their worst days. The only thing he knew was that by the time he got back from the holding cells, the paperwork for this call would take him to the end of shift. The worst thing about this job was the paperwork.

His lower back throbbed. He was acutely aware of his belt riding low on his spine and his inability to adjust it while restraining the man. And his feet were aching again. And it was hot, too hot for the middle of the night. And he had to take a leak, which wasn't going to happen any time soon. And neither was stopping for a coffee. The stench of the man was churning his stomach. Even with the windows down, he wouldn't get the smell out of his car for hours.

He looked to the woman in the doorway talking to Peterson. Blonde, five six, 125, mid-thirties. Blue housecoat. Bare feet. Mascara-stained cheeks.

At the living room window, a small girl peered through the curtains. Long brown hair. Six or seven years old. Pink nightie. The tattoo was a good likeness. What was the girl's name?

The man wrenched sideways, teeth bared. "Do you see me now, bitch?" he yelled. "*You see what you've done to me!*"

Mike twisted the cuffs, placed his hand firmly on the perp's neck, and shoved.

4

Kate took a sip of cold coffee and immediately regretted it. She checked her watch, another mistake. There were still two hours remaining until shift end. The patient board was almost clear. Most had been discharged, or were awaiting admission, and walk-ins didn't come to emergency at this hour. The Waiting Hours had begun.

The nurses' stations had settled into the endurance segment of the night. Conversation and gossip had dissipated an hour ago. Exhausting the litany of kid trouble, husband trouble, restaurant recommendations, rumoured liaisons with hound dog paramedics, and the ever popular, boundless gripes about the ineptitude of the latest batch of baby nurses. The old adage of nurses eating their young had been proudly upheld.

For the entertainment portion of the evening, patient stories had been swapped and notes compared. The grosser the story, the higher its value. The most shocking were destined to become classics. The best revolved around excretions and secretions, specimens brought in household containers, and inventories of stomach contents, which all contributed to their growing list of foods to be avoided.

Kate personally hadn't eaten Chinese food for three months after a patient vomited during chest compressions. She also didn't eat leftovers stored in plastic containers, unless they were the red, festive kind. She had never seen a patient bring in a holiday container, but dreaded the day when it would happen.

They told terrible stories about horrific deaths, devastating maimings, and grotesque indignities involving body parts and orifices, which made them laugh until their eyes teared and their stomachs hurt from spasms. Laughter was the most defiant and life-affirming thing they could think to do when they couldn't do anything else.

At this time of night, most of the nurses were huddled in the cocoon of their stations, ringed by the closed doors leading to their patients' rooms. They watched EKGs blip past, checked on blood results, and slipped in charting codes to warn and amuse. *ATD*—acute Tylenol deficiency. *DFO*—drunk and fell over. *JPS*—just plain stupid. *TMB*—too many birthdays. Fluorescent lights hummed, monitors beeped, IVs pumped, and vital machines alarmed. These were all good sounds that said "alive."

She had two frequent flyers—one in heart failure and a diabetic with a renal infection. She had paged and re-paged the appropriate specialists hours ago, but both patients were stable and therefore low priority. Hospitals had no capacity for slow deaths.

Buzzers sounded for rooms 27 and 6. They weren't hers. At this hour, it would be patients needing to urinate, needing reassurance, needing someone to remind them that they hadn't been forgotten. The majority of her charges had gone home with a few cosmetic stitches, IV hydration, blood work recommending follow-up, a rapid heartbeat recalibrated with meds, two broken toes splinted . . . garden-variety cuts, bumps, and bruises. Fortunately, they had all been grateful patients and families. It shouldn't matter, but it did.

There had only been one emergency, Motorcycle versus Pavement. The twenty-eight-year-old male had road rash from shoulder to hip. The gravel she tweezed from his flayed elbow and torso half filled a kidney dish and dinged against the metal pan like hail. He was conscious and chatty while they worked on him, and didn't flinch when she scoured his ragged flesh with a scrubbie and iodine. He had applied the tourniquet around his thigh himself. It was brittle, army-issued rubber tubing, a talisman from two tours in Afghanistan that he still carried in his front pocket for luck.

Tattooed on his upper calf was a helmet atop a rifle propped upright in a pair of military boots. Bones piercing the skin obliterated the name and date. En route to the operating room, he thanked them for taking care of him and told her she had beautiful eyes.

Kate stood and stretched. Her scrubs smelled stale and antiseptic. Her skin was dry from the air conditioning and she was cold. Her core body temperature had dropped and her hypothalamus was fighting to regulate her sleep-wake cycle. She put on her sweater and took a walk to stimulate her circulation.

The outer corridor was stark bright, washed in a sickly yellow light. She paused in front of the windows overlooking the parking lot. It was dark. There was too much glare to see if the sky was brightening. In the reflection, a petite blonde-haired woman with a short, severe ponytail, blue sweater, and scrubs stared back at her. Kate looked tired.

Farther down the corridor, a.k.a. the boarding room, two elderly patients slept on stretchers waiting for admittance. They didn't belong in ER and the hospital didn't want them. The system was jammed from budget cuts, bed shortages, and political standoffs as to where they should go to die. The hallway was their purgatory. Their accompanying paramedics, unable to sign off until their charges were admitted, were playing games on their mobiles. They didn't look up. She gave the ER entrance a wide berth, so as not to trigger the sliding doors. On the other side of the glass wall, beyond triage, a handful of long-haul walk-ins were sprawled on the tattered vinyl waiting room chairs. Some were curled up with their heads hidden beneath thin hospital sheets, breathing in germs. Others stared blankly at the mute overhead TV screens.

She recognized two as "treat 'em and street 'ems" who dropped by a couple of times a month to plead for pain meds. Antipsychotics and opiates brought a good price on the street. They had been in the waiting room when her shift started ten hours ago. It appeared, by the dried blood under his nose, one had been in a fight. So long as they didn't cause a commotion, security allowed them to sit in the air-conditioned room with free TV and Wi-Fi. Come dawn, they would accept defeat and wander back out to the street. She had to admire their self-control, determination, and deluded will in this one aspect of their life.

Kate smiled at the security officer tucked in the corner, who was fixated on a bank of monitors. Black-and-white images of the parking lot, hallways, waiting rooms, and corridors dissected the screens.

"No movement," John said.

He was young, a wannabe cop who couldn't pass the physicals. He cropped his hair military short. His skin was pasty, and there were dark circles under his eyes. He was struggling with night shifts.

She leaned over his shoulder and quickly located her vehicle. Zeus was asleep, exhausted from the day's accomplishment. She had walked and watered him on her first break, and now he'd sleep through the night. The windows were open a crack and a vent-lock propped up the back hatch for ventilation. Lately, there had been multiple news stories of dogs left unattended in suffocating vehicles. She had already treated one Good Samaritan who suffered extensive bites when he'd smashed the window of a running, air-conditioned car. The Doberman didn't think it was being rescued.

When she switched to days, Zeus would stay with his sitter, Sara, and her dog, Max, fellow SAR members. He'd spend his days going on walks, chasing balls, and sleeping on the couch in front of a fan. Whenever she dropped him off, her heart tightened a little with envy and regret, and also a slight pang that he could be happy with someone else.

She and John stared at the image of her vehicle, locked in its hypnotic stillness.

"Thanks," she said.

He nodded and his eyes scanned the static images clockwise then counter-clockwise. She loved the emerg department. They took care of each other. After eight years, she was one of its veterans. As a contract employee, she had the perfect arrangement that accommodated her training and SAR calls. The charge nurse was always trying to rope her in for extra shifts, and every few months she was courted for a full-time position, but she preferred the flexibility. Still, it was nice to be appreciated.

The screens flickered through the various cameras. The corridor around the corner from where she was standing popped up on screen. A police officer was leaning with his back against the wall. They didn't sit like the paramedics. If she took a step forward, he would turn to assess her. On duty, he wouldn't smile.

He was stationed outside the isolation room, guarding one of her patients who wasn't really a patient. He was a domestic brought in handcuffed, awaiting a psych consult. The guy had been restrained on the gurney after refusing to settle down. It was almost time for her to check on him again.

Her thumb worried the antiseptic pad taped to her palm. The thin slash across her lifeline wasn't deep enough for stitches, but the pain cut sharp. It would remind her to stay focused on the terrain next time. She opened her hand wide, so the wound wouldn't heal tight. Her watch beeped. She headed back to the enclave of her station.

Her heels were tender. The last time she went in to pull blood, the domestic hadn't paid much attention to her apart from the usual vitriol of curses. He cried the entire time she was in the room. A portrait of two children was tattooed on his left arm. She wasn't gentle taking his blood and used the strongest adhesive tape to affix the cotton ball. Before leaving, she covered him with a warm sheet.

By the stench, his blood alcohol level would be significant. The nurse's pool had him at .19. She had guessed higher. The pot was at twenty bucks, and she felt her odds were good. He had been flagged high risk for self-harm, but psych beds were more rare than geriatrics. He wouldn't be admitted until morning for a seventy-two-hour observation. The officer who'd brought him in was excellent at calming him down. He made the need for restraints sound like a gift and a privilege. One would have thought he really cared about the guy's well-being.

The hum and beep of the emergency department warmed her. Bed 27 had thrown up. The timid newbie on her first shift was heading in with a kidney pan. The kid had literally been given every shitty job tonight. She'd toughen up, though. She was smart. She had already made it past the maximum hour they wagered she would crack.

Kate called up to the eighth floor. It took five rings for the duty nurse to pick up, which irritated her. It irritated her more when she had to identify herself as daughter. "No change" was the answer, and the nurse on the end of the line went silent. Despite assurances that she could call any time, the implicit tone was *Don't.* Kate didn't like her.

Gratefully, no one on this shift was working when her mother had been brought in. Her colleagues would have felt obliged to awkwardly comfort her and suggest compassionate leave. They'd second-guess her ability to do her job and would surreptitiously look in on her patients. There was nothing she could do on the eighth floor. Here she could still do something. She checked the computer records. The tests were in. The blood alcohol level was .23.

"Pay up, my lovelies."

A collective groan greeted her. A couple of sore losers headed to her computer to verify the results. She grabbed a warm sheet for the domestic and held it tight to her chest. Heat bloomed over her heart. The paramedics would be stopping by soon with fresh coffees. She took a sip from her cup and regretted it immediately.

5

The clear blue sky was nauseating in its intensity. Tamara focused on the parking lot and withered patch of grass sprouting by the red picnic table that only smokers used. Her ears struggled to adjust to the sudden expansiveness of sound unbound by cement walls and white noise. The smells of warming pavement, parched grass, and gasoline churned. She felt dizzy.

Bluebird Taxi pulled up to the curb. She had called fifteen minutes before, ensuring he would be there, but it was an unnecessary precaution. He was the same driver who'd dropped her off last night and whom she had been requesting these past few weeks. It worried her that she was relying on one driver. Not many people had shifts longer than hers, but cabbies were the exception. Studies proved sleep deprivation correlated to diminished reaction times, but she assumed there were safety checks in place and that he went home to sleep. At any rate, he never appeared to be compromised by fatigue.

"Good morning," said the driver. "Which way you wish to go today?"

As always, the car was cool, clean, and quiet. The ID badge pinned over the visor said his name was Hassan. He might have been in his sixties or he could be an older-looking fifty. Regardless of the season, he always wore a cardigan over his thin, slouched shoulders, even during this heat wave. In the rear-view mirror, she could see deep pouches under his eyes, and when he tilted his head up, his teeth were yellowed. He was a smiley man. He spoke with a Middle Eastern accent, overemphasizing the vowels. On the passenger-side dashboard, he had glued a small bud vase that held three red silk roses. Stencilled in yellow paint on the glovebox were the words FASTEN YOUR SEATBELT PLS. The letters were thin, not commanding, but merely a friendly reminder.

She told him to head up Neptune, then take Fenwick across to Johnston and—

He stopped her. "You tell me when you want to turn."

She tightened her seatbelt, sat up straight with her feet flat, knees together, hands on knees to simulate the best outcomes of crash test dummies. Her colleagues tried to persuade her to get her driver's licence, even offered to teach her, but she knew she would be overcautious and overreactive. She'd likely cause an accident. And bicycles were out of the question. She had taken too many bike-related calls. She had tried buses. Twice. The second time, she froze on the steps, unable to get on or off. The driver had to hold her hand and help her back to the street. Taxis she had learned to manage.

She liked that this driver didn't engage in banal conversation. He kept his focus on the road and didn't try to talk her into taking a more direct route or challenge her need to avoid left turns, which were statistically proven to be ten times riskier than rights. She knew where accidents happened. Without question, he circumvented high-risk intersections, blind corners, and high-incident off-ramps. He was careful and steady. The additional fare was a small investment for her safety and peace of mind.

His window was cracked a few inches and warm air slipped over her shoulders and cooled her neck. She breathed in deep and held her breath. She exhaled long and slow. One-two-three-four. She was doing well. She was outside and she was calm. Practise. Practise. Practise. She breathed in the faint sun-baked almond smell of her hair.

It was going to be another scorching day. Seventeen breeze-less days since it last rained, with sustained temperatures nearing forty. Last week, the annual sail-past of tall ships had to shamefully leave harbour under motor. August had broken all daytime highs and triggered an epidemic of calls related to heat exhaustion.

Slumbering houses slipped past as the cab wove through side streets to avoid the main thoroughfare of Pleasant Street and the risk-laden Five Corners. The pre-rush-hour commute was statistically one of the safest, but at this time of year sunrise was in the driver's eyes. She took another breath. Her skin flushed hot. The bridge was fast approaching. She had considered moving across the harbour to be closer to work and avoid it, but the thought of uprooting her life was overwhelming. She preferred her personal world to be uneventful.

"Right at the next block, please."

The driver nodded pleasantly and smoothly took the corner.

There had been a call on this street last week, a heart attack. The man's wife made the call. Sometimes there weren't alternative routes to avoid her work. When this happened she looked for evidence of skid marks, shards of shattered taillights, indications of blood spilled, or a shoe overlooked on the sidewalk, but usually there weren't any signs. This did not reassure her.

She thought there should be colour-coded marks to warn and commemorate. Some houses would be completely covered in red or purple dots. Red for crimes and purple for sorrow. She recognized the house number. It was a well-kept bungalow painted a solid blue. She thought it would be white and she hadn't imagined the pots of geraniums on the stairs. She added a purple dot to its white door.

The public didn't know that most emergency calls were from repeaters and most crimes weren't random. Most were wars, criminal on criminal, or domestics that had been transpiring for years, or families with long histories of illegal activity. Houses that had made 911 calls when she started her career were still calling, but now the calls were coming from subsequent generations. The public didn't know how much hurt there was behind closed doors.

Her team was trained not to profile an area or a caller. But it was hard to ignore the facts. Some areas and people had red dots all over them . . . poor white people, poor black people, poor mad people. A disproportionate number of calls came from neighbourhoods that predominantly shared her own skin tone.

Sometimes those calls made her angry, angry that so many lives were being wasted. Angry that people didn't try to do better. Angry that people didn't stand up and demand, *Enough!* She knew the reasons that led to *them* and *us*. She had lived the reasons. As a child she knew the degradation of being followed by security guards assuming she was shoplifting, and the burning shame of names hurled by little white girls in expensive store-bought dresses, and the judging eyes at the checkout when she was counting out dimes to buy a box of macaroni. And later, all the smiles she lied to assure everyone else it was okay when hers was the only backpack searched at the local bar, and all the times she deafened her ears, and all the silences she agreed to so as not to make others uncomfortable. She knew all the reasons. But that didn't mean she accepted the alternatives.

Choices made to be tough, because tough meant power and status, and sometimes money. Choices made, not realizing they were still powerless, because now they were warring each other and poisoning their veins with drugs, hurting brothers, fathers, husbands, while suppliers and profiteers from elsewhere were recruiting twelve-year-olds with candy crack and new sneakers.

Angry probably wasn't the right word. Perhaps it was disappointment that made her jaw clench when she heard a voice cadenced with street slang, or took yet another call about shots fired in the north end where she grew up, or when she pulled up a profile of a black man or woman with priors that filled her screen. She was disappointed that another life had been lost. Disappointed that the story in the next day's news would only serve to fuel the ignorant, while disregarding all those who had succeeded and all the reasons why others had not.

It was only a silverfish flash of emotion, and once she swallowed it was gone. But still there was a flash. She wondered if her white co-workers had a similar reaction when they saw white faces making headline news or if they even identified as being part of the same community. Skin colour didn't seem to bond them. They appeared to congregate by economic class and interests. Perhaps because they were the majority, they didn't have to acknowledge each other. They just were.

On the job, her team was perceived as colourless. They were Integrated Emergency Services personnel, voices on the end of a line. They prided themselves on being family. But sometimes there were careless comments and jokes that forced her to paste on that smile. Her colleagues seemed to forget that she didn't look like everyone else in the room, and there was an unspoken expectation that she should forget, too. And sometimes she almost could. But outside of work, she was a black woman. It startled her when someone looked at her braids or face for a moment too long. It reminded her that she didn't look like them and they had noticed.

Maybe it was anger. Maybe she was angry—angry that she had to work so damn hard not to be mistaken as poor, uneducated, and other.

The cabbie smiled into the mirror. "Bridge," he said.

She took a deep breath. One, two, three, four. The cab slipped through the toll booth and onto the old suspension bridge that was being retrofitted. She clutched the door handle. According to legend a Mi'kmaw chief's daughter or lover, depending on the storyteller, stole away to be with a soldier. The chief killed them both and cursed the bridge that had brought their worlds together. Three bridges would rise and fall—the first in wind, the second in silence, and the third in death. The first collapsed during a hurricane, the next floated silently away on a calm, sunny day, and the third . . . the third was still standing. A sacred ceremony supposedly lifted the curse when this bridge was opened, but she wasn't convinced one chief's words were more powerful than another's.

Her heart beat faster. She talked herself back into the now. Five things she could see: the seat, her skirt, the handle, the headrest, her shoes. Four things she could touch: the seat, her skirt, the handle, the headrest. She was cheating. Three things she could hear: the tires, her breathing, the click of the dashboard flowers against their vase. Two things she could smell: coconut and air freshener. One thing she could taste. She couldn't taste.

The taxi wheels hummed onto the bridge deck. She cast her gaze upward, following the strobe and arc of cables. It was like being inside a child's game of cat's cradle, except that she was being held aloft with steel string and iron fingers. Five things she could see . . . She checked the towers for signs of sway and scanned the aging cables and wondered whether she would see the unravelling or would the line just snap? There was corrosion on the girders and the paint was peeling.

On a windy day or if the traffic was heavy, the platform bounced. Surely the vibration of forty thousand cars crossing daily, and the accumulated weight of two lanes of traffic stopped during rush hour, factored into its structural integrity. How could all the factors—the effects of salt air, spalling, stress fractures, engineers' qualifications, the skill of the ironworkers—be accurately calculated? Four things she could touch: the headrest, the window, the seat, her skirt . . .

The cab zipped over the centre span. She glanced to the water below and its 177-foot drop. Three things she could hear: the wind rushing past, the staccato of girders . . . The cab's shocks bottomed out as it lurched over a deck-plate seam. She grabbed her seatbelt. She had read a book that said she should confront her fears. It was a shitty book.

The cabbie said, “It’s going to be another beautiful day.” He glanced at her in the mirror and back to the road. “You should look at the water. It’s on fire with the sun.”

She forced herself to look away from the bridge and out to the becalmed harbour. It was molten with light. A huddle of construction workers erecting the new barriers flashed past. She breathed through her mouth. A walking path and bike lane were also being added. Her heart beat faster. Engineers had always said the bridge couldn’t support additional weight, but a new engineer was hired when a claim was filed for damages incurred from “things being thrown or falling off the bridge.” When pushed by reporters to be more specific, the spokesperson had cited television sets, tools, car parts—anything that could be thrown from a high place. One, two, three, four . . .

Tamara glimpsed a man’s head appear above the railing, straining to pull himself up in a tangle of harnesses. He looked young. Too young to have any experience.

She had taken those calls of “things” falling off the bridge. Everyone at IES had. There had been an increase since the announcement of the barriers going up. Some things were never found, swept away by the current; some things landed in people’s backyards, on roofs, on parked vehicles; some got snagged on girders or pilings; some made it to the water. Left behind were cell phones, shoes, socks, photographs, empty beer bottles, jewellery, and even a book with a highlighted passage. Tamara would like to tie a ribbon to mark each spot. She would leave the tails long to kite in the wind. Something beautiful to deter others from looking down.

One of her calls had come from a construction worker welding a bottom deck plate. He called while still in his harness. She imagined him suspended in the air, swinging slowly beneath the bridge. He said a woman had fallen. He said she seemed surprised to see him there and had reached out. She was young and wearing a yellow dress. She was pretty. He said, maybe she wasn't reaching out—maybe she was trying to keep her dress from billowing over her head. He said he could see her down below in the water and she looked like a flower. Just like a flower after a hard rain.

The car hit a bump and Tamara grabbed the seat. The cabbie glanced up to the rear-view and tilted his chin so she could see his reassuring smile.

6

When he pulled into the driveway, Mike's two boys were waiting for him at the bay window. Caleb had on his big-kid diaper and *Daddy's Boy* T-shirt. Held fast was his stuffed green crocodile, Snappy, the subject of an ongoing laundry battle with his mother despite her insistence that crocodiles *liked* water.

Baby Connor's belly bopped-bopped against the window and his hands slapped smudge prints on the glass and his pudgy legs pumped froggy-style on Lori's lap. She was pointing at Mike. He could see her enunciating "Da-da." Each utterance sent Connor into spasms of shrill joy.

Mike grabbed his kit from the trunk and waved to his boys. He tipped his police cap, tossed it in the air, and lithely caught it. For the finale, he swirled it on his fingertips, before tucking it under his arm. It was their signal: Daddy's home!

Caleb jumped from the window seat and disappeared from view. Lori watched Mike's face closely. Her forehead was creased, the way it was when she was worried or serious. He smiled, and the tension softened around her mouth. He was back safe.

He bent over to pick up the tricycle abandoned in the middle of the yard and pain stabbed his back. His friggin' belt. His body was starting to feel the wear and tear. Christ, he was only thirty-eight. He straightened and redistributed the weight of his holster. It would feel good to get the belt off . . . and his boots. The soles of his feet were burning.

He stepped into the foyer, avoiding the stroller, diaper bag, Caleb's superhero backpack, swim noodles, cooler, and cookie crumbs. He had about fifteen minutes to change back into Daddy. They had a rule that the boys couldn't see him until he had put the policeman away. Mike untied his laces and tugged off his boots. He had a hole in the big toe of his black sock. Another dead sock. The boots smelled rank. He'd have to spray them later. He tossed them outside onto the porch and headed down the hall to the bedroom, unbuttoning his shirt as he went.

His vest was back at his locker. It was too filthy to bring home. The germs, the blood, the spit, the puke—god knows what else was on it. Lori hadn't made the bed. His pillow was propped like a body alongside where she slept.

He unholstered his Glock and removed the magazine. Make it safe. The mantra from basic training was still drilled into him after all these years. He racked the slide and ejected the cartridge. He checked the barrel and set the pistol on top of his dresser, with the muzzle pointed towards the wall. He retrieved the second magazine from his belt and set it beside the first. He counted the ammunition. He always counted it. Merely checking that the magazines appeared full wasn't enough. When he got to thirty, he was halfway to returning to his family. He cleared the chamber of the plus-one round. Thirty-one. The gun went into the lock box in his sock drawer. Groaning, he reached for the ammo safe on the top shelf of the closet and secured the magazines.

From front to back, he removed each item from his utility belt—always front to back—and laid them on his dresser in precise order.

Right hip: weapon holster—check. Key—check. Cuffs, rubber gloves, CPR mask. Check.

Left hip: Taser holster, baton, radio, flashlight, pepper spray. Check, check, check.

His Taser, labelled No. 3, was back at headquarters charging. Everybody knew No. 3 was his. In a pinch, he would use No. 7, but he didn't like it. He unclipped the keeper hooks of his utility belt, detaching them right to left. With the release of each hook, the weight tugging on his back lightened. He unclipped the fourth keeper and the belt slipped from his hips. His back slumped forward with relief.

He considered whether he could wear the trousers another night, but tossed them aside along with his shorts. He sniffed his shirt's armpits and balled it up. One black sock was tossed in the trash and the other in the laundry basket. He was almost home.

He turned on the shower and held his hand under the soft downpour. He flipped the tap to cold, stepped in, and lifted his face to the spray.

When he walked into the kitchen, Caleb threw himself around his legs. Lori had prepared a hungry man's breakfast of pancakes, bacon, orange juice, and sliced strawberries. She had cut the boy's pancakes into dinosaurs and trucks. There was no denying Lori could cook. She recapped the evening and night he had missed. Caleb had wanted to go swimming, so she made arrangements to go with so-and-so's mother, and tomorrow there was a birthday party for some other name. Caleb chattered about a dream Snappy had, something about a dragon and a hotdog. Lori said someone was coming to repair something and something else about thirty-seven degrees. Maybe it was the air conditioner that was being repaired. She was thinking of a barbecue for supper or maybe she'd pick up something on the way, whichever he preferred. It didn't matter to him. She talked, he smiled, and said yes yes yes.

When he couldn't talk anymore, she told the boys to kiss Daddy goodnight. Before leaving, she asked if he could take a look at the sprinkler because it had lost pressure. She kissed him on the mouth and told him there was lunch in the fridge and reminded him not to forget the sprinkler. She looked him in the eyes to make sure he was listening.

Mike pulled down the roller blind and drew the blackout curtains. He turned on the television, hit mute, and eased into bed. His body relaxed into the cotton sheets. Lori's shampoo perfumed his pillow. He kicked off the top sheet, and warm air cooled hot skin. His body was heavy and the bed seemed to float. He flicked the channels past the news and talk shows and settled on a rebroadcast of a community football game.

The previous night's calls flowed and ebbed: the house with towering stacks of empty cigarette packs and hundreds of lighters lining the windowsills, the man with the gangrene arm who said bugs had crawled up inside him, the ponytail girl who kicked her boyfriend's car door and broke her foot, the gold-chained shit-head who spat at the safety divider from the back seat until they bagged his head, and the guy with the tattoos of his kids, who cried all the way to the hospital. Green and white shirts ping-ponged across the TV screen chasing a ball. After a while, it began to look like a constellation imploding, expanding, and imploding again.

He thought about the steak he was going to have for dinner and hoped it would be a rib-eye. He thought about giving the boys their bedtime bath and tucking them in. He thought about the day after tomorrow being a day off and Lori asleep beside him, her arms embracing him, the lift of her breasts, the softness of her nipples. He thought about how beautiful she was, even after two Caesareans. He thought of nothing as his hand stroked his sleeping dick.

Just before he dozed off, he reached over and turned his police radio on loud.

7

Kate accelerated to beat the yellow light and hung a sharp left through the intersection onto the main street. She shifted down to third gear. Her palms were sweating, her head pounded, and she was cranky from being overheated. The dashboard gauge read thirty-eight degrees outside. Ten minutes ago, she had been shivering. She glanced to Zeus's crate and cranked the air conditioner back on high. He had slept the entire highway run.

A car pulled short into her lane and she tapped the brakes. Zeus jostled against the crate and stood up. She hated driving in this town. She would check on her mother's house and then straight home to sleep. First, she'd make herself a proper breakfast with fruit, if she had any in her fridge. Squinting into the glare of overtired, she lowered the visor. A jumble of Day-Glo signs zipped by shouting out fast-food joints, pawnshops, thrift stores, and good-enough used cars.

The strip club had a new name, but the faded billboard displayed the same ageless girls from back when she was in high school. She changed the CD, hoping Van Morrison would carry her the last few miles. Zeus's ears pricked back and forth with the traffic. She was cold again. She switched off the air conditioner and rolled down the window. Muggy, exhaust-tinged air wafted in. Zeus's nose swung up.

Reacting late to the brake lights of a Buick, she geared down. The vacant big-box store's parking lot was empty. The remnants of yesterday's flea market had been swept away. Somewhere on the asphalt grey was the spot where her mother had fallen. She gripped the wheel tighter and slowed to a full stop behind the lumbering car signalling left, stalled by a steady rush of traffic heading from the suburbs to work.

A jacked-up truck with monster wheels roared up on her bumper. Its stereo thump-thumped. Gas and asphalt fumes leeched through her window. Without the benefit of a breeze, the temperature inside the jeep was climbing. Zeus was panting. She rolled up the window and switched on the air conditioner. Tapping the steering wheel, she waited for the car to turn. It had already missed two openings.

She tried to conjure the harness racing track that had once stood where the parking lot was now, her favourite teenage spot for a toke. She used to sneak through the fence and sit against the stable's weathered boards, listening to the bugle's trill and the announcer's tin voice calling—*and they're off! Captain Jaimie's going for the lead. Noble Stuff along the rail, Inga's Dream coming up the backstretch, Potato Butt a length behind, and Noble Stuff takes the lead . . . !* She loved their names and the rumble of their hoofs thundering around the last bend and galloping for the wire. She loved the smell of hay and dirt, and the soft neighs and shuffle of the horses tethered in their stalls. It was her place of happy.

When she was sixteen, the track was razed for the big-box store and promises of jobs. Old men cried and young ones threw rocks and beer cans. The vibration and roar of the bulldozers flushed swarms of rats across the highway and into the new subdivision. The crowd cheered. She still had a photograph of the fleeing rats. It was shot with an Instamatic. The rats looked like ink smudges, partially obscured by a blurry close-up of a man's extended middle finger. She regretted not taking the shot of the old men crying just off-frame. That was the day the town died, but nobody knew it then.

The car's taillights flashed hesitantly as it crept slowly across the open lanes. C'mon, c'mon. Kate popped the clutch. Her wheels squeaked on the hot pavement and she swung around the Caddie's big-ass tail and pulled to the outside lane. The pickup grumbled up alongside her on the inside and slowed to keep pace. The windows were tinted black. The truck's engine whined a challenge and it squealed ahead. The town was filled with idiots.

Up ahead, a tall, skeletal man stepped off the curb into her lane. Despite the sweltering heat, he was wearing a bomber jacket and jeans. The truck accelerated and swerved into her lane, swiping past the man. A head appeared out the passenger window and screamed obscenities. The man stepped back onto the curb as the truck and a gob of spit sheared past.

She checked her rear-view mirror and stopped to let him cross. He didn't look up. He tapped the edge of the curb twice with his toe and stepped into the street. She held on tight to the gearshift and forced herself to watch his awkward, stilting gait. His eyes were fixed on the pavement, following an imaginary line. With one hand he clutched the sagging waistband of his oversized jeans. Tattered cuffs ground against the pavement under the crumpled backs of filthy, laceless sneakers. The soles flopped against bare heels. He looked in worse shape than most of the treat 'em and street 'ems who wandered in and out of emerg.

In her side mirror, she glimpsed a car speeding up the inside lane. The man's head was down and he was about step past her fender. *Look up*, she willed. Anger biled under her tongue, he was going to get hit. She leaned on the horn. The sound pierced him mid-step. He froze as though seeing the pinpoint of a sharp-shooter's mark on his chest. It reminded Kate of the moment after a bullet strikes but before a body crumples. The car wailed past. In the stillness after, Van Morrison moaned.

The man looked at her. His face was gaunt and his hair was long and matted. Nausea balled in her stomach, but she didn't look away. There wasn't any recognition in his eyes. He scuttled across the street. Taking a half step back before stepping over the curb, he tapped it twice with his toe. She watched his thin back as he retreated down the sidewalk in a stuttering half walk, half run.

Drive.

Zeus shifted in his crate to face her. Her fingers loosened their chokehold on the steering wheel.

Drive.

One foot released the clutch, the other accelerated, and she lost sight of her brother.

The narrow gravel driveway was choked with alder brambles and the bowers hung heavy with summer's weight. Kate glanced up to the dappling of light and leaf brushing over her windshield. A tire dipped into a pothole and briars scratched the mirrors. The overgrown lane opened onto her mother's front yard. Parking under the shade of a crimson maple, she kept the vehicle running in neutral and redirected the vents to deflect the coldness back to Zeus.

The cut on her palm throbbed and the bandage's edge had lifted. She could smell the previous night on her scrubs. This was a mistake. She should have gone home. There was no need to check now. Her brother wasn't there. She needed to sleep. She rolled down her window and the warm smell of trees spilled in. Birdsong fluttered from the boughs. Living in the city, she had forgotten that sound. She picked at the bandage sticky with adhesive and peeled it off fast. The pain was sharp and deep. She ran her thumb along the thin scab, straight as a knife blade.

Tucked at the rear of the property, the small farmhouse looked as tired and sad as the town that had built up around it. Through the splay of untamed forsythia and honeysuckle hedges, she could see the neighbours' vinyl-clad houses butting against the property lines. The narrow lot was the last remnant of what had once been farmland, long ago paved over by a labyrinth of streets named after clear-cut trees.

Her mother's property was considered an eyesore and she'd been served with numerous citations to tidy the yard, which she self-righteously ignored. When the neglected wild of trees and bush finally obscured the view from the street, the neighbours stopped complaining. They were certain the next owner would raze the house and the trees.

The house had always been white, but the peeling layers of leaded paint had dulled to a gloaming grey. It was scarred by subpar renovations, a sagging porch, and moss-eaten roof. A corner had been scraped bare to its weathered cedar shakes, another of her father's many abandoned projects. He'd had dreams of fixing things, but only succeeded at tearing them apart. After he left with the family station wagon and the racetrack's best beer maid, handiwork wasn't high among her mother's priorities.

She looked to the mound of tires, gutted motors, and cement blocks overrun with tall grass and wildflowers—a monument to the rusting remains of her father. She was another of his abandoned projects. Her brother said he remembered what he looked like, but he'd been only four. His descriptions resembled characters from the books he was reading and popular TV shows of that time. One winter, he convinced her their father was the skipper on a famous island with a banker and a movie star and once they were found, he'd come home again. But the show was cancelled before they were found.

She squeezed her hand closed. The pain held solid and barbed. Zeus rustled in his crate. She should let him out for a run. Around the porch, a patch of grass mowed to within an inch of its life had burned brown with thirst, but the rest of the yard was knee-high wild. There would be ticks. A monarch butterfly careened over the hood and windshield. A childish part of her heart reacted with the disappointment of being found.

Her mother said butterflies were sent by faeries to determine whether it was safe to come out and play. They only appeared when people were away. Their gowns were spun from spider webs and jewelled with dewdrops and ladybugs. They always sang their words and wrote their stories on the bellies of clouds, and they were experts at hiding.

As a child, Kate practised walking barefoot on the gravel so she could sneak up on them. She never succeeded. They left evidence behind, though—a half-eaten strawberry on a rose-petal plate, a dandelion necklace on the windowsill, an acorn bridge spanning a puddle, or a letter under a rock addressed in tiny print to *The Giant Girl*. She was eight when Sally Mosher told her faeries weren't real and that she had seen her mother stringing buttercups in the trees. But by then, Kate already knew. She didn't tell her mother. Soon after, the faeries moved away and she chose to believe they were living happily ever after.

Kate leaned forward to watch a squirrel run up the trunk of a towering pine, but lost sight of it in the broken limbs severed by the last hurricane. The same winds had toppled the crown of the ancient oak where the faerie queen lived. Her mother had cried. The rotting stump, pocked by woodpeckers, still guarded the house. Boat builders and furniture makers made multiple offers for the virgin wood. Instead, her mother piled its broken pieces in the back lot, even though they didn't have a working fireplace and were always in need of money. She talked about hiring an artist to carve the stump, but when Kate offered to arrange it, she refused. Ruth said she didn't know what it was supposed to be, other than a tree.

She forced herself to look at the upstairs window shielded with blankets. It had been three years since she'd been inside the house. After another pleading call for help. Another nauseating drive bleeding shame and fear and hope all the way to the front door. Only to be told again, It's okay, it's better now, would she like some tea? She couldn't play pretend anymore. She wanted doctors and hospitals—what her training told her could work. Her mother wanted love to be enough. Kate had begged and threatened and cajoled and finally played the only bargaining chip she had left—her. She wouldn't come back if they didn't get help. She's pretty certain she cried. Her mother said, "How can you be so cruel? He's my son."

Now they talked on the phone once a week about trivial, safe things—the weather, supper, flea market finds, crime reports, and only near the holidays would she be asked if she was coming over, and Kate would ask if he was back on his meds, and the conversation would veer to celebrity divorces and botched plastic surgeries—other people's tragedies that made her mother feel better. She picked at the scab. Blood welled in the crease of her palm.

Her brother hadn't recognized her. And she hadn't called his name. Her throat knotted. She swallowed the bitter pill of her training—*some can't be saved*—but her heart spat out the words. Zeus growled softly.

A woman was walking up the driveway. She had the stained knees and broad sun hat of a gardener and the gait of someone who took pride in knowing her neighbours' business. Kate balled her hand into a fist to stanch the wound.

"Kate?" It was Mrs. Carson who hated dogs and kids and led the charge filing complaints. Kate didn't have the energy to smile back. "I haven't seen you in ages." She rested her gloved hand on the open window.

"Yea, it's been a while." Not since she was a teenager and Kate lit her garbage cans on fire after Mrs. Carson threatened to poison her dog when it peed on her manicured lawn. Her mother called her Mrs. Catpiss.

"I'm so sorry about your mother." She didn't bother to explain how she'd heard.

"She'll be fine." Kate didn't offer any more. She would probably have to trade off if Mrs. Carson came to emerg on her shift.

"Oh, that's good." The words fell hollow between them. "We thought she might be thinking of selling." She eyed the house as though calculating the cost of demolition. It was probably lowering her property value. Her eyes narrowed and she trod on gravel words: "And your brother, how is he?"

Kate thought of all the times Mrs. Carson watched from the curb and never once approached her weeping mother.

"Good." Neither blinked. "I'll tell him you said hi and you'd love for him to stop by for visit." Grinding the gears, she backed out of the driveway. Zeus's claws scrabbled and he braced himself with a sit.

The clock mocked her with another lost minute. It was already past ten in the morning and she couldn't sleep. In less than eight hours, she would be back at the hospital. She rolled over and Zeus snuggled against her belly. Her bedroom smelled stale with dirty laundry and floors that needed vacuuming. The cheap fan oscillating noisily at the foot of the bed was in the wrong position and the weak drafts barely reached her. She was too tired to get up and adjust it and, more importantly, she didn't want to wake Zeus. He was dreaming.

She stared at the slash of light under her too-short blackout blinds, recycled from her last flat. Sirens bleated in the distance. Car tires hummed past the window. In the small park next door, a kid was bouncing a ball off a netless hoop. It didn't sound like he was making any baskets.

Maybe if she got under the covers, she could trick her brain to sleep. But she was already too hot in a T-shirt and panties. She should take a shower, but worried it would wake her more. She should eat something, but she couldn't decide whether she was hungry for breakfast or supper. If she didn't sleep soon, she might as well get up. She could get groceries, pay the light bill, put on a load of wash, hang some pictures to offset the hooks heavy with leashes, ball caps, and survival gear, or finally decide on a colour to paint the room other than landlord white.

She closed her eyes and pushed back images of her brother's boned fingers clutching his waistband. She tried to recall her mother's last phone call. I love you, Ruth said. Love ya, too. She didn't think she had said *I*, and there might have been a pause before replying.

She focused on what else could be done. She could disinfect the cut. She could turn off her pager. She could set another alarm. She could visit her mother. She could find her brother. She could buy some fruit. She could . . .

Her breath fell into slumbered pace with Zeus.

8

911. What is your emergency?

Tamara tasted the metallic sourness of panic. She couldn't decipher what the woman was screaming. In the background, dogs shrilled hysterically.

What is your emergency? Her mouth was sticky and dry. She struggled to control the fear rising in her throat. *Where are you?* The woman's guttural howls were coming from somewhere too deep for humans to know. She activated a trace to unlock the location of the private call. Her fingers fumbled over the keys. *Tell me what's happening.* The monitors flickered, text garbled, and her screens flashed dead, blinding her to the scene. Screams pierced her headset and she gasped awake.

Her chest was slick with sweat. Sheets tangled her feet, and the silk scarf bundling her hair had slipped off. She looked to her clock: 2:35. Day or night? The windows bled light around the tight edges of the blackout shades. It was day. She loosened the scarf's chokehold from her neck and a torrent of braids dropped to her shoulders and slapped her back. She let herself breathe.

Slowly, she depressed the plunger on the French press and inhaled the coffee's rich bloom. She poured with equal care, then added one sugar and a frothy head of warmed milk. A perfect cup. She rinsed the spoon, wiped the stray grounds from the counter, and curled up on the far end of the couch.

The room was soft with cushions and throws. Diffuse light filtered through the white sheers and gleamed over her hardwood floors. The countertops and tables were clear of mail, newspapers, and smudges. Everything was in its place. She sipped her coffee and it made her happy.

Flicking past the news channels, she paused on the weather station. It was forty degrees, another record-breaking high with five more days of sun in the forecast. The program cut to a rapid-fire headline of the world's wildfires, tornadoes, droughts, and grief. She switched it off.

The shouts of children playing seeped through her closed windows. She presumed they were her elderly neighbours' grandchildren. Through the sheers, she sometimes watched them take out their garbage, mow their lawn, and haul in groceries. It was a white neighbourhood. People kept to themselves, which suited her fine. They smiled and nodded hello to each other, but there was no expectation of conversation.

Tucked away from the city's extremes of the south end's privilege, the midtown's bars, and the north end's poor, her area was a pocket of postwar homes whose owners took pride in keeping them looking the same. Hers was an unassuming one-and-a-half-storey on an unassuming street that rarely saw traffic or emergencies. The real estate ad touted it as a fixer-upper with one previous owner, *location, location, location*. If she walked down the steep hill, she could see the harbour and bridge and the first hints of the community where she grew up. But she didn't do that. Just the thought of going outside made her shoulders tense. The world was a dangerous place. The air conditioner purred its comfort. She drank three-quarters of her coffee and set it aside.

The floorboards were cool beneath her bare feet as she watered the spider plants and hibiscus. She plucked off the dead leaves, pulled the pots farther from the window to mitigate the blanching sun, and clocked each a quarter turn to keep their stalks upright. They were healthy and strong, and the hibiscus blooms were trumpeting. Tomorrow she would mist their leaves.

She sat at the piano and gently lifted the fallboard. Running her long fingers across the keys, she checked her fingertips for dust. The hundred-year-old upright had been her grandmother's. It was plain. The beech wood bore no embellishments. She preferred the straight, simple lines that concealed the true beauty within—the bronzed harp and strings gilding the spruce soundboard, the piano's heart. Sometimes, she played with the front panel open so she could watch the hammers strike the strings.

It had cost a small fortune to refinish and tune, and she had been advised that it wasn't worth it. But she knew the piano's low, sweet resonance. As a child, she would lie on her belly under the bench and listen to her Granny Nan's husky alto filling the world above her, *Touch me, Lord Jesus,* while she watched her cracked, thick heels and the soles of her feet on the foot pedals, step-step to the holy hallelujah choir, *Guide me, Jehovah, through this vale of sorrow.* She would press her ear to the floor, hugging the vibrations lifting from the boards. *Touch me, Lord Jesus, with Thy hand of mercy . . .*

She laid her hands on the keyboard. The ivories were cool against her warm skin. She sat tall with her fingers arched, wrists straight, so unlike her grandmother's hands with their bent wrists and thick, arthritic fingers seemingly plucking music from the keys. She brought her hands back to her lap, cupped them palms up, and waited for the lightness to enter her muscles. Her arms rose and her fingers arched, bowing to the keys.

The opening measure of Debussy's "Claire de Lune" lifted. She leaned into the slow ripple of notes. As the melody and harmonies mingled in their slightly irregular wash, her eyes closed and she moved within its gentle ebb. She was barely aware of her neck craning forward or her head rocking slightly so her ears could follow the notes flowing from her hands, reverberating back to her through the heart of the wood.

If she could have seen herself, she would have seen the fluidity of her arms rising and dipping to the keys, elegantly summoning the sounds to the surface. Softly, so softly, she caressed the notes, pouring them towards her chest. Her shoulders lowered into the swells. Her breath slowed, deepening between the crests, the music washing her away . . .

The doorbell buzzed, long and hard. Her hands stiffened over the keys. Her eyes opened, but their focus was distant, still lost in the music's fugue. Bereft of sound, emptiness pressed against her.

The buzzer sounded again. An interminable bzzzzzzzzzzzzzzzzz.

"I'm coming."

She peered through the peek hole, unlatched the chain, turned the deadbolt, unlocked the handle, and opened the door.

Heat stifled her lungs. She pulled the door partially shut behind her, as though she could keep the sweltering air out.

The boy who delivered her groceries stood on the step with two grocery bags in hand. His bike, with its oversized rusted wire basket bolted to the fender, was unceremoniously dumped on its side. Its front wheel was still spinning and a fresh tread mark of gnawed grass marred her lawn.

"Got your groceries." He hoisted the bags up like weights. His thin twelve-year-old's biceps were surprisingly sculpted. His hair was shorn shorter than the last time she had seen him, and he had two blade cuts marking his left and right temples. One line was slightly higher than the other. The boy's brow was damp with sweat. "Some hot out." He peered over her shoulder gauging the temperature inside.

She should have had the money in hand. She always had the money in hand. "I'll be right with you." She stepped back into the living room to retrieve her wallet.

"I like your piano." The boy had entered her house. "Was that you playin'?"

She didn't like that he had stepped inside. "No, I was listening to a CD." She counted the bills, considering whether to tip him less.

"You don't have much stuff."

She surveyed her possessions: a worn couch, ten-year-old television, vintage record player, CD player, piano, four plants, and two walls of overstuffed bookcases that didn't contain the surplus stacked on the floor. She thought, *That's right, you tell them I don't have anything worth stealing.* And then she thought, *I need to get an alarm system installed.*

"You want 'em in the kitchen?"

"No." Too loud. "I'll take them."

She set the bags on the floor behind her. She wasn't going to turn her back on the boy even if he was a child. He smiled. He had a wide smile that made him look innocent. She fished a five-dollar bill from her wallet. It was prudent to bestow the full tip plus a little extra to keep him on her side.

"Can I play you somethin'? I just learned it."

He was moving towards her piano. Before she could find words, he had sat on the edge of the bench and pulled it closer. The wooden legs scraped the hardwood. His untied laces swept the floor and his sneakered feet reached for the pedals. His hands plunked down on the keys. The juvenile plink of "Twinkle, Twinkle, Little Star" jarred her ears. His finger jabbed the notes.

She tried to moderate the rage rising from her belly. Her ears flushed hot. The word *STOP* was stuck in her throat. The opening refrain finished and she was considering the repercussions of physically grabbing the child and wrenching him from the piano, when the boy's posture changed. He shuffled his bum closer to the seat's edge and launched into a second refrain.

But this time, with his body cupped into the piano, the music exploded with a percussive rhythm as his hands jumped across the keys. His left foot thumped out a beat and his right depressed the sustaining pedal and the piano's voice opened louder. His shoulders and head rocked with the sway. She wasn't sure what she was hearing. It was still "Twinkle, Twinkle," but his hands were slapping—pawing—the keyboard and the notes were licking each other into wildness.

She could hear the rhythm-and-blues roll, but somewhere deeper inside of that she discerned the strains of Mozart's twelve variations of "Twinkle, Twinkle." The music galloped and the boy's head nodded time. As he reached the third variation's transition into the fourth, he stood up, pushing back the bench. His arms spanned the keyboard, faster and faster he grabbed the notes, wrapping them in a crescendo, the keys almost escaping his thrashing fingertips. Pulled back into syncopated pace by flopping wrists, the pounding heartbeat rose through the floorboards into the soles of Tamara's bare feet.

The boy reined the rolling notes into an abrupt stop and the sustain held the room. In its thin fade, he turned to her, grinning, saw the money in her hand, and took it.

"Thanks! See ya later." He ran out the door, leapt off the top step, and mounted his bike in a move worthy of an action hero. Pedalling up the street, he looked back and waved.

Tamara shut the door and secured the locks.

She tried to calm herself with the unpacking of groceries and the orderliness of her fridge. Beverages to the right and condiments to the left. Fruit, vegetables, and meats in their appointed bins. Milk in the milk receptacle. Butter in the butter tray. She placed the orange juice container to the right. The boy had brought "with pulp" rather than "no pulp," as if there wasn't a difference. She shut the fridge and made a mental note to mention it to the grocer on her next order. She wanted to support the family-run store, *57 years in business* their sign said, and loved that each year they hand-painted over the number to add another. But she'd been a customer for three years—always "no pulp." She expected better. She expected people to do their jobs. She looked at the piano. The bench was askew. This irked her more than the botched order.

The fan hummed a disinterested metronome. She straightened the bench and checked the keys for smudges. For good measure, she wiped them with the soft hem of her dress. The piano appeared untouched. With one hand, she walked the notes of "Twinkle, Twinkle" up to *star*, and slid the fallboard shut.

The boy had disrupted her precious quiet time before shift and thrown off her schedule. She went into the bathroom and tried to forget his small hands thrashing her piano. She craned to see the top of her head in the mirror. Her fingers traced the tracks of bare scalp between her tightly woven rows. The pressure made her follicles ache dully. Losing her protective head scarf had caused two braids to tangle and frizz. She would need to have them redone.

Her face scowled back at her. It was the same scowl she had perfected in childhood when Granny Nan pushed her head to the side to leverage the hairbrush. Her hair had always been her grandmother's bane. When she was a toddler, Granny Nan preferred a multitude of short, stubby pigtails interwoven with pink ribbons. By the age of six, she had taken to pressing Tamara's unruly curls straight with her cheek pressed to the ironing board. When she was ten, Tamara cut off her hair with the kitchen scissors.

Granny Nan didn't punish her. She swept up the freshly ironed locks, threw them in the garbage can, and didn't speak to her for two weeks. Tamara didn't understand then that Granny Nan was trying to protect her. Trying to make her look like the other girls, the white girls, so her life would be easier. She was grooming her for better jobs and a way to move through the world without drawing attention. Tamara didn't understand that she was afraid for her or that the pain came from love.

Through junior high, she wore her hair natural, high and wide, using only a pick to keep it from tangling. But then came high school and boys, and they liked girls with straight hair. When she asked for help with the chemical relaxers, hot combs, and flat irons, Granny Nan wept. *Praise Jesus, hallelujah.* The lye brews burned her scalp and fumed their eyes, but her hair was smooth. Granny Nan cupped her face in her hands, looked her in the eyes, and told her she was beautiful. They both ignored the lingering pungent smell of burned hair.

She missed Granny Nan's strong hands roughly tugging her hair. She missed hearing her pounding out Jesus on the piano. That boy had the same natural ease. The music came easy to them. They didn't have to look for it. Granny Nan had tried to teach her, but couldn't name the notes she was playing. As a child, Tamara would sit beside her grandmother and attempt to memorize her hands flittering over the keyboard. She spent hours transcribing the music, but when she would play the pages back, they sounded nothing like Granny Nan. She pushed away the notes repeating in her head. All the years, lessons, practice, and money invested as an adult to achieve her Grade 8 level, and the boy had just sat down and diminished all her work.

She roughly worked apart the two thin braids, though she knew she should be gentler. Her stylist would reprimand her. She had finally found one whose work she liked. Edie was expensive, but her salon used only the highest-grade East Indian hair, nothing synthetic, and after a botched glue-in and three months of bad wigs, she was willing to pay. She did her best to protect her hair. She avoided rain, showers, and humidity, and slept religiously with a silk head scarf and pillowcase. Grannie Nan would be proud of her. Even so, she was lucky to get five weeks between appointments.

If she could pull off the powerful look of popular celebrities, she would crop it short again. But that would require being a foot taller, twenty pounds lighter, and possessing a different face, with high cheekbones and oversized eyes. She puckered her lips. She had nice lips. And she was a nice colour. Not too dark. That's what Granny Nan said. Easier in this world.

She could see the boy's small hands against the white keys, his fingers barely spanning the scales. His hands were dark, darker than hers. He used his thumb to play the black keys and his fist to pound out chords. She squeezed the tube of dry shampoo. Her nose crinkled at the antiseptic smell. She rubbed her fingertips along every exposed bit of her scalp, paying special attention to the hairline because it was most vulnerable to breakage. Softly, she towel-patted away the residue as she dissected the notes the boy had played.

She repeated her hair care process with a tube of unprocessed castor oil, then again with moisturizer, and finally sealed the shafts with coconut oil. It took forty-five minutes and she was no closer to understanding how the boy had bent the music and her hair was still fuzzy. She pulled out a small pair of scissors and clipped away a flyaway strand that wasn't her own. The extensions were beginning to shed, which she blamed on her headset at work.

It was supposed to be high-grade virgin hair that had never been cut. At least that's what was advertised. She pulled on a single loose strand. It came out long and kinked. It amazed her that a woman in India had the same hair colour as hers. The shops said it was hair willingly donated as an offering of thanks to their gods. But she knew that wasn't true. When sourcing cheaper suppliers online, she had found articles with a different story.

The hair wasn't a joyful offering. It was a plea for mercy, a sacrifice to heal an only cow, dying child, ailing parent, or a broken heart. The women were giving up their beauty, their desirability, and future prospects in return for a miracle. And it wasn't just women, it was children, too—girls and boys—ten thousand penitents a day bowing their heads on the steps of the Temple of Tears to the specially appointed cutters. Their hair swept away as it fell. Unaware that behind the holy walls, it was being sorted, washed, sun-dried, baled, and sold. She wondered if there was a sound to all that hair falling, or only the swish of straw brooms on ancient stones.

The boy's brilliant notes tumbled in her mind. The gods were cruel.

She dropped the loose strand of virgin hair into the trash bin. She didn't know this girl. The girl had given her hair willingly. The tears had been washed away. For all she knew, maybe this girl's prayers came true.

"911. What is your emergency?"

Monday night—no, Tuesday morning now—and Tamara had already logged twenty-three calls. The heat was drawing the crazy out of people. She was grateful for the next three days off. She glanced at the time: 1:26 a.m.

"Ma'am, did you get the licence plate number?"

No. It was almost always no.

"What kind of vehicle? Do you know the make? Colour? Closer to blue or black?" Her voice didn't betray her impatience. She rolled her neck side to side, stretching the muscles to consciously lower her shoulders.

"Blue, you think. How long ago did you pass the vehicle? An hour?" She stopped typing. "Yes, I have the information. Yes. Thank you for your assistance." She disconnected the line.

She was thirsty. The air was dry in the room tonight. She scanned the hive. Every call-taker was engaged; even fire dispatch was monitoring a burning dumpster. She pivoted to the snack carousel and grabbed a water bottle. Her lips were parched. She needed to remember to take vitamin C and D tomorrow. It had been five days since she had been in the sun for any length of time.

Active and incoming calls scrolled down her monitor:

10-68 Impaired Driver

10-81 Break and Enter

10-30 Mentally Unstable

She checked her other monitor for the responses: On site, false alarm, arrived at scene . . .

The security door buzzed and Constable Mike entered. A wave of welcoming hands, including hers, lifted to greet him over their half-walled partitions. He was carrying two trays of coffees and teas and a handful of raffle tickets.

"For you, lovely lady, two sugar, no milk, as you like it." He placed the cup on Tamara's console with a flourish.

"How much is this going to cost me?" It always cost something.

"May I suggest five dollars and three chances to win a dinner for two? All proceeds going to a good cause."

"It always is." She reached for her purse.

"Or ten dollars for seven chances . . . ?" He fanned open the tickets.

Constable Mike was a good one. He took the time to drop by and acknowledge they were part of the team. He didn't complain about the GPS systems recently installed in the squad cars, or talk too much, or flirt. He just dropped in and said hi. He had their respect. She sifted through her wallet. She only had a ten-dollar bill, having used her last fiver to tip the grocery boy.

"I want my change." In fourteen years, she had never won a raffle. She swung around on her chair. "911. What is your emergency?"

"Help, you gotta help us!"

More than one person. A man was sobbing, choking on his own tears.

"What's your name?"

"Antoine!"

The voice cracked high. A boy.

"Antoine, how old are you?"

"Fourteen. We need help!"

"What's happened?"

"He's shot!"

Tamara's hand flew up in the air, a signal for assistance. Something big was going down. Her supervisor came to her side and peered over her shoulder.

"Tell me where you are, Antoine."

"The park."

"What park?"

"By the water."

"Which side of the harbour?"

"The dark side."

Slang for this side of the harbour. "What do you see around you, Antoine?"

"I don't fuckin' know! Oh— There's blood everywhere!"

"Tell me what you see."

"There's a school . . ."

"What else do you see?"

". . . the bridge . . . I don't know what to do."

"Are you in the park, Antoine? Is the school beside you?"

The boy was hyperventilating.

"Talk to me, Antoine. Help me find you. Is there a school?"

"Yes." He choked on the word.

"Are you at the turn to the bridge?"

"Yes!" he wailed.

Constable Mike read over her shoulder as she typed:

10-34 Shots Fired. 14-year-old boy reporting shooting incident. Possible wounded.

She nodded confirmation as she typed in the address located just down the road, minutes away. Mike headed for the door, leaving behind the drinks and the bag of raffle tickets on her desk. Her fingers raced to trigger the response. Code 3. In the cubicle across from her, Colleen took over logistics. Tamara glanced to her left and saw her call hit "active" at the top of the screen. Red alert. Police and ambulance dispatched.

"Who's been shot, Antoine?"

"My friend!"

"What's his name?"

"Devon!"

"Are you injured, Antoine?"

"No." Snot and tears choked his throat.

"The police and ambulance are on their way."

"He's dying, he's dying."

"How old is Devon?"

"Twelve. He's my friend."

12-year-old boy shot, name Devon.

"Do you know who did this, Antoine?"

"No! Noooo! The blood won't stop!"

"Can you see where he's been shot?"

"He can't breathe . . . his neck. Blood's squirting all over."

"Antoine, if I talk you through it can you help Devon? Can you do that?"

"I don't know . . . it's all coming out."

"Antoine, the ambulance is en route, but we want to slow the bleeding. Can you put your hand on the wound?"

"Like the doctors on TV?"

"Yes, like on TV. Can you do that?"

"Yes." The voice sounded so small.

"The ambulance will be there soon." She looked to the screen and hoped it was true. The vehicle markers were converging. "You'll hear the sirens soon, Antoine."

"He's—he's—he's making sounds."

"Is Devon on his side?"

"Yes."

"You're doing really good, Antoine. Put your hands on the wound."

"I don't want to hurt him."

"You won't hurt him. You're going to slow the bleeding. You can do this."

Tamara heard a clunk and then nothing. She leaned forward, straining to hear. A gasp gurgled in her ear. In the distance she heard, *I'm doing it! I'm doing it!* She realized Antoine had dropped the phone beside the wounded boy. It was his breathing.

"Devon? Can you hear me?" A low moan. "Devon?" She leaned closer to hear the whimper of a reply. Her ear cocked towards the ground. A choking cry responded. "Devon, I don't want you to talk. Help is coming. The ambulances are coming. I'm going to talk to you." She could hear a rasping inhale, sucking inward, starved for air. Two boys, twelve and fourteen. In the park. At 1:36 a.m. Black boys. Antoine and Devon. She knew the moment she heard Antoine's voice. The breath exhaled, a stuttered gargle, followed by a broken inhale. It was wet and suffocating.

"Help is almost there, Devon."

She strained to hear the sirens in the distance, but heard only Antoine's hoarsening calls for help, which abruptly stopped. She thought he might be crying.

An inhalation, long and thin, keened.

"Devon, stay with me." She could hear the caterwaul of sirens. "Can you hear the sirens, Devon? They're coming for you. They're so close . . ."

The breath caught and gurgled and slowed and slowed and slowed . . .

"Devon, you stay with me." She covered both ears and bowed her head to blot out every other sound. "I'm right here with you. I'm right here."

But there was no more breath.

"Devon?"

Tamara pressed her hand to her headset, trying to filter out the sirens and Antoine's frantic cries, *We're here! We're here!* She bent in close to see the boy lying on his side on the grass in the park at night. Sneakers, jeans, and a T-shirt because it was warm, even though it was night. Antoine kneeling over him with his hands on his neck, red soaked . . .

Colleen's voice jarred her back into the room, urging her to let go. "Police and paramedics are on scene."

Antoine was screaming. *I'm helping! No, no, nooo! I'm doing what she told me to do!* His voice was pulling farther away. *I did it! I did what you told me to do!*

The line went dead.

Tamara looked up and the other call-takers respectfully looked away. She removed her headset and passed it to her supervisor. Then, for the first time in her career, she walked into the quiet room.

9

Trauma Room 2 was prepped for incoming, and the team activated for the ambulance en route with a Code 1. Male, twelve years old, gunshot wound, unresponsive. ETA one minute. Two doctors and four nurses were watching the clock. Kate put on her gloves. There was no need to talk. They knew their roles.

Dr. "Spider" Patel, the on-call vascular surgeon noted for his fine stitching, was at the foot of the gurney. His head was bowed and his eyes closed. Kate assumed he was meditating or visualizing the body's circulatory pathways. His favourite sci-fi film involved a microscopic submarine. She could imagine him peering through tiny portholes at veins and capillaries.

Beside him, Dr. Savoy rocked side to side. It was a tic not to be misinterpreted as nervousness, but rather was a sign of restless anticipation, much like a thoroughbred at the gate. He earned the nickname Mapmaker for his ability to chart wild medical terrain and locate the true source. Nurses adored him and bemoaned the fact that he was married. He kept a collection of recovered objects that included glass shards, metal projectiles, and a set of crumpled motorcycle handlebars. Some were wins and some were losses.

The nursing team was positioned around the gurney at head, heart, and feet. Rhonda, the primary nurse with fourteen years' experience, had the head. She was Kate's mentor and appropriately feared by the newbies. She always worked the right side of the room. Kate had the heart. Monitors, vitals, IVs, blood, fluids, and meds were divvied between them. Amy, who was always where she needed to be, was acting as relay, replenishing blood and fluid bags, restocking supplies, and manning the defibrillator. The youngest, Donna, detailed and logistics oriented, with only four years on the floor, was scribing. Her documentation of procedures and vitals was unerring and legible.

The overhead fluorescents hummed. The team practised stillness, breathing in and out. Someone swallowed. Kate made visual checks of the crash carts and trays, taking inventory of the IV bores, sharps, cath lines, tubes, leads, sutures, towel packs, scissors, scalpels, meds, and painkillers. She had never found an item missing with Rhonda as primary. She rolled her neck and loosened her fingers. She was already overly warm in her protective gown, booties, and latex gloves. The siren's wails bled through the walls, Code Blue.

"Rock and roll," Dr. Savoy said.

The trauma room doors slammed open and a fury of paramedics and a stretcher crashed in. One paramedic was straddling the boy, performing CPR. A police officer jogged beside, guiding the gurney and holding an IV bag above his head. Its line snaked down to a thin brown arm. Kate momentarily registered that it was the same cop who had been in the corridor the previous night. The boy, strapped to an adult-size backboard, was so small that the paramedics were using the bottom half to hold their kit. The lead paramedic was squeezing the Ambu bag with one hand and firmly holding the oversized mask around the boy's nose and mouth with the other, while leaning in to apply pressure with his elbow to the blood-soaked dressing. His gloves and arms were red. His eyes were dilated, flooded with adrenaline.

"Gunshot wound to the neck. Left side. Elapsed time seven minutes from call, eight minutes in transit, fifteen minutes down. No pulse."

The team moved in a choreographed dance. "One, two, three—lift."

The boy—small, so small—rose into the air. All had miscalculated the weight of his body and for a moment he seemed to rise from their fingertips and they had to pull him back down.

Dr. Savoy, standing at the helm, took control. "Stop compressions," he said in a calm voice.

The paramedic leaned back, sweat dripping from his hair onto the boy's face. With two slices, Kate cut the T-shirt from the thin body and slit the jeans up the sides. Cardiac leads were applied. Lines and tubes snaked across the body. The finger sensor was clipped on, adjusted to grip the child-size fingertip. The blood pressure cuff wrapped around his arm twice. There was no pressure.

"Resume compressions."

The paramedic leaned in. He smelled sour. Kate located a vein, but the IV bore was too large and she reached for a narrower gauge. It went in.

Rhonda was still placing the leads. "Take over compressions," she said.

Kate leaned in and the paramedic slid back. Her hands spanned the breadth of the boy's chest. Palms to his sternum, she pressed down, and his ribs bowed. She hummed the count in her head. A hundred beats per minute. *One, two, three, four* . . . She played her version of a famous song on continuous loop in the back of her head, *Ah, ha, ha, ha, stay alive, stay alive . . .*

IV lines, cardiac leads, and gloved hands snaked around her. Blood and saline flowed through tubes. Another sharp was inserted in the back of the boy's hand. *Ah, ha, ha, ha . . .* Voices collided, documenting actions. Monitors beeped—heart rate, blood pressure, respiration—all alarming RED. The neck dressing was removed, spraying red. Kate averted her face.

Behind her, Dr. Savoy's steady voice guided them. "Stop compressions. Suction."

Dr. Patel hunched over the patient, and she could see the thin balding spot on the back of his head. The bullet was a through-and-through. The carotid artery was nicked.

"Jeezus," Patel said as he sutured the wound, hoping his web would hold.

"Resume compressions."

One, two, three, four . . . The wound was reduced to a mere leak.

"Hold compressions. Intubate."

On first attempt, the tube was too large, and Rhonda tossed it to the floor with the growing debris field of discarded packaging, bloodied dressings, and clothing.

"Do we need a trach?" It was simply a question, with no pressure either way.

"Let me try again." Rhonda tipped the head farther back and the tube slipped in.

"Ventilate. Resume compressions. Charge 40."

Kate slipped her hands under the lines that were warm with blood and saline. Oxygen hissed and the defibrillator whined.

"Push .31 milligrams of epi." Dr. Savoy raised his hand and halted them. "Stop. What's his estimated weight again?" He adjusted the dose to .21 mg.

Ah, ha, ha, ha . . . Kate's forearm muscles were tightening and her underarms were wet. The defibrillator alarm shrieked, ready.

"Clear." She raised her hands from the boy. The small body twitched.

"Resume compressions."

Amy tossed away an empty blood bag and hung another. Alarms screeched. Kate was looking into the boy's open eyes. He had brown eyes and blue lips.

"What's his name?" Savoy was staring at the monitor, as if the answer was there.

A stranger's voice responded, "Devon." There was someone else in the theatre with them. Was it the cop?

"Charge 80."

Kate was puffing and her arms were trembling. Dr. Savoy leaned in, blocking her view. He shone a penlight in the boy's eyes. "Devon." When he pulled back, she was looking into clouded pupils. *Ah, ha, ha, ha . . .*

Rhonda said, "Switch," and Amy took her place. Catching her breath, Kate glanced to the vitals monitor before compressions resumed. The heart rate was flat. The line jumped jagged, *one-two-three-four . . .* Amy was counting under her breath. The elapsed time in the room was fourteen minutes. The paramedics were still there and so was the cop, watching their every move. *Back the fuck up*, her mind growled as she reached for an empty fluid bag.

More compressions, more shocks, more drugs. The bags were emptied again and more blood was rushed in. Beyond the trauma doors, she glimpsed a huddle of police officers and paramedics. Their heads turned, awaiting word. In that moment, she hated them for expecting her team to do more. The dressing around the boy's neck was sopping red again. *Ah, ha, ha, ha . . .*

"Charge 80." Dr. Savoy's arms were crossed. She pressed the charge button on the defibrillator and its whine shuddered up her spine. Amy was counting louder. A rib cracked and they pretended not to hear. Rhonda touched Amy on the small of her back, a touch that said *It's okay*, and took over compressions.

Savoy asked, "Is the family here?"

The cop answered, "The mother's en route." From his hand dangled one sneaker. The other was still on the foot.

"Clear," Savoy called, and hands lifted. She pressed the paddles to the still chest and fired. It was the tenth one.

"Stop."

The doctors stared at the monitors for the smallest blip. The nurses did not. The machine said *heart dead*. But Kate had known that before she applied the first compressions. She had looked in his eyes. The alarms squealed. There was blood on their hands, blood on the floor, blood on the boy.

"I'm calling it." Dr. Savoy's voice was calm, but she could see the hand hidden behind his back and the tremble of his fingers. He had two sons, ten and thirteen. Only he and Donna looked to the clock.

"Time of death, 2:26 a.m."

Latex gloves were snapped off, alarms silenced, oxygen shut off, and IVs shunted. Dr. Patel touched the stitching over the carotid as if feeling for a pulse, searching for anything else he could have done. He closed the scalpel incision with clean, tight stitches, and Rhonda dressed the wound with fresh white dressing.

Kate cleaned the face and neck. Someone closed the eyes. A clean sheet, folded in half and half again, was draped over the body, up to the neck. The cleaners arrived and the aftermath was swept into bags.

The paramedics had left, but the cop was still standing in the corner. He looked older than he did last night. His shoulders were slumped and his vest was stained like his hands.

"You should wash up," she said, and their eyes met.

His eyes said, *I don't know what to do.*

Hers said, *Get out.*

She was standing between him and the boy. He stepped around her and laid the sneaker on the foot of the gurney. His boots squeaked against the polished floors. The door swung shut behind him and the space felt bigger.

Kate accompanied Dr. Savoy to the family meeting room. Security was stationed outside. A small woman sat alone at the head of the overbearing, cheap boardroom table. Her bare arms, lean and muscular, were crossed tight, protecting her heart.

Dr. Savoy explained in a neutral voice what had happened and what had been done. He kept his folded, calm hands on the table. The woman appeared to be listening, but Kate wasn't certain that she was hearing. She didn't look up. The doctor waited patiently for questions, and when they didn't come, he said what he needed to say. "I pronounced him dead at 2:26 a.m."

This was when the silence usually broke. It was the one word families waited to hear—despite all the other words that meant the same thing. But the woman didn't cry out.

"I want to see him," she said. Her voice was as dead as her boy.

The mother noiselessly followed Kate down the corridor, past the security monitors and the rooms with the sprained ankle, kidney stone, and blistering sunburn. Kate's fresh scrubs rubbed stiffly against her legs. Her skin felt raw from the antiseptic soap, and her ponytail elastic was pulled too tight at the nape of her neck. The handle of the trauma room door was cold. The boy's mother didn't falter as she entered.

The room had been cleaned and the harsh overhead light had been partially dimmed. It was eerily silent. The boy was still hooked up to the muted machines, a practice intended to help families understand the enormity and finality of the moment. But Kate didn't think they needed that help. The woman, who was looking down at her son, didn't make a sound. Only when she reached for his hand, where the IV was still connected, did she hesitate.

Wordlessly, Kate cut the tubing below the shunt. She couldn't remove the IV, because there would be an autopsy, so she taped the line to his forearm, adhering it with the gentlest paper tape to mask the adhesive tugging at his skin. She had to remind herself that she couldn't hurt him. She pulled up the sheet and tucked it over the IV to hide it from view. She did this for the mother. The mother took his hand in hers.

"The buzzer is here if you need me." She took care to shut the door behind her so it barely clicked.

The howl began as she reached her nurses' station. It tore from the belly and ripped the throat and raged through the walls. The sound didn't match the juvenile charts of grimaces and clenched lips used by nurses to identify pain on a scale of 1 to 10. This pain shuddered up spines, bristled hair, gutted souls, and devoured hearts.

Kate checked the clock. It was 3:05:21 a.m. 3:05:22. 3:05:23. *Ah, ha, ha, ha . . .*

We take care of them, her mind reminded her. *We don't care about them.*

The call buzzer sounded for the patient in room 4. Her charge. *We take care of them*, her mind snarled. *We don't care about them.* Sedatives would need to be prescribed. She paged Dr. Savoy. The woman with the shattered heart was scaring the other patients. Someone had to do something, but no one was moving. The charge nurse, Momma Jo, finally made the long walk. The trauma room door opened and shut, and the unnatural sound stopped.

Room 4 buzzed again. Mr. Blue Pill. Male, sixty-six. Racing heart, sustained erection. DFB—dick for brains. In the corner, his much too young red-faced girlfriend wanted to know why someone wasn't helping him.

"It shouldn't be long now." Kate used her softest, most reassuring voice. She noted the patient's clenched lips, furrowed brow, and twitching cheek. A five on the pain scale. "Are you cold?"

Her stomach growled. She was ravenous for a burger, salty fries, onion rings, too much ketchup, a chocolate milkshake, and hot fudge sundae. She would settle for a bag of plain chips from the vending machine.

"I'll get you a warm blanket."

Kate sat in the parking lot with the window down. The air smelled dew green. Doctors and nurses, with coffees and bagels in hand, disappeared from view behind the sliding ER doors. A new crop of casualties was already lining up for triage. Her eyes wandered the brick building, counting the floors. She couldn't find her mother's window. Zeus shuffled in his crate, sated from his early run, water, breakfast, and hugs. He spun around and settled down for another nap. She started the engine.

The bandage on her palm was limp and lifting at the edges again. Adhesive stuck to the steering wheel. She peeled it off. A flash of pain flared up her arm and set her chest, throat, and eyes on fire. Hot tears streaked her cheeks. She gagged on the choking grief, but not a sound escaped her lips. Zeus scrambled up, whining and pawing. She raised her wounded hand to shield her face from the security cameras.

"I'm okay." She wiped her cheeks dry. The night was over.

Zeus remained standing, stiff and alert, staring at her flooded eyes in the rear-view mirror, until she had to look away.

10

The morning sun was blinding, and night hadn't brought any relief from the heat. Bluebird Taxi was waiting for her, though Tamara had forgotten to call. The driver stepped out and opened the back door. She wanted to protest that he didn't need to do that, but her feet were stepping forward. The door shut softly behind her.

The air conditioner hummed. White noise plugged her ears. The vinyl seat was cool against her back and legs. She noticed the cabbie's ID was now displayed on the back of his seat, at her eye level. *Hassan Ahmad.* He looked younger in the black-and-white photograph. She looked into the rear-view mirror and met his eyes. They were soft and patient. Brown like hers.

"Fasten seatbelt, please."

She secured the belt around her waist, surprised that she had forgotten.

"Stay on the main street, please." She rested her forehead against the chilled window. Iron railings flickered past, blurring dark leaves, heavy with dust and drought, and flashes of old headstones glinting in the rising sun. She looked to the sky. It was going to be another relentless scorching day. She missed the rain. The railing abruptly ended and the trees thinned, giving way to sidewalks and school crossing signs.

The cab slowed. Up ahead, several vehicles were stopped, though it was just after seven and well ahead of morning rush hour. A barricade blocked the road: LOCAL TRAFFIC ONLY. Hassan shifted in his seat, placing his hands at ten and two on the steering wheel. Chilled air wafted into the back seat, carrying the faint scent of his underarm deodorant.

"We'll take a right?"

"No, keep going." She sat up straighter. The taxi crept forward. A copse of stunted maples gave way to a school's parking lot crowded with squad cars, SUVs, media vans, and the mobile forensic unit. Officers walked with purpose, talking intently on radios. A K-9 team, led by a tugging German shepherd, cut across the field towards a birch grove. Hassan stopped for the police officer barring the road. He dabbed his brow before rolling down his window.

"Hello, good morning." Hassan nodded. His smile was broad. "We go through to bridge, please."

Tamara could see the officer's torso, holster, and gun. Dark stains sullied his vest and the front of his pants. A deep, unfriendly voice responded, "Local residents only. Take the detour."

"I'm sorry, I can't." Hassan looked to Tamara in the mirror.

"I'm not asking you."

Hassan's shoulder flinched. The officer bent down to peer through the side window. Tamara looked up at Constable Mike. In the daylight, she thought he didn't look well. His skin was sallow and dry, and dark circles distended under his eyes. His lips were pressed tight and there were no laugh lines. He had blue eyes and the whites were bloodshot. She thought, *His shift is over.* But knew why he was there.

She rolled down her window.

"I have to go this way," she said, and he understood she was saying *I'm sorry it went bad.*

Stiffly, he straightened up and waved the cab through. "Don't stop," he said to the cabbie, his voice hard and threatening.

"No, sir. Thank you." Hassan cautiously pulled ahead and swung around the police car, taking extra care not to touch the brakes.

Tamara craned to see the narrow footpath carving its way through the dun grass away from the sidewalk's safety. Amidst the dappled shade of green leaves and white birch trunks the forensics tent looked almost serene with purple ribbons trailing from the treetops. The cab turned left towards the bridge and Tamara shut her eyes.

OFFENCE/INCIDENT REPORT

OFFENCE/INCIDENT TYPE	LOCATION OF OFFENCE	TYPE OF AREA
SHOOTING	**VICTORIA RD**	**WOODED**
TYPE OF OFFENCE	DATE OF OFFENCE	TIME OF OFFENCE
MURDER	**24/08/2009**	**0126**
Beat Badge#	REPORTING OFFICER	
	CST MIKE BRANDT	
COMPLAINANT	HOME ADDRESS	HOME TELEPHONE
ANTOINE LUCAS	**xxxxxxxxxxx**	**xxxxxxxx**
RACE SEX	DATE OF BIRTH	SIN
BLACK M	**MINOR- 14**	
CODES	DESCRIPTION OF ITEMS	VALUE
D-DAMAGED E-EVIDENCE L-LOST R-RECOVERED S-STOLEN		
CODE	V-VICTIM S-SUSPECT M-MISSING	ADDRESS
HOMICIDE	**V- DEVON JOHNSON**	
	DATE OF BIRTH	HOME TELEPHONE
	MINOR-12	
RACE SEX	HT WT	EYE /HAIR COLOUR
BLACK M	**-------**	**BROWN/BLACK**
EMPLOYER PHONE	DATE OF BIRTH	HOME TELEPHONE

NARRATIVE:

ON THE NIGHT OF 24.08.09 AT 0126 HRS, I CONSTABLE MIKE BRANDT WAS AT IES AND HEARD A CALL COME IN NEAR MY LOCALE. I ARRIVED FIRST ON SCENE FOLLOWED BY PARAMEDICS. I LOCATED TWO MALE JUVENILES ON A PATH CUTTING ACROSS GROVES CORNER.

DEVON JOHNSON, 12, HAD BEEN SHOT AND WAS BEING ASSISTED BY ANTOINE LUCAS, 14. THE VICTIM WAS NON-RESPONSIVE ON ARRIVAL. ANTOINE DID NOT SEE THE SHOOTER. THE SINGLE GUNSHOT SEEMED TO COME FROM THE ROAD. HE DID NOT SEE A VEHICLE.

PARAMEDICS WORKED TO REVIVE VICTIM. I STAYED WITH THE OTHER JUVENILE UNTIL BACKUP ARRIVED. I THEN ACCOMPANIED EHS TO HOSPITAL. VICTIM PRONOUNCED DEAD.

RETURNED TO ASSIST SECURING CRIME SCENE.

END OF REPORT

11

Mike stirred to the squeal of children's voices. He wrenched awake, alert to the muffled cries of distress. No, it was laughter. He was lying naked on his back under a cotton sheet. His skin was clammy from the stale heat in the room. What day was it? He looked to the clock: 5:10 p.m. He had slept in. His heart tightened, but then he realized his police radio was silent. Lori must have turned it off. It must be a day off.

The hoots and hollers were coming from the backyard. A play date. He thought he smelled barbecue and his stomach growled. Was tonight the night they were having steak? No, that was last night. He heard the back door open and Lori's voice spilled in. *Who needs a drink?* He heard several women answer enthusiastically. Outside his window, the patter of a sprinkler fanned back and forth. It would be good to run through the spray with Caleb. It wasn't too late in the day.

Mike swung his legs off the bed and sat up with his feet flat to the floor. He winced at the hitch in his back. His head felt thick, muddled with a low-grade pain as though he had been drinking. He yawned and pondered the small paunch at his midriff. Sucking in his belly, he stretched his arms high above his head to release the tightness.

He must have had a shower last night, or rather this morning, but he couldn't recall doing so. His gear was on the highboy dresser and his work belt and holster were hanging from the back of the door. All was safe. Yawning, he donned a T-shirt bearing his unit's emblem and his baggiest shorts. His shoulders drooped under the lightness of the fabric. He was going barefoot today. His toes waggled happily.

On his way to the bathroom, he barely acknowledged the tightly bound garbage bag beside the laundry hamper containing his uniform's pants and shirt, or the words that he had written with permanent marker—*Do Not Open. Dry Clean Only*. He had a long, satisfying pee, then filled the sink with lukewarm water. He lathered the soap and washed his hands, then washed them again, and again. He found the nailbrush and scrubbed under his nails and between his fingers. Rinsing, he could still feel the stickiness of warm blood. He doused his face and checked his hands again.

He stepped into the hall towards the clink of ice and Lori's mutterings. His thought of surprising her with a hug from behind and a kiss on her neck deflated when he saw the kitchen counters strewn with bags of hotdog buns, chips, pop, paper cups, empty beer bottles and popsicle moulds. On the island a large crocodile slab cake shouted in crayon colours, *Happy 4th Birthday, Caleb!*

"Good. You're up." Lori cracked a tray of ice cubes into a bowl. "Everybody's here and it's time to put the wieners on. You can do that." She loaded a tray with rum and Cokes. Her eyes said, *We'll talk about this later*.

Moving towards the open patio door, he saw the colours first. Exclamation marks of fun: turquoise wading pools, red plastic gingham tablecloths, orange umbrellas, and the stark, sun-white day. Christ, he needed a coffee. He stood at the threshold, obscured by the screen and the room's shadow, conscious of his blanched legs, exposed feet, and the thinness of the fabric separating him from them.

The adults, wives of his colleagues, had migrated into small groupings, laughing at shared jokes. They held their drinks as though nobody had a care in the world. The women were dressed in floral dresses and capri pants that flattered each body. Mike wondered what it would feel like to be so at ease.

The barbecue was smoking. The backyard was perfumed with suntan lotion and bug spray. On the deck was a stack of unopened presents mostly wrapped in blue paper festooned with superheroes and cars with giant eyes. Hordes of boys were charging each other with balloons fashioned into sabres, the parents watching and not watching. The disorder unnerved him. Nobody was in charge.

He located baby Connor on his grandmother's lap. His sunhat was askew and the chinstrap tugged at his neck. He was gripping a popsicle stick. Red juice stained his face and dripped down his chest. Mike bristled at his mother-in-law's inattentiveness. His own mother had always been so particular about her only son's appearance. She believed one must always be prepared to meet their Maker. Into her seventies, she was still curling her thin hair and insisting on wearing a blazer, skirt, nylons, and low heels, even though her fingers could no longer fasten buttons or pull up zippers. In the end, she met her Maker in a crumpled, stained hospital gown and diaper.

"Daddy!"

Caleb ran towards him, arms wide open, *Birthday Boy* emblazoned across his chest, a child-size police hat on his head, and at his hip a plastic gun and holster.

Mike adopted his best civilian guise and stepped into the day.

The party was over. Gift bags had been bestowed, guests hugged out the door, picnic tables cleared, and murky wading pools dumped. From the kitchen, the sound of dishes clattering was more emphatic than usual. The baby was already asleep. Mike had rubbed Connor's mildly sunburned shoulders with aloe vera and tucked him in. He would have to talk to Lori about her mother. She was getting too old to watch the boys. People assumed accidents were something that happened away from home, but he knew that most happened right in front of you.

"I'm dried, Daddy."

He stopped rubbing the towel and lifted it to reveal his son's pouty face and mussed hair. Caleb's entire body had tanned to a deep, rich brown with the exception of the bathing suit line highlighting his little white bum.

"Okay, PJs on and bedtime."

Caleb draped his arms around his father's neck and leaned in as Mike pulled on one pyjama leg followed by the other. He breathed in vanilla bubble bath and that other smell that only children have, something that reminded him of fresh-cut grass.

"Okay, birthday boy, away we go." He hoisted him up.

Caleb wrapped his legs around his father's waist and tucked his wet head against his chest. It always surprised him how little his son weighed and how much he had to adjust his hold to not crush him. Caleb was limp in his arms and he thought he might be asleep, but then his son reached out, miming for his stuffed crocodile propped on the toilet seat cover. Mike leaned down to retrieve Snappy and his back muscle tugged.

Caleb squirmed to loosen his father's grasp. "Too tight."

He redistributed his son's weight onto his hips and groaned upright. "There's too much cake in your belly, little buddy."

At nine o'clock the sun's orange cast suffused the blue walls in Caleb's room. The salvaged stop sign and one-way street marker above his bed gleamed. Mike pulled the blind down and night instantly fell. Stars painted on the ceiling glowed an alien yellow-green. He checked the safety lock restraining the window. Hot air streamed over his hand, drawing through the narrow opening.

"I want my birthday present with me," said Caleb.

"Tomorrow we'll make the bed when you're not so tired."

"No," he whined and clung tighter to Mike's neck. "I need it to go to sleep."

Mike looked at his son's face and tried to imagine its visage as a man's, but could not. His hand was on his son's chest and he could feel the thump of his heart so alive.

"I guess that would be okay." He flipped the boy on his back and flew him once around the room before floating him down onto his bed. Caleb heaved the bedcover embellished with soccer balls onto the floor.

"Hey, hey, Mommy's not picking that up."

His son winced at the disappointment in his voice. "Sorry." The *r*'s rounded into *w*'s.

"I'll get it this time, but only because it's your birthday." He shoved it into the laundry basket. "I'll be right back."

Caleb watched his daddy disappear into the light of the door. He looked up at the stars above his head and pulled Snappy closer. Snappy smelled like laundry. Mommy had washed him for the party. Snappy didn't like going round and round in the washy machine. Even if Mommy said crocodiles liked water, Snappy didn't. Caleb counted on his fingers: 1, 2, 3, 4. He was four now.

He told Snappy about his cake, chocolate, his favourite, and about stepping on balloons that went pop-pop-pop, and the fizzy root beer that came out his nose, and hot dogs catching fire, and Aiden puking blue and green, and everybody singing "Happy Birthday" to him, and Daddy not coming downstairs to say good morning. He held his hand up and saluted four fingers.

Daddy said, "Close your eyes."

Caleb scrunched his eyes shut. A waft of warm air and soft cloth fluttered onto him. He lay perfectly still while a tickle of hands straightened the covers over him.

"Okay, open your eyes."

He was swathed in a red and blue comforter. There were two police cars going in different directions, almost as big as his whole bed, and squiggles to say the sirens were on. He reached down to touch the sun-yellow police shields adorning the cars. Skirting the floor were roads with street lamps and high buildings at night, some windows were lit up yellow and others dark, and bad guys were jumping over rooftops with bags of loot.

"You like it?" Mommy asked. Caleb couldn't see Mommy. She was standing in the doorway and all he could see was the light around her.

He didn't know all the words to tell her that the bad guys thought they had got away but the police cars were waiting on the other side of the bed to catch 'em and take 'em to jail for a time out. He was in the police cars and on the roof and in the streets and in the cars and he could drive off the bed and down the hallway to patrol the kitchen and windows and doorways and nothing bad could ever happen to Daddy or him or Baby or Mommy because now he had all the superpowers to keep them safe.

So he settled on the best words. "I'm the good guy. The end." He squirmed under the covers, pulling Snappy close.

Mike bent down and kissed him on the forehead three times. Always three times; Caleb insisted that was the magic number. By the time his mother leaned in, he was asleep.

The stringent eucalyptus ointment made Mike's eyes water. No matter how far he twisted his naked body, he couldn't reach the middle of his spine to apply the salve. Lori stepped out of their bathroom, rubbing away moisturizer on her cheeks and neck. Her white tank top highlighted the soft distension of her belly and the milk fullness of her breasts. Silvered stretch marks radiated down her inner thighs.

"Give it to me." She took the ointment and sat beside him. He shifted sideways, irritated that he needed to rely on her to reach the tender spot. It wasn't how he wanted her to see him. His skin flinched from the cold salve and the gentle pressure of her touch. She rubbed the cream in a widening circle. Its heat flared.

She said, "Tell me."

The hot prickled his skin and he thought maybe she should stop.

"Not this one," he said.

She worked her fingers deeper, kneading the muscle that was rigid across his lower back. "Tell me."

"No." He moaned as her fingers probed the aching hurt.

"This is the only way we make it together." Her voice was soft, a whisper behind him. The pain wormed deeper. "Why did you forget your son's birthday?"

Her hand stopped on the small of his back and pressed deep. Warmth bloomed against his spine, numbing the pain. The sensation was no longer hot or cold but liquid.

Her hand burned under his skin.

"Why were you late coming home? Did you go for breakfast with the guys again?"

"No."

She rubbed the small of his back, melting away the hurt. He squirmed from her probing touch. "Tell me."

He couldn't tell her about the boy he knew was dead before he reached for a pulse. Or how he made a rookie mistake and looked him in the eyes breaking the first rule to never look them in the eyes.

He couldn't tell her about the meat smell of warm blood. Or the strength of a fourteen-year-old boy who doesn't want to let go. He considered telling her how the boy curled into him, burying his face against his chest, but then he would have to tell her about the sound that tore from the kid's throat.

"Two friends in a band were up late writing songs. It was hot, so they took a walk because they couldn't find the right words to describe what it felt like to be in the street in the middle of the night. So they walked to find the words . . ."

Lori's hand was on his back. Heat flared from her fingertips.

"One of them got shot. He was twelve. He didn't make it."

Her hand fell away, and cold flushed his skin. She stood and wrapped her arms around him and he leaned into her breasts to breathe her in.

"I couldn't help him."

"Shh." She kissed his forehead. He fumbled for her breasts. She lifted her shirt and slipped off her panties. He was awed by her softness. She laid his hand on her heart. He kissed her in gratitude and in hunger. Straddling his lap, she guided him inside her, her nipples against his chest, her long hair smelling of sun and coconut. He tasted salt on her neck. Unable to stop, unable to wait for her, unable to escape the boy's staring eyes, he came.

12

Spooned against him, Lori listened to her husband's restless dreams and held the spasms of his legs and the shudders of his body. When his sleep breath arrested, she nudged his shoulder and breathed in with him. She whispered in his ear, "Tomorrow will be a better day."

She wondered how much longer she could keep telling herself that.

13

On Wednesday, the mall was crowded with teenagers and the elderly. The media had been advising people to go to air-conditioned malls, theatres, bars, and restaurants to escape the heat. They were heeding the call.

Strapped in his stroller, Connor was crying, and Caleb was dallying, focused on his ice cream cone rather than on where he was going. Lori was navigating the stroller, and Mike, cranky that he was there on his day off solely to spend his mother-in-law's birthday gift certificates, had been relegated to lugging shopping bags. Somewhere between the fifth or sixth pair of rejected sneakers, when he suggested Lori come back another time, she gave him a warning growl. "I'm not doing this alone."

To keep himself mollified, he scanned the crowds, checking body language, glancing at bags, purses, and pockets, guessing heights and weights, and memorizing distinguishing features. When some glared back, he switched to covert mode, looking quickly, then recalling as many details as possible before confirming accuracy. His success rate was high, though occasionally he was surprised to discover that a shirt was blue, not green, and hair was curly, not straight.

He had lost Caleb. His son was twenty feet behind them, shoving the sticky remains of his cone into a garbage bin.

"Get over here!"

Caleb ran to them, wiping his hands on his T-shirt.

"You don't go off on your own. You know better than that. Hold on to the stroller."

He pushed open the glass doors and the smell of asphalt, exhaust, and heat assaulted them. Connor kicked off a shoe. When Lori bent down to put it back on, he kicked off the other. Mike scanned the lot in the general direction of the minivan. He hated the minivan. Lori said it was practical and economical. She had tied a pink scrunchie to the antenna to set it apart from the wash of other grey vans. She had a habit of not taking a visual reference when she parked and later wandering aimlessly searching for it. She said she had other things on her mind when she had the kids and that she *always* had the kids.

His attention lingered on a man leaving the mall. Caucasian, six two, 260, Montreal Canadiens T-shirt, jeans. Cropped red hair. He used his body to open the door and leaned against it to light a smoke. It took him three attempts to spark the lighter. He was coming out of the Black Raven Tavern—*Beat the Heat $2.99 Draft*. Rows of taxis lined the curb, but the man headed to the parking lot.

"Ready." Lori had the children in tow again and stepped into the crosswalk. Caleb raised his hand and looked both ways. The stroller bumpity-bumped along with the back wheel's wobble. "Don't you touch those shoes again, Connor! Do you hear Mommy?" Connor responded with a shriek, and a glob of snot blew from his nose.

The man was definitely staggering.

"What?" Lori said. She followed his stare. "You're not on duty."

Kicking and arching, Connor was priming for a tantrum. Caleb tried to distract him with Snappy, but that made him scream louder.

"I'll just get the plate number." He stuffed the bags into the back of the stroller. "Call it in for me. Suspected DUI. South parking lot." He ignored the tightening of her lips and furrowed brow. "I'll be right back."

"Me come!" Caleb moved to follow his father. Lori grabbed his arm.

"Put your hand back on that stroller and do not take it off!" She watched Mike's retreating back and sniped, "You're *just* getting the licence plate."

Mike slowed when the man dropped his smoke and bent to retrieve it. Perhaps he could help him make the right choice and everyone could go on with their day. People make mistakes. Terrible mistakes.

He approached, using his friendliest smile. "Christ, I can never remember where I parked." The man stared back. "Didn't I see you in the tavern?" Mike shielded his eyes from the sun and casually scouted the lot. "Nothing like a beer in this kind of heat, huh? Specially at those prices."

"You got that right." The man slurred his words and resumed course.

"Ah, there's mine. Goddamn minivans, can't tell them apart."

He followed the man to his truck. Red. Licence plate CMJ 2X2. Retrieving the keys from his front jeans pocket, the guy dropped his smoke again but this time didn't bother to pick it up. Backup wasn't going to get there in time.

"Damn, that's not my van." Mike removed his ball cap and wiped the sweat from his forehead. "I only had one beer, but shit, this heat, huh, it might as well of been three. Maybe I should grab a cab?"

"What are you doing, bud?" The man had the key in the lock.

He went for the non-threatening casual-buddies script. "Just looking for my van."

"Well, it ain't here." The *so fuck off* was implied. He unlocked the door.

"I think you've had too much to drink to be driving. Don't you? There's a cab right over there. You can get your truck tomorrow."

Mike sized up the bulge of his arms, working hands, and extra sixty pounds. He reviewed the strike points—knees, solar plexus, throat—he had a thick neck. Two elderly women strolled past the pickup. A few vehicles down, a woman and teenage girl were loading shopping bags into a hatchback. No sirens were in earshot. The man opened the door and got in.

Mike put his hand on the door and quietly said, "I can't let you drive." He glanced at the seat and floor for a crowbar or empty bottle that could be used as a weapon. The man had one hand on the steering wheel and the key in the ignition. His knuckles were bent and flattened. A fighter's hand.

"And who the fuck do you think you are?"

"I'm a cop. I need you to step out of the vehicle."

It was the narrowing of the man's eyes that gave him away. Mike sidestepped a hard right, grabbed the perp by his shoulders, and yanked him forward and out of the truck. But rather than being thrown off balance, the man tackled him. Two hundred and sixty pounds drove into his chest, and vise-like arms constricted his ribs. Mike's sneakers scrabbled for the pavement as he was lifted off the ground. He couldn't breathe. Pain seared down his leg.

For the first time as an officer, Mike was not in control. He slammed the man's ears with palms wide open, to no effect. Fisting two hands together, he came down hard against the clavicle and bulging neck. The man swung around and rammed him into the side of the pickup box. Metal buckled against his back.

That's when it happened. He could taste it on his tongue. It clawed through his skin. He wanted to kill this man. He wanted blood.

He drove his fist upward under the man's rib cage, boring for his heart. Lungs expelled stale cigarettes and sour beer and the man's arms dropped. Mike dug into his collarbone, wrenching him down and forward. Flesh tore under his fingernails. Grabbing his wrist, he rotated the perp's arm behind his back. Hurling his full weight on the fat bastard, he slammed him face first into the pavement. They hit the ground hard.

Jabbing his knee in the man's back, he leaned into the contorted arm to amplify the pain, pinning the man's head with his other elbow. The perp was swearing a fucking blue streak. His lip was split, he was spitting foam and blood. Mike ground his cheek into the asphalt.

"*Shut up!* You're under arrest for assaulting an officer and intent to drive under the influence—"

With each indictment he jarred the perp's arm farther up. His muscles quivered with adrenaline overload. His grip would leave marks and if he applied any more pressure he would snap the wrist or arm. He wanted the perp to resist and give him a reason.

A siren pierced his eardrums, and tires lurched to a stop a few feet away.

He looked up and saw a woman and a teenage girl with their mouths open as though they were screaming bloody murder. Across the way another woman on her phone with a crying baby in a stroller was trying to shield a small boy's eyes. The boy was standing stock still with a green crocodile limp in his hand, and the front of his shorts was stained wet.

"I'm a cop! I'm a cop!" Mike raged as officers converged with weapons drawn.

14

Beddie-bye. Night, night. Caleb kissed Snappy three times on the snout.

The bedroom blind was down. The door closed tight. If he opened the door he would find Daddy and Mommy and baby Connor there on the other side. He knew this was true because he'd done it before. He ran his new toy car over his birthday comforter, tracing circles around the big police cars. He didn't push the button to make the siren wail. He was supposed to be asleep. The stars were glowing on the ceiling and it was night outside.

He whispered, *WhooWhooWhoo*. The bad guys were on the rooftops. The bad guy was in the parking lot. Daddy stopped the bad guy. Caleb spun the toy car to a stop, blocking the robbers about to jump onto the next roof. *Freeze!* They froze with their loot bags on their backs.

The bad guy hit Daddy. Daddy hit the bad guy. Caleb's not supposed to hit baby Connor, not even a little. Not even when he takes his cars and sticks them in his mouth. But Mommy didn't yell at Daddy, or the bad guy, when they were hitting.

The toy car slowly patrolled the edges of the bed. All was quiet in the town. Some windows on the buildings were yellow, but most were black. Everyone thought they were safe in bed. They didn't know there were bad guys on the roof.

There was a big bang when Daddy felled against the truck. There were bad words not allowed. Daddy hit the bad guy and the bad guy hit Daddy and they felled down—all fall down. The sirens went *whoowhoowhoo*. Mommy tried to make him not see, but he saw. He saw Daddy and a bad guy and they felled down, then he couldn't see, then he could, and then there wasn't a good guy and a bad guy. There were just two bad guys. The one with the meanest eyes looked right at him.

Hot wet welled and spread under his bum. He squirmed in the bed. He had on big-boy underwear because he was four and didn't need a diaper anymore like his baby brother. When he had to pee he told Mommy and she took him to the toilet because he was *too big for the potty*. But he didn't tell Mommy in the parking lot, because the hot peed down his bare leg and into his sock before his brain knew he had to go. He touched the fresh wet spot on the sheet.

Daddy was there and then he was gone. Daddy runned away and the bad man made him pee.

He should call Mommy. She would make the bed good again and tell him it's okay he was still little. But through the walls and under the door he could hear Mommy and Daddy growling.

He opened his mouth wide, baring all his teeth, and Snappy chomped down on the bad guys.

15

Across the lower screen of the muted television, the banner read: *Friday 5:10 a.m., 22°C, expected high 39°C*. Mike looked at the black socks on his feet and sighed. He checked his watch—5:14—and rolled back the time. Fridays were always a crappy workday.

He looked at Lori fast asleep. All of yesterday, she had given him the silent treatment. She took the boys out and wasn't back for supper, and when they finally did return, she ignored him and didn't bother to say goodnight. Three days off and one was spent being punished by his wife.

What was he supposed to have done? Let the asshole drive away? His family was driving on the same roads. He winced as he applied antiseptic to the road rash on his elbow. Clocking sideways to the mirror, he assessed the deep purple bruise branding his lower back. As he rotated his waist gingerly, a twinge stung his side. He looked at the sag of his belly and sucked it in. He flexed his arm and was somewhat comforted by the hard bicep. He'd done the right thing; even the boys on scene said so. They took the collar and kept him out of it. His word was good enough and less paperwork for them.

He pulled on his regulation black T-shirt, followed by his freshly dry-cleaned black shirt. At least it was short-sleeved. He stepped into his pants. The sky-blue stripes running up the legs and the blue and white badge on his right shoulder popped bold against the dark fabric. He looked assertive and official. It wasn't all his fault. An asshole had been drinking and about to drive. Lori was supposed to call it in, take the boys to the van, and wait for him. She wasn't supposed to be there. With the boys, no less.

He buttoned the collar. It was tight. He undid one button. It wasn't fair to punish him for doing what was right. He couldn't turn it off and on. She liked being a cop's wife when she was attending community picnics and charity events. Everything was fine as long as she didn't have to see the shit he really did to make a living.

He immediately regretted blaming her and swallowed the bitter taste of 5:00 a.m. and his own bullshit. She was right. He should have just taken the plate number. He was off duty. Lori groaned and rolled over in bed, twisting the sheet. He followed the long line of her tanned legs to her bare thighs to the peep of polka-dot underwear. When they first were married she didn't wear underwear to bed. He felt a tug at his crotch and looked away.

A serious news anchor was mouthing the day's top stories. A photo of a smiling boy appeared on the screen. He skimmed the unfamiliar face. A headline flashed beneath: *Devon Johnson, 12, Murdered*. He looked at the child's face again, unable to reconcile it with the boy he had seen. The news cut to a crying woman speaking into a microphone. *Mother Appeals for Witnesses to Come Forward*. Someone's hands held her trembling shoulders. He shut off the TV.

As he tightened his belt, his back recoiled from the leather snaking across the bruise. He sagged forward and donned his utility belt. Bracing against the pain, he straightened, and loosened the belt another notch. He loaded the belt clips in reverse order: pepper spray, flashlight, radio, baton, Taser holster, CPR mask, gloves— He had forgotten to use his gloves that night in the park. He looked down at his work belt. The black leather hid most stains. He ran his nail along the ridge of his holster, and a dark brown crust shaved under his nail. He wiped his nail on his pants and finished dressing: cuffs, key, weapon holster. Check.

He retrieved the ammo safe from the top shelf of the closet and extracted the magazines. Lori continued to snore soft, even breaths. He pulled open the upper sock drawer and pushed aside the tightly balled socks, all black. He unlatched the lock box and removed his gun. The cold metal in his hand pulled his shoulders back and made him stand taller. He set the gun on top of the dresser. He checked mag No. 1, counted fifteen bullets, and slipped it into the pouch on his belt. He checked mag No. 2, counted fifteen, and looked in the ammo box for the chamber single. But it wasn't there.

He tried to process how that was possible. He checked the sock drawer to confirm he hadn't dropped it. His mind calculated the height of the dresser plus a chair plus the height of Caleb and remembered that the ammo box had been locked. He looked down at the hardwood floor, but he would have heard it drop. He slowly pulled back the gun's slide. Inside was the bullet. Live in the chamber.

His eye twitched. He slipped in the mag and holstered his weapon. He told himself the gun had been secured in the lock box. It had been a brutal seventeen-hour shift and he had been exhausted. He knew that wasn't an excuse. Just now, he had taken the gun out of the lock box with his finger on the cocked trigger.

He told himself, *You won't do that again. You won't do that again. You won't do that again.* He didn't want to think *Nobody knows*, but he did.

He went to the bed. Lori looked happy. The tightness around her mouth and eyes was relaxed. Watching her sleep felt intimate, even illicit. He was seeing her free of her life, of him, the children, and worry. He was seeing who she could have been. He had given her a heavy burden as a cop's wife. She had married him and the job and all the risks it entailed, both on and off duty. How many of their "blue family" had divorced or been ravaged by booze or worse? How many funerals had he attended for self-inflicted wounds? Too many. He knew how rarely she truly laughed, and then only with the children.

He had promised himself that he would never bring the ugliness of out there into their home. But he had, he had brought it home, cut it open, and let it bleed all over his family. He would do better. He kissed his fingers and softly touched her cheek. Lori groaned and rolled away.

He tiptoed out of the bedroom and went to the baby's room. Connor was on his back in the crib. His cheeks were flushed and his hair damp. By the smell, his diaper was full. Rumpled at the foot of the crib was his blanket. Mike debated covering him, but decided the risk of waking him was too great. He brushed his fingertips ever so gently over the wisps of the baby's flyaway hair. *You won't remember that day.* But it stank of absolution. He would do better.

Gently, he pushed open Caleb's door. He was on his side on top of the covers. His pants were off and his bare bum was exposed. Snappy was in one hand and the toy car in the other. Mouth agape, he was breathing deeply. There was no fear of waking him. Mike kissed him three times on the top of his head. Three times, the way Caleb liked it.

They had said their proper goodbyes at bedtime, knowing Caleb wouldn't be awake when his daddy left. Three kisses, responded to with three "I love yous." There had to be three. Before night shifts, Mike would get down on one knee so his son could throw his arms around his neck, stretch on his tiptoes, and recite the words fast in his ear. Then Mike would wait while the boy ran to his room, calling, "Is you still here?" He was expected to reply "Yes, yes, yes" to the patter of bare feet retreating down the hallway and wasn't allowed to leave until he heard his son's bedroom door shut and his muffled, "All clear!"

Any deviation from this protocol resulted in a titanic tantrum that turned Caleb's face apoplectic. Lori said it was a phase and Mike should humour him. But lately, Caleb had been applying the same system to his mother and baby brother. It was no longer cute when it added twenty minutes to every departure. It would need to be addressed. As would the "gifts" he kept finding in his pockets at work: a rock, an uncooked macaroni noodle, a dead housefly. He reached into his left trouser pocket and extracted a bent beer cap.

As he pried himself up from the bed, his hand slid across a cold, wet spot. He pulled back the comforter. Caleb's pyjama bottoms were crumpled in a sodden ball. He let the comforter fall back in place. He had to get to work.

Using the long shoehorn to wedge on his black regulation boots, he planted his foot on the hallway bench to tie the laces. He finalized his checklist:

- ✓ important papers—top drawer file cabinet
- ✓ medical, house, personal insurance—paid in full
- ✓ family services contacts—side of fridge
- ✓ emergency funds—top of fridge
- ✓ wills—up to date
- ✓ three "I love yous"
- ✓ five goodbye kisses
- ✓ Eyes he had looked into—
  - ✓ one mother
  - ✓ one father
  - ✓ nine suicides
  - ✓ seven motor vehicle accidents
  - ✓ three ODs
  - ✓ one shot boy

He looked back to the living room at the toys piled in the corner, the Kool-Aid-stained carpet, crooked family photos above the couch, and bag of empty beer bottles he was supposed to take to the curb.

He would do better. He put on his hat and walked out the door.

16

Kate refused to open her eyes, fearful of the light threatening to pierce her brain's throbbing membrane. She swallowed the after-taste of too many beers and the acrid regret of illicit smokes. She should've had the IV.

She tried to reconstruct the night but lost the trail after three bars. She retraced her steps back to the point last seen, her monthly girls' night out—dinner and wine at a decent restaurant with five of her sister nurses. Much to the chagrin of the waiter and other patrons, their requisite anatomical stories were ribald, disgusting, and deliciously inappropriate for a public space. Apart from the snorts and belly laughs, it had begun as a respectable evening.

There had been a cab ride to an unfamiliar club where they drank concoctions that tasted like orange popsicles. They got louder, more beautiful, and their legs longer. Amy tied a cherry stem with her tongue, which Kate thought could only happen in the movies. She remembered buying a round of something topped with whipped cream at the bar. Beside her, an older woman with teased blonde hair and a low-cut white tank top and a braying notice-me laugh was hitting on a much younger man.

"I'm sixty-two, can you believe it? California, all my life." Her breasts were more pert than Kate's and perfectly symmetrical.

"Belgium! Really?" The Californian leaned in with both hands on the man's thighs, exposing her white lace bra and vodka-infused heart. "I've always, *always* wanted an international friend," she slurred. "Speak French to me." Instead, he asked to pay his tab.

The woman laughed, wobbled herself upright, and downed her sex in a glass. "It's been raining in California," she said, her head held high. "The rain just keeps falling and falling . . ." She looked directly at Kate when she said these words.

There was another club, but she couldn't remember the where or how of getting there. She remembered strobes of nipple-shaped shooters, thumping music shocking their hearts, barefoot stomps, shouts of "I love you!" in each other's ears. A small terrier of a man insinuated himself into their inner circle, hands groping.

"Do you want to get out of here?" he hollered to her over the beats. He had soft eyes, and for a moment she undressed him and imagined them screwing. It might even have been nice.

"It's raining in California," she said. "It just keeps raining and raining." Laughing, she spun away, needing to pee. He grabbed her arm, too tight, and rubbed his crotch against her leg.

"Live a little, babe."

"Fuck off," she said and shook him off.

"Stuck-up bitch."

It wasn't the words but the tone. It had the same bile of the DUIs, crackheads, and SOBs with busted noses, heads, and knuckles who railed and spat at the nurses charged with revealing the secrets of their blood. She grabbed the man's balls and twisted, snarled in his ear, "Down, boy." A melee of arms and citrus perfumes yanked her out, out into the breathless night.

She remembered squatting to pee on the sidewalk, shielded by staggering friends, horns honking, and then up, up into a hotel. Mini bottles were emptied and stale peanuts devoured. They danced a conga line to a Latvian polka over the beds, shedding their tops down to their bras. The two youngest puked in the bathtub. She remembered someone calling the Good Guys, and two gorgeous paramedics arrived with party packs of IV fluids, but they refused to come into the feral room or run the lines, citing professional limits and their own personal safety.

The city's finest ER nurses tried to find a vein and failed in fits of laughter and pin-cushioned arms. Finally, Betty, who didn't drink and was on speed dial, was called. She replenished the young one's fluids with one simple prick, which they all admired and profusely complimented her technique. With hindsight churning her head and stomach, Kate deeply regretted puncturing the other fluid bags for a raucous, pissing water fight. They had all agreed, "Save the young ones first." Next time, frig the young ones.

She opened one eye. She had made it home. Mounded in the corner was a tangle of blue scrubs in need of laundering. Splayed on the floor, her little black halter dress was inside out and her panties and bra were nestled beside a half-empty bottle of scotch. The trail of clothing led to the bed: jeans, sneakers, and a man's black T-shirt.

She reached behind her and met hot skin. An arm encircled her waist. Tattooed on the forearm, in black and grey, was the head of a Belgian Malinois, and scrolled beneath, "Annabelle" in commemorative cursive. On the strong, tanned hand was a wedding band.

"Morning," Riley said and kissed her shoulder. "I'm glad you called. I've missed you."

The room tilted and bile rose in her throat. "Where's Zeus?"

Tripping over her shoes, she swung open the bathroom door and Zeus scrambled to his feet, his tail wagging Good morning! On hands and knees, she made it to the toilet and vomited. Between retches, she fended off Zeus intent on herding her away from the thing that was hurting her.

It was going to be a hell day and it was only mid-morning. Kate followed the red dots mapping the hospital's floor to the elevator, disregarding the blues and yellows. It was a simple system, but she had already been accosted twice for directions. It astounded her that people could get lost inside a building.

An aborted, stifling half-mile run and a too-long cold shower had failed to detox her pores, and she couldn't stomach the eggs and bacon Riley had made in her kitchen, as though he belonged. Mercifully, she had no recollection of what he said was a mind-blowing night and she pushed away the tenderness of his see-ya-later kiss before he went home to his wife.

Zeus's nails clacked against the cool, polished floors. His light nylon "Working Dog" vest wasn't deterring the delighted smiles and reaching hands of enamoured passersby. Without her scrubs or rescue gear, she was merely a woman with a dog. It didn't help that Zeus looked everyone in the eye and wagged *hello*.

A forceful, overweight woman with two canes blocked their path to the elevator. "Oh, my! What a beautiful pup!"

Zeus submitted to a rash of sloppy head rubs, and Kate waited for it to be over. This was her penance. She had convinced administration to grant him therapy status and therefore access to her mother's room, contravening hospital policy. Admin cited health concerns, which seemed absurd in a realm of superbugs. In the end, they made an exception for one of their own.

The woman kissed Zeus's nose and yammered on about how he looked exactly like her childhood Labrador. Gripping his snout, she stared into his eyes. She cooed and asked him if his name was Teddy, and actually waited for him to reply. Zeus glanced uncertainly to Kate. His tail swished the floor. "You have the same eyes as Teddy, don't you, sweetness?" The elevator doors opened and Kate ushered Zeus in. She feared the woman would follow.

"Teddy was the best dog," the woman said. There were tears in her eyes and she waved until the elevator doors shut. Kate noted the woman's yellow skin and swollen ankles, and triaged her as CTD—circling the drain. She caught a whiff of her own stale-alcohol breath. She should have had an Aspirin and more water. She really needed to take better care of her kidneys and stick with beers.

It was rest period on the eighth floor. The hallway lights were dimmed and the corridors thankfully empty. She hated this floor, and they weren't thrilled about her either. She ghosted past the nurses' hub station, ringed by rooms and radiating corridors. There were no closed doors here, no expectations of privacy. Consults happened in the hallways and patients' doors were always open. Everything could be seen and overheard. She didn't like it.

As a visitor, she discovered she could walk the halls unseen. If by chance eyes met, she only had to look at the floor to regain invisibility. But everyone noticed Zeus. She'd see the questioning in their eyes as to whether rules were being breached. When this happened, Kate leaned back on her heels and walked as though this was her house. No one had ever questioned her.

It was harder for her to be seen. The shunning felt deliberate when she was standing at the desk waiting to be acknowledged. It was worse in her civvies than her scrubs. The impatient look of *What?* infuriated her, even though she had given the same hard look to timid family members who dared open their STAFF ONLY door rather than ring the buzzer.

Compared to the ER, this place was a slow-motion eddy of days and nights and rounds and shifts. It was a place in waiting. The indifference of day after day had infected the floor with a general malaise. There was no sense of team or pride, and the patient load was impossible. Nurses were doling out care five minutes per patient per hour. She had timed it. Inevitably, the insistent robbed from the meek. The unit jittered with an uncertainty that wasn't eased by the false bravado and rabbit-shit fear of the rotating third- and fourth-year residents. She didn't trust it.

Zeus's head swung towards every open door, indicating *someone's there*. She looked too, drawn to the anonymous bodies curled tight, cloaked in blue gowns exposing vulnerable spines and buttocks, waiting for permission to go home. Here were the patients she didn't see or think about. When patients left ER they were alive and that was the end of the story. There was nothing to gain knowing the outcome. But here, their stories were still being written.

Their acquiescence and quiet resignation unnerved her. Buzzers—rung for help to pee, to stand, to lessen pain—often went unheeded until too late. Patients made their humiliations small and apologetic. Forgiving when nobody came and grateful when someone finally did. She wanted them to shout and throw things. Behaviour she wouldn't tolerate downstairs in the ER.

Zeus veered around a wheelchair laden with stuffed animals, chocolate boxes, and empty vases. Inside the room, a tense family awaiting discharge looked up expectantly. On the edge of the bed, a grey-skinned woman clutched a plastic bag stuffed with personal belongings, defying anyone to snatch it away. They'd hear the same parting words she so often said, "Good luck," before their names were wiped from the board.

She stopped at the threshold of her mother's room. Zeus plopped to a tight sit with one paw on her boot. Kate breathed in the stringent chemicals and dead air and steeled herself with the armour of a nurse. *Okay*, she thought and breathed out.

Zeus trotted to the bedside with his nose high, cocking his head to take in the person on the bed. He sniffed the motionless hand, nuzzled his snout under its palm, and coaxed it to pat his head. The hand flopped back onto the bed. He looked up at Kate.

"She's sleeping. Beddie-bye."

He lay down on the cool floor, chin on paws, eyes on her.

Kate stepped closer. The ventilator had been replaced by an oxygen mask. The saturation levels were minimal, a good sign. She checked the urine bag. It was clear. Dried blood flecked the IV insertion site. The surrounding papery skin was mottled black and purple around old stabs. Kate wondered how many bruises she had inflicted in the ER. Bruising wasn't a concern for them.

She didn't find anything amiss, unlike the day before when she had walked in on her mother bleeding out because a baby nurse hadn't inserted the IV properly. When the nurse finally answered the buzzer, Kate was in the midst of inserting a new line. She didn't give a shit that she made the newbie cry. Half the nurses on this unit wouldn't last an hour in ER. And god help them, they knew not to send the baby doctors in while she was there. A special meeting was convened to address her concerns, but it wasn't her job to train them up. Zeus's head lifted. Kate smiled a fake calm and he settled back down. The upside was that Ruth was moved to a private room. Kate wasn't sure if that was for her mother's benefit or to mollify her.

The woman in the hospital bed looked nothing like her mother. Her face was lax, and skin slumped over her cheekbones in a slight frown. Her mother always had a lipstick smile. This woman had chipped nail polish. Her mother's nail polish was immaculate, cherry red to complement her hair, Clairol No. 5. Ruth would never go out into the world looking so exposed.

Her mother's brain was flooded with blood, but there was no outward sign of damage. In the scan, the blood appeared white in a terrain of x-ray grey. It reminded her of the satellite imagery used for ground searches. Somewhere in that vastness, her mother was lost. All they could do was wait. Some came back.

"Hi, Mom."

The silence widened between them. Daughter was a harder role. She took a seat in the only chair in the corner and watched her mother breathe. The oversized clock mounted to the wall ticked away seconds. She squirmed in the sticky vinyl chair. Across the hall two young residents were in the room with Mr. Stroke Man. From her vantage point, she could see his sunken, off-kilter face. They asked him the same questions every day. "Do you know where you are?" "What time is it?" She wished they would close the door. "What day is it?" The day always stumped him. "Saturday," his deep voice boomed. Once a week, he would be correct.

It was Friday, she told herself. But she had to think about it. She flashed on Riley naked on her bed and the scars on his chest, and her standing above him. Had she danced for him? Ruth would be appalled if she knew her daughter. A dull headache pulsed behind her eyes. She still had to go to the house today.

"What's your name?" She should look away. Mr. Stroke's mouth opened in a wordless, gaping *O*. They asked him again and his face twisted in mute anguish. They asked him if he was in pain. "Point to your nose." He touched his forehead. A drawing was held up. He said the words loudly, so he'd be heard: "Teacup, dog, spoon." "Point," they said, and his finger drew aimless lines in the air. "Good job," they said.

Zeus laid his head on her lap and his soft eyes stared up into hers. She rubbed behind his ears. "It's okay." But her heart was beating fast.

He spun around and his tail waved welcome. Nurse Pam of the floral scrubs, so much cheerier and hopeful than the utilitarian blues Kate wore, entered the room.

"Hello, handsome boy!"

His ears cupped the warmth of her voice.

Nurse Pam had a natural ease with animals and people. She tried to answer every question, sought out what she didn't know, smiled often, and remembered everyone's names. She walked as though she knew she was the luckiest woman alive and by the grace of god she'd go home that night and had no right to complain. Pam would make a great ER nurse. She went directly to her mother's bedside with Zeus trailing behind her. His vest had slipped slightly and his tail swooshed-swooshed against the thin fabric.

"Hello, Ruth. I'm here to check your vitals. Oh, what a good strong heartbeat you have today. Some hot out there. You're not too hot are you, dear? I'll be back later to change your bed. That'll feel good, won't it? Nice clean sheets. I'm going to take your temperature now, it might be a bit cold." She expertly inserted the thermometer into her mother's ear. "Her vitals are good today." It took Kate a moment to realize the warm voice was directed to her.

"She did very well coming off the ventilator. Didn't you, Ruth? It must feel so much better having that out." She updated Kate on the stats, meds, fluids, and latest CT results. There was a small reduction in swelling and no indication of further bleeding. The docs were weaning blood pressure meds, but keeping her in an induced coma to allow the brain to rest and heal. She spoke to her nurse to nurse and knew every detail of Ruth's chart. Pam had been at the special meeting, but didn't seem to hold a grudge. She brushed aside the hair plastered to Ruth's forehead, intimately touching her mother. Something Kate couldn't yet do. In truth, she had never touched anyone as tenderly as Pam had just done. The thermometer beeped. "All done. It's perfect. Good job."

She patted Ruth's arm, slipped the rubber tip off the thermometer, and tossed it into the bin without looking. "I think we'll have a nice sponge bath later and moisturize your skin. And before I leave tonight I'll do something with your pretty hair."

Kate looked to the thin red strands and grey roots pressed flat to her mother's skull and the bangs brushed aside, revealing deep furrowed creases. Her mother had always been self-conscious about her forehead. A doctor had asked if she knew her mother's wishes. Would she want to be resuscitated? She had wondered how many times she had heard that same question posed in the emergency room. Hearing it, though, was completely different from asking it.

As a nurse, she knew what she was expected to say. This was a sixty-two-year-old woman with a brain hemorrhage and uncertain outcome. Consider the bed shortages, the costs of a prolonged hospital stay, the risks, and quality of life. She was supposed to draw on her medical training and be impartial. Instead she said, "Yes."

She said it with conviction and authority, not having the slightest idea if it was true. Ruth hadn't liked to talk about death. It was too depressing. She preferred the small joys in life: discovering twenty dollars in a coat pocket, a ladybug alighting on her arm, the taste of vanilla ice cream melting on her tongue. Her mother believed in angels. "Yes," she had said and saw the doctor's eyes recategorizing her from "nurse" to "family." She was emotionally involved and couldn't be relied upon. Even Nurse Pam had looked away.

"I'll see you later, handsome boy."

Kate didn't want her to leave. She wanted her to stay and keep talking to her mother. "Thank you." The smallness and gratitude in her voice embarrassed her. She hoped Nurse Pam knew she meant it.

"You're welcome."

Zeus's ears followed her footsteps down the hall and his tail thumped twice when Pam's bright voice sang out another patient's name. Kate checked the clock—under four minutes, a real pro.

She went over to the bed, laid her fingers on her mother's wrist. A steady pulse of blood thrummed.

"It's Friday, Mom."

On her way out, Kate kept her hand loose on Zeus's leash. Masked and gloved cleaners popped in and out of rooms, littering the halls with soiled laundry bags and rolling carts stacked high with the desiccated remains of breakfast trays. It reminded Kate that she hadn't eaten yet. Her stomach growled. She squeezed closer to the wall to allow a gurney to pass. The leash tightened and she looked back at Zeus.

He was bowing, his bum high, his paws stretched forward, scratching at a closed door. He whimpered a high-pitched keen and looked to her expectantly. She had trained him well to have a distinctive alert.

"Live only," she said.

All Kate had to do was go inside, but she was rooted to her mother's porch. A line of ants paraded across the boards. Fat spiders lazed in the corners of trembling webs abuzz with trapped wings. Zeus waited with his head between his paws. His eyes flicked upward to check her face, but she gave him nothing to read.

The door was open. She breathed in mildew, cheap perfume, and potpourri. Somewhere a clock was ticking. The fridge hummed. Behind the vintage orange curtains that cast the room in perpetual sunset, a fly's furious bumble hummed and stalled.

Her mother didn't believe in pulling back the curtains. Anyone could look in.

Olive greens and sickly browns clashed with cellophane-sheathed lampshades and dog-gnawed walnut side tables. The furniture hadn't changed position in three decades. In the entranceway, school photographs smiled back with missing front teeth, bad haircuts, and questionable fashions. The collection stalled after her brother reached grade nine and she was left suspended in grade six with a bowl cut, sloping bangs, and a purple plaid jumper. She looked happy. They both did. Later, she would see Ruth staring at these photos looking for signs of what was to come.

A swath of bills and junk mail littered the floor. The softwood bore the claw marks of stray dogs Kate had brought home. She claimed they followed her, but in truth she lured them with pilfered food. The neglected, abused, and wounded seemed to find her. Sometimes she went looking. She cut one dog loose. Robbie the collie had mange and oozing sores under his rope collar. His paws were swollen and bloody and the ground trodden bare from endless circles. When the owner came raging, a neighbour from two houses over, her mother answered the door with a rusted, unloaded shotgun and threatened to judge him right then and there. Ruth feared dogs, even the pups. She didn't trust their teeth, but she always let them stay. You don't turn your back on what's hurting. That's what she said.

The last dog in the house was Bear, a decrepit deaf, half-blind mutt her brother had held captive to his chest for four and a half hours before relinquishing him. He said the dog's heartbeat was keeping him alive. He was sixteen.

She should deal with the mail and empty the fridge. She should take out the garbage and open a window. She should go inside. She should go in. Make sure the stove was off and plants watered. She should check for wet clothes in the washer. She should go inside.

But that would bring her closer to the bathroom door that her brother had shut and didn't open for three days, and the window he broke, and the floorboards stained blood-dark from his cut hand. It would mean walking past the kitchen table of untouched meals when he deemed that only Kate's leftovers were safe to eat, and the locked cupboard where her mother hid the knives, and the latches on the bedroom doors when he started wandering the house at night.

She couldn't avoid the stairs and him clinging to the banister and doorframes when the police escorted him out. He was seventeen and had stopped wearing clothes. She remembered thinking that his skin was too thin to hold his bones together and that she was too young to see a boy naked and know he had hair down there. Under the stairs was the cubbyhole where he hid when he refused to be taken away, because in his mind he wasn't sick. Once he hit nineteen, he knew nobody could force him to go to the hospital against his will. He was always the smart one.

He was the one she was always trying to impress but could never surpass. He was her teacher and protector. He'd drop the needle on his turntable and extol the colours of jazz and Bird and Davis and Parker and Coltrane. He'd read passages to her so she could hear and taste the language of Shakespeare and Proust and Hunter and Ginsberg. She was ten and pretended she understood just to be in the room with him.

Kate swallowed. Her lips were dry, and her tongue stuck to the roof of her mouth. Zeus's ears pricked back. If she moved a finger now, he would sit up. He was studying her for the slightest tell. She had taught him to watch her eyes. But really, he had taught her that she could speak with her eyes and he would follow wherever she looked. Go left. Go right. Come close. Stop there. He always won the game, unless she closed her eyes. Then he'd jump up and lick her face until he could see her again.

If she closed her eyes now, perhaps she could erase the image of angels obscuring the rubble of their lives. Hundreds of porcelain faces, white gowns, and stiff upright wings cluttering the floor, chairs, couch, tabletops, and shelves. A narrow pathway wended from the front door through the living room to the kitchen and up the stairs. She couldn't go in.

As she reached to shut the door, Zeus pushed his way past, assuming a down stay across the threshold. His ears forward, he stared straight ahead.

"Let's go."

His hindquarters tensed.

"Now."

He spun around and resumed his previous position. His eyes flicked almost imperceptibly to the left. She followed his focused gaze above the angels' heads and forced a smile to hide whatever expression was in her eyes. She felt it spill down into her chest.

"Find live," she whispered.

He bolted forward with his nose to the floor, breathing in thirty years of socks, bare feet, and shoes. His head bobbed side to side but his route was direct. At the cubbyhole door, he bowed and barked his sharpest bark. His tail swept angels onto their backs.

She followed his path. Wings brushed their obscene hope against her legs. "Good, boy." She rubbed his head and gave him his reward. "Good, good boy."

He took the frayed rope with the tethered ball deep into his mouth and chomped down a joyful squeak-squeak-squeak. Tossing his head high, he pranced past her, nudging his ball into angel faces before lying down in their valley. Careful that their praying hands couldn't reach his just reward.

Kate made her face smile, her eyes soften, and her voice warm. She steeled herself against the stench of urine, filth, and sweat and opened the cubbyhole door.

"Hello, Matthew."

In the kitchen cupboards, Kate found a stockpile of mac and cheese, Matthew's favourite childhood food. He stood in the corner watching her, and Zeus, at her feet, watched him. There wasn't any evidence that he had been eating. Food was rotting in the fridge and the sink and dish rack were empty. They stood in silence for eight minutes while the water boiled. She had opened the screened side door, and Matthew stared at the ragged mesh ripped long ago by eager paws. His shirt was unbuttoned, revealing the sharpness of his ribs and too-thin neck. His muscle tone had deteriorated, a sign that his body was feeding on its own protein. The timer dinged and he flinched.

She described her movements to minimize further agitating him. "I'm going to drain the noodles now . . . I'm getting butter from the cupboard . . . I'm getting milk from the fridge . . ." But the milk had spoiled, so she substituted water and thickened it with ketchup. She set two plates and two spoons on the table. She couldn't find the forks and knives.

"I'm hungry," she said. "Sit down."

He hesitated. So she sat. He took one step forward, two steps back, three steps forward, one back. His eyes wandered around her outline as if she were shining.

He said, "Your eyes look different."

"Sit down." She picked up her spoon and he sat across from her. She scooped noodles onto her plate and a mound onto his. Zeus lay beside her with a paw on her boot and his eyes on the filthy socked feet under the table. His nose was up, breathing him in. Kate took the first bite. "Eat."

Matthew picked up the spoon. His gnarled nails were chipped and blackened. He held the spoon over the plate, but didn't touch the food.

"It's good," she lied.

Keeping his eyes on her, he lowered his spoon to the macaroni. She swallowed the gag of rubbery, artificial flavour that had become her breakfast and lunch. He watched her eyes. She swallowed spoon after spoon. He did not. With only a few spoonfuls remaining, she slid her leftovers towards him. He touched the back of her hand with his spoon, as though expecting it to pass through her skin.

"Eat," she said.

He ate what remained on her plate.

"When was the last time you had your meds?" She kept her voice light and non-judgmental.

He stuffed his mouth, squirrelling noodles in his cheeks.

"When was the last time you saw your doctor?" He had lost an incisor, and a thick tartar obscured the remaining front teeth. His brown hair flecked grey was matted in ratlike tails and the follicles were pulled taut against his scalp. She wondered if he had lice. A rash or infection, greenish tinged, mottled the side of his nose. His skin was jaundiced and the circles under his eyes were dark. He looked much older than the three years that separated them. "Swallow," she said.

He did. She reached across the table and filled her spoon from his plate. She chewed the cold, limp noodles and swallowed. She kept her eyes fixed on his. She was his poison tester. He scooped a spoonful from his plate.

She filled her spoon again as he wadded his cheek. "Do you know what happened to Mom?"

He looked at her hard, his eyes sharp as broken glass. "They took her and won't let her come back." Macaroni stuck to the roof of his mouth. She wondered if he had been at the flea market when it happened.

"Who took her?" She held his fierce, unblinking stare. "Swallow," she said.

He spat the orange mash onto his plate and abruptly stood. Zeus scrambled and pressed hard against her legs. A low grumble rumbled from his throat. She silenced him with a wave of her hand. He had never growled before.

"Eat your dinner," she said, pretending nothing had changed and Matthew wasn't staring hard at Zeus. She scooped another heaping spoonful from his plate and hoped she had ground the meds into a fine enough dust. There were only three pills in the bottle she had found hidden behind the butter. Expired, no refills. She had used them all.

"You can see Mom," she told him. "I can take you there." She had his attention. "But first you have to bathe, put on clean clothes, and eat more food. Then we can go." And so their old game had begun. *Listen to my voice. Listen only to my voice.*

"They won't let you." He looked behind her when he said this. She wondered if *They* were in the room.

"I can help you, Matthew." She believed it, just like she had every other time. This time it could work. This time he could get better.

His eyes found hers. "Katie . . ."

He hadn't called her that since childhood. She was ten years old again, looking up at her big brother. His voice was weary, disappointed, maybe even loving.

"They're not afraid of you anymore."

He walked out the door, leaving her at the table with the bitter taste of medication on her tongue.

17

When Tamara called Bluebird Taxi's dispatch she was told Hassan's shift didn't start until one.

No, she didn't want another car. She would call back.

The woman on the other end of the line sounded irritated. A smoker, Tamara speculated from the deep, wheezing breath. Older. Overweight. Sore knees. White. Poorly educated. The whir of a fan crackled across the phone line. Hot. She leaned forward to better hear the woman's rasping breaths. Perhaps she used a puffer.

"Is there something else?"

Yes, she wanted to say, but didn't speak. She cradled the phone tighter and imagined the woman sitting in her battered office chair with the armrests digging into her ample waist. Maybe she was staring straight ahead trying to visualize her, too. Would she hear the confidence and diction of her voice and assume she was a privileged white woman with money to waste on taxis? She heard an end-of-her-rope sigh and the line went dead.

But Tamara kept listening. She listened past the gap of dead space and through the dial tone. She hummed to its tuning pitch. Mmmm. Closed lipped, it slipped away. AAAaaa. Open mouthed, she caught it again. She listened to the intertwine of calming notes undulating F and A until they were interrupted by the clipped, mechanical command, "Please hang up now. If you need assistance dial the operator. This is a recording. Please hang up . . . now."

She appreciated the non-human identification—"this is a recording"—though perhaps it would be more accurate to say, "this is a representation of a humanoid voice. Do not talk to me, I will not hear you. Do not presume I care."

She also admired the pause between "hang up" and "now," with the emphasis on "now." Strong, emotionless, practical. You are incapable of performing this task. That is okay. I will tell you what to do. Now.

She recoiled from the shrieking tone, pitched two octaves higher, reaching for the alarmist sphere of smoke alarms, sirens, and crying babies. She forced her ear back to its piercing squeal. It shuddered down her back and rattled the words free: *Don't hang up*. That's what she wanted to say. She hung up and the sound's residue wormed in her ear.

She hadn't been outside since Tuesday, having spent most of her three days off in bed, cocooned in the covers. She followed her hunger to the fridge. The milk was sour, the lettuce slimy, and the strawberries had softened under a downy mould. She drank three sips of black coffee and forced herself to eat a mottled banana. She sat in the white hum of the room and wondered if there was such a thing as absolute silence.

The air was heavy like church and death. She opened the window a crack. Heat spewed in. She shut it tight and turned on the fan. Standing before its oscillating blades, she tried to discern the rhythm of its purr until her skin goosebumped. She watered her wilted plants, not bothering to wipe away the droplets on the sill. She looked at the piano and then the bookcase, but settled in front of the television, not turning it on. She waited for Hassan's shift to start.

She practised being as inanimate as the couch, the piano, the bookcase, a book, a single page, the period at the end of a sentence, the white space between the words . . . until the clock reached one. She dialed Bluebird Taxi, relieved to hear the same cranky voice. She requested Hassan's car and gave her address.

Ask me, she willed.

The woman recited back the address.

Ask me. She cradled the phone with both hands and replied, "Yes, that's correct." *Ask me again, "Is there anything else?"*

The line went dead. She cupped a hand over her ear and hummed in perfect pitch.

Hassan wasn't wearing a sweater today, but he still had on a long-sleeved shirt buttoned crisply to the collar. His hair had been trimmed, highlighting the grey distinguishing his temples. She glared at the sun and its blistering heat. Her cotton dress was already limp and her underarms perspiring.

"Beautiful day, yes?"

She slid across the cool vinyl seat and he turned to look at her directly. She was acutely self-conscious of the silk scarf wrapped around her head and the two loose braids coiled in the grocery bag on her lap.

"You don't work today? I waited this morning, but no call. You're good?"

"Yes. I took an extra day off."

It was the first sick day she had ever taken. Her supervisor suggested she take two, but she declined. The cab's interior smelled lemon-polished and freshly vacuumed. The silk flowers in the vase had been replaced with real wild roses. The dashboard gleamed and the words FASTEN YOUR SEATBELT PLS. seemed especially kind.

"I hope for a better day for you." He watched her eyes. She couldn't lie, so she looked away. "You are Tamara, yes?"

He said her name like a love poem. The short *a*'s equally weighted, the *r* sliding, *Sa-HA-ra, Ta-MA-ra.* Her name sounded like it was being played only on the black keys. The melody was so different from the lower register and plodding heft that she was accustomed to hearing: Ta-MARE-a.

"Dispatch said a lady, Tamara, asked for me and I knew this address." He was pleased with this fact. "This is you. Tamara."

She wanted him to stop looking at her now. She wanted him to drive and not make left turns.

"I am Hassan." He twisted farther and pointed to the identification sign on the back of his seat. "You can call me Hassan, please." With that he turned to the wheel. His eyes found her in the rear-view mirror. He tapped the yellow stencilled words: FASTEN YOUR SEATBELT PLS.

Tamara tried not to flinch as Edie unwound two more braids. Granny Nan said her sensitive scalp line would toughen up, but it never had.

"I told you, you need the scarf to keep it good. Look at this mess." Edie detached a straggle of hair.

"It came off."

"Then you wrap the scarf around the pillow if you can't keep your hands off your own head."

There was no arguing with Edie. When she'd opened shop four years ago, word spread fast. Her extensions, relaxers, and cornrows were pure art; even her flat-iron work hardly smoked. She could coax the most stubborn hair into docility. "Look at that one," Edie said, nodding towards a young man sitting under the dryer at the back of the shop. His hair was twisted in long, glistening curls coiling well past his shoulders. Edie leaned in confidentially. "All his. He has better hair than most women who come through here." She smiled broadly at the boy, revealing the small gap between her front teeth that made her look perpetually young and reminded Tamara of a runway model. She had always wanted her own small, distinctive gap. Edie shouted over the dryer, "I'm telling her you're getting your locs today, Trevor. The ladies are going to be chasing you around the block. Guaranteed."

The young man tried to hide his hopeful smile and slumped lower into the vinyl seat under the neon pink dryer hood. Splaying his legs wider, he cast his eyes to his unlaced white sneakers, unmarred by scuffs. They looked expensive. Tamara worried for him. Two years ago, a boy had been found stabbed to death. The only thing missing was his sneakers. Edie tugged at her hair and uncurled a three-inch strand.

"See how much it's grown? I told you I'd bring your hair back. You're using the coconut and olive oil every day?"

"Yes."

Edie selected a weft of long hair from her stand. Tamara's scalp whitened as the track stitched across her temple. Pain needled her skull, pore by pore. Edie had pianist's fingers, long and strong. A thin braid, perfectly symmetrical, spooled from between her palms. Tamara concentrated on the display of Styrofoam heads lining the glass shelves.

Unlike the white mannequin heads, the black mannequin heads had eyes with irises and pupils. Huge eyes, but oddly, blue. The irises almost filled the whites. The eyes looked upward, as though the phantom bodies belonging to the heads were on their knees. The faces were painted with dark eyeliner, thick arched eyebrows, blush, and cherry lips, and coiffed in wigs coyly christened Asia Blue, Angel, and Juicy. The heads were precariously perched on foot-long necks no thicker than Tamara's wrist and appeared sacrificial, if not brave.

"That's right. Listen to her, she knows what she's talking about." Edie had a habit of speaking to the perpetually chattering television mounted high in the corner. "She's always right, that one. Ah, now here they go, listen . . ."

Braid number two was taking shape. Tamara was queasy from the relentless jumble of sounds. Deep in her belly, the air conditioner rumbled low. On her lips was the metallic taste of refrigerated air, but her brow was sweating. Her eyes followed the philodendron's tendrils snaking up the red walls to the gloss-black ceiling where haphazard staples thwarted their escape to the window's light.

"When are they going to take hold of their own lives?" It took a moment to realize Edie was speaking to her. "I see the same thing coming through this chair all the time. I tell them to pick themselves up. Life's made them forget who they are." Edie's fingers pecked around the strands of the virgin's sorrowful hair entwining hers. Tamara's stomach churned. "But *I* see them. Weddings, proms, funerals, new jobs, christenings, babies, grand-babies, cheating men, new men, lazy men, good men, I see them getting sick and well, and well and sick—I see them needing to look their best, even for the worst." Heat radiated from Edie's hands on the nape of her neck. "And I listen. I give them new hair and they walk out of here taller."

Tamara wanted to walk out of here taller. She wanted to tell Edie about the bad call, but she didn't trust herself not to cry. And if she started to cry, she didn't trust herself to be able to stop. She counted one, two, three, four and focused on her reflection, ignoring her torso and shoulders. She imagined herself as a mannequin's head, earless—deaf. All she had to do was breathe and let the room fall away. Focus on her day's plan. Hassan was waiting for her and soon she'd be home. She'd make herself a real meal, lay out her clothes for work tomorrow morning, have a shower, and read a book. Her shoulders loosened, soothed by the familiarity of routine. She tested the words in her head: *911. What is your emergency?* Nothing felt amiss.

Edie reined her up by her hair. "Sit up straight. Why are you slouching?" Tamara extended her foot-long neck. Edie spoke to all her clients with the authority of a mother. Or how Tamara imagined mothers spoke to their daughters. It was her house. Her rules.

She couldn't remember her parents. When she'd emptied the contents of Granny Nan's house, she had found a newspaper clipping in the dresser. It didn't say much. Car went off the road, two dead. She was five. Granny Nan was babysitting that night. "They're with Jesus now, baby girl. He needed them to come home." For a long time she hated her parents for choosing Jesus over her.

In elementary school, while the other children were drawing Mother's Day and Father's Day cards, her teachers let her draw whatever she wanted. Mostly she drew cars. Cars going over cliffs, cars on fire, cars crushed under trees, cars hitting deer, cars upside down—until the teachers took her crayons away.

Edie's hands stopped. "Oh no. His mother was here just last week. Oh, that poor baby."

She followed Edie's gaze up to the television. A police spokeswoman was speaking directly to the camera.

"We're looking for the public's assistance . . ."

Edie shouted to the young man under the dryer. "Do you know that boy, Trevor?" She tied off the braid with an elastic band and picked up the scissors to trim the end.

"Yeah. We all did." The young man's foot bounced up and down.

The screen cut back to the news anchor, looking appropriately concerned. "Anyone with information pertaining to the shooting death of twelve-year-old . . ."

Tamara shut her eyes tight. She stuffed her nose, ears, eyes, and throat with Styrofoam. She scoured away the irises and pupils, scraped off the blush, cherry lips, and brown paint, and hollowed out her head. She smothered the words, black against the white, that would force her to remember. *911. What is your emergency?*

She burrowed deeper and ran the scales of the A-flat melodic minor. Four octaves, ascending and descending. Securing every note with an unwavering touch. She ran the notes over and over, filling the white with black, obliterating every memory, every imagining. *911* . . . Faster, faster. Leaping to the D-flats. D is for Devon. Twelve years old. The notes ricocheted off the back of her eyes. She crashed into C major and became the keys, became the hammers striking the strings, CDEFGABCDEFGAB, became the vibration of just C in the knotted whorl of the heartwood . . .

"We're done."

The room returned to the natter of the television's regular programming. In the corner, the dryer droned, and above it, the air conditioner rattled. Edie nudged one of the braids, checking its alignment, and coaxed it forward. She took Tamara's chin in her hand, turned her face left then right, gauging her reflection in the mirror, then tugged hard once on each new braid. Tamara flinched.

"There you are, beautiful girl."

Hassan didn't notice her coming out of the salon. The engine was off and his window down, yet he appeared nonplussed by the simmering heat. He was reading a book propped against the steering wheel. Its yellowed pages were dog-eared and loose.

Insect legs of panic scuttled up Tamara's throat. She was exposed on the street, but couldn't interrupt his reading. Her heart quickened and her palms flushed. She breathed through her mouth and told herself, *He'll turn the page soon.* Five things she could see: a taxi, a Bluebird sign, a tire, a door, a taxi driver reading a book.

His face was relaxed. The corners of his mouth sagged down and his lower lip pouted in serious contemplation. His reading glasses were low on the bridge of his nose and he leaned ever so slightly into the pages. He was inside the story, following the characters into their limitations, their wants, their hearts, giving them life word by word, compelling them towards a fate as yet unknown. She could tell by the way his fingertips lightly rested on the pages that he loved, ached, and feared for them. She couldn't break that private communion. She could wait.

Four things she could touch: her skirt, her braids, her purse, her watch. Three things she could hear: cars whooshing past, laughter, and somewhere a radio busting rhymes. Drawing courage from the cab and Hassan so near, her heart rate slowed and the heat of her panicked blood receded. Two things she could smell . . . She inhaled exhaust and the sweet rot of garbage bags lining the curb. She lifted her eyes and broadened her view of the street. She stood very still. No one seemed to notice her.

The majority of faces looked like hers. The forty-degree temperature had driven people out of their homes and onto their front steps, so unlike the fair-skinned migrations of her neighbours into their cloistered, canopied backyards. Kids sucked on freezies, their tongues stained purple, red, and orange. Shirtless men and skirted women, their flip-flops kicked off, cooled themselves with handheld battery-operated fans. Conversations were shouted jovially across yards.

It had the lazy, easy feel of a community street party despite the early rush-hour traffic with its rolled-up windows nudging past the rowhouses towards the bridge and out, out of the city. The neighbourhood didn't betray its historic scars. An explosion that had flattened houses, shattered glass, blinded a thousand eyes, splintered trees, snapped iron railings, and hurled church bells, an anchor, fish, and torsos onto rooftops and into fields. There wasn't a high-water mark from the tidal wave that followed or scorched stones to commemorate where timber houses burned and black snow fell. She couldn't imagine the volume of 911 calls had there been phones.

One thing she could taste. Coconut oil on her lips. Five things she could not see. The layers rebuilt. The strata of greengrocers, cobblestone, and tramways giving way to sailors and kitten heels; acquiescing to neon signs, dance halls, movie theatres, furriers, and jewellers; receding from public housing, artists, students, and gentrification. A street constantly in the throes of dying and being reborn.

This part of the city was choked with two hundred years of red and purple dots. Now it was covered with the more common yellow, orange, and black marks of drugs, addiction, and mental illness. And reds . . . there were still so many reds. Salvation Street. Hope Street. Save Yourself Street. Step inside to bad coffee, good intentions, praying hands, caring hearts, and not enough money. Not much had changed in appearance since she had lived here with her Granny Nan.

Heat wrapped around her bare legs and arms and sucked at her breath. Devon's mother had walked out of Edie's salon, perhaps even paused at this exact spot. What was the colour of grief spilling from the soles of her feet? She looked down at her sandals. There wasn't an inch of sidewalk here that wasn't stained. These were the facts: people lived, people died, people were cruel, people were kind, some were rich, more were poor, there was seldom justice, some suffered more than others. Life was a momentum of loss, but life persisted nonetheless, perhaps even because of that loss. Granny Nan used to tell her, *I live for you.*

Across the street, a toddler chasing bubbles screeched with

each pop on the end of his fingertips. A barbecue was smoking. A man was laughing and a little girl was clipping a pink barrette in his hair. A woman stood up and waved to an old woman pushing her walker up the street. There was so much more that couldn't be seen.

She couldn't have done any more to help that boy. He was one boy, who was now a red dot. Granted his dot was larger than others and would be remembered longer than some, but he was still a dot, and no longer a boy who would become a man. The colour pooling at her feet was the same delicate pink as the roses in the dashboard vase. *I will live for you*, she promised. Hassan turned a page and she reached for the door handle, but it was locked.

He swung around as though she had a gun. "*Aasef. Salam.*" Then remembered his English. "Hello. I didn't see you. Come in." He slipped the paperback under the front seat. The lock clicked and Tamara got in. The seat was hot, too hot. The car had superheated, but Hassan wasn't sweating. "I'm sorry. I'll make it cold for you."

He turned on the air conditioner and she leaned into its relief. The chill fanned her face, but it was the white noise she craved. The combination of every tonal frequency cancelling the others out, becoming everything and nothing simultaneously. She hadn't realized she had shut her eyes until she opened them to find Hassan studying her face. Surprisingly, the car was still parked. She could have sworn they were moving, which she attributed to standing too long in the sun.

"You look nice," he said. Perhaps her eyes betrayed her discomfort at having been seen unguarded and he quickly qualified, "Your hair looks nice."

She reflexively reached for her virgin's hair and ran her fingers down the comforting plaits. "I'd like to go home now." She had been outside too long.

The meter was stopped at $5.75. He turned it on and it immediately flipped to $5.85.

"You should have kept it running."

Bowing his head as though apologizing for the need of money, he shrugged the suggestion away. "You're a good customer."

The turn indicator clicked patiently while he waited to merge. He wanted nothing from her and for that she was grateful. She would give him a generous tip. "Hassan." She said his name with care. "What are you reading?"

"You like books?" In the rear-view mirror, his eyes enlivened and he missed an opportunity to merge.

"Yes," she said.

"I love books, Tamara." He said "books" the same way he said "Tamara." She wondered where his home had been. "I learned words in English books. The same stories I read before are a different music in this language." He eased into traffic.

She didn't ask for the name of the book again or how the music differed. He needed to focus on traffic. She reached for her seatbelt, which they had both forgotten she had to fasten.

The delivery boy was late and Tamara was hungry. Ravenous, in fact. She had planned a menu of Greek salad, homemade spaghetti sauce, fresh pasta, and to finish, ripe peaches and ice cream. But the ingredients hadn't arrived yet. She would have been more irritated, but it was true that after Edie's, even she felt taller.

She had already laid out her clothes for the morning, selected a book to read, tidied the house, and changed the bed. Beethoven's Piano Concerto No. 1 in C major, opus 15, was trilling from the record player, dashing through the living room, around the kitchen, ducking in and out of bedrooms. One of her favourites.

The final movement reminded her of young lovers playing a giddy hide-and-seek for a covert kiss. She could see the long skirt hiked above the ankles, a rush of crinolines darting down hallways past doors and hidden cubbies. Cheeks flushed, chests heaving until they were alone together, for one—oh so gentle—illicit touch before their sweet, forlorn parting.

Beethoven himself played the concerto's debut in Prague. He was twenty-eight years old and blissfully unaware that in two years he would be losing his hearing. He dedicated the work to his pupil, a Croatian countess. Perhaps it was more than a kiss that was stolen. Tamara was pleased with her coquettish mood. She was feeling better. Her hair was fixed. She was feeling strong and ready for work tomorrow.

Beethoven's notes leapt and pirouetted on the piano. She tried to imagine his hands. A stout, broad-chested man, just five foot two, his fingers would have been short and thick. He was known to snap strings and break hammers. One of his students said he demanded too much from his pianos and pushed them to the breaking point.

She looked to the piano to confirm that the fallboard was down. Today she would retrieve the groceries at the steps. She turned up the volume. Vinyl was still her preference when listening to classical music. The crackle and tone placed her in the concert hall, front row centre where she could have a clear view of the hands.

Her favourite run, the final cadenza, was approaching. The rondo was soaring and falling, the notes climbing upon each other's backs, the orchestra receding, giving way to the piano gradually quieting . . . the individual notes caressing each other, fading . . .

The doorbell buzzed. She lifted the needle from the spinning record. She unlocked the bolts, placed herself between the door and the doorframe. Furnace heat blasted her bare legs.

It was another boy. Older and white. At the curb, a woman kept watch in a running car. This boy set the groceries on the step and handed her the receipt. She reached in her wallet for a fifty-dollar bill.

"Where's the other boy?"

"Devon's dead." The boy's eyes glistened. "Some fucker's gonna pay."

She declined the change and gave him a ten-dollar tip. It was too much, but it was all she could say. He took the money. His hands were hot. He ran back to the car and didn't look back.

She hauled the grocery bags into the house and locked the door. She carried them to the counter, put away each item, folded the bags, and tucked them in the drawer. She should make supper now. She went to the television and turned it on, muting the sound.

She didn't have to wait long to see his face. A photograph filled the screen. He was wearing a toque jauntily askew, exposing one ear. He had on a puffy coat and checkered shirt. At a doorway, he was looking up into the camera. Close up. Smiling to the picture taker, "Here I go." He didn't look like the boy she had imagined.

The image cut to a woman corralled by microphones. Tamara turned up the volume. “If anyone knows who did this to my baby, I’m asking you to come forward.” She looked directly into the camera, her eyes hard and dry. “You do the right thing.” The anchor man returned. “Weather’s next, we’re keeping an eye on a tropical depression in the Atlantic . . .”

She shut off the TV, went to the piano, and opened the fallboard. She sat straight with her hands on her lap. She pushed the bench back, scooted to the edge, and splayed her leg honky-tonk over the side. Her fingertips grazed the keys and she pulled them back. Leaning her shoulders in, she curved her body into the piano and cocked her ear. Feeling like she might fall, she dropped her wrists and attacked the keys.

“Twinkle, Twinkle” burst from her unbridled hands, cantering into the jump and bounce of notes stumbling, the rhythm careening uncontrolled. She reined in hard, forcing it to gallop, beating down the melody. It pulled and yanked to free itself from her stranglehold. The music reared and fell apart beneath her hands. She slammed the fallboard down. The strings’ harmonics bled. She couldn’t breathe.

She couldn’t breathe.

Her lungs sucked air. Her heart pounded her rib cage. Help. She needed help. She reached for the phone and it crashed to the floor. Wheezing, she fell to her knees, her fingers fumbling for the numbers. Pressed to her ear, the phone rang and rang . . .

“Bluebird Taxi, how can I help you?”

18

Hassan focused on the strobe of bridge struts and the percussive rhythm of his tires slapping against the cement seams. He liked bridges. He appreciated the in-between. The view reminded him of the Tigris, but not as beautiful. Tamara's hands were clasped tightly on her lap. She had never sat up front in his cab before.

He knew that the woman, Tamara, was afraid of the bridge and it saddened him that she was deprived of its beauty. He wished she would look up and out. She was different when he dropped her off at work. With each step that took her closer to the door, she stood taller. Her stride became more confident and her head lifted higher. She was no longer small. On their drive together, she seemed to gather her strength. It pleased him that he could give that to another human being.

But something had changed between the salon, home, and now. "I need to cross the bridge," she had said. He hadn't asked for the address. He knew where they were going and wondered how she knew the dead boy.

The bridge deck merged with solid land and her hands released. Palms flat on her knees, her fingers worried the cotton fabric of her skirt. She seemed to be mumbling something under her breath. He slowed for the toll booth and tossed the coins without making a full stop. They jangled in the basket and the arm lifted. Accelerating up the hill, he checked the bobbing wild roses in the vase to assess the smoothness of her ride. She sat up straighter as he eased around the right-turn corner. The barricades and caution tape had been taken down.

"Stop," she said.

But it wasn't safe. He promised, "Just up ahead."

She craned to look back and her braids parted, revealing her slender neck. He pulled into the empty school parking lot, a right turn, and kept the car running. He would like to turn off the air conditioner, but she didn't seem cold. They stared straight ahead, his arms goosebumping under his cardigan.

When he had picked her up, she had been standing at the curb. He had never seen her waiting outside before. She looked small and sad. He had pulled up close, but when she didn't get in, he nudged the passenger door open. He understood the loneliness of the back seat.

She placed her hand on the glove compartment's stencilled words and then touched the sprig plucked from the bush outside of dispatch. The flower bounced under her fingertips. She had long, delicate fingers and the nails were cut short. He didn't need to remind her to put on her seatbelt.

The woman, Tamara, was looking at him. He had never seen her from this angle before, face to face. Even in their hurt, she had beautiful brown eyes. Classical eyes. The eyes of Queens and Muses. Eyes that reminded him he was an old man. The faint scent of coconut perfumed the car. He said, "Shall I walk with you?"

"If you keep the meter running," she said.

He heard, *Yes, please.*

They walked the two blocks side by side down the sidewalk. The evening air had the same dusted heat of Baghdad. The sun was low and the world golden. They could be walking towards Al Mutanabbi Street after supper, just like he had done so many times as a young man. He could conjure the harbour into the river Tigris, maple trees into date palms, and cement into clay. He could summon the markets crowded with vendors and the aromas of shawarma grilling on spits, simmering chickpea *lablabi*, and wood-roasted *masgouf* river fish—the taste of freedom.

Tamara clenched her purse like a shield. She seemed uncomfortable in the outside world. Her lips were pressed tight, not inviting conversation. She had said she liked books. She would have appreciated Al Mutanabbi Street's bookstalls, stationery shops, and literary cafés and marvelled at the array of books from around the world laid out on blankets and plastic sheets paving the street, books harking back to the golden age when art, culture, and science were revered. He would like to tell her about Bayt al-Hikmah, the House of Wisdom, that sheltered four hundred thousand original manuscripts, and the caravan of a hundred camels that transported precious manuscripts from Khorasan to Baghdad, and the scholars who translated the words of Aristotle, Plato, and Hippocrates.

This was the time of day when Hassan would have made his way to Shahbandar to listen to the writers and intellectuals, men and women, who gathered unconstrained. The café's blue and white walls were tobacco stained from decades of discourse, and paint-chipped wooden benches were polished from the rub of every seat taken. Paintings of holy sites and ancient streets were displayed alongside faded black-and-white photographs taken when the British flags came down and King Faisal I and his pet leopard stared forcefully into time. The samovars were always filled with sweet strong black tea infused with cardamom. It was dirty and hot. There was rarely electricity and when there was, the fans made no difference to the heat. It was glorious.

He would like to tell her how the men gathered for poetry chases. Anyone could make a challenge. A labourer and a university professor could face off. One competitor would start with a line of poetry and the opponent would respond with another line beginning with the last letter of the last word. It was a great feat of skill and memory, an ancient Arabic rap. And every Friday night, there was a literary salon and writers would read their work to the standing-room-only crowd. He wondered if she would like that story.

Or maybe he could tell her about how his mother kept his supper warm when he'd come home late from university, and how he'd make excuses to run to the market and return with strangers in tow. The first few times he did this, she was angry and embarrassed that she hadn't prepared enough food. He tried to explain he needed others, at least two others. Friends or strangers, Sunni or Shi'ite—it didn't matter. What was important was listening and learning and telling each other's stories. From then on, his mama kept extra food warming. All these years in this country and he could still taste her lamb stew, but couldn't replicate it. The spices weren't alive here. Maybe Tamara would like that story better.

His leg pained, but he didn't slow. He kept pace beside Tamara and wondered what her stories might be. She was breathing through her mouth. He noticed her surreptitiously touch her skirt, her purse, her hair, and the back of her neck. She was counting.

He could only share his stories of Before. He couldn't tell her about the After, when books were burned and paper became as precious as gold. When newspapers, publishers, theatres, and film companies had to register typewriters and photocopiers and private ownership was banned. When professors, writers, and students were detained in the Palace of the End and the President for Life commissioned a calligrapher to write the Qur'an with twenty-seven litres of his own blood. Or how his mama used to stuff the cupboards full with newspapers, because every paper had a picture of the Anointed One on the front page and couldn't be thrown away for fear of insult. Before he had to leave.

Long before the shock and awe. She didn't need those stories.

He wasn't there to see Al Mutanabbi Street and his beloved Shahbandar destroyed by a car bomb. Though sometimes it felt as though he were. He has dreams of books on fire. Sees the walls imploding around him as he sits on his favourite bench drinking tea. He can even taste the sweetness. He is always about to speak just before it happens. He holds papers in his hands. He has written the greatest poem. In his dream, he is not the young man of then. He is the age he is now.

In his dream, other men have gathered around him. They are poets and former political prisoners. They show him pictures of their confinement, as though sharing wedding photographs. The men tell him how they survived. In the photos, they are hunched in groups, thin and hollow eyed. They show him their scars. He does not show them his.

He is about to stand to speak his poem when the windows blow. Unlike life, which he imagines would be starkly divided as before and after with no between, in his dream there is between. He is seated as the books fly past. Covers open, pages aflame. They lift like a murmur of swifts. Words separate from papery skin, a swarm of cursive script combusting. The paper in his hands, his magnificent poem, flutters to reach the others. Each *abjad* lifts from the scorching pages, right to left. The words of Abbas Chechan, Saadi Youssef, Abu Nuwas, Dunya Mikhail, Muzaffar al-Nawab, Al-Mutanabbi . . . absorbing his words into a blinding light that breathes just one word, *Allah*, before the world explodes.

He does not die in the dream. He is lying on his back amidst rubble and scorched books. He has glass in his mouth and cannot speak. It crunches against his teeth, shears the inside of his cheeks and lips. Pages float above him, a gyre of flames and smoking sky raining cinders, the words extinguishing into ash. Falling on him like snow in the desert. Bones and blood and paper. The taste of poems on his tongue.

Only then does he awake.

The entire street no more. Thirty-eight people no more. Thousands of books no more. Baghdad no more. He heard that Mohammad al-Khashali's four sons, who were working in the café, were killed in the blast. They say his sons are with the books and manuscripts they loved. They say, *Al-Hamdu Lillah*. As Allah has willed; praise be to Allah.

He heard that the day after the bombing, a poet stood on the remains of Shahbandar on a hill of broken-backed books and spoke for those who could not speak. Another poet stood all day at the edge of the gaping remains of an upper storey, his arms spread wide, a wooden crate on his head the size of a child's coffin. Saying nothing. Men looked up at him and wept.

Tamara stopped before a shrine of teddy bears, balloon bouquets, roses, carnations, red and white, white and red, blood and bones. Photographs of a smiling boy were propped against a makeshift cross with DEVON scrolled in rainbow crayon colours.

"This is the wrong place," Tamara said as though she might cry. "This isn't where he died." Her breath was ragged and one hand was clutching her skirt.

"We keep going," he said, and she stepped forward.

He followed her along the trodden dirt path to the birch tree bower where the police tent had been and the grass was trampled. She knelt and parted the parched blades until she found where the bone-dry earth darkened to burnt umber. She laid her hands on the stained earth. "I should have brought him something."

He had never spoken the words out loud before, but he remembered them all and gave them to her. He tried to carry the music of his language into the translation of hers, knowing he would fail.

"I wrote the letters of your name in the sand, and they were washed away by rain.
I wrote them on the roads, and they were wiped away by feet.
I wrote them in the air, and they were blown away by wind.
I wrote them on people's faces, and they were lost to me.

I wrote them as tunes, and they flew away.
I wrote them in days, but the years erased them.
Shall I write it in the depths, so it shall continue to pulse through veins?
Where shall I write your name?"

Tamara, the woman with shining eyes, was looking up at him. "Did you write that?"

"No," he said. "A poet whose name is lost." And it was not a lie. They were words he had read as a student. Anonymous. Unlike this boy. There wasn't a name to write.

"Amen," she said and bowed her body in perfect *sujud*: forehead, nose, both hands, knees, and toes touching the ground. She might have been praising Allah, except the words she kept repeating were *I'm sorry*.

He looked away, according grief the respect it deserved. *Don't worry about the eyes with tears*, his mama used to say. *Worry about the eyes without*. He wondered why this one boy had garnered so much attention.

In Baghdad, some streets would be rendered impassable with teddy bears and balloon bouquets.

It took six right turns to get back onto the bridge and eight more to reach Tamara's front door.

"Thank you, Hassan." She said his name softly, as though it might break, and asked if he could pick her up tomorrow morning for work.

"Of course." He didn't tell her that he was working the night shift. She paused unlatching the handle, and he thought she might speak again, but she didn't.

"Tamara . . ."

He eased the wild rose from the dashboard vase. The flower drooped between them, its petals already withering. He was embarrassed by its decay and odd lack of scent. It wasn't worthy. He wished it was a branch of night-blooming jasmine, but she took it anyway. He watched until she was safely inside before pulling away.

The sun was low, so he headed towards the Hill. Up the steep, manicured mound, over the humped shoulders guarding its stone citadel. He drove until he cleared the scrape of buildings and could glimpse the dimming harbour and awakening bridge lights. The tour buses had departed and the star-shaped fortress's dry moat, stone walls, and cannons were retreating in the gloaming night. He parked close to the guardrail, opened the trunk, retrieved his kit bag, and locked the doors.

After checking to make sure that he was truly alone, he stepped over the rail and headed down the steep incline towards the illuminated town clock that had been keeping time for a mere two hundred years, and unrolled his prayer rug. He removed his shoes and set them aside. Dried grass stuck to his socks. He opened his water jug, filled the basin, and dipped his hands into its warmth.

"*Bismillah*," he said. In the name of Allah.

Three times he performed ablutions: washing his hands up to his wrists, his mouth, his nostrils, his face. Cleansing his right arm, then his left. Running his wet hands through his hair from his forehead to the back of his neck and ears. He was almost cleansed. He passed his wet hands over his sock feet. The horizon was bleeding red.

He stepped onto the prayer rug facing *Qibla*. Even though he had long stopped believing that the Eternally Merciful One was listening, the melodic words of each *rak'ah* were all that remained of his homeland. He raised his hands to his ears.

"*Allahu Akbar*." Allah is great.

He crossed his hands over his heart, even though he knew he would burn in the fires of Jahannam a thousand years for his crimes. And that was just.

"*Allahu Akbar*."

The holy words lifted from his throat and reverberated in his chest. The sky flamed pink and red. He thought, Poets would have words to describe these clouds.

19

Mike took a swig of cold beer and gave thanks to the setting sun. He was a lucky man.

Caleb, with Snappy in hand, ran screeching through the sprinkler again. Connor, seated on a blanket, gleefully clapped his hands at each running pass made by his big brother. Mike looked back to the kitchen, where Lori was tidying up. A boisterous bouquet of sunflowers, daisies, and delphiniums shouted from the table. After work, he had grilled chicken, potatoes, and even remembered the vegetables. Caleb helped him set the picnic table with paper plates and cups for easy cleanup, and together they braided a dandelion crown for Mommy. His sons laughed at his big, fumbling fingers, and Caleb sprinkled the popped-off yellow heads on their napkins.

Throughout dinner, he kept the baby on his lap, poured the drinks, and encouraged every rambling story Caleb could imagine. Lori had laughed, more than once. He did everything right, and by the time he had scooped the bowls of ice cream he knew he was forgiven for his lapse in judgment at the shopping centre.

"Last run. Time to get in your pyjamas."

"Noooooooo . . ." Caleb protested. Mike would have done the same.

"I said one more. Make it good."

"Okay, okayyyy. This is last time, I gonna jump over the very, very top. You watching, Daddy, you watching?"

"Yeah, I'm watching." Mike took another sip of beer.

Caleb set Snappy on his brother's blanket and ran back to the starting position. "Heres I go!" He crouched down to make himself fast. "One, two, thee, four—GO!"

His expression said he was running faster than any human being on earth, faster than a lion, faster than a car, faster than a plane, he leapt and water sprayed his chest and face. "One more—I didn't jump high enough!"

"That's it. Get your brother." Caleb furrowed his brow. Mike worried it could all go wrong here. Defuse and distract. "Remember I'm going to read you a story tonight. Your choice."

"Anything?"

"Yep, anything! Pick up your toys." He gathered up the empty beer bottles, surprised to find four instead of three. He turned in time to see the boys in a tug-of-war over Snappy and Caleb slamming his brother in the chest. The baby toppled back and after a shocked delay screamed bloody murder. Lori looked out the window, and Mike waved at her to stand down, he had this.

He strode over and picked up the baby, whose face was blaring red. He squirmed, railing at being held. "What did you do?" he said to Caleb.

"Nothing."

The kid lied right to his face. He didn't even twitch. "Caleb . . ."

"He fell over."

Mike brushed the dead grass from Connor's back and hair. The baby rubbed his snot face on his shirt. Mike jiggled him up and down, back and forth, and the sobs subsided. He was going to be a tough kid. "You have one more chance, Caleb."

His son's chin lifted defiantly. "He stole Snappy! He was bad!" He hid the toy behind his back.

"So you hit him." It wasn't a question.

"He was bad!"

"You could have hurt him. You know you don't hit people."

Caleb's eyes narrowed.

"What do you say to your little brother?"

"I sorry?" His bottom lip was trembling.

"Tell Connor." He knelt down with the baby on his lap.

"I sorry." Caleb leaned in and hugged the baby. "I love you, I love you, I love you." Connor hugged him back.

"Okay, then." Mike had solved another crisis. "Let's get ready for bed." He stood and his back pinched. He grunted upright and headed for the house. Caleb didn't follow.

"What are you waiting for?"

"Do I have to go to jail now?" His cheeks were blotching red.

"No, Caleb." His little boy was so soft. It worried him. "Let's go inside."

"I love you, I love you, I love you."

"I love you, too." What he meant was *You're my son forever and ever. I will always protect you.* Connor was squirming and his diaper was full. "Yes, stinky boy, I smell you. Let's get you cleaned up."

"IloveyouIloveyouIloveyou."

He looked back to Caleb. The kid liked to push it.

"Get in the house. Now." He didn't leave room for debate.

By the flinch of his cheek, he knew Caleb heard him. Mike trailed him inside. He didn't know how Lori did this day after day.

20

Tamara clipped the obituary from the newspaper, careful not to lose any words. She folded up the Arts and Life section and the arbitrary words she had filled in the crossword while reading the adjacent notices. She appreciated the juxtaposition of comics and death side by side.

4 down, Vast expanse: *Him*

JOHNSON, DEVON, 12, was a caring, fun-loving boy, who loved music, piano, riding his bike, and his friends.

6 across, More acute: *Antoine*

An honours student and recipient of a Maritime Conservatory Music bursary, he was preparing for his Grade 8 piano exam.

After school, he worked part-time at J&J's Grocery delivering groceries to those unable to get out. Often, if they had a piano, he would stay and play for them.

Devon is survived by his mother . . .

22 down, Dyeing art: *Devon*

> A Home Going Service will be held Monday, August 30, 10:00 a.m. at Cornwallis Baptist Church. Donations can be made to the Devon Johnson Music Fund.

She trashed the remaining unread pages and carried the small square of paper to the living room and opened the piano stool. She pushed aside the music books, then laid the clipping alongside two other small squares, yellow and brittle, and closed the bench.

She ran her hand over the silk scarf bundling her braids. Tonight, her hair would stay in place. She checked the door, shut off the lights, and headed to bed. Somewhere far off, a siren wailed.

911. What is your emergency?

The words were calm and comforting. She smoothed the silk wrap encasing her pillow, adjusted the fan's direction, and turned off the lamp. Her eyes adjusted to the moon's light. The sheets smelled clean and cooled her skin.

She breathed in the sweet scent of the wild rose sprig. On her side table, she could make out the water glass and the flower's bowed head. She touched its petals and thought about the taxi driver's hand and his thick, short fingers and the white scars marring his misshapen knuckles. And how gently he held the stem between his fingertips. An older man's hand that reminded her that she was younger. But not too much. And about how his words sounded like music. She couldn't remember the poem, but she could hear its rhythm. It sounded like a river. He was a nice man. She saw it in his eyes. Younger eyes that smiled easily.

Her Granny Nan always said, *The eyes will tell you everything*. She shut her eyes.

Tomorrow was another day. Tonight she would sleep. Tomorrow she would work. Tonight she would sleep. Tomorrow she would work, and the day after that, and the day after that . . .

26 across, Ocean motion: *blue*

Blue was the colour of the dress she would wear to his funeral.

21

Zeus groaned when Kate kicked off the sheets. Her bedroom was stifling. She checked the time again. The red light glared 2:28 a.m. The night was never going to end. Outside, through her open window, university students whooped and serious drunken young men murmured about serious things. The power pole outside her window was humming and Zeus was snoring.

Enough.

She eased out of bed, snuggling the covers against Zeus. On her way to the kitchen, she tripped over her boots. Zeus watched her, but didn't bother to get up.

She opened the fridge and the light blinded her. Drinking from the orange juice container, she leaned into the open door. Cold air rolled up her belly and over her breasts. She shut the fridge and the room went black. She held her ground until she could discern the room carved from streetlight. The voices receded.

Her skin felt dry and her eyes stung. She shouldn't have had that coffee and wondered if a beer would help, or a whiskey, but she was out of whiskey. She traced the kitchen counter to the catch-all drawer and rifled through it. Something sharp jabbed her finger. She weaseled around it until she felt the pack. There were two cigarettes inside. Months old, forgotten by a friend. She turned the stove burner on high and waited for the snaked coil to glow. Lighting the smoke, she inhaled deep and held her breath. Then she remembered the smoke alarm overhead.

She hurried to the living room, cranked open the casement window, and exhaled through the gap. Her head floated and she leaned against the sash to steady herself from the nicotine rush. The street was empty and the houses were dark. She took another long drag and her shoulders dropped.

She hated days off, too much time to think. She wasn't good at waiting. Something would eventually happen. Her mother would live. Her mother would die. Her brother would return. Her brother would be lost. There was nothing she could do but wait for whatever was next. Now was the time to rest and gather strength for when she was needed. Now was the time to sleep. Follow the nurse's creed: *Keep yourself intact*. In a few hours, she would be back at work. She focused on the glow of the cigarette's ember. Zeus brushed against her bare leg. She reached down and rubbed his ears, keeping the smoke high above his head.

"Some things are just sad," she said.

Zeus cocked his ears. He was a good listener, but tonight she didn't feel like telling him her stories. The red tip flared in her reflection. Headlights skimmed the street. She didn't retreat from the window. She willed the driver to look up. She wanted someone to see her. Maybe even smile. Someone who would remember her fondly and twenty years from now affectionately tell the story of the Woman in the Window. Her nipples were erect and the cigarette burned low.

The car drove past. She looked down at her body, pale and stark in the street lamp's light. She laid her hand on her belly and conjured Riley's arm holding her close. Zeus pressed harder against her leg.

"I know," she said. "He's with her."

She let the cigarette smoulder until she could feel its burn.

22

Hassan pulled into the international departures lane and eased in behind another parked cab. The night was grinding along. There had been only four calls and another three hours remained before he could pick up Tamara to drive her to work. A security officer leaning against the wall assumed an official stance. Here, his skin colour made people nervous. He checked the rear-view mirror. His fare was slumped forward with his head on his chest. "We're here."

The man's head snapped forward, sucking up drool. Bleary eyed, he took in the fluorescent lights and low building. He groped for his wallet in his breast pocket. It was an expensive suit, tailored. He passed Hassan a wad of twenties and opened his smart phone. The cab's interior glowed blue. Hassan counted out the change. Men like this preferred him counting out the change. The man waved away the bills. It was a decent tip.

"What time is it in London?" He tapped numbers into his phone.

"I don't know, sir." Men like him preferred "sir." He popped the trunk and hauled the luggage to the curb. The two sleek hard cases had the sheen of sports cars. He considerately extended the handles. The man climbed out of the cab with the phone to his ear.

"I dunno. I just got here, I'm checking in . . ." He squinted at his expensive watch. "It's four thirty here." The man looked from his bags to the door to Hassan, then headed for the revolving doors.

Hassan shut the trunk. "Have a good flight, sir."

Men like him were always surprised when he didn't carry their bags. He settled into his seat and took a sip of his lukewarm tea, extra-large, three sugars, three milk. In the side mirror, he watched the man struggle with his suitcases, refusing to relinquish the phone propped to his shoulder. The car radio glowed 3:31 a.m. The man's expensive watch was not good with time.

He looped around the partially constructed ten-storey hotel. Billboards proclaimed *Coming Soon*, but the project was bankrupt. The shell of steel girders and cement floors jutted ragged and abandoned. He heard it was being torn down. This country liked to tear things down rather than use what it already had.

He settled back into the vinyl indentation of himself, thankful he owned such a good, solid, reliable car. It wasn't easy finding parts for a ten-year-old Buick, and its size made it challenging to park, but it was a real automobile of chrome and metal. The weather report came on and he turned up the radio. Continuing hot and sunny. A storm forming off the coast was gaining strength due to the elevated water temperature and was expected to become a Cat 1 hurricane. Early projections were indicating a possible landfall. He shut off the radio. Forecasters had been wrong before.

The last one wasn't supposed to make landfall and look what happened. The roads were a mess for days with crushed cars, blocked streets, and lingering power outages. He had a good couple of weeks ferrying passengers to work, restaurants, and pubs.

Another storm like that and he could buy new tires and maybe replace the shocks.

He headed down the side road leading to the cargo and freight compounds, until he reached a dead-end hemmed in by warehouses—his favourite waiting place. He couldn't risk napping now for fear of not hearing his alarm. He would sleep after he picked up Tamara. He nosed the hood close to the tarmac's fence and shut off the lights and engine. It wouldn't be long before a security vehicle pulled up and blinded him with their spotlight. They knew his car and his name, but never remembered it.

He rolled down his window. The night chirped with crickets and frogs. Moths and crane flies ricocheted around the coned lights embedded in the runway. He had flown only once, eleven years ago on a one-way flight. Even if he could afford to travel now, he had nowhere to return to and no desire to go elsewhere. He was content circumnavigating the globe in books. He had walked Scottish moors, huddled in bunkers on the Western Front, climbed Kilimanjaro, voyaged the Congo River, run with wolves, and stood on the deck of the *Pequod* as surely as he was sitting here drinking cold tea.

It was true there were things he would never know: the taste of cut sugar cane, the sound of a trumpet in Brazil, the smell of a glacier, the colour of Diwali, the undulation of the northern lights, the smell of the fish markets in China, the neon shock of Times Square . . . but he was not a writer. It would sadden him to see such life and not have words to describe it.

The clock ticked over another minute. Tamara would be sleeping now. He wondered if she travelled in her dreams. He hoped so. Her eyes seemed filled with stories he would like to someday hear. He drained his cup to the slurry, syrupy bottom.

A high-pitched whine screamed to its frenzied pitch. The frame of the car vibrated up through his bones and quivered the dregs of his tea. He leaned forward to widen his view through the windshield. A quaking roar and a jet appeared, engines screeching, climbing impossibly skyward. Red-green-white lights and wings sheared the night. Pale faces opaque in windows. The landing gear retracted, groaning against the folding of its mechanical limbs into its tin underbelly . . .

He watched the plane's lights until they were lost in the stars. It was flying east into the sun rising and rising. He lifted his cup to the sky: *Safe journey*. High beams blasted the interior of his cab. He raised his other hand to show he meant no harm.

Hassan lowered the visor to the blaze of morning and checked the rear-view mirror. Tamara hadn't said a word since getting in the cab's back seat. The black-eyed Susans brightening the dash he had snipped fresh from a south-end garden went unacknowledged. She kept her eyes downcast and concentrated on her hands on her lap. When they crossed the bridge, she shut her eyes, and didn't open them again.

He worried he had done something wrong. When he'd picked her up, he held the door open and said, "Another beautiful day," but she didn't respond. After yesterday, he thought she might sit in the front seat and her smile would say *Good morning, Hassan*, and they would talk about books.

He pulled up close to the security door. The surveillance

cameras and severe concrete building tightened his heart. It happened every time, even though there weren't guards posted at the steel door. His eyes and his heart chose to believe different things. Tamara unfastened her seatbelt and slipped her security badge over her head. She handed him the fare and refused the change.

"I'll pick you up this evening?" Not wanting to transgress further, he hesitated to use her name.

"Yes. Please," she added, without looking up. She remained seated. "Hassan, yesterday . . . that wasn't me."

He wasn't sure whether she meant the woman with the new hair or the woman who sat in the front seat or the woman who cried.

She said, "Some days are just . . ."

"Yes," he said. "Some days are."

She reached into her purse. "I thought you might like this. It's not new . . . I've read it, but . . ." She passed him a hardcover book. It had weight and its jacket was smooth and glossy. The end cuts were unspoiled and the spine pristine, unlike his thrift-store buys. "A small thank-you for yesterday. If you don't like it, I have others."

"It's perfect."

Before he could thank her with proper words, she stepped out of the cab.

"I'll be here," he said, but the window was up and she didn't hear.

With each step, she settled into her stride. He watched her back straighten, neck elongate, and chin tilt up. It must be an important job that required her to be that strong. She swiped her badge and stepped inside. *There she is*, he thought.

The glass building prickled his sleep-deprived eyes. He lowered the visor and opened the book. Not a single page was dog-eared or inked with marginalia or brittle with mustiness. It didn't matter that he had read it before.

He lifted it to his nose and inhaled the new pages. It smelled like the sun-warmed skin of his wife.

23

Mike wrenched the steering wheel hard left and barrelled up the centre line, forcing the traffic to part. The siren wailed to clear the intersection. *Move!* Cars braked in front of him. Revving his engine, he nudged tight against the bumper of a sedan. In the passenger seat, an elderly man excitedly motioned the driver to pull over. Brake lights flashed as the car lurched curbside. Mike veered around it, glaring at the grey-haired woman clutching the steering wheel, and accelerated through the red light.

10—30. Proceed with caution. 34—year—old male. Caucasian. History of mental instability. Suspect armed with knife. Mother knife wound upper shoulder. Guns in house. Officers on scene. Bus en route. Request for backup.

He swerved hard as a pedestrian ran across the road. His tires fished on the searing asphalt. This was his third call since shift began and it wasn't even noon. Nineteen calls yesterday. The city was losing its friggin' mind in the heat.

He sped through the residential street with its two-car garages and manicured lawns. Triple his pay grade. The onboard computer spewed directions. He typed through the turn—10-23 Arriving on scene. The screen showed the blips of three cars converging and two on site. He shut off his siren.

Up ahead, two police vehicles were jackknifed across the street. Gawkers and media weren't on scene yet. He slammed to a stop. As he stepped out of the car, he unfastened his Taser and weapon holsters. He reflexively touched his chest for assurance. Bulletproof vest. Check. The house looked like any other house on the street.

A woman, mid-forties, was sitting on the curb. On closer approach, he reassessed her age to be mid-fifties. Eyeliner smeared her eyes. Her tank top and pants were spattered red. She wasn't wearing a wedding ring. Kneeling beside her, Constable Raylene Wade was applying pressure to the shoulder wound. She had the reputation of being a steady cop. Ten feet from the front steps, a second officer had his gun drawn. He was young. Mike couldn't remember his name.

On the doorstep was a man. Naked, thin, butcher knife in hand, screaming incomprehensibly. Blood trickled down his arms and legs from what appeared to be bite wounds. Inside the house, a German shepherd barked hysterically. It clawed at the aluminum screen door's glass. The thin metal flexed with each pounce.

Mike hitched up his holster and his lower back twinged. The mother's pupils were dilated in shock. Raylene's eyes said she had it under control. The woman pleaded with him. "Please don't hurt him. Please. He's sick."

"Ma'am, what his first name?"

"He didn't mean it. I was vacuuming and it was too loud. He doesn't like things loud. My son wouldn't hurt me."

The rookie was yelling at the man to drop the weapon. His

voice was hoarse and his inflection shrill. He was scared. He was aiming point-blank at the man's chest.

Mike urged the mother along. "We're here to help him, ma'am. Tell me his name so we can help him." His voice was controlled, belying his urge to scream at the woman to stop wasting time. He took a precious moment to look her in the eyes. *Trust me, I'm all you have.* Her lips tightened and the corner of her mouth trembled. He had her.

"Luke."

He said the name loud and certain. "Luke!"

The man looked at him, his eyes wild and sunken. Mike approached slow and calm, taking his position alongside the rookie. His kept his hands low, slightly raised to show he didn't have a weapon.

"Luke, your mom's hurt and we need to help her. But we need you to put the knife down. Can you do that?"

The man looked down at his hand as if trying to comprehend the object. The rookie had a death grip on his pistol. His carotid was pumping and his neck muscles were taut. Mike relaxed his own shoulders and opened his arms wider—an invitation to engage the man. *I'm in charge now. It's going to be okay.* The officer took his lead and lowered his aim.

"Luke, I need you to help me."

The man's belly was hollowed, his pelvic bones sharp and angular. His skin was jaundiced, his dick shrunken. He looked older than thirty-four. Blood streamed down his shins. A flap of flayed skin above his left knee exposed muscle and tendon, but it didn't seem to bother him.

"Luke, I can see you're hurt, too. You and your mom need help."

The man's calf was twitching. His adrenaline load was in full dump.

"Baby, listen to the policeman. They're not going to hurt you. You have to go with them to the hospital."

The man sighted his mother with the knife. "I'm not going back there!"

Mike glared at Raylene: *Shut her the fuck up.*

The man swung the knife towards Mike, then at the rookie to ward them off. "I didn't do that!"

The rookie raised his weapon. Mike held up his hand. *Don't fuckin' pull that trigger.*

"Luke, once you put the knife down, you can tell me what happened. I know you want us to help your mom."

"It wasn't her."

The man's anguish was real. Mike could almost believe him. Poor bastard.

"Luke, this can end now. This is just one bad day. You can have a thousand good ones once you get past this one." He heard the hollowness of his words. He was sick of saying them.

The ambulance wailed up the street. The man thrust the knife in the direction of the sound and took a step back. Teeth gnashing, the dog hurled itself against the door. Slobber fogged the glass. It clawed at the barrier and the aluminum frame shuddered. The man stepped forward.

The rookie hollered, "Do *not* move! Do *not* take another step forward!" The rookie had taken a step forward. His feet were planted. He had assumed the "stand your ground" position.

Mike raised his voice above the siren and the barking dog. "Luke, listen to me. Listen only to me." *For Chrissakes, shut the goddamn siren off.* The man's eyes darted from Mike to the approaching ambulance. He was rocking side to side. He covered one ear with his free hand. Mike was losing him.

"Luke!"

"Shut up shutup shutupshutup . . ."

"Luke!"

The man slapped the knife blade against his chest. A thin red line welted over his heart.

"Luke, talk to me! Let me help you."

The ambulance came to a stop. Its sirens ricocheted off the blank, mute houses and throbbed against their chests.

The man wielded his broad knife high, about to charge. "*Shut up!*"

Mike Tasered him.

One probe penetrated his chest. The other barbed his stomach. The man's torso clenched rigidly and his pectoral muscles spasmed. Tremors locked his right arm and knife hand mid-air. His mouth wrenched open. He looked down at his chest as though a wasp was stinging him and not 1200 surging volts of electricity.

Tethered to the perp by the fifteen-foot lead, Mike reached for a second cartridge. He should be on the ground. The man raised his left arm, the one punctured with dog bites, and ripped the lead from his chest. His body slumped as if pulled from a pike.

Mike ejected the cartridge and loaded the second charge, stepping between the man and the rookie's clear shot. He walked briskly forward, two steps, three . . . The man raised the knife and he fired again. The probes caught him on his thigh just below his testicles. This time he dropped the knife. His knees lurched forward, and he catapulted off the front steps onto the sidewalk. He landed on his chest, his body shuddering and frog legs kicking.

Mike was aware of the mother screaming and sweat stinging his eyes. He was standing over the man still riding the current. He had to force himself to stop pulling the trigger. The electric hornet's buzz died and the man rag-dolled. The rookie, who had managed to put on gloves, yanked back the man's arm. His grip slipped on the slick skin. *C'mon, c'mon, get the cuffs on.* Fumbling for his restraints, the young cop looked to his belt, and the man bucked him off.

Mike threw his weight on top of the naked man. He was acutely aware that he didn't have his gloves on. He drove his elbow between the man's shoulder blades. Gripping his forehead, he pulled his head back. His pant leg was rubbing against the man's bare ass. Urine pooled on the sidewalk. The rookie grappled for control of the arm. A fourth officer, Brickhouse Bill, *thank fuck*, arrived as the man started to rise, hoisting Mike like a child's piggyback ride.

Even with three two-hundred-pound officers dog-piling the scrawny crazy to the ground, Mike could barely hang on. They wrestled in the tangled grunt of testosterone, B.O., sweat, blood, cement, and crushed grass. The rookie finally managed to restrain the man's arms and legs, kneeing him once in the ribs for good measure. Only then did the man stop resisting and begin to howl. He howled just like a dog. Even the dog stopped barking.

Two more uniforms arrived, Steve and John, *the friggin' A team.* Mike nodded his appreciation. They'd be talking about this one over beers. He pushed himself off the already bruising man, and pain stabbed his back. His arms were smeared red and his ears were ringing. The sirens and the screaming woman had stopped, but the man was still howling. The other officers picked him up by his elbows and feet. Bill yanked the probes from between his legs and passed the lead back to Mike. Blood and flesh stained the barbs. They carried the howling man face down to the gurney, his dick dragging across the cement.

Mike bent down and retrieved the other cartridge. He picked up his cap and saw the flash of his family's smiling faces in the photograph tucked inside the lining. He pulled the cap on tight, groaning as he forced himself upright.

The mother was in front of him, her eyes as wild as her son's. He was about to say they would take good care of him, when she spat in his face. The warm, thick wetness gobbed his cheek. His defensive training kicked in and he gripped her face, smothering her nose and mouth, obliterating her eyes, and shoved her hard. Hard enough to drive her to the ground. Her neck snapped back, her head bounced on the lawn, and her shirt hiked above her stretch-marked, flaccid belly. Blood bloomed from her shoulder wound.

"You said you wouldn't hurt him. You said . . ."

She collapsed into incoherent sobs as the paramedic and Constable Wade stepped between them. Raylene had her hands on his chest, walking him backward from the scene. "It was assault. We'll charge her."

He didn't want that. What he wanted was for her to do her job. What he wanted was to scream at the five-eight girl cop pushing him back, who smelled of shampoo and suntan lotion, *Where the fuck were you? Your job was to clear her from the scene! Your job was to have my back!* Instead, he wiped his cheek on his flak jacket's shoulder and walked away. The fucking paperwork on this one was going to be a nightmare.

Inside the house, the enraged dog threw itself against the bulging door. Bloody paws smeared the glass. Its mouth was a white froth and its eyes were on him.

He stared the dog down. His hand on his gun. Wanting it to break through.

Forty minutes to shift change. Mike was parked behind the church watching time run down as he wrote up his notes. It had taken eight pages to record the morning's events in his notebook and over an hour to two-finger-type the incident reports into his computer. He cranked up the air conditioner another notch and looked out at the neighbourhood. No one had spotted him yet.

A chunk of his day had been lost waiting for ER docs to medically clear the perp. Just a corridor over, his colleagues dealt with the mother's complaints. More time was lost at the mental hospital waiting for admission and custody transfer. He hated waiting. The first hour, the guy kept howling. The second hour, his voice went hoarse and his bays sounded more like a beagle's. The last hour, he finally shut up and stared at Mike. He refused all offers of water, food, or clothes and allowed only a blanket to be wrapped around his naked body. When Mike handed him over to the psych attendants, the man finally spoke. He said, "I see you."

Mike had stared back at the oddly elongated facial muscles, the lengthened jawline, sallow skin, constricted pupils, and unblinking ice-blue eyes. Eyes more animal than human in their piercing intensity and focus. The remains of the man were trapped somewhere behind those mad, glassy eyes. "I see you, too," he said, which set the guy off howling again.

He scanned his tightly lined notebook pages.

Volume 17. Pg. 87.

Brandt

His handwriting never betrayed the emotion of his day. He took great care to make his notes neat, legible, and compact to maximize space. He restricted the narrative to the facts, leaving himself out of the story as much as possible.

7:15 a.m. Overdose. 348 Oakland Road. 52-year-old female. Found in bed by neighbour . . .

9:36 a.m. (Bob?) 30+ No fixed address. Erratic Behaviour. Possession of crack cocaine . . .

10:45 a.m. Mentally unstable Luke Collins, 34, wielding knife. Mother T. Collins, non-fatal stab wound, right shoulder. Resisted arrest. Taser deployed.

He flipped past the notes documenting his actions and the events justifying the use of Taser and restraints, until he reached the end of the entry. He had nothing to justify. If he hadn't used the Taser, the perp would likely be dead. He didn't write that down.

After the bodily assault, I pushed T. Collins (mother) back to protect myself. She tripped and fell. Witness: Constable Raylene Wade. Declined pressing charges due to extenuating circumstances and emotional state of the assailant. Accompanied mentally unstable to ER (medically cleared by Dr. Lee) Accompanied mentally unstable to Admission. Custody transferred 1:40 p.m.

He drew a hard, straight line

---

and started what he hoped was the last entry of the day.

3:00-5:20 p.m. Canvassed neighbourhood of U. Square with Const. J. Ellison. D. Johnson case.

He was grateful he had been assigned with Ellison for the afternoon. James was a community cop, one of the first black officers to receive commendations of excellence, a good guy and a friend. Hell, he was probably Mike's best friend. He had been at his wedding and Caleb called him uncle. When he came by for a barbecue, he always brought a bottle of wine for Lori. James could make him laugh even when everything was going to hell. That's the kind of guy he was.

There was something about him that invited people to talk to him, and a real smile that made others smile back. Despite walking a beat, he was easily sixty pounds overweight, and couldn't chase down a toddler. But people didn't run from him. He really believed he could make things better.

He coached afterschool basketball. Fundraised for art, basketball, and music programs. He was spearheading a scholarship in the dead boy's name. His motto was one child at a time. There had been a write-up in the local paper about his own experience as a lost kid and the mentor who saved his life. It was the first he'd heard about his friend's troubled past.

James once had his three-year sobriety coin and maybe would again. Mike was reticent to admit it, but his friend wasn't much fun sober. He couldn't open up to people; couldn't find that smile. He had cut back a lot and kept his drinking mostly to his days off. Lately, there were fewer sick leaves and fewer times his phone was off the hook. He was still a good cop. He believed in second, third, and fourth chances. Sometimes those he collared couldn't look him in the eyes. He always said shame was a good first sign.

Being assigned an afternoon with James was like a day of R&R. It was the sergeant's way of prescribing an unofficial attitude adjustment. But foot patrol made Mike uneasy. It was too exposed. He couldn't stroll like his partner, and people sensed it.

We're just here asking about the boy who died, Helen. James knew everyone's names. *Anything you know or heard that could help us?*

No one had a bad thing to say about the boy. He was an artist, a musician. No drugs, no gangs, no grudges. No reason why. Every story was the same—nobody knew anything, nobody heard anything. Before moving on, James would ask about their sons, daughters, and husbands. Who was working, who was in jail, who was getting married, who was in university? He held grandchildren and let them wear his cap. In every house, fans and air conditioners hummed. He was offered iced tea and lemonade, while Mike stood silently apart, surveying family portraits, cheap toys, and outdated televisions. Public housing all had the same floor plan, and most walls bore the original builder's white paint, making the houses seem both temporary and permanent.

Outside in the courtyards, teens held each other closer, knowing that if it could happen to Devon, it could definitely happen to them. Some girls cried. Boys looked at the ground. Nobody heard nothin'. Nobody knew nothin'. They were lying.

James mentioned anonymous tips and reward money. Mike watched their eyes, but no one blinked. One boy with long locs and unscuffed white sneakers asked, "What you gonna do when you find 'em?"

"We'll take them in to answer for what they did." James could lie like that.

"I'd shoot 'em like a dog," the boy said.

"I wouldn't shoot a dog," James said.

Mike held his pencil poised above his notebook. Somebody knew something. He had no doubt something was coming and when it did it was going to be bad. Criminals taking care of criminals. Judge and jury with civilians caught in the crossfire. He wrote:

No leads

and drew another hard line.

The car radio squawked. He cocked his ear to the static.

Car vs pedestrian. Quinpool and Harvard. Bus on scene. Requesting detour and traffic assistance. Car 163 responding.

He looked at the map, relieved he wasn't needed. He had called in a 10-99, *Taking a break*, almost thirty minutes ago. He knew his car icon was flashing inactive on the IES monitors and the new GPS system was signalling dispatch every hour to check on his status. Standard procedure. *We have your back even when you're hiding.* It was a pain in the ass.

Ten-zero, radio check, Car 322.

Mike radioed back. "Ten-two. Good check."

Each time it had been Tamara checking in. She was working dispatch today as part of the regular rotation through call intake, dispatch, and fire. Her team handled it all.

Male thirty-five years old. Head injury. Said he was assaulted with a baseball bat at Midtown Motel. Does not want to press charges . . .

Female unconscious. Suspected heat exhaustion. EMS on scene . . .

Bike vs car. Parties involved fighting. Corner of Cunard and . . .

Report of dog locked in vehicle. Parking lot of . . .

Her voice was always calm and in control. She enunciated carefully. She listened. Really listened. She could decipher the white noise and dirty static of their radios' crappy technology, no matter how degraded or clipped. She told them what she knew and only what they needed to know, directed radio communication so nobody stepped on each other, and she never sent them down the wrong street. She was the best of the best. No one said it, but they all considered Tamara good luck and hoped she'd be the one guiding them in on a bad call. He hadn't seen her since that morning in the cab. Listening to her now, though, he knew she had got through it. She was tough. Nothing cracked her.

"Car 322. Off-shift in twenty minutes."

Ten–four. Copy that.

She wouldn't send him out now unless something bad happened. He stretched his legs. A late-model Jeep, black, two-door, stopped at the small park adjacent to the church. A female—Caucasian, mid- to late twenties, five six, athletic build, blonde, blue T-shirt, jeans—got out and opened the back. An unleashed dog, black, jumped down in violation of Animal Bylaw A-300. The dog curled into a snug sit against her left leg. Its attention focused solely on its handler.

He watched them enter the greenbelt and was surprised that she walked like a cop. The dog pranced at her side. She had an orange ball-tosser. The car thermometer read 37.8. It wasn't worth giving up the air conditioning. He was definitely having an off day. The entire week had been off. He blamed it on the damn heat.

He stared at the blank space beneath his last entry. Notebook 17 was almost full and would soon join the others in the fire-safety box at the back of his closet. He flipped through the pages, glimpsing short passages, and five to six hard, straight lines per page. His rookie notes had been more extensive before he realized that he only needed a few lines to recall every detail of an event, regardless of how much time had passed.

Without his crib notes, he couldn't conjure a single name, place, or incident. Not even from the previous day. He had to see the words. Once read, he would be back in the room or on the street, able to recall the weather, the smell, and forensics. If he read the names, he could see them shouting, crying, bloodied, denying, drunk, stoned, afraid, fearless, combatant. He could walk up to the bodies and see the colour of their eyes. The bottom corners of some pages were marked with three squiggly lines indicating they held children's names. *Don't look here.*

The radio squelched, followed by a piercing repeating tone signifying, *Listen up. This is a real emergency.*

Two—car MVA, 102 westbound. Need ambulance. Injuries reported. Car 274 and 357 responding. Rollover. Two trapped severely. Fire responding. Car 357, ETA?

The garbled interference and clipped siren of car 357 cut in: Three minutes.

Mike typed in his last notes on the computer. He filtered out the non-stop chatter of the radio and tuned his ears to only his car number, which was unlikely to be called this close to shift end. The shrill repeating alarm was more difficult to ignore. He flicked the air conditioner up another notch.

He was lucky to have found this spot behind the church. It couldn't be seen easily from the street. Every cop had a spot like this—a place to drink a coffee, catch up on paperwork, or simply take a breath. It had taken him a year to find.

The public expected him to be on call 24-7. If he parked in the open, cars pulled up alongside him to complain about potholes, and people crossed the street to tell him about a party three nights prior. Parking lots were the worst for a litany of dented doors and scratched fenders. Nobody ever approached just to say hi. If they did he would wonder what they were hiding.

When he saw the Grumblers coming towards him, he'd stare them down with his most unapproachable look and make them wait before he rolled down his window. He never spoke first.

He'd cut them off: *Is this an emergency?* When they said no, he'd recommend they call the non-emerg line and file a complaint report. He wasn't outfitted with a 4.6 L 250-horsepower car, weapon, and bulletproof vest for annoyance complaints and dinged cars. They'd insist that he come see the scratched paint and ask him to check surveillance cameras.

Upgrading. Two—vehicle MVA rollover with injuries. Entrapment. Fatalities. Three ambulances and medevac en route . . .

He would like to tell the Grumblers what happens to paint jobs when two vehicles collide head-on at 100 km/h. And what first responders would find on the scene and how it would keep them awake at night and haunt them in the days ahead. He'd tell them how far bodies are found from their shoes, their legs, their heads, and guts, and how unbelievably long intestines are when they spill outside their soft belly. Then he'd like to ask them if they still wanted to file a report for their dented door. Inevitably, they would say yes. And he would do what he always did: take down their name, make, and model; verify the scratch; and wish them a good day.

He shifted in his seat. His back seized, and pain ratcheted up his spine, exploding behind his eyes, momentarily blinding him in its blackness. He leaned to his left and the pain ebbed. He breathed out.

At ER he had been checked over. Minor bruising, but the doc's probing fingers almost buckled his knees. Likely a muscle pull, maybe a repetitive strain injury. He suggested age was a factor, which pissed Mike off. He filled in the necessary forms documenting the latest workplace scuffle, adding to his long medical record for insurance protection. He had never filed a claim.

The doc recommended better shoes, more exercise, Epsom salts, massage, physio, and an over-the-counter relaxant and anti-inflammatory. Mike had tried them all at maximum strength and dosage. The doc suggested rest. When he said he had two more shifts this week and didn't want to use his sick leave, the doc gave him six codeine pills and reiterated several times, "*One* tablet at bedtime."

He reached in his shirt pocket and retrieved the pill bottle. Across the street, the black dog was running away from the woman. She whipped the orange handle and a yellow tennis ball arced through the sky. The dog charged ahead of the soaring ball. Power rippled every muscle. Its hindquarters drove in tandem, an accordion of legs exploding into each elongated stride. It was beautiful in its pure physicality. His body had felt like that once. The dog's gait slowed a fraction of a beat, its head swung up and twisting it leapt, plucking the yellow orb from blue sky.

Mike leaned forward and flinched. He opened the nearly empty four-litre jug of tepid water at his side and swallowed a pill. By the time he got home the med would just be kicking in. He picked up his handset. "Ten-seven. Car 322 out of service."

Ten-four. Copy that.

The radio went silent, and then, Have a good night. Thanks for the day.

He could barely keep his voice in check and the tears from his eyes. It was ridiculous that he was so grateful for those words. Pain was stripping him bare.

"You, too."

The alarm fired again.

Engine 15, Medic 17 responding. MVA rollover with injuries. Entrapment. Fatalities. Medivac ETA 1 minute.

A taxi rounded the corner. Bluebird. The driver hit the brakes hard, surprised to find him there. Mike glared at the man. Middle Eastern. Late forties, early fifties. He looked familiar. Another minute and Mike would have been on his way home.

The cabbie bowed his head. His hands clenched the steering wheel. Mike wondered what he was waiting for. The driver kept his head low and timidly backed up. *That's right*, Mike thought. *This is my spot*. The steering belt squealed. The cabbie raised his hand, an open-palmed apology. Mike watched the taxi, its signal light needlessly flashing, retreat around the church. Shift was over.

He flipped his notebook to the top of the day and drew a long diagonal slash down the page through all the entries, locking them up in the past. The line cut through names, addresses, phone numbers, and incidents, confining them behind a single, impenetrable bar until he reached the end of the page.

Soon he would need a new notebook.

"Again!"

Mike hoisted Caleb above his head and spun. Cradling his son's waist in perfect equilibrium in the palms of his hands, he was amazed by his lightness. The boy's sneakered feet helicoptered and sun flickered through his outstretched arms. Tethered by his tail, Snappy whipped around.

Caleb screeched when Mike draped him over his shoulder, dangling him upside down by one ankle. He wrapped his leg around his father's arm as he slid down his back, shrieking with sheer joy at the possibility of falling. Snappy's head touched the ground.

"What's that on my back? Is that a fly? Should I swat it?"

"*No!*"

Mike hoisted Caleb over his head and flipped him, allowing a moment of freefall before catching him in his arms. Squealing, the boy was somersaulted to the ground and immediately tried to shimmy back up Mike's leg. "Again!"

"Do you have to play so rough?" Lori was smiling, but she had assumed her best serious-mom pose. "And what about your back? Do you think you should be doing that?"

Mike winked to Caleb. "Uh-oh, we're in trouble."

Lori crossed her arms. "My mom's here. What time are we supposed to be there?"

Playtime was over. "Daddy has to go—the fun police are here."

"Don't tell him that." This time, she wasn't smiling.

Caleb grabbed his legs in a monkey hold. "Daddy stays with me."

"No, Mama's right. Mommy's always right." Mike looked at Lori, hoping to make extra points. "Look at your mommy. Doesn't she look pretty?"

"She looks like a *girl*." Caleb burrowed his head between his father's knees. Snappy flopped against his calves.

"Okay, that's it, let's go in." Lori was taking charge, though Mike could tell she was pleased by her son's unintended compliment. "Nana brought you a homemade pie. Apple, your favourite." She rolled her eyes at Mike. "Who makes pie in this heat?"

Lori really did look beautiful in the evening light. She was wearing the blue dress, the one that silhouetted her legs when backlit. Nestled between the soft roundness of her cleavage was the turquoise pendant he'd given her at Christmas. He marvelled that a mere dress and stone could bring out all that beauty.

"What are you smiling at?"

"I just feel good, babe." And he did. He felt great. Pain-free.

Lori was already at the screen door. "Don't wind him up any more."

"All right, climb on up." He crouched for Caleb to hop on his back. Small arms wrapped around his neck. Mike was amazed at the effortless rise straightening his back. He should have had these pills months ago.

"I not letting go." Caleb had a solid grip.

"Oh no? You're stuck to me? You're coming with us?"

"Uh-huh."

"Who's going to look after Nana and Connor while Mama and Daddy are away?"

"Nana."

"And what about Snappy? Nana can't look after Snappy and crocodiles aren't allowed in restaurants. Are you going to leave Snappy here alone?"

"No!" Caleb pressed the stuffed toy tight against Mike's throat. It smelled sour and sticky.

"Duck your head." He nodded to his mother-in-law as he stepped through the patio doors and into the kitchen. She had the baby in her arms. Connor was trying to grab her glasses. She was patting his diapered bottom and yanking her head away—"No, no, no. Those are Nana's"—which only made Connor stretch farther to reach the forbidden rims. He slapped his grandmother's cheeks.

Betty was getting old. He hadn't noticed how much she had aged. She must be in her late seventies by now. Lori's dad had been dead for six years. Her mom was alone all the time, except when she visited their house, which was often. Betty did a lot for their family. Without question she came whenever they called. And yes, it was true that Caleb sometimes had a scratch on his knee, or she let him eat too much junk food or watch inappropriate shows, and Connor's diaper wasn't changed as often as they liked, and she didn't always rinse his soother when it dropped on the floor before popping it back in his mouth . . . but she loved the boys. She had raised Lori and look at the woman she'd become, an amazing mother. His wife. His friend. She was everything that was good in his life. His mother-in-law did her very best.

"Hi, Mom."

Betty and Lori looked at him. It was the first time he had called her Mom in seven years of marriage and five years of dating.

"I have to get my wallet and I'm ready."

"You stay!" Caleb tightened his chokehold.

Betty shifted the baby onto her shoulder. Connor grunted, trying to wriggle free, kicking her in the belly. "Caleb, you and I are going to have such a nice time together. We're going to play and I brought stories—"

"You go away!"

"Caleb, you do not speak to your Nana like that."

Caleb responded with sniffles and ragged breaths. Soon there would be real tears. Lori breathed in deep, her warning sign for

Enough. Mike was distracted by the soft rise of her breasts, but he knew if he didn't intervene the situation would escalate. He kissed her on the cheek. *I've got this*. She smelled of sun and talcum.

She pulled back and looked him in the eyes, a question still formulating in the crease of her forehead.

"Caleb's going to help me get ready. I'll be right back."

He galloped down the hall to their bedroom and reversed up to the bed doing his best version of a big truck's *beep, beep, beep*, until Caleb's toes touched the mattress. "Okay, ride's over." But the boy held on.

"Caleb." He used his soft but non-negotiable voice.

The boy's slim arms loosened and he slid down his father's back. He was still so small. His cheeks were flushed and his lower lip quivered. Mike had never been more afraid than the first time he held his firstborn son.

"Mommy and Daddy are going out tonight for a grown-up dinner. Daddy needs to do something nice for Mommy because she does so many nice things for us. I need you to help Nana and be a good boy for her. Can you do that for me?"

He got a reluctant nod. It was a good start. "Because what do deputies do?"

"Serve and protect."

"That's right." He picked up his wallet from the dresser. They had plenty of time before their reservation. He double-checked the locked gun box and scanned the top of the dresser to confirm everything was in its proper place. He had checked the gun three times to ensure it was empty and counted the bullets twice.

He glanced at himself in the mirror. Good enough for a date. Maybe even good enough to get lucky. One of the benefits of shifting to nights was a free evening and morning to turn around his schedule. He checked his five o'clock shadow. Lori had liked his scruff when they were dating. She'd liked the scratch of it against her neck when they nuzzled on the couch, in the car, in bed, on the beach, in the street. When she leaned into him, her head rested perfectly in the hollow of his shoulder, and when they spooned, their bodies fit together as though moulded for each other. He sucked in his gut.

He could still be that twenty-six-year-old who picked up his girl in his '72 red Camaro with bucket seats. Sure, the seats were duct-taped and the wipers didn't work, or the heater, and the last two months he'd driven without reverse gear, but it was a Camaro. And she liked it. He flexed his bicep. He was still in good shape for thirty-eight. Screw the doctor. He might not be able to run a 3:06 PARE test anymore. But he could hold his own.

Dinner and a movie. Maybe she would neck with him in the back seat for old times' sake. He could take her down to the waterfront for a walk. No, not on a Saturday night, it would be swarming with drunken university kids. Better to avoid the area than have to look the other way. She was choosing the movie, so no car chases or blow-'em-ups, but he didn't care. He was going to put his arm around her, eat popcorn, and be a regular guy out with his girl.

"Don't go, Daddy." Caleb was standing on the bed with Snappy hugged to his chest. God, he was a good kid. Such an easy child. All heart. A little soft, but he'd grow out of it.

"We won't be gone long. Do you want one last ride to the door? Then you're going to be a big boy and take care of Nana, right? I'll be in to kiss you goodnight when we get home."

Caleb snuffled. "Promise?"

"Promise."

"Promise the bad guys won't shoot you?"

"Caleb, we're just going out for dinner and then I'm taking Mommy to a movie. There won't be any bad guys there."

"What if they come here?"

Mike assessed whether or not he was being played by the stall tactics of a four-year-old, but his son's eyes were welling.

"The bad guys know not to ever come here. But if one made a mistake and forgot whose house it was, what would you do?"

"Get the phone and lock me in the bathroom."

"And?"

"Call 911."

"That's right. And then what would happen?"

"Police cars would come whoowhoowhoo."

"And would you hang up the phone?"

"No, not till the bad guys is gone."

Mike knelt down to his son's height. He squeezed the crocodile's mouth and its soft teeth flopped up and down. "And you'd have Snappy with you, so you wouldn't be afraid. Snappy and his big teeth."

"And he'd grow bigger than the room and his teeth would be big as my head and he'd bite the bad guy."

Mike needed to hurry this along. "And you wouldn't open the door for anyone, no matter what you heard, not until the person on the phone said it was safe. Even if someone was knocking on the door and said they were a policeman."

"I don't open the door, till phone people say oh-kay."

"That's right. But you don't have to worry about any of this because Nana's here and she would never let bad people in the door." Mike ruffled his hair. "Okay?"

Caleb's gaze didn't waver as he scrutinized his father's face for lies. Maybe his son was going to be a cop someday.

"Daddy . . ."

"Yeah . . . ?"

"There's bad guys everywhere. You can't see them all."

"You know what, buddy? Daddy has to go. Hop on." He scooped the boy up, slung him onto his back, and headed down the hall.

"Check under my bed, Daddy."

"Nope, gotta go."

"You have to look in the closet!"

"I already checked. Everything is safe."

Lori was waiting at the door. "We're going to be late, as always." *As always* was directed at him. He lowered Caleb to the floor. "Say bye to Mommy."

She bent down and kissed Caleb three times on the top of his head, reciting, "I love you, I love you, I love you."

Caleb wrapped his arms around her legs and pressed his eyes tight. "I love you, I love you, I love you."

Mike kissed Connor's belly. "Bye, little man."

"Three times!"

Mike looked up at Lori. It would be the simplest solution, but they were going to have to deal with this soon. He kissed Connor two more times. His chubby hand opened and closed in his version of a wave. "Ba, ba, ba."

"Bye, bye, baby boy."

"We have to go." Lori was breathing in again.

"Okay, kiddo, where's my kisses?"

Caleb slung his arms around his neck and kissed him hard on his cheek three times. Mike reciprocated, already thinking about the steak he was going to order. He stood and smiled generously at his mother-in-law. "If you need anything, call. We won't be late."

He waited for Caleb to complete his round of love yous before disengaging his arms from his legs. "See you soon, big boy."

He followed Lori out the door. He was planning to open the passenger door like a real gentleman.

"It didn't work! Do again!"

Caleb was on the front step. His grandmother had him by the shoulder. "Come back inside."

Caleb screamed, "I love you, I love you, I love you!"

Lori had already opened the van door by herself. "Just keep walking."

"You have to say it!"

Mike went to the driver's side and took out his keys.

"Daddy!" Caleb was wailing. "*Daddy!* You have to say it! I love you, I love you, I love you!"

The van was hot and smelled of sour milk and wet sneakers.

"IloveyouIloveyouIloveyou! *Daddy!*" He slipped from Betty's grip, and stood on the bottom step screaming, red faced, tears wetting his cheeks.

"We can't leave him with your mother like this." Mike got out of the van and walked slowly to the stairs. "Get back in the house, Caleb." He used his quiet this-is-the-end-of-the-line voice.

Caleb retreated to the top step. Betty held the screen door open for him. Snot hung from his nose. His eyes were rimmed with tears. Mike looked down on his son using his full height. He waited. Without his work boots, he felt shorter.

Caleb's heaving breaths slowed to short gasps, then sniffles, and the tears stopped spilling.

"Are you done?"

Caleb shook his head. "You have to say it."

His boy was stubborn like his mother. "Caleb, I want you to go to your room and not come out until Nana says you're allowed."

He didn't budge. He bit his lower lip.

"For every moment you stand there, you're going to lose something you like. Do you understand?"

Caleb nodded.

"Do you want to stop now?"

He shook his head.

"No video games."

Caleb stared up at his dad. "Say it."

"No TV." Mike looked at Betty to confirm she'd heard.

Caleb sniffled. "Say it."

"No apple pie."

Caleb nodded. He was willing to pay that price. "You have to say it."

The kid was tougher than Mike gave him credit. It was time to end it.

"Do you want me take away Snappy?"

He saw panic flicker in his eyes. But then his son's chin tilted up and he breathed in like his mother. He gave Snappy a hug and laid him on the steps at his father's feet. His entire body was quivering.

"Mike, the reservation . . ." Lori had her window down. "Get in the house, Caleb! Now!"

Mike looked down at his son. Just this once it would be so much easier. He said, "I love you, I love you, I love you."

Caleb exhaled. He wiped the snot and tears from his face with the back of his hand. "Now you'll be safe." Gently, he picked up Snappy and went indoors.

Mike looked back at the van. It was going to take more than an overpriced steak and crème brûlée to make Lori smile again.

24

Mike was sleeping open-mouthed. The tension was gone from his jaw and the creases on his forehead and around his eyes had softened. He looked younger. Lori hadn't seen him so peaceful in years.

It had been a good night. A great night. After they had implemented the no-talk-about-kids-over-dinner rule and imbibed two glasses of a good pinot noir, they had forgotten who they were and became a couple out on a romantic date. They flirted with each other. The room was sultry and the jazz sensual. They indulged, refusing to think of the cost and the bills it might have paid. She slipped off her sandals and rested her feet on his shoes, legs slightly apart and dress hiked coyly. The night hummed electric like their honeymoon in Puerto Vallarta, when they had stayed up dreaming the future until the neon sky lit the sea.

He had been funny tonight. His eyes shone in the candlelight. He was still so handsome. She had known the first moment she saw him. Those ice-blue eyes and movie star's jawline. Tall, athletic. His confident, easy stride and quiet, respectful integrity. She would have slept with him that night. But instead, he walked her to the door, kissed her on the cheek, and asked if he could see her again. She had been so flustered, aching with the heat of want, she pleasured herself that night imagining him as she writhed on her futon. It would be another two weeks before they had sex. It was wild, unfettered, and as tender as she had hoped.

He'd been that boy again tonight. She had been surprised by their mutual hunger and the heat of his hands. Before they reached the bed, their clothes were off, discarded on the floor. They didn't pull back the sheets or close the blinds. Their bodies found each other and tangled closer. They came at the same time. She couldn't remember the last time they had stopped breathing together and the children hadn't woken.

After, they curled into each other, recounting the night so they would remember: the steak *best ever*, the accompanying wild garlic, loganberries, capers, and mushroom bouillon *unbelievable*, the summer berry tiramisu *intoxicating*, the ricotta, coffee, and honey gelato *orgasmic*, the walk along the waterfront *magical*, and even the movie Mike had admitted *life-affirming*.

She asked him, What was your favourite part?

This, he answered.

Her eyes had teared. He must have thought that she was overwhelmed by her love, and not the guilt of the nights spent wondering who she would be if she left him. She did still love him. She nuzzled against his chest. His hand cupped her breast, and groaning, he nudged her closer.

If only the children would sleep through the night, this could be her heaven.

She would try harder. She would try harder . . .

25

Mike woke clenched in pain. His face contorted in a silent scream. He curled his knees to relieve his back. Lori was lying on his arm. He slipped the appendage free, cringing with every tug, and rolled onto his side. With clamped teeth, he tried to ride the fire and will his muscles to relax, but to no avail. He leveraged himself onto his arm and slid off the bed. White-hot pain seared. There were tears in his eyes. He crawled to the dresser and, using the handles, pulled himself to his knees. He could go no farther. He was trapped.

What the fuck was this? Nothing had ever forced him to his knees. His body had never betrayed him before.

"Lori . . ."

He heard her rustle in bed. It was still too dark to see.

"Lori."

She woke like a mother, fully awake and alert for danger. "What's wrong?"

"My back, I need you to get me something." He tried pulling himself up again, and the pain drove him down.

The nightlight switched on, revealing him naked on his knees, hanging on to the dresser, his back arched as if he were being flogged. He wanted the light off. He wanted her to go back to sleep. He wanted her to not look at him. She jumped out of bed.

"Baby, what's the matter?" She had never see him like this before.

"I need you to get something for me. In my pants, there's some pills." The effort of speaking sawed at his spine.

She rushed to the door. He hung on. The hardwood floor crushing his knees.

"I don't see it. Which pocket?" Her voice lacked the practised calm she used with the children.

"Right lower."

She returned with the pill bottle. "How long have you been taking this? This is codeine."

"I know what it is!" It came out louder and angrier than he had intended. "The doc prescribed it. Just give me a pill."

She padded to the ensuite and he could hear water running.

"I don't need water!"

She returned with a glass of water and handed him one pill. He swallowed it without water.

She said, "When were you going to tell me?"

"Give me another one."

"It says one pill."

"It says *as needed*. Give it to me!"

She threw the bottle at him. It bounced off his chest and rolled to a stop just out of reach. She walked away.

"Is this what you were on tonight?" She said it like the answer mattered. She was behind him and he couldn't see her.

"What the fuck does that mean?" He growled the words. He didn't want to talk. He wanted to be left alone until he was himself again. He leaned tentatively forward, his fingers nudging the bottle.

"What did the doctor say?"

"It's a pulled muscle." If he rocked his weight gently onto his heels, the pain loosened. "In a couple of days it'll be fine." Another inch and he had the bottle. He ground the pain into his back teeth, refusing to show her. It did say one pill only. But he needed more. Now. He swallowed a second pill and tried to breathe.

"I knew something was wrong when you were tossing Caleb in the air."

"Nothing was wrong! I was playing with my son! *This* is nothing!" He forced himself to stand. He couldn't hold back the whimper that escaped his lips. He tried to straighten to his full height and stitched over heavily to the right. He leaned on the dresser. "Just give me a few moments and I'll be fine."

"Where does it hurt?"

Before he could stop her, she had her hand on the small of his back. The shock ripped through him. "Don't touch me!"

"I'm trying to help."

"Just let the meds kick in."

"Those aren't meds. It's an opiate. It converts to morphine."

"What are you, a doctor now? Did you learn that from your afternoon shows?" Too far, too far. This had nothing to do with her. "I'm sorry, Lori, you have to let me get through this. Please, go back to bed. I'll be fine in a few minutes."

"You'll be stoned in a few minutes." It was the righteous tone in her voice that pissed him off.

"*You* wrestle a crazy bastard to the ground with a ten-pound belt slung around your waist and sit in a shit car seat twelve hours a day! That's my job! I don't get to call my mom for a break. So if I need a goddamn pill, from a *doctor*, I'm going to take it!" The pain, the fucking pain was throbbing behind his eyes now. He wanted her to shut up and go away.

"I knew it wasn't you tonight," she said.

"What the fuck does that mean?"

"You weren't the prick you usually are."

Now, she chose to attack him? Now? He could hear sirens in the distance. They never stopped. Four in the morning and somewhere shit was going down.

Her cheeks had flushed. "It's always your job! There's no time, day or night, when you're not bleeding cop!"

All he had wanted was for her to get him a pill and go back to bed. He hadn't asked for anything else. He never asked for anything. "If it wasn't me you were screwing tonight, then who were you with? Because you sure seemed to be enjoying yourself, baby!" Sirens were wailing nearby. It was odd to hear them on this street.

"I thought the man I had married had finally come home!"

Oh Christ, she was going to cry. He wanted to put on his clothes. He didn't want to be standing with his ass hanging out like he was about to be strip-searched. Couldn't she see the pain he was in? Crap, now the baby was crying and that would be his fault, too.

He wanted to say he was sorry, this didn't involve her, that he couldn't think through the vise grip crushing him, if she just stopped talking and let it ease, everything would be good soon. Instead he was shouting. "I've never left! I've been here for you every day! Everything I do is for you and them. Every bit of shit

I walk through, every horror show, I do it so they don't have to ever see it! You expect me to come home and sit at the table and talk about grocery lists and crayons and chores and bills and fucking bills . . ." He knew he should stop, but the electric pain was frying him inside, jump-starting his tongue and short-circuiting his heart. He would have kept going if the doorbell hadn't rung.

Instinctively, his trigger hand reached for the revolver case forgetting that it was unloaded. It was after four in the morning. Nobody came to the door at this time of night.

Lori wiped her eyes and eased open the bedroom door. Red and blue, red and blue ricocheted through the windows.

From under the bathroom door, hard white light spilled.

26

Daddy said, daddy said, daddy said if the bad guys come lock the bathroom door.

Caleb's bare feet were cold on the tile floor. He was standing on his too-long jammy bottoms that got wet when the shouting woke him up. The pee was hot but now it was cold. The bad guys were in Mommy and Daddy's room.

The portabelly phone was heavy and he was holding it with both hands. His ear didn't reach the listeny piece when his mouth was on the talky piece, so he kept his mouth pressed to the talky. Someone was saying his name from inside the phone, far away. He slid the phone down to his ear.

A man's voice said, "Caleb, are you still there?" Caleb nodded. "The police are there and are looking for the bad guys. Can you hear me? Can you say yes?"

"Yes."

"Caleb, where are your mommy and daddy?"

Mommy and Daddy were gone eating ice cream in the big people's restaurant. He had kissed them three times. He had said IloveyouIloveyouIloveyou. He had done everything right. He had been good for Nana, ate apple pie, let baby play with his toys, said *See ya later, alligator,* and Nana said *After a while, crocodile,* and kissed him three times, and he kissed one-two-three and touched the birthday present cars chasing robbers on the roofs, one-two-three, and pulled the covers up around his neck so the monsters couldn't suck his blood, and checked no fingers or toes were over the edge—

"Caleb?"

"They gone," he said.

The door handle turned and Caleb took a step back. The bad guy that sounded like Daddy was saying his name. Knock knock, let me in, said the wolf to the piggy pig pig.

The voice in the phone said, "Are you still in the bathroom, Caleb?"

"Say the magic words," Caleb whispered.

"Can you say that again? I couldn't hear you."

"He's at the door."

"Caleb, I'm talking to the policeman now and he says it's safe to open the door. Your mommy and daddy are there."

Those weren't the right words.

The knob rattled. Shadows flickered under the door. Mommy was saying his name, but that wouldn't work. Only the policeman could make the door open. Daddy said.

"Caleb, the police officer is going to knock on the door. His name is Constable Harvey. Then you'll know it's safe."

"Three times."

"What did you say, Caleb?"

"Him knock three times."

Caleb stepped behind Snappy. The crocodile's green chenille head was touching the ceiling and his tail overfilling the bathtub. Snappy's button eyes were blacker and shinier. His white felt teeth had hardened to razor bone. Caleb laid the phone on the toilet seat and pulled up his soppy pyjama bottoms.

Knock. Knock. Knock, said the door.

Caleb took hold of Snappy's soft paw.

If it's not them, you bite their heads off, he said. And Snappy licked his lips.

27

Just after midnight, Kate had been woken by the shrill pips of her pager and mistook the sound for her alarm. She had fallen asleep on the couch next to a plate of cold pizza on the floor and the television hawking lonely, full-busted girls. It took thirty-one minutes to deploy, having lost several minutes locating her keys and boots while Zeus waited patiently at the door. En route to the ground search, she confirmed with the hospital that she could switch shifts. Go, they said. Go find them.

The area of probability was a densely wooded park not far from the city. For the past two hours, they'd been searching the ravine's dense bush. Ranging twenty feet ahead, Zeus's lit red collar bobbed and his reflective vest weaved. His light disappeared and reappeared, warning of a dip ahead. It was good to be in the woods.

It had been a shit day at work. Swamped with the elderly. In ER they didn't really care about the old dying. It was accepted they'd had their time and should be grateful, but today she couldn't push it away. She had avoided looking into the eyes of family members hovering nearby, as doctors called for tests delaying the diagnosis of old age and scripts to either send them home or up to the eighth floor. Twice she pulled up charts to hurry along the process to get them in or out. They were running out of time to wait. The afternoon was worse, when a howling unstable was brought in. The ER hated unstables, even more than the elderly. Really, they hated their own helplessness.

They couldn't hear their poor stories, couldn't help them, couldn't do anything. Of course they felt for them, but they had to put up walls or they'd suck you dry. Poor, poor man, they said and got on with their day. Kate hadn't said a word. She had picked at the scab on her palm, kept her head in her paperwork, and made sure he wasn't her patient. After he was transferred, she gorged on brownies, chocolate, and iced lattes with the others and refrained from their barbed jokes. They weren't wrong. The ER wasn't the place. There just wasn't any other place.

Treading carefully, she trained her flashlight on the uneven ground below and her headlamp on the terrain ahead. The soil was thin, and roots humped from a tangle of decaying deadfall. Stands of old-growth hemlock had given way to the choke of spruce and weedy hardwood. Her flashlight flickered over the green curl of leaves, yellow mushrooms, and the blush of red berries. She pushed aside a branch, then let it lash back. Behind her, Heather grunted.

Over the walkie-talkie, Riley's calm, strong voice punctuated the night. As incident commander, he had deployed her to the south sector and assigned his wife as team lead. It was her first mission. Riley at least had the decency to pull her aside to apologize. Nobody else was available. Would it be a problem?

"Can she do the job or not?"

"Yes." He adjusted his voice from lover to commander. "She can."

"Then what's the problem?"

Her boots kicked through a carpet of rust needles. The understory was tinder dry. The fire hazard sign at the entrance was red-lined extremely high. Trees gave way to a rock slab mottled with lichen. Clomping heavily behind her, Heather was already out of breath. Above them, night's blackness opened to stars and a deepening blue sky.

Kate stopped and retrieved the bottle of talcum powder from her pant pouch pocket. She gave it a quick squeeze and the fine dust fell unperturbed. She lowered it to ground level and squeezed again. It settled over the rocks. The gully was a dead pool. Scents could be drawing down over the ridge.

Mosquitoes churned in her ears. She swiped her face and bug spray fumed her eyes. "What's our heading now?" They had been looping erratically, backtracking, and sawing forward through bush at times too dense to penetrate. Twice they had crossed open paths that would have led a lost person out.

Riley's prized military compass glowed green in the reflection of Heather's safety glasses and her red headlamp illuminated the map pencilled with plotting points. She was outfitted in new, expensive brand-name gear and boots. Even her reflective orange vest was crisp. Kate glanced at the crescent moon and drew an imaginary line south, found the Big Dipper, followed the pointer stars to Polaris, the cardinal point, and sited their direction. They had swung west again.

Heather breathed heavily. "South-southwest. Bearing 225 degrees?"

"Are you asking me?" She hated sentences that ended in a question mark. Either she knew or she didn't. Guessing wasn't an option.

Heather lowered her head to double-check her calculations. Her diamond ring glowed blood red in her lamplight. Zeus, trained to check in and maintain contact, circled back and looped away again.

"We're losing time," Kate said.

She ducked under a sprawl of limbs and followed Zeus's bobbing light, not waiting for confirmation. Heather scrambled clumsily to keep up. Kate heard the satisfying tear of fabric but didn't look back. An owl hooted and the woods pulsed with the hum of crickets and the deep-throated throb of bullfrogs. Heather's breathless voice relayed their coordinates to base camp. At least she could read a compass and was decent with a map. Earlier, though, Kate needed to correct her and tell her not to walk in front of the dog. Basic search knowledge—don't contaminate the dog's scent area.

Nosing the ground, Zeus circled a spot and sat. Her headlamp flashed green off his eyes and flared white off a teacup garlanded with bluebells. Her amazing dog was on the scent. Kate dropped a red marker and glanced back to see if Heather was recording the find. Her lover's wife's sleeve was ripped and her vest gobbed with spruce gum. Zeus's nose lifted. She wondered if the gully was indeed funnelling the scent over the ledge, giving him a false direction. They had circled this area twice. She might need to take him up the ridge to check the perimeter. He chose southwest again. Trust him.

"Confirm with Command there are no other search teams within a kilometre."

At least a kilometre. Zeus had been known to pick up scents at .7 kilometres. She quieted the restless energy of hope and widened her gap between Heather's overly enthusiastic walkie relay. The object find meant nothing other than that Zeus was on scent. It could have been dropped hours ago. They had found other articles on other searches and never recovered a body. Zeus's collar wove back and forth.

The point last seen was a modest fifties bungalow not far from the park. She checked her watch. Fifteen and a half hours had passed since the person went missing. As per protocol, the SAR teams weren't deployed until after the K-9 trackers proved unsuccessful. Now they were searching an area contaminated by police, K-9, family, and volunteers. Just like in the ER, searches had golden hours and delays increased the risk of negative outcomes. The deployment protocol was a constant prick of irritation. Trackers were trained to police and apprehend, not find. And were known to mistake "lost" for "eluding capture." SAR dogs didn't bite their finds.

Heather stumbled. Her flashlight beam careened across the twisted trunks and shattered limbs of hurricane-damaged trees. Kate picked up her pace. Laden with extra water and first aid supplies, her backpack scraped a low-hanging bough, showering her with needles. Riley had asked if she wanted to be taken off the active list, seeing as her mother was in hospital. In a moment of too many whiskeys and the false security of his embrace, she had mistakenly confided in him. His only concern was whether she could do the job. The mess of life wasn't part of their exchange. He didn't know about her brother. And never would.

She glanced back at Heather. Her head was down, watching her feet. She held the handset to her mouth like a respirator. Kate shifted the pack biting into the small of her back. Riley worried about her ability to separate work and personal, yet he entrusted her with his wife. He didn't worry that she could blow up his life. It both irritated and reassured her that he knew her so well.

Zeus was leading them to lower ground. His collar skittered along a buffer of nettled bush. His sweeps were tightening and his trot quickening. He had found the scent cone.

The missing person was a Wanderer, a seventy-eight-year-old female with mild to moderate dementia. When the teams were informed, they knew what that meant. Wanderers walked in straight lines and would keep going until deflected or stopped completely by an obstacle. They left roads and paths to follow visual breaks in the landscape and were known to walk into marshes and lakes as though on solid land. Unable to conceive of turning around, they'd push deep into impassable bush until hopelessly hemmed in. A twig whipped her cheek.

Zeus was working closer. The red light bobbed in and out of the knotting branches. Nettles and burrs grabbed her legs. Heather's nasal voice chattered unnecessary coordinates and Riley didn't correct her. They were veering southeast, moving towards the outer edge of the area of probability, a five-kilometre radius from the heart-shaped pond where the missing person had walked daily for thirty years.

Her name was Freda, but there was no point calling. She didn't know her name anymore. She was last seen at breakfast wearing a blue nightgown. Her eighty-year-old husband went to the bathroom and when he returned she was gone, along with her cup of tea. Her slippers were still under the kitchen table.

Deadfall cracked underfoot. She hoped the noise would flush wild animals out of the area. It had taken a long time to suppress her fear of Zeus being attacked. She had proofed him to avoid wildlife, but she was still hypervigilant to the danger of stray or unleashed dogs, and would never quell her worry over hunters' traps. She swiped her flashlight over a copse of jagged stumps and splintered trunks, white as bone. Hale young saplings rose from the remains. After the hurricane, surviving trees blanketed the ground with pine cones and acorns and showered the forest floor with whirling maple samaras. She wondered how they knew to attempt to save themselves.

A red blur and white-tipped tail burst from the thicket. Heather gasped. Kate panned her flashlight and caught Zeus's vest in the light. He was still, facing the direction of the retreating fox. His nose flared, but he swung back, intent on his purpose. Good boy. She swiped a mosquito from her nostrils and stepped over the broken spine of a tree, steadying herself with the trunk of another. There wasn't any pattern as to why some trees had fallen and others stood unscathed.

She had been working the night of the hurricane. That was six years ago, but sometimes she still had dreams of being caught in its wind and lifted off the ground. When the storm began, people ignored the warnings and were in the streets with their arms outspread, leaning into the gale. But when it truly arrived, and the rain roared sideways and waves surged over the city, people cowered in their basements and under support beams as trees fell. The wind sounded alive and vengeful. Transformers exploded, raining fire, poles toppled, power lines roiled and arced, windows blew, roofs failed. They had to evacuate a whole ward.

When the eye passed overhead, she had stepped outside. The air was thick with tropical heat and the sweet breath of dying trees and silence. She had never truly heard silence before. It made her feel small and afraid, as if she had trespassed and found herself inside a stillness humans weren't meant to witness and knew it couldn't last. When she looked up, there were stars and, oddly, she thought she heard birds.

She had lost sight of Zeus's collar. Branches clawed her arms as she wended her way around a thatch of spruce. Zeus barked. She stopped short, and Heather bumped into her.

"Sorry."

She raised her hand to silence her. The barks were loud and insistent. Her flashlight pierced holes in the blackness. Zeus emerged from the briars to her right. His tongue lolled and his sides were heaving. Burrs tangled his fur.

"Show me," she said.

He led the way, adjusting his pace so she could keep up. He spun in tight, joyful circles, coaxing her forward. She leaned into the dense undergrowth, pushing it back. A gnarl of upturned limbs carved her light. Zeus bounded ahead, bowing at the colossal roots of an upended skeletal tree. He barked, loud and deep and sure, *Here, Here, Here*. Kate slowed her breath and cloaked her heart, preparing for what was ahead. Another raised hand stopped Heather from coming closer.

"Call it in."

Zeus's tail circle-wagged and he ran squirming back to her. His nose bumped her leg and she retrieved his toy from her pocket. "Good boy," she whispered and tugged twice before letting him win. He tossed his head in victory and plopped down on the ground. Reassured that he had indicated "live," she proceeded. But Zeus couldn't discern the degree of alive.

She saw the hem of a blue nightgown squirrelled in the cage of ancient roots, snagged in the bramble. Spindled legs streaked with dirt and blood flared under Kate's glaring light. The still body was slumped to its knees against the heart root. Wide eyes blinked.

She knelt beside the woman. "Hello, Freda," she said. "I'm Kate. We're here to take you home." The woman's fingers clenched the rich loam, and startled sowbugs scuttled over her quaking hand. The earth smelled sweet and the woman sour.

"I'm going to check you over to make sure you're doing okay." She triaged the ABCs—airway, breathing, circulation. Took note of hypothermia, dehydration, lacerations, and bruising. She ran her hands over the trembling limbs. No pain response. No obvious broken bones. The woman's piercing eyes, swollen with bites, studied her face. Her breathing was unobstructed. "Very good, Freda, thank you."

She draped a thermal blanket over her and held a water bottle to her crusted lips. The woman suckled it with both hands. Her opaque eyes stared back. Kate pointed the flashlight away to soften its spill, and the tree's silvered-grey heart clogged with mud and stones illuminated. Pacing in and out of the light, Heather radioed in their coordinates. She was speaking too fast and her voice was pitched high, betraying the emotion of her first find.

"Hold your light here and talk slower. Tell them we have a find and require assistance." Code for alive.

Heather's eyes were shining as though she might cry. Apart from that, she had shown promise as a team lead. Riley would be pleased. Kate tipped the bottle away and cold fingers touched the back of her hand. The old woman caressed the younger skin in long, reassuring strokes, then slipped her hand in Kate's and held on.

The hand was small and Kate could feel every bone under the papery skin. The palm seared into hers. Gently and professionally, she turned over the woman's hand to expose her wrist. Her rabbit-pulse thrummed wild against Kate's fingertips.

"It's okay," the old woman said, her voice soft as moss. "Don't be afraid." Freda's oceanic blue eyes flooded Kate with her love. "I've found you. You're safe now."

Kate switched off the TV, silencing the infomercial selling pain-free miracles in four easy payments. She checked her watch. Another hour before dawn. Her body ached for sleep, but the night was still pumping inside her. Dangling off the couch, Zeus's paws twitched and his legs jerked. He was burrowed against her belly, keeping her close. She ran her hand over his soft, warm fur. He groaned.

She had treated the superficial scratches and nicks on his paws and forelegs with antiseptic, and after a massage to loosen his muscles, prepared a special meal with his favourite foods—egg, apple, raw salmon, steak, and raspberries. He emptied two bowls of water and fell asleep during his brushing, unfazed by the nettles, burrs, thorns, and ticks she had removed. He hadn't stirred since. She managed a shower for herself.

She stood under the warm spray until the water went cold. Pine needles, sweat, bug spray, and a spider circled the drain. The needles had hived her neck, her forearms were scratched, and a whipping branch had left a welt across her cheek. The scab on her hand had split and peeled. Soon it would be just another scar tattooing her with stories.

Zeus's nostrils crinkled and flared. He was dreaming. His eyes were partially open and his pupils rolled back, revealing the soft pink tissue of his flickering third eyelid. His paws paddled air and his tail thumped once, twice. He was happy. She hoped he was dreaming of her and not just his ball.

The faint song of birds drifted through her open window. They sounded lonesome and uncertain in their solo performance: *Anybody out there?* She strained to hear a reply. There. Far off. The birds paused between the call and answer. *Do I know you?* More songs tentatively awakened, exalting the first light she couldn't yet see. The chorus, *Oh my god, you're alive too? Give thanks, give thanks!* Zeus's tail whomped faster and his ears pitched back to the sound of its swish. His unseeing eyes opened and his legs stretched rigid. He sighed, and his eyelids slumbered shut.

She suppressed a selfish urge to wake him so she could see his confusion and loving recognition of her. *Her!* He would nuzzle his head close or sprawl on his back for a belly rub. *Give thanks, give thanks, you're here! How wonderful!*

Her legs seared pins and needles. Zeus was a dead weight. She needed to eat. She needed sleep. She closed her eyes and was lifted into the whirling night of Freda's blue eyes, chopper blades, flailing trees, and the basket slowly spinning, ascending into blinding light . . . She relaxed into the wind. Allowed herself to be carried up, up to the star sky, past red berries, swollen bites, and fox eyes. She rose through the swirl of birds calling, her mother's still hand, petrified roots, sharp and boned as her brother's ribs . . . she fell. Before she could catch her terrified heart, she landed in the soft cushion of the couch and Zeus's heat. His head craned back. *Hello*, his tail wagged. Twenty minutes had passed.

Zeus rolled over, pressing harder. She rubbed his hot, soft underbelly. The birds were singing *Get up!* The crows had joined in. If she started her day now, at 5:27, she could do what was needed, get home early, and then sleep until tomorrow's shift. At some point, her body would shut down her mind. The longest she had stayed awake was three days, and by then she was seeing deceased patients at the foot of her bed. They didn't say or want anything. They just waited for her. She slipped her arm from under Zeus's head. *Stay*, he coaxed. She nuzzled his neck. He smelled of woods and air and summer. "Nighty-night."

She squirmed out of his nest. Head on paws, he watched her pull on jeans and T-shirt, finger-brush her hair into a ponytail, and slip on her boots. She avoided making eye contact. When she picked up her keys, he scrambled for the door.

"No, you stay home." His tail drooped. His unblinking eyes were soft with disappointment. "Aren't you tired?"

He jumped up, paws on her chest, and licked the tip of her nose.

Damn it. She grabbed his leash and Zeus barrelled out the door.

The hospital corridors were empty and the patients asleep. The night nurses' heads were lowered, and when they looked up, there weren't questions in their end-of-shift eyes. She had come in through emergency to say hi, drop off coffees and teas, and ascertain if the search had mattered. But she already knew it had.

Regardless of the outcome, the family had their loved one home.

Amy was on duty and said Freda had been transferred to IMCU and was expected to recover. Her sweet husband of fifty-seven years held her hand the entire time and cried when the docs told him she couldn't go home. The woman was raving about a little girl lost in the woods. They gave her a shot and that settled her down. Amy admonished Kate to go home, she had done enough.

The eighth floor's hall lights flickered on. The day shift was coming on. Outside, morning yawned orange and magenta. Zeus bounded into her mother's room and nuzzled Ruth's hand. To Kate's ire, the overhead bed light had been left on again. The oxygen mask had been replaced with nasal prongs. Saturation still high. Vitals stable. Catheter clear. Wrinkles puckered the corners of her mouth around the feeding tube, and her thin lips were chapped. She gently pinched her mother's forearm to check hydration. The skin was warm and supple. Kate clicked off the harsh light. In the dawn's glow, her mother appeared to be sleeping. Her forehead, normally creased, was smooth, and the slightly upturned corners of her mouth could be mistaken for a smile.

"Mom," she whispered. "It's me, Kate."

A small, childish part of her expected Ruth's eyes to open or her hand to twitch. There were stories of people awakening after months, years, even decades. Some even returned intact. But then there were others who slept lifetimes and the families who waited beside them ever vigilant. Ever loving. Ever believing. Taking up a bed.

Years ago, she had watched the news stories with Ruth about a comatose girl and holy statues in her room that supposedly wept. The girl's mother hung cups filled with cotton balls on crucified feet to catch the oil and gave it away for free. Pins were sold for fifty cents and blessings could be had for a quarter. There was an eighteen-month waiting list to be in the child's miraculous presence. The garage was converted into a hospital room and a picture window installed.

The room was pink and lace curtains framed the bed. Kate had envied its prettiness and begged Ruth to paint her bedroom pink. Her mother refused, so she strung a lace-edged tablecloth over her window and laid in bed pretending to be in a coma. She imagined pilgrims streaming past her second-storey window and her mother lovingly brushing her hair like the other mother, until Ruth doused her with a pot of cold water. Get up and live, she had said.

The fifteenth anniversary of the girl's accident was commemorated by wheeling her gurney into a football stadium filled to capacity with ten thousand believers. She had on sunglasses and a tiara. She was laid out in an air-conditioned room, specially built for the occasion. It had a bulletproof window. Believers said she was a living saint who could commune their prayers directly to God. The Church said no. Ruth said, Whatever helps them live. Kate hoped the girl wasn't aware. Recently, she read the girl had died. She was twenty-three. Two bishops attended the funeral, testament to a mother's unwavering love.

"Mom, can you hear me?"

Ruth breathed in and out. Someone had placed the angel, which had been in the locker with her mother's personal belongings, on the bedside table. One lopsided wing was snapped and shoe prints sullied its dress. The doll's downcast, frozen eyes looked down on Ruth and its open arms beckoned.

"Mom . . ." She watched her mother's unresponsive face. "I saw Matthew."

The oversized clock ticked and tocked. The climbing sun shafted through the windows and blazed Ruth's cheeks. "Mom . . ." She wanted to see her oceanic blue eyes. But there was nothing to see. She spun the angel around to face the wall.

"Let's go." But Zeus didn't scrabble to his feet. He wasn't by the chair or on the other side of the bed. She checked under the bed. Her mouth soured metallic.

"Zeus." She said his name calmly, expecting his quizzical head to pop up. The heart monitor beep-beeped and oxygen hissed. The back of her neck flushed hot and her hands chilled. He would lose his clearance if he was caught roaming the halls. He had never left her side before.

The corridor was empty. His dominant turning direction was right. She chose right, but before she took a step, she felt his stillness. He was in the room across the hall, seated near the foot of the bed, calmly watching.

"Zeus," she whispered. His ears pulled back. "Come." She used her most neutral voice. He didn't budge. She entered the room, averting her eyes from the patient. Zeus remained seated, intently staring straight ahead. She grabbed his vest strap and firmly tugged him to a standing position. He had never disobeyed before. She glanced to the bed, hoping Mr. Stroke was asleep, but Mr. Stroke had been replaced by Mr. One Leg.

The man was young, near her age. He was sitting on the edge of the bed staring down at where his leg used to be. He seemed oblivious to their presence. His arm was pockmarked with raw striated wounds, and visible on the leg's stump was the partial tattoo of a rifle stock and helmet. Kate's calf muscle seized as she remembered the rash of gravel and shattered bone. He had said she had pretty eyes. She didn't know his name. She tugged Zeus's collar sharply and hauled him out and down the hall.

"Bad dog," she hissed. "Bad, bad dog." His ears flattened and his tail wagged submissively.

Zeus was panting, standing over her. She must have fallen asleep. It was hot. She had forgotten to turn on the air conditioner. The afternoon sun blazed through the living room window. Wiping drool from her chin, she stumbled up to let him out to pee. He bounded into the duplex's small fenced yard and lifted his leg on the first fence post. On the shaded side of the house, the heat was almost bearable. The yard next door was choked with weeds and likely hid fleas and ticks. The neighbours were a nightmare. She'd have to consider moving again, but the rent was cheap and it was close to the hospital, dog-friendly, and had a fenced yard. Not an easy find.

Zeus wandered off, sniffing dandelions. He found his blanched bone under the overgrown hydrangea and plopped down for a good chew. She switched on the air conditioner. It rattled awake. She slid the roaster pan over to catch the drips. It was on her list to repair or replace, but not today.

She had only slept four hours. A half bowl of soggy cereal was on the floor beside the couch. She still had on her boots. She plopped down on the ratty, comfy chair that Zeus chewed as a pup and yanked them and her socks off. She sighed the release. The wood floor was salve to her feet. Her instep was bruised, her toenails dull and scuffed, and her heels callused. They were working feet. She wiggled her toes. She liked her feet. They were strong and dependable.

She stripped off her deodorant-stained T-shirt and padded to the bedroom. The rumpled sheets, untouched since Riley's visit, held the tangle of their imprints. Strewn on the floor were dirty scrubs, a little black dress, and a near-empty whiskey bottle. Enough, she said.

She said it again louder to convince herself. She had to stop living like a student. She had to take care of herself, stop drinking, and eat better. She had to keep strong. She had to stop screwing another woman's husband. She reached in her back pocket and retrieved the folded topographical map. She smoothed the creases and stuck it on her wall alongside the others, then stepped back to assess the collage of overlapping, concentric circles, tracing the areas of probability. She didn't sort "live" or "dead." She classified them all as "found." Enough.

She stripped the sheets and pillowcases that smelled of adultery. Balled up the dress and scrubs and hauled them to the washing machine. She didn't bother to separate colours from whites. She crammed it all into the drum and pushed the hot water cycle. The dress would likely be ruined. She scratched at the scab itching her palm. Plucked a thorn from her baby finger. Clouds of dog hair wafted over the floor. The house needed cleaning.

Enough, she said and grabbed a cold beer from the fridge. She switched on the radio loud, not caring if the shouty next-door neighbours who woke her day and night were home. She craved bacon and pancakes. She was out of bacon, but there was just enough instant pancake mix, and she was certain that she could substitute water for milk and one egg for two. Butter sizzled in the pan. Zeus barked once at the door. The neighbours thump-thumped their disapproval and Kate hurled the pan at the wall.

Approaching the two-mile mark of their run, her pace was good. It was cooler beneath the treed canopy. Thankfully, the secondary path was free of people. Most were seeking shelter from the heat closer to the water. It was only her, her breath, Zeus, and the crunch of gravel underfoot. She needed to decompress, and running was the quickest and most effective way to get out of her head and back into her body. She had to regain control.

She adjusted her track to the shift of Zeus's head warning her of bends ahead. Her feet scuffed gravel and his head whipped back. Satisfied she was okay, he pulled ahead. He was barely breaking a trot. His tongue lolled, its pink wetness catching cooling air. Her own breath was even and controlled and her heart beat steady. She focused on the rhythm of his paws and the song playing in her head. Something about Sunday morning coming down, one of her mother's favourites. Zeus's ears pricked forward and his head dropped. There was a crow on the path.

He glanced back to her. "Go," she said, and he was gone. Outdistancing her in two strides, he widened the gap impossibly in four, reminding her again how much he limited his canine being to be with her. He bore down on his target and pulled up short. His rear end dropped, his front paws stomped, and he snorted a breathy woof reserved for flushing birds. The crow lifted and settled high on a limb, cawing its displeasure. She was breaking training rules allowing him to critter, but she was in a why-the-hell-not mood, let him be a dog. They were approaching the final bend, an uphill stretch. She leaned into the climb, every stone digging into her sneakers' thin soles.

She burst from the dark bowers into ocean sky. Her lungs sucked in the wide open of salt and seaweed. A surge of reserve energy flooded her body. She rounded the final stretch to the parking lot and Zeus fell apace alongside her. Phlegm clogged her throat. She spat it out. She scanned the cliffs for the praying man she sometimes saw early in the mornings bowing to the sea. But he wasn't there. The ache of disappointment surprised her. He seemed so vulnerable and brave showing his heart to the world. He was a moment of breathless beauty when there were so few she could still see.

She veered off the path and headed towards the craggy shoreline to survey the praying man's vantage point. Her legs quivered as she slowed to a walk. Hands on hips, she gulped hot air. All around her, families and lovers dallied in the laze of summer.

She filled Zeus's drinking pouch with water. He nudged her hand away before she could fully set it down and drank it all. She filled it again before taking a long swig from the bottle for herself, then splashed the remainder over his belly, flanks, and hot black coat. He shook and rolled in the grass. He didn't like the tingle of wet on his skin. Righting himself, dust and dead grass clinging to him, he looked to her expectantly. One ear was folded down and his head cocked to one side like a goofy puppy. He was ready to play. Her silly boy made her smile.

"Okay. Wait." She tossed the ball a short distance. He watched it bounce and roll and stop. His muscles flinched in anticipation.

"Release." His hindquarters kicked up a puff of dust. He pounced on the ball.

The ocean was shimmering white-hot. Far off at the harbour's mouth, a behemoth cruise ship and its accompanying pilot boats were entering the Narrows. She watched the moving city glide towards the anchor of land. She had enough money. She could step on board and disappear into the fugue of open bars and everlasting food, cocoon herself in scripted days of massages and salsa dances, wrap herself in Egyptian cotton and float through the stars in a king-sized bed to the ooh and aah of fireworks. Maybe they had dog pools and served biscuits on silver platters.

Zeus dropped his ball at the cliff's edge and lifted his nose to the south. His nostrils flared. She wondered if he could smell the ship's three thousand souls. Or if he had caught the scent of the Bahamian winds wafting ahead of the churning storm, carrying the sweetness of hibiscus or the acrid destruction and primordial brine of fifty-foot seas. The ship lumbered into harbour. Beyond, she tried to see what the praying man saw, but was blinded by the sun.

Zeus grabbed his ball and bowed. His tail wagged. The ball dribbled between them. She assumed the steal position. Hands outstretched, she crabbed forward. His backside rocked with anticipation. She tiptoed closer, reaching slowly. He scooped up the ball and spun in circles and stopped. Somewhere a commotion of shouts and a name frantically hollered and hollered. Bearing down on them from the trail, a Rottie mix was rapidly expanding the gap between its pursuing owners. Its head was lowered and its eyes sharp in prey drive.

Zeus turned to face it, his tail high and ears alert. The ball dropped from his mouth. She gave him a hard "Stay" and grabbed the only weapon at hand, a large rock, and braced herself between him and it. Intent on Zeus, the charging dog didn't slow. Its shoulders were hunkered, hackles up, jaw open, lips curled.

She made herself alpha-large. Screaming her throat raw, she strode directly into its path. The dog startled and slowed. She barked at it to "Sit!", her arm raised high to pummel it. She roared again, so it would understand she *would* kill it.

The dog sat. The owners arrived breathless and indignant. "He just wanted to play! Are you crazy?" She could see herself slamming the rock into the side of their heads. Yes, maybe she was. She said other things out loud to them, which confirmed their suspicion. She didn't drop the rock until the dog was dragged from sight. Zeus hadn't broken his stay.

"Release," she said. He looked at her uncertainly, then, abandoning his ball, submissively approached. She clipped on his leash and tried not to touch him with her trembling hands. "Get your ball." She made her voice light, but had to tell him twice. He set it at her feet.

She sprinted the last leg to the parking lot, pushing hard. She pushed until her lungs constricted and her heart pounded. Pushed until her calf muscles tremored and her stomach lurched. Pushed until she could think of nothing else: not the praying man, not her family, not herself. Only the imaginary line she had to cross.

Zeus adjusted his stride from trot to canter and back to trot again, encouraging her onward.

———

The smell of barbecues and hoots of children seeped through the buffer of trees and bush encircling Ruth's home and into the house. Zeus clattered down the stairs. It was a clean search: Matthew wasn't there and hadn't returned. Kate was shamefully relieved. This was her last duty of the day. She rewarded Zeus with the raw knucklebone she had picked up on the way. "Stay."

He nuzzled the bone between his front paws, only his eyes acknowledged her. She wasn't sure if he remembered the night's search or the hospital or the near attack. Dogs seemed able to cast off the past. Even those abused possessed an ability to forgive and trust and love again. Maybe they chose to forget. She should be more like her dog. But she wasn't as noble. As she headed up the stairs, Zeus's earlier disobedience still gnawed at her. *Let it go*. She needed sleep. Her emotional fortitude was compromised. If she was in the field, or on the job, she would have herself removed.

The bedroom doors were closed and the upper storey's heat was oppressive. The overpowering scent of air fresheners and potpourri couldn't mask the musty, mildewy undertones. She would open the windows and go home. Matthew wasn't there. There was nothing else she could do. Eventually, he would come back. He always did. She stopped at his bedroom door. She hadn't been inside for years. Nobody was allowed in his room. She turned the knob and nudged it open.

Heavy curtains and bedsheets shrouded the window, smothering the light. The ceiling fixture was missing its shade and bulb. She took note of the exits, window and door. Gagging, she breathed through her mouth.

She relinquished her mind to her training. She ran her finger down the door in a long diagonal line, marking the disaster site. Stepping in, she kept the wall to her right, so she could retrace her steps back to safety. Cautiously, she found her footing on the uneven terrain. Paper crackled underfoot. The risk of fire was high.

Beneath the window was a partially collapsed bed. The bare mattress was filthy, and on the floor was a balled-up comforter. In the debris, she recognized the flattened husk of a tin robot; the ragged paw of a beloved childhood bear; the crumbled carcass of a record player; jumbled Walkmans, headphones, and spooling cassette tapes. A sock. She had trained for this. This encountering of the unimaginable. Her heart was quiet.

Mounded against the opposite wall were the vinyl shards of Matthew's treasured record collection. Walls of books had caved. Their soft spines were broken and splayed, their covers wrenched away. The pages had been ripped into smaller and smaller pieces, burying the floor in knee-high paper drifts. She stood in the crush of the eviscerated words. Everything had tumbled in the quake of his life.

Carefully, she retraced her steps. Her hand didn't leave the security of the wall. She shut the door and drew another diagonal line through the first. Her finger hovered at the bottom of the phantom X. She traced the number *1*. Then added *D*, for dead.

In her respirator mask, her breath was hollow and mechanical, the rubber seal slick with sweat. She tilted her head to widen her peripheral vision as she filled the garbage bag with the corpses of books and the detritus of a lost life. She tore down the layers shrouding the window. Dust motes clouded the room. She hammered the windowsill with her palm and the wood frame groaned open. She would have broken the glass to let in air. The sun was low, casting the world in a golden lie.

She shovelled the paper carcasses into the garbage bag—Atwood, Hemingway, McCarthy, Vonnegut, Murakami, Achebe, Lessing—books he'd wanted her to read when she was ten. She preferred happy endings with no surprises. The bad guy was caught. The girl got the boy. Nothing that tore out her heart. She tied off the bulging bag and dragged it to the hallway, heaved it beside the others. Zeus kept guard outside the door, his ears twitching forward and his eyes studying her. She swiped the hair from her goggled eyes and re-entered the room, navigating the cleared path to the bed.

Sweat and dirt caked her arms. Her hands were wet inside her mother's dish gloves. She dragged the single bed away from the wall. The mattress, blackened from sweat and body oil and god knows what, held the imperfect impression of a body. The bed legs tore through crumpled pages and dirty clothing. She shook open another bag and crammed the filth inside. She would burn it all.

She was breathing heavily. The respirator was harsh and the lens clouded with condensation. She had to calm down. She swayed in the heat, reached for the wall, and heaved the bag into the hall. One corner remained. The damage here was more pronounced. Flayed pages, shredded in strips, jammed the door from fully opening. She whipped open another bag and waded into the disjointed words. The paper slipped from the clumsy grip of her gloves. She bent down, scooping up the crackling remains, crushing them against her chest to stuff into the swelling bag. She swung the door away to breach the corner. Air caught in her throat.

The mechanical inhale and exhale of the respirator rasped her ears. She read the collage of ragged strips butted together like a ransom note papering the door.

> But in the world according to Garp we are all terminal cases.\ You must go on, I can't go on, I'll go on. / "Like a dog!" he said; it was as if the shame of it must outlive him.\ It was a fine cry—loud and long—but it had no bottom and it had no top, just circles and circles of sorrow./ He never sleeps, the judge. He is dancing, dancing. He says that he will never die.\ That may be, Nora said, but it's all pretty unsatisfactory./ One bird said to Billy Pilgrim, "Poo-tee-weet?" | Yes, she thought, laying down her brush in extreme fatigue, I have had my vision.| Then there are more and more endings: the sixth, the 53rd, the 131st, the 9,435th ending, endings going faster and faster, more and more endings, faster and faster until this book is having 186,000 endings per second./ Yes, I said. Isn't it pretty to think so? \

She looked down at the pages at her feet. Each fragment was a story's ending, only the ending. The last sentences. Each ending was punctuated with a taped yellow pill. Her brother's medication. She clawed apart the words, shearing through the madness. The words stuck to her skin and she scoured them off. She could barely breathe. Zeus scrambled up, growling.

She stepped into the hall to find Matthew at the bottom of the stairs. His eyes were wide, fixated on her towering over him. He took a step back. A low warning vibrated from Zeus's throat. "Sit." For the second time, he hesitated before obeying.

Matthew was trembling, and she remembered she was faceless in the goggled mask. She cloaked her eyes, steadied her breath, and removed the respirator.

"It's me, Mattie. It's Kate."

He studied her face, then tentatively stepped up a tread. Snarling a full-throated growl, Zeus broke his sit-stay. Kate grabbed him by the scruff, marched him to the back of the hall, and yanked him to a sit position. "Stay!" She turned her back on him.

Matthew was almost to the landing. Laceless shoes flopped from his heels. He had on the same pair of crusted running pants, and his grimy shirt was buttoned askew. It was sweltering and he was wearing a water-stained leather coat. The polyester lining hung limp from the soiled cuffs. In his bony hand was another bag of books. He clutched it like a shield between them.

"What are you doing?" He addressed the bulging garbage bags.

"Cleaning up your mess." Her voice was neutral, but her jaw was tight and her spine rigid. He dropped to his knees and rifled through one of the bags, pulling out the severed paper. His face contorted in a mask of grief, an agonized collapse of mouth and eyes.

Through the matted knots of grey-streaked hair, the back of his neck was mottled with dirt. She could count the vertebrae on the thin Braille of his spine. His pants, sagging from jutting hips, exposed the crack of his bare behind. His heels were blistered and callused, and the soles of his sneakers worn through.

"You've lost how it ends!" The words bled from him in a deep, primal anguish. A sound she had only heard before at work. And then she did what she was trained never to do when a mentally unstable patient was distressed. She touched his shoulder.

She felt it before she saw it. A direct blow to her solar plexus knocked the breath from her chest and sent her flying onto her back. Choking for air, she barely caught Zeus's collar as he leapt over her, teeth gnashing. His weight arrested mid-air, wrenching her sideways. His collar cut into her fingers. She grabbed hold with both hands and he dragged her onto her stomach. His claws scrabbled, and losing his footing, he crashed to his side. Thrashing upright, he pulled her forward. His raging bark pierced her eardrums. She gasped for the words that needed air to be said. *STOP! SIT! STOP!*

Matthew slammed the bedroom door and the lock clicked. She released her strangled hold. Zeus hurled against the door. His claws dug into the soft wood. His eyes were wild and the whites exposed. "ENOUGH!" The word came out hard and broken. She kneed him away. It was the humiliation that enflamed her, but it was hate that obliterated her. She kicked at the door. The frame shuddered. "OPEN THE FUCKING DOOR!"

Zeus was barking, darting between her and each crash of her boot. He charged, spinning sideways to stop her leg. She slammed her shoulder into the door again and again and rained her fists against the wood. Zeus was barking, shrill and sharp, a bark she hadn't heard him make before. He was barking, she realized, at *her*. His ears were pinned back and his tail cowed.

She knelt before him and he nuzzled his head to her pounding chest. His ears flicked forward with each whispered "Sorry."

He pressed harder, nudging her to her feet. He circled her legs, prodding her towards the stairs. He shepherded her away.

Kate pressed the numbers slowly. Her chest ached a blooming bruise.

"911. What is your emergency?"

She was waiting on the front steps when the cruisers pulled in. White smoke billowed from the fire barrel at the side of the house. Paper ash drifted in the deadened evening air. Zeus was nestled between her legs. She rubbed his chest to assure him that all was well. He glanced uncertainly up at her when the first cruiser pulled in. His bum shifted and he leaned in harder. An officer stepped out of the vehicle, but didn't move beyond the safety of his door. To her dismay she recognized him as the cop from the hospital. She couldn't keep any part of herself private. He looked crisp and pressed like he was just starting his shift. She could taste her shame. A second car pulled in behind. The cop she recognized said, "Is the dog restrained?" He spoke with surprising authority, considering how small he'd seemed in the trauma room.

"No," she said. "But he won't hurt you."

"You'll need to secure the dog, ma'am."

Maybe he didn't recognize her. "I have to get a leash from my truck."

She stood, and the second officer, who was younger, stepped out of his vehicle. His hand was on his holster. Zeus hugged her leg as she walked past them into the shade of the old maple.

Slowly she opened the hatch, so the officers could see what was inside, recognize her SAR kit, and understand that she was not a threat. She retrieved a lead and tethered Zeus to the hitch. "Good boy. Stay." She patted him on the head. Only then did the older officer step out from behind his door. They were afraid. She could smell it. She approached them calmly, so they wouldn't be afraid.

"Do you have any weapons on you, ma'am?"

"No." She understood they had a protocol to follow.

"Any in the house?"

"No," she said. "My brother's stopped taking his meds and needs to go to hospital."

"Where is he now?" The first officer asked all the questions. His pupils were constricted and his blue eyes shining. She noted his tight jaw and too-straight back and dark circles under his eyes. He was on something.

"He's in his room, upstairs." She knew the magic words she needed to say to have him involuntarily admitted. *He tried to kill me. He tried to kill himself. He's going to kill you.* Only an immediate threat would trigger a response. The officer was leaning back on his heels. His cheek twitched. He was grinding his teeth.

"He needs help," she said. "He's not dangerous, he's . . ." How could she explain *You'll need to break down the bedroom door. He'll be in the corner. He'll scream. You'll need to restrain him to carry him down. Don't let him grab the railing. Once he's in the back of the car he'll stop resisting. He'll just give up.*

Instead, she said, "I'm a nurse." As though that would explain everything and they could trust her assessment. The officer recognized her then. She could see it in his eyes.

"He's not eating. He's not communicating. He's unable to care for himself..." She wondered how many checklist symptoms she had to recite to convince them. She didn't tell them about the pain over her heart with every breath.

"And you can't get him to admit himself?"

"No." She repressed the urge to bite back at the unspoken *Did you try?* "He doesn't think he's sick."

"You know what happens if we take him in." She heard the emphasis on *you* and the lack of a question.

"He's inside," she said. Her mother's angels would provide some comic relief back at the station. She couldn't blame them. No one wanted to be here. The pain in her chest spilled hot against her ribs and her eyes burned with heat.

Zeus reared, baying, straining his tether. The officer took a step back, closer to the hood of his car. The line whipped behind Zeus, who was trying to slip his collar.

"Zeus!" She marched towards him. "Stop!"

The second officer, the young one, drew his weapon and aimed it at Zeus. Kate held up her hand to the cop—a warning, a stop. "Don't you *fuckin'* point that at him!"

Zeus's barking reached a frenzied pitch. He was going to snap the line. She continued towards him, adding an emphatic hand command and the bore of her eyes. He ignored her.

The older officer's voice hardened to a deep growl. "Stay away from the dog, ma'am."

She turned to face him, taking in his paunchy belly and crooked lean that favoured his right side. He was big and hopped up and afraid of dogs. "I need to calm him down." She used her most professional voice, the one reserved for small children and the elderly. She turned her back on him. Zeus lunged, strangling against the collar. He didn't understand that now wasn't the same as before.

"Enough!"

The front door opened and Zeus assumed the down position. His eyes were fixed on the danger. In the swell of silence, the officers and Kate turned to stare at Matthew in the doorway. He had taken off his coat and pulled up his pants. He was barefoot and wearing a ballcap.

"Is everything okay?" His voice was casual, concerned, and calm.

"Are you her brother?" the older officer asked. His voice had changed to a friendly banter.

"Yeah," Matthew said, but didn't look at Kate.

"Your sister called us because she's worried about you."

"It was a misunderstanding. She was in my room. You know how that is with sisters." He actually smiled. She almost laughed at the audacity of the performance.

She said, "Maybe you should show the officers your room?" But then she remembered the evidence burning in the barrel. No one moved.

The officer tugged on his belt and hitched it over his hipbone. "Your sister says you haven't been taking your medication."

"She doesn't know," Matthew said. "She doesn't live here. I'm good. I'm fine."

He had passed the test. He was lucid and communicative. Harmless. He didn't meet the criteria. The officer glanced to his backup. She saw the *stand down* exchange. The younger officer holstered his weapon.

"If there's another *misunderstanding*," he said, "we'll have to come back and sort it out. Do you understand?"

"Yes." Matthew smiled through thin lips. "Have a good day." The door shut softly behind him.

Her voice wobbled, "That's not him."

The older officer's back flinched. When he turned to her, she saw the weariness in his eyes. He looked to the ground, searching for platitudes. "Sometimes us coming by is enough." When he looked back up, his eyes were sharp and insistent. "Did he do that?"

Her hand went to her welted cheek. Her elbow and chest pulsed pain, but the welt was all they could see. Everything else she'd said was true. He was sick. Her word should be enough. He needed medical help, not an assault charge. "No."

His eyes said she was lying and she could feel him pull away. "If the situation escalates or you feel you, or he, are in danger, you call and we'll be here." The second officer was already in his cruiser.

"So, we wait?" She hated the smallness of her voice.

The officer paused at the door of his vehicle. "You know how it is," he said and his voice was small, too. Wincing, he lowered himself into his car. He would need another hit soon. He rolled down his window and her heart leaned in for the words that could save her.

"There's a burning ban in effect," he said. "With a substantial fine." He added the pause so she would understand he was doing her a favour.

"I'll take care of it."

In the upstairs window, Matthew was there and then he was gone.

28

Mike knew where to find him. The kid would eventually show up on the corner. It didn't matter how many times he was busted, he always returned to his regular spot. Dumb as a bag of nails. Or he just didn't give a damn. The kid never ran. He handed his stuff over like it was candy, knowing he was underage and they couldn't touch him. His preferred operating hours were eleven to midnight. Bedtime hours. It was ten to eleven.

Mike stretched his legs the best he could, careful not to jar his back. This night was never going to end. Everybody at the station knew what had happened at home. At call they asked if he wanted coffee, chatted him up about how the new squad car handled, if he'd seen last night's ball game, and the frigging weather . . . talking, talking about nothing while their eyes and relentless smiles said, *You okay?*

He was called to the duty desk and questioned whether he wanted to take vacation time. For Chrissakes, his four-year-old son had a bad dream, thought bad guys were in the house and—like he'd been taught—called 911. It was no big deal. But the cops who came to the door, one he had friggin' trained, came into his house and looked around like he had something to hide. Now Lori wasn't speaking to him. But oh, she had plenty to say to her mother. And every time he moved, she watched him like he was under house arrest.

And the cops, his *brothers*, treated him as though he was one of *those* dirtbags. Separating Lori so they could question her privately. Looking for bruises and handprints on his little boy's arms and legs. Hell, he had carried child victims from their homes himself. Bare-assed and snot-nosed. Silent even in their tears. Only to be returned to their assailants after a mandated anger management course and counselling sessions at a parent resource centre. And there was nothing he could do about it except wait until the next time they were called. Keep building the evidence and compiling a baseline, until the bastard or bitch could be put away. Always too late.

Like the guy at that farmhouse. Batshit crazy, six foot tall and weighing maybe a hundred pounds. His hair ratted up under his ball cap, shirt three sizes too large, pants sagging off his hips, and filthy feet. If he took his goddamn pills, they wouldn't be called out there. Then *he* wouldn't have to look the sister in the eye and walk away. *Good luck*. Is that what he had said? It's what it sounded like. His last pill was on the edge of wearing off at that call. The woman—whom he was certain he'd seen before at the hospital, but couldn't remember when—had pissed him off.

The brother couldn't help it. He didn't even know his mind was lying to him. But her . . . she had a sharper edge. She wasn't afraid of the police. She stood with her feet apart like she was ready for combat and her eyes judged him with contempt like *he* wasn't doing his job. Like it was his duty to come in and clean up *their* mess. There was nothing he could do—that was the friggin' law. Everyone had rights. Which meant standing by until someone was in imminent risk of dying—either the poor sick bastard or whoever got in his way. And she knew it. There wasn't enough money, not enough beds, doctors, social workers, not enough people who gave a damn. He hated unstable calls. Hated the misery of them. Hated his impotence.

And that woman *was* lying about something. Something had happened for her to make that call, but then she clammed up. So what was he supposed to do? Forcibly drag the guy off to the hospital, fill out five hours of paperwork, only to see him back on the street a few hours later? Another casualty of government cutbacks to balance budgets. It was cheaper to have them on the streets than in hospital beds. And this one lived only blocks from Mike's own home. They were all lucky the dog's leash held. It would have been a public relations disaster, because it would have been shot. His right calf muscle cramped. He rubbed around the jagged scar, a lifelong reminder of the ten stitches and rabies shots he endured at the age of six.

"Come on, kid, where are you?"

All this shit was because of his friggin' back, which was a direct result of his job. He should file a compensation claim, but it would go on his record and next time he'd be denied benefits because of a pre-existing condition. Gotta love the lawyers. He had tried to get help. Two walk-in clinics before his shift started and the same useless scripts for massages, over-the-counter meds, and rest. He was on his own.

He didn't bother telling the docs that he wasn't sleeping either. Not just last night, when Lori banished him to the friggin' couch and its jabbing coil springs with the sun blasting through the living room window at five o'-friggin'-clock in the morning because she wanted sheers so she wouldn't feel closed in. And the fans were in the bedrooms, so even without a sheet, he was soaking in sweat. And after breakfast Caleb crawled onto the couch with his friggin' stuffed toy that smelled like piss. And when he finally did get to sleep, despite the baby crying and Lori banging dishes, he was woken a couple hours later by pain so intense, a bullet would have been merciful. All on a day when he was supposed to be turning around for nights. One ailment per visit, please. He considered himself a tough guy. He wouldn't ask if he didn't need it. Just because they couldn't see it, didn't mean it wasn't killing him.

He stiffened as the kid approached the corner. Right on time. What the hell was a kid his age doing out at this time of night anyway? But he knew his history. He had taken him out of the house twice. No mother. Alcoholic father. Three younger siblings. The kid was probably fourteen now, soon he wouldn't be able to plead out in youth court. He had his hoodie pulled over his face and his hands tucked in his kangaroo pouch pocket. If he wasn't always looking at the ground, he might have noticed the squad car parked a block away. He doubted the kid weighed more than seventy pounds. It was tough to be out alone without handlers. He was a self-starter.

Kids were different now. The only trouble he got into as a boy was stealing a pack of gum from a corner store. He was seven. The police were called and the old cop scared the shit out of him. Gave him the talk. Told him he didn't think he was a bad kid, just a dumb kid making stupid choices. He didn't think Mike would do it again and was willing to give him that trust, man to little man. There was no need to call his parents.

He had the same sickness in his belly now as when he stole that gum and the cashier grabbed him by the shirt, and his friends ran out with their pockets crammed with chocolate bars and chip bags. The old cop made him look the storeowner in the eye and apologize. The man barely spoke English. All the kids called him the Paki.

The old cop said, "This is who you're stealing from. You don't know nothing about him. You don't know where he's come from or how hard he's had it. You don't even know his name. This is Mr. Patel. He has two girls and one boy, all getting good grades despite little shits like you beating on them every other day. He has two budgies and his wife sings to them. He's been robbed three times, twice at gunpoint, and once with a knife. He's had his cheekbone fractured and 'Go home Paki' spray-painted on the front of his store, even though Mr. Patel is Indian."

The cop made him shake Mr. Patel's hand. Then cuffed him on the back of the head and told him to get the hell out of there. That's the moment Mike knew what he wanted to be. He understood the power of changing the direction of a life. He never went back to that store. Mike flicked on his headlights, roared up to the corner on the wrong side of the street, and flashed the red lights once for business. The kid didn't run.

He rolled down his window. "Sean, what are you doing out here again?"

"Oh, *man*." The kid said it like he had been tagged out of a child's game. "I'm just out for a walk."

Mike got out of the car. A low grunt in his throat absorbed the pain. "I told you I was going to have to take you in if I saw you out here again. I know you're not stupid, so why are you acting it?"

"Gotta pay the bills." The kid, all freckles and acne, didn't stand any higher than his chest.

"There's other ways to pay the bills, kiddo. Empty your pockets. You know the drill."

Sean shuffled to the cruiser and pulled out a baggie packed with prescription bottles and laid it on the hood. He hadn't changed his modus operandi.

"How many times this year you been picked up, Sean?"

"Twice."

Mike rolled the bag over in his hands. "The judge isn't going to like that. Did you go down to the job bank like I told you, or talk to that youth counsellor?"

The kid shrugged and looked down at his frugal red high-tops. The same canvas shoes that were too dorky to wear when Mike was a kid were shit-hot now.

"Sean, I don't want to be doing this until we're both old men. You've gotta make a change. You hear me?"

"Yeah."

"Get the hell out of here." He sounded generous and forgiving with an appropriate undertone of warning.

The kid glanced at the baggie, as if calculating his losses. He shuffled back up the hill without looking back.

Mike breathed in the stink of the harbour and fermenting sewage. It made him sick to his stomach. He eased back into the car and opened the bag. Yellow pills, white pills, blue pills. Ups and downs, and no in-betweens. There was one bottle of pain killer with maximum codeine.

He popped the lid. It was more than he would need.

29

"911. What is your emergency?"

Tamara leaned in close to the monitors and made note of the time. She was twenty-six minutes into the Waiting Hours. Adrenaline spiked her veins, flooding her brain into high alert. The phones hadn't rung for over an hour. The bars were closed. It was past assault, DUI, and domestics time. They had moved onto fire, mass casualty vehicular accidents, and suicides. Her colleagues' heads rose like gophers alert to the possibility of danger. They turned to their monitors, put down their cold pizza slices and adjusted their headphones in preparation.

It was a payphone call. The fumble of the phone clattered in her ear.

"911. What is your emergency?"

"The goddamned doors are locked and I can't get in."

She analyzed the deep growling voice held tight in the vocal cords, the slurring consonants. "Robert?" she said.

"Who else'd be calling this time of night?"

She mouthed the word *Robert* to the others, who groaned and celebrated their luck. She leaned back in her chair. "Where are you, Robert?"

"I'm where I'm supposed to be and they've locked the god-damn door."

He was piss and vinegar. She couldn't help but smile. He had made it through the winter.

"It's three thirty in the morning, Robert. They've probably gone to bed."

"That's what *I'm* trying to do! Now they're gonna write me up and say I wasn't here, and I'm here!"

"What do you want us to do, Robert?"

"I want you to call 'em and tell 'em to let me in!"

That wasn't an option. "Have you tried knocking on the door?"

"If *I* wake 'em they'll be pissed. They won't be pissed at you."

It was difficult to counter that argument. She visualized the phone booth and a small man overcompensating for his build. Missing teeth, judging by the lisp. Poorly educated. Something was broken in his body, arthritis or fractures, something that made him speak with a tightness that squeezed the words out of him.

"It's a nice night, Robert. Is there somewhere you can nap until morning?"

"You want me to sleep in the street? I used a quarter for this?"

"I think you'll have to knock on the door, Robert."

"Fer shit's sake. Hold on." The receiver clunked against metal and glass.

She wanted him to come back. She wanted him to stay on the line. She looked to the other call stations. Colleen was reading a book. Karl was doing stretches at his desk. Wendy was drinking a bottle of water and staring out the window overlooking the parking lot. A cruiser was pulling in.

The phone clattered in her earpiece. "I did it!"

"Good," she said. She wanted to tell him she was happy he had made it through the winter and ask him how old he was, where he came from, and where he had been. And who had hurt him.

"What's good about it? I'm still standing outside talking to you and I have to piss. Hold on."

The phone dropped again. She should hang up and wish him luck, but she wanted this pause of a non-emergency. She heard running water. The old bastard was relieving himself in the phone booth. The stream thinned in spurts and stops.

He picked up the phone again. "So what're you gonna do? I ain't got all night."

"Are you asking me to send somebody by? Maybe take you to a shelter for the night?"

"I ain't goin' to no goddamn shelter!" The receiver hammered against metal, ricocheting through her earpiece. She pulled the headphone away from her ear.

"Robert, you have to calm down."

"You don't know what it's like! I can't get a break. I'm here where I'm supposed to be. What else am I supposed to do?"

For the first time, in all the years she had listened to his voice, he sounded like he truly wanted an answer.

"I want you to get your break, Robert." And she meant it. She could hear his broken breath close to the mouthpiece. "It's beautiful out there tonight, isn't it? Maybe you could sit on the doorstep and listen to the night. Listen to the world waking up and that smell of morning making itself new again. The sun's only a couple of hours away. That wouldn't be so bad, would it?" She would like to sit on that doorstep with him.

"The bastard's turned on the light. Gotta go." The line went dead.

She disconnected. 3:43 a.m. The security door clicked and Constable Mike walked in with a tray of teas and coffees. The room cheered as he made the rounds to each station, stopping to chat and share a joke. He never got an order wrong. He moved with ease and confidence and his smile was wide open. End of shift would fly by now.

Like everyone in the room, she had discreetly read the transcript. His name was whispered in the locker room. One of their own. They shook their heads and said it could have been any one of them. She would never call 911. She'd drag herself to hospital first, or if desperate call a private lifeline. Mike was one of her backdoor contacts.

"How are you?" He perched on the edge of her console and set down an herbal tea, two sugars, no milk, no caffeine.

"I'm good." She wanted to ask the same of him. His face was soft and relaxed and his eyes were bright and unconcerned. "Better now." She took a sip of the sweet, hot tea and it was true.

"I have your tickets." She handed over the bulging bag of bills he'd left behind the night things went bad, a fundraiser for at-risk kids. He turned the bag over in his large hands that could leave a mark.

"You sold them all?"

"It was for a good cause." They always were. At her feet, her purse bulged with raffle tickets. His smile was small. She waited for him to tell her more, so she could tell him more. Furtive eyes watched them over half-walled cubbies.

"Do you think we're gonna get that storm?" he said.

"What storm?"

30

Kate was on top. Her hands bore down on Riley's wrists and her thighs clenched his hips in feral need. They were free of awkwardness, knocking limbs, and apology of bodies. Grinding against his torso, she drove him deeper, wanting more. His spine arched. Not yet. She pressed him down. Her hair was wet and her skin slick. His hands on her waist steadied her thrusting hips, insisting on more. She didn't care about his wife. She didn't care about tomorrow. She wanted Now.

She woke to tears on her cheeks and the scent of freshly laundered sheets. She slowed her breath and wiped away the tears. It was night. She was home. She had kicked off the covers. The humming fan oscillated cool air over her hot skin. Her nipples were hard and swollen and her chest clammy. Flush with shame, she covered her nakedness with the sheet. Zeus watched from the edge of the bed and offered his head for her to pat.

Dawn bloomed inky blue, thorny with the silhouettes of trees over the sleeping suburban street. A mosquito droned in Kate's ear. She swiped it away and rolled up her window. She was parked across from a modest white vinyl-clad bungalow. It had a large fenced yard with several spindly maples. The grass was green. Riley had been watering it.

He didn't turn on the house lights and kept his head down as he crossed the street. He looked nice, even in bed pants and a T-shirt. He had pulled on boots, but the laces weren't tied. He wasn't as tall as she thought of him. Her hand went to her bruised chest. Just this once, she would tell him everything. She'd lean into him and he'd put his arms around her, tell her it was going to be okay, and help her find the path out. He walked up to the passenger side but didn't get in. She unrolled the window.

"What are you doing here?" His words were clipped and accusatory. The corners of his eyes were crusted with sleep and his hair unbrushed. It was the first time she had seen him unsettled. "What's wrong?"

"Is she sleeping?"

He looked nervously to the house. The windows reflected nothing. It was a nice starter home. The straight and narrow garden beds held compact plants, nothing too unruly. A sign at the end of the driveway proclaimed their names and at its base was a cast stone dog that looked like his beloved Annabelle.

"Do you sleep on the right side of the bed here, too?"

Riley was breathing hard. "What are you doing, Kate?"

Her eyes welled. "I don't know." They could drive to the ocean, watch the sunrise, rent a cabin where no one knew them, gorge on bad movies and popcorn, read the paper with coffees and croissants, and talk, just talk. Kiss each other's scars and bruises and make it better. She didn't even know his middle name.

"I don't know," she said. "Do you?" She really hoped he had an answer.

"You can't be here." He stepped away. "Go home. I'll come by later." An orange cat sauntered across the road. Down the street, a light came on in an upstairs window. It was a nice neighbourhood. He and his wife would be happy here.

"That's okay." She put the truck in gear. "Don't."

31

The words were humming electric inside him. He couldn't hear her downstairs. He couldn't hear her outside the door. In the moon night, her truck was gone. He had waited and she, light radiating from her head and eyes, and her dog on fire, were gone. He had waited and they had gone.

She could come back.

He broiled with the words collecting on his skin. He stripped off his shirt and the words fell to the floor and swarmed his feet like fire ants.

She had stolen his story. Ripped away the ending he had almost found. She had walked through the valley of his mother's angels of death and said his name like she knew him. She said her name was Kate.

Lies. She tried to poison him. Tried to lock him up. Unleashed the dog on fire. Only the strength of Words kept the door from shattering. She hurled flames with her fists and the paper burned. She wanted him dead. Katie.

He ran his fingers over the brittle shreds of papery words, ragged tape, and poisoned pills he had buried inside their power. In the dark, he couldn't read the savaged words, but he knew what they said in his heart.

You must go on\ Yes, I said. \ the shame of it /
—loud and long—/ the judge. He is dancing, dancing |
But in the world \ That may be/ One bird said / I have had
my vision / there are more and more endings

Words crawled up his legs. He brushed away the ones that didn't belong to him. Words bored into his skin. He scratched his arms to let them out. Words hatched from his feet. He kicked his sneakers off.

She said her name was Katie.

Lies.

But when he drove his fist into her heart, the light shattered and he saw her. And she looked afraid. He remembered he remembered he remembered. Another beginning. Of him and her before he was erased. He needed to find another ending.

It's not safe here.

Words climbed up his legs, over his chest, and scuttled around his neck. They brushed against his lips and circled his ears.

Run.

The space between the letters whispered answers he couldn't hear.

Run.

The words stung his tongue, swarmed his throat, and wormed into his eyes.

Matthew opened the door and ran.

32

As of 9:40 a.m., maximum sustained winds have increased to 105 miles per hour, a Category 2 hurricane. The eye is located 645 miles offshore. A turn to the north with an increase in forward speed is expected tonight. Rain and wind warnings are in effect. The public is urged to closely monitor alerts—

Hassan switched off the car radio. Every ten minutes, on every station, meteorologists were prognosticating the hurricane's track. Some mapped it passing three hundred miles offshore. Others were forecasting landfall anywhere from the south shore to a direct hit up the city's harbour. Everything depended on the wobble of a turn. Half a degree northeast or west would smite or spare. All agreed it was gaining strength. Satellite images showed it measuring seventeen hundred miles across and widening.

Scientists were sounding the alarm about above-average ocean temperatures. Ecologists, oceanographers, and climate experts were presenting tipping-point scenarios. Researchers compared the trajectory of the last hurricane against current conditions and warned the public to prepare for the worst. Special news features replayed archival interviews and devastation highlights. Junior reporters were sent to the hardest-hit sites of six years ago to assess the recovery.

The city was on high alert. Sales of Kraft Dinner had soared, generators were sold out, and battery supplies were low. Emergency preparedness broadcasts warned people it was never too early to prepare. Dog behaviourists offered advice on how to mitigate pet trauma. Psychological counselling was in high demand. A weeping woman interviewed in the street said she couldn't live through another storm.

Hassan thought it was a lot of fuss for maybe. It would blow or it wouldn't blow. Now, it just resulted in too much traffic on a Monday morning. He glanced at Tamara in the front seat. She hadn't commented on the white carnation bobbing in the dashboard vase. She looked regal in her blue dress. Her braids were pulled back and clipped loosely by a barrette at the nape of her neck. Her look was befitting a sombre occasion.

He felt less certain about his light tan suit. The shoulders were tight and the waistband was cutting into his belly. He had borrowed dress shoes and his toes were pinched. They were black shoes and he was self-conscious of the weight and exclamation of his feet. When she had asked him to go, he hadn't hesitated. But there was an awkward moment clarifying whether he was driving or accompanying her.

He knew a funeral wasn't a first date, but he had prepared as though it were. He trimmed his nose hairs, shaved his cheeks smooth. Applied cologne and washed it off. Bought new underwear and socks. Clipped his finger- and toenails. He even tidied his one-bedroom apartment and changed the sheets. When he pulled out the fridge to sweep behind it, he realized how ridiculous and humiliating hope could be. Still, he had a bath instead of a shower, and soaped between his legs.

He dug out his only suit from the back of his closet and dropped it off for same-day dry cleaning. It was the suit he'd worn when he arrived in this country. His only suit. It had been too large then, a gift from the benefactor who had helped him cross the Turkish border. He had worn it from Ankara to Istanbul, across the Aegean into Greece, and onto the plane. The trouser cuffs were still chalked with dust and the suit's collar was ringed yellow. It smelled sour with despair, which the dry cleaner with a wave of his hand assured him would be gone.

Inside the lapels and trouser seams were the hidden pockets where he'd stitched in pages of poems with white thread. The inner weave of the inside breast pocket still held the imprint of his passport and fake travel visas. It had never held names, numbers, photos—nothing that could have led back to what had been left behind. Rendezvous points, times, allies, and contacts were kept in his head. Everything else was written in the scars on his skin. What couldn't be written was sealed in his fused, crooked bones.

He took a deep breath as the traffic leading to the church stalled at the intersection. The dry cleaner was correct. He smelled brand new. He turned left and Tamara didn't notice. Cars were parked on either side of the already too narrow street. The sidewalk teemed with young people unified by black T-shirts. They congregated in small groups hugging each other.

There was nowhere to park. Around the corner, the Presbyterian church had three massive lots. Half a block north, the abandoned Catholic lot was chained to trespassers. But the small Baptist church, hemmed in by buildings and its facade flush to the sidewalk, didn't even have a drop-off zone. He stopped close to the entrance, waving traffic past. Removing the Bluebird

Taxi light had been a good decision. He opened the passenger door.

Shrinking from the crush of mourners, Tamara hesitated with one hand on the dash and the other gripping the seat.

"I'll find you." He offered his hand, noting how close and perfectly aligned he was to the curb. It was an effortless step. Her hand was hot and she held on tight. He walked her to the door and ran back to the cab under a honk of complaints.

33

Night shift had ended hours ago and Mike should be home sleeping, but he had volunteered to clean up the mess. The shrine of flowers and stuffed toys had become a distraction. There had already been two fender benders, three complaints of jaywalkers, and one near miss because of rubbernecking. And now there was the threat of high winds. City workers wouldn't touch it for fear of sparking a riot. With the funeral happening today, everyone would be at the service. It was the best time to clean it up. Besides, he wasn't tired yet.

He had gone for breakfast and had the Hearty Man's Special: eggs, bacon, sausage, and hash browns. Yogurt or fresh fruit weren't on the menu, just greasy, cardiac-inducing goodness. He'd even had a cup of coffee, knowing Lori would disapprove. He hadn't called to say he'd be late. He would blame it on paperwork. It didn't matter. He'd be in shit either way.

He gathered the bouquets in his arms, a crackle of cellophane and blurred condensation. The brown, mummified roses and wilting carnations smelled dusty and sweet. He didn't read the cards. He had already gathered the teddy bears and drawings and placed them in clear bags. There was a right way and a wrong way to do this job.

It had to be approached solemnly, with ritual. It couldn't be rushed. He carried the relics in both arms with the ceremony and dignity of a folded flag and gently laid the flowers in his open trunk. He was doing everything right. If someone was watching, they'd see him demonstrating proper respect and care. The trunk was almost full. He would put everything curbside in dark bags on garbage day. It was the simplest way.

He felt good walking back to the site. He was upright and strong. The harbour was ablaze with morning, and windows flared molten. He was golden. Two little pills and he was whole again. He pulled up the wooden cross and hoped it would fit in the trunk. He carried it flat in his arms, bearing the painted word DEVON like an offering to the sky. He looked up quickly, wiping the word from his mind. People didn't understand how dangerous distractions could be.

A car with tinted windows rounded the corner. He straightened his back and lifted his chin. He was in full uniform with the cross level in gloved hands. His stride was a measured march. He was doing everything right.

The tinted window slid partially open. An arm extended. Male. Brown skin. Middle finger saluting.

He memorized the licence plate.

34

Kate downed her third coffee of the morning. She was only a few hours into her eight-hour swing shift to relieve Amy, who was fighting a cold. After Riley's, she'd gone home intending to sleep, but kept seeing him in the bed, at the stove, on her couch, in the shower . . . so she laid down food and fresh water for Zeus and left. He'd be fine until lunch break. She managed a couple of hours' sleep in her jeep in the hospital parking lot and showered at work. It was the only good choice she had made in days.

It had been a deep, dreamless sleep and when her watch alarm went off the sky was purple and pink and the moon and sun were sharing the translucent blue. Curled up in the seat hidden from view, she had heard the murmur of voices passing nearby. It was like being inside a tent.

She felt surprisingly good despite her lack of sleep. The hospital was in a buoyant mood, prepping for the approaching hurricane. Pain meds, suture, and dressing supplies were being stocked in anticipation of the upswing in chainsaw lacerations. She had agreed to work multiple shifts day and night. She could grab sleep as needed and relieve nurses with families or those dealing with extensive property damage. Special allowances had been made for Zeus to crate in the storage room. And as for

Riley . . . they would get past it. They were both professionals. She didn't think she would even miss him much.

Two young women slinked past her station, shielding their eyes from the probing sun. Purple Jesus punch casualties. Their mascara had run and lipstick smeared their cheeks. Their high heels clicked unsteadily as they wobbled by in rumpled short skirts and vomit-stained tops. Night shift said the girls wanted their gurneys side by side so they could hold hands. One girl sang hit songs out of tune and begged the other to join in on choruses between retches. Through slobbering tears, they told each other, *I love you, I love you.* Four paramedics kept them company for five hours. The girls loved them, too.

"Have a good day." Kate was feeling magnanimous. Everybody screwed up now and again. The girls slipped through the sliding doors, pretending not to hear.

Despite her personal life being in ruins, so far it was a good day at work. Word had spread about Zeus's find and she had been given her choice of doughnut and her first coffee was hot. Her colleagues were calling her Tracker and diverting her intake of frequent flyers and Advil pain. The jokes were particularly sharp and the atmosphere was almost giddy in anticipation of the possibility of major trauma within the next forty-eight hours. She pulled her next chart, a four-year-old boy with a possible arm fracture, Caleb Brandt.

She passed through the sliding doors into the waiting area. The boy, his mother, and infant sibling were seated close to triage for rapid admission. The baby was asleep in a car seat and the boy was curled in his mother's lap. His face was flushed from crying and his arm was wrapped in an ice pack. He hugged a green stuffed toy that resembled an alligator.

"Hi," Kate said. "Is this Caleb?" She reached for the toy's leg. "I hear he's hurt his paw. Is that true?"

The little boy snuffled, "I'm Caleb."

"Oh." She checked the paperwork. "They must have written it down wrong. It's not a green alligator, it's a boy."

She looked to the woman. "You're the mother?"

"Yes." The woman had the stoic calm of someone accustomed to taking care of things. But her eyes were fearful.

"Come on back with me and we'll get you fixed up."

The little boy, supporting his arm with his stuffed toy, slid off his mother's lap.

"Have you ever been to the hospital before?" He swung his head in an emphatic no and sniffled. She walked slowly to give the mother time to gather the baby and led them to a private room. All eyes waiting in the common holding-pen glared as they passed by. Children first.

"I'm going to put you on the bed, okay?" She lowered the gurney as low as it would go, which wasn't low enough. "I'll help you up." Cradling the boy, taking care not to jostle his arm, she sat him on the edge. He was trembling and moaned softly. He smelled of suntan lotion. She raised the head of the bed to an upright position. "You can lean back." Uncertain, he complied. "My name's Kate and who's this?"

"Snappy."

"Oh my, I hope he doesn't snap *me*." The boy relinquished a small smile. "I'm going to unwrap this and take a look. I promise I'll be very gentle." The boy stiffened, but he was trying to be brave.

"Tell me what happened?"

"Mommy hurt me."

"Caleb!" The mother's face reddened. "It was an accident." She burbled, "We were late for swimming lessons, the baby was crying, Caleb didn't want to get in the van, then he didn't want his seatbelt on . . ."

Kate waited patiently for the woman to move past the why and get to the what.

" . . . and I slid the van door shut. I thought he was in. I didn't see his arm." The woman's eyes were dark-ringed from lack of sleep. The baby keened a shrill protest.

Kate prodded her to the ending. "So his arm was caught in the van door?"

The woman nodded. "I put ice on immediately, but it looked like it was swelling." Absently, she unstrapped the baby from the car seat and tugged him out before the latch released. Half awake, the baby kicked and whimpered. The mother untangled his leg and rocked him back to sleep against her breast. The infant looked healthy and cared for.

The boy's forearm was faintly bruised and reddened. The shape of the bruise seemed consistent with the crush of a van door. She lifted his T-shirt and checked his torso, front and back. There were no other signs of bruising or abuse. "I bet it hurts?" He nodded emphatically. "Does it hurt more now? Or did it hurt more before?"

"Before." His eyes roved over the vitals machines in the corners. His fingers were white from clenching the toy. She checked his chart. No previous visits for broken bones and he didn't appear to be afraid of his mother. It likely was an accident.

"Can you move your fingers?" She placed his hand tenderly in hers. They wiggled. "Excellent," she said. "Do you want to lie down? I'm going to get the doctor now." The bed lowered and his eyes widened.

"Will I have to gets a needle?" He snuffled. "Snappy doesn't like needles."

"No, I don't think so, but we might do an x-ray. They'll take a picture of your bones. How cool is that?"

Caleb didn't look sure if that was a good thing.

"Afterwards you can have some juice. What's your favourite kind?"

"Apple."

"Apple it is. And would a cookie help? Chocolate chip?"

"Yeah."

She tucked the sheet under his chin and over his stuffed toy. He was a beautiful boy. "Will Snappy need a cookie, too? He's been such a good alligator."

"Crocodile."

"Of course he is. Would you like a cookie later, Snappy?" Caleb nodded. She patted the toy's head and turned to the mother.

"He'll be fine. It may look worse than it is." The woman looked as though she might cry. "Would you like a tea or coffee?"

"Tea. Thank you." Her *thank you* was steeped with a mother's gratitude.

The door to the exam room slammed open and a police officer filled the room. It was the same cop who had come to the house. She couldn't understand how he found her, or what horrific crisis had happened to bring him here, and who had her brother hurt?

"What happened?"

The intensity and bark of authority made Caleb jump. She noticed the boy's reaction and the wordlessness of the mother.

The cop wasn't there for Kate and her fear sloughed off. She stepped in with her most professional voice. "It was an accident. There's some bruising and hopefully that's all."

The cop's shining, drugged eyes narrowed in recognition. She could see his confusion, but they were professionals and could pretend they didn't see each other.

"He'll be fine," she said.

He turned on his wife. "Where were you?"

The woman's jaw clenched, her neck flushed red. She bit back. "Where were *you*? I've been calling and paging. You were supposed to be home hours ago."

The little boy was hiding behind his stuffed toy. Only its wide mouth and fabric teeth were visible over the sheet.

"I'm going to get a tea for your wife. Do you want anything?" She was trained to redirect and de-escalate. "Caleb's been very brave. He let me meet Snappy." The boy lowered his toy. His eyes were brimmed with tears. The officer's shoulders softened and he went to his son.

"A coffee?" she offered.

"No," the cop said, not looking at her. His wife added, "Thank you." "Hey, kiddo. You okay?" He stroked his son's hair.

"Say it," the little boy said.

The police officer glanced at his wife and leaned in closer. Kate noticed his back spasm and the flinch of his cheek. During the doctor's exam, she would check the boy's legs and backside.

"I love you, I love you, I love you," the cop said, punctuating each with a kiss.

"Again," said the boy.

35

The church was overflowing. Breathless. Shoulder to shoulder. Paper fans wafted under noses, churning hot air across cheeks. A video screen had been set up in the basement to accommodate the excess of grief, and the air conditioner moaned, overwhelmed to capacity. Standing at the back of the church, Tamara dabbed sweat from her brow.

Dozens of young people, stark in black shirts, punctuated the crowded rows of straight-backed chairs. Leaning forward in their seats, they stared at brand-new sneakers firmly planted to the floorboards, their shoulders resisting the sermon, rejecting forgiveness. Every young man in the congregation had crisp razored lines over his temples. His mark. Devon's. Edie's salon had been busy.

Tamara swayed in the heat. The smell of coconut oil and hair products was making her lightheaded. She breathed through her mouth. The church was smaller than she remembered. Her bare arm brushed against Hassan's tan linen suit. She could smell the soft scent of his soap.

The sun slashed through the windows, across the pulpit and casket. White. Small. Closed. Thank God. An enlarged photograph of him. The same one used for television and newspapers. Him smiling on his way out the door.

In the front row, she could see the back of a red velvet chair and the top of a woman's head. Her hair was cropped short. No other family members sat with her. The woman was still and erect. The mother.

Tamara and her Granny Nan had sat in those same red velvet chairs. Her feet didn't reach the floor and she didn't understand why they were being punished and not allowed to sit with the others. She had on a short dress and Granny Nan slapped her legs when she kicked the chair rungs. There were two coffins then. The pastor had kept saying her parents' names, and when she stood to look for them in the congregation, she was swatted again. And when he sang, she danced and couldn't understand why everyone else was crying.

Sandwiched between the wall and broad shoulders, Hassan shifted beside her. Pastor Linda's voice rose and fell, speaking of terrible injustices and the inadequacy of words. She spoke of home-going. Her voice softened them through the pain, carried them up to the steeple of anguish, held them close in the weeping of goodbyes. *I will be your Light. I will keep my hand in yours.* Her words churned between the oscillating fan blades, wobbled at the roof peaks, and wafted down to roost in their caged hearts. Amen.

Hallelujahs rose from the congregation, and the Revival Choir stood. Their shimmering blue and golden robes blossomed in the whiteness. One lone voice sang out "Precious Lord, Take My Hand" as hundreds of hands reached upward. In the red velvet chair, the mother did not move.

In the wake of shuffles and rustle of tissues, a boy rose from his seat and made his way to the pulpit, giving the casket a wide berth. He faced the congregation, his head down. His whole body quaked. In his hand, he clutched a CD player. He set it on the pulpit and adjusted the gooseneck microphone to its speaker. Every breath was held. Willing him to speak. Waiting to be released.

Pastor Linda laid her hand on the boy's shoulder. He looked up and out. His eyes were glistening. White-hot.

He leaned into the mic. "Devon was my best friend."

She knew his voice immediately. Antoine who had made the call. Antoine who did everything she had asked him to do. Antoine who looked as young as he had sounded. His scalp glistened where razor lines had been cut into his hair.

"We were working on this . . . Devon and me. He said it was one of your favourites." He said this to the woman in the red chair. "It was gonna be a surprise." The words caught in his throat and his thin chest heaved. He nodded and the young people in the congregation stood. Antoine pushed the Play button. Head bowed, he placed a trembling hand to his chest.

The room leaned in closer. A voice spoke. His voice. Laughing. Alive. "Take one. We ready, yeah? Here we go . . ."

A piano stool scraped across the floor. He breathed out and the notes lifted, one by one. A simple, pure refrain. Sombre and sober. Broad hats nodded in recognition. Some inhaled its exquisite pain. Others prayed. Praise Jesus. Praise the Lord. Many looked up to some place beyond the rooftop.

Another scrape of the piano bench and she knew the boy was drawing himself closer to the keys. His sneakered toes were reaching for the pedals. It was coming. He was taking it to church. His left hand rolled the octave into a tremolo and the bass chords started to billow.

Antoine, head down, began tapping his heart like a kick drum, slapping the snare of his bare arms. His teen choir followed their conductor. Clapping hands, stomping feet. Fluttering wings. The melody broke free.

Antoine drummed his chest as his youth choir clap-clapped in syncopated beat. They sang, heads high, their voices thin and wavering. *Some glad morning when this life is over, I'll fly away . . .*

Antoine was drumming his ribs, his fingers snapping, his feet stomping in and out of the half-steps walking across the blues scale. *I'll fly away, O glory . . .* All around her voices soared as the piano revealed itself to be percussion and string.

She could hear it all. The blues, the jazz, gospel, and classical—all of time resurrecting. A riff descended the pentatonic scale in free fall. Suspended. His foot lifted from the pedal, clearing the sound. The piano's inner voice opened to ascend on the breath of its own expanding choir. There was the call. There the response.

Antoine's face had lifted and he was drumming his chest with both hands. Palms open. His eyes fixed on the rafters. Cheeks stained wet. Drumming the hollows of himself. Antoine was singing. His voice slipped between the lines like jazz. Countering the other voices. *I'll fly away . . .* The beats of his heart. *I'll fly away . . .*

The music scrabbled against the windows and skimmed the roof peak. The floorboards bounced, vibrating through Tamara's soles. The murmur of song flew over them and into them. *O glory!* The notes churned and dipped, rising in an orchestrated swirl. She was clapping. She was stomping. She was singing. *When I die, hallelujah, by and by . . .* She was weeping. *I'll fly away.*

The boy, Antoine, was pounding his chest with closed fists. Hands uplifted all around him. Holding him up.

The woman in the red velvet chair stood. Her dress was the same bruised colour as her grief. The woman was small, but her legs were strong. She wasn't singing. She wasn't crying. She went to Antoine and wrapped her arms around him tight. Her son's name freshly tattooed on her sinewy forearm. She clasped Antoine's pummelling fists to his heart as he pleaded with her, broken-winged, *I'll fly away*.

Tamara heard her Granny Nan singing and her momma and her papa. *O!* She heard the voices of the sixty-seven-year-old white male cardiac arrest rising from the sidewalk *I'll fly away, O glory* and the girl in the yellow dress levitating from the bridge *I'll fly away, in the morning* and the baby choking in its mother's arms, soaring *When I die* and the ninety-seven-year-old woman who never woke *Hallelujah, by and by* and the paramedic bleeding out his own life's blood *I'll fly away* and the crumpled bodies unfolding from twisted metal *I'll fly away*, the born and the unborn *O glory*, swooping into her chest, flapping against her rib cage *I'll fly away*, clawing at her throat *In the morning*, thrashing against her skull *When I die*, a blurring white light of wings exploding *Hallelujah!* behind her eyes. *By and by*, she flew away.

Tamara.

Her forehead was cool and damp. Water trickled down the nape of her neck. She reached for her hair. Her hair clip was missing and her braids were loose. She opened her eyes. And wondered why there was a damp cloth in her hand. Heaven was a waiting room with a cheap sofa, wooden chairs, and bare walls. Hassan was kneeling beside her. She smiled. She didn't remember calling a cab. He smiled back and she saw the worry ebb from his face. A woman said, "I'm calling 911."

"No!" She bolted upright too quickly and the room heaved. Hassan's hand caught the small of her back to steady her.

A woman with an ample bosom and wide hips stood at the end of the couch peering down. She was a vision of lilac. Purse and cell phone in hand, this was a woman who took charge of things.

"I'm fine, really. There's no need to call." She couldn't have her name flashed across her colleagues' monitors. "Please," she begged Hassan.

"She's okay," he assured the woman. "Too hot, that's all. Perhaps she needs water, yes?" He fanned Tamara with the church bulletin, studying her face to see if he was telling the truth.

"Yes." That was all she needed. "A glass of water, please."

The woman slipped her phone into her purse and trundled to the nearby water cooler. Hassan guided Tamara to lie back down, and as he did so, he discreetly inched her skirt hem below her knee. His fingertips barely brushed her skin.

She smiled weakly. "I'm so embarrassed."

The woman handed Hassan the paper cup. "No shame in giving yourself over to the Spirit." The woman's eyes were murky with cataracts. She squinted at Tamara. "Do I know you?"

"No." No one here would know her now.

The woman squinted harder. The door opened and the room filled with the shuffle of high heels on wood floors, gulping sobs, and the fading strains of the organ. An apologetic white-haired woman peeked in. "He's going now."

The lilac woman considered her obligation to the living or the dead.

"I'm okay, really. You should go."

"I'll stay with her," Hassan promised.

The lilac woman with milk eyes studied her, then relinquished her watch. "You stay as long as you need, child. There'll be somebody around to lock up."

The door shut behind her. The room was vast in its quiet.

"You need more water." Hassan guided her upright again. His hand was warm through the thin dress fabric. He brought the cup to her lips and she took it with both hands and guzzled it down. The water was cold and chlorinated. She emptied the cup.

Still on bended knee, Hassan kept his arm extended in front of her as one might for an unsteady toddler. His suit coat was puckered tight around his shoulders and his knee smeared with dust. She noticed his waistband was constricting his belly and the weave of his jacket pocket held a permanent imprint of a wallet, or maybe a passport. Loose threads betrayed hand stitches along the lapels. She wondered if he had borrowed the suit for the occasion.

"Please, get up." She motioned for him to sit beside her and he did. Her shoes weren't on her feet. Her black flats were set neatly by the couch, revealing their shiny, sweat-stained linings. They had been her special-event shoes since university. Her bare toes left round prints on the cool floor. "How did I get here?"

Hassan wanted to tell her how he caught her as she fell, a crumple more than a fall; and how light she was in his arms; how the path cleared as he rushed her into the hall before most had noticed; and that for a small man, he had strength that belied his size; and that he had held others before her, dead weight, in his arms. But he wasn't certain the question was intended for him.

She brushed a dusty footprint from her skirt. "I'll pay to have your suit cleaned."

"No need." He tucked his shirt into his waistband. His underarms were wet and his shirt was sticking. He should have bought a new suit. A grey suit like the others were wearing.

Tamara listened to the hum of the hollow space. She could smell the clean soap smell of the man sitting beside her. She wondered if this was what unafraid felt like. Or maybe her dehydrated mind hadn't yet caught up. She looked to the ceiling to see if part of her was up there.

"I was with him when he died," she said. "That's my job—911. Listening and waiting for others to arrive." She didn't want sympathy. It was just a fact. She was trying to explain. "I think he could hear me. I think he knew I was with him."

Hassan lightly laid his hand on hers. His gnarled fingers were rough with scars. One thumbnail was thick and misshapen. The heat radiating from his palm made her want to cry. His eyes were downcast. He was listening. He was waiting for her to speak, which frightened her even more. She extricated her hand under the ruse of straightening her dress.

"I need to use the washroom." She stood. And so did he.

"Thank you for everything, Hassan." *Everything* seemed a paltry word. She suppressed the urge to shake his hand or give him a hug, fearing she wouldn't let go. "I'm sorry I brought you here."

"This is where I was supposed to be," he said.

She didn't know what to do with his words and so she put on her shoes.

"I have to go."

She walked past the washroom, through the church of empty chairs, forgotten bulletins, and caged hallelujahs, and out the door.

Sun blazed her scalp and panic gnawed her stomach. She hadn't walked these backstreets since she was a child. Five things she could see: a crumbling foundation, cracked sidewalk, full dumpster, vacant lot, choked weeds, asphalt mirage, chalked hopscotch, pink and yellow . . . she had lost count. She wasn't far from Edie's salon. She breathed in and out slowly. Sweat beaded her forehead and stung her eyes. Two things she could smell: rotting garbage and mowed grass. Three things she could hear: traffic on the road above, her own frantic breath, the shuffle of her practical flats. Something she could feel: her shoes, their leather stiff with age. With each step, they pinched her toes, and a blister was welting on the back of her left heel, sawing at her Achilles tendon, and the pavement's heat was seeping through their paper-thin soles. Pain, she could feel pain.

She wiped her brow. It was too hot. She was following her feet, trusting they would get her home. She stopped under the shade of the only tree by the school and focused on quelling her trembling arms. She counted the stairs leading up to the door, the narrow gashes of windows positioned too high for escape, and the red bricks until her heart settled back into her chest and she could see the squat building as a whole—her elementary school. A place she had loved and that had made her feel safe.

Despite the protests, it was being shut down. The city would forget the gleaming hardwood gym floor and painted murals of giraffes and palm trees adorning the halls. They wouldn't remember that there had been laughter, singing, and music. Or that there had been first kisses, best friends, and first-place ribbons. Or that children drew angels and baby Jesuses with black and brown crayons, or that she had sat in the third seat of the third row in Mrs. Gregor's class and earned the most gold stars alongside others who became lawyers, doctors, athletes, musicians, and artists. People wouldn't remember that.

They'd remember the stories of concealed weapons, drugs, bomb threats, and the body of a woman found in the window well. And the codes of conduct sent home with six-year-olds stipulating the penalties for profanity, violence, theft, vandalism, racism, harassment, sexual misconduct, and weapons possession. She looked up at the sneakers strung in the power lines and imagined yellow dots, thick as ivy, climbing the lamp pole, choking the sidewalk, and infesting the schoolyard.

She deciphered the graffiti on the steel armoured doors cladding the gymnasium. Only five numbers were written in legible script. It was a date. She opened herself to see the whole. She saw the negative space forming the letters of his name. *RIP*. Alongside, spray-painted by another hand, bled the words *SOME FUCKER WILL DIE*.

Devon was twelve. He rode a bicycle. He had grass-stained knees. Some fucker *should* die, she thought.

Horrified she could have such thoughts, she hurried past the building, her left shoe slapping against her heel. She ran from the polite, dun-yellow script tagged on the brick corner: *Nothing is okay*. She ran from this outside world that held so much hurt.

She cut through a front yard no larger than a cemetery plot

overflowing with delphinium, phlox, and black-eyed Susans. Dusty heads hung heavily against a greying picket fence. A plastic Santa was perched on the veranda roof. Her feet led her to the only footpath that wended through the brick row houses fortifying the outer walls, demarcating them and us.

Inside the Square, air conditioners buzzed. A white cat, framed by hot pink curtains, watched from a window. The meagre backyards fenced in by timber rails were crowded with plastic toys bleached dull from sun and generations of use. Somewhere children were laughing. She smelled fabric softener and fresh-cut grass. Summer clothing bannered compact clotheslines. Beside every back door was a chair. She looked along the rooftops. The hard lines and blue sky were sharp and nauseating against the public housing's red brick.

She hobbled past the missions, food bank, parents' resource centre, and community policing station and into the bower of Middle Lane. Backyard fences penned the narrow path. Two young men had been shot on this path, two more red dots. More had died in the park beyond. Her feet slowed at the third door on the left. The door was painted red now and the windows upgraded to vinyl. She remembered the house being taller and her upstairs bedroom window larger. Across the street, the neighbours' houses seemed closer and the patch of sky above smaller. But mostly, she noticed the absence of Granny Nan's chair at the back door.

Her childhood had passed through that door. Bandages and reprimands. Popsicles and peanut butter sandwiches. Macaroni and cheese casseroles in times of need and sorrow. Thrift-store finds and anonymous Christmas hampers. Back-door chats. No secrets, no lies. The women holding all the stories. And the door propped open on Sundays for Granny Nan, pounding on the piano, bringing Jesus to the neighbours. As a child, she couldn't remember there being any coloured dots. It was home, and when she thought of home, the colour was confetti pink and yellow and robin's egg blue.

Sometimes purple crept in. But Granny Nan didn't tolerate purple for long. *There are lions and there are deer*, she would say. *The lions want the deer, but they must both run. Why do they run?* she'd ask her granddaughter. *To live*, Tamara would reply. *To live happy*, Granny Nan would declare with conviction. Tamara was never sure that was right. But it was how Granny Nan chose to live.

Old friends would drop by for tea, and when the light was right—dark and holy—Granny Nan would speak of her first home, her true home. From under the kitchen table, Tamara would listen to her voice, soft as a hymn, describe the house her father had built overlooking the harbour, and the train tracks below, and the view from her bedroom window of her beloved church. She spoke of the peal of the church bell, sunrise services, spirituals sung, and baptisms in the sea.

Her voice would lift as she recalled days spent picking wild blueberries and swimming in the Basin. Do you remember, she would say, the older boys playing hockey on Tibby's Pond and baseball in Kildare's Field? Such handsome boys. And the little ones pretending they were cowboys with tin cans tied to their heels for stirrups. And the men, her father and brothers included, scavenging the city dump for lumber, windows, and furniture to sell back to the city or use to reinforce their own walls. So many treasures found. And the music—oh, the music! From the choir to Portia White and Duke Ellington paying visits. And the ladies, their hair done up fine. And the pretty dresses. So many happy memories.

The women's voices murmuring, conjuring names of long-lost aunties, uncles, and cousins, would lull her to sleep between their nylon-stocking toes and crisply pleated skirts. She'd wake to rolling laughter and feet stamping. The women would laugh and laugh until they cried, and soon after that the chairs would be pushed back and the kettle put back on to boil.

Only once did she hear Granny Nan talk about the night the bulldozers came in the middle of night. And how she woke to the church gone, reduced to rubble and boards. She thought she was dreaming, or the world had ended, or she had acquired a rare affliction that made her see only the ugly of the world. When she told that story there was a long time between the tears and the kettle boiling and purple choked the room. Granny Nan never spoke about the typhoid, raw sewage, contaminated wells, incinerator, slaughterhouse, rats, moonshine, or why black people lived there and white people didn't. She chose to remember the good and leave it to God to remember the bad.

Tamara breathed shallowly. The piano was no longer blocking the hallway. Her single bed with its orange yarn coverlet had long ago moulded. The green electric clock that ticked too loudly and the nubby gold chesterfield that pockmarked her bare legs were decaying in the dump. Granny Nan wasn't sitting at the gold-flecked table waiting for her to come home. She felt the choke of gone.

She was thirsty. She was tired. She was hot. Her feet throbbed. The voices of the choir crashed against her temples. *I'll fly away*. Fists drummed against her chest. She closed her eyes and concentrated on one note—A—until she silenced all the others. She didn't look back.

She huffed up the hill in a broken walk-run, following the only street leading out. Her too-tight shoes slipped and slid. A white van roared down the hill and veered to a stop in front of her on the wrong side of the street. Her skin pricked danger, but it wasn't a police van.

The driver stepped out and smiled. A soft, kind smile. He was older, his black hair greyed. He was wearing a suit that was loose on his large frame, and his tie was limp around his neck. He opened the back of the van and extracted two large arrangements of white roses. He set them on the curb.

"Can you manage these?" Not waiting for an answer, he reached into the van and dragged out a cooler. "They can go by the stairs."

Tamara looked at the house. Two folding banquet tables were draped in white tablecloths, with barbecues positioned at each end. The door swung open and a woman who could have been her Granny Nan filled the frame.

"You got the ice, Harold?"

"Yeah, I got the ice." Harold was pulling a second cooler from the van.

"And the propane?"

"If you told me to get it, I got it, Dottie."

"Umbrellas?"

"And chairs. You want to unload it, old woman?"

"I want you to get that van gone in the next ten minutes." Dottie looked up and saw Tamara. "Whose girl are you?"

"Nobody's."

"Everybody belongs to somebody."

"I've been away a long time."

Dottie squinted for a better look. "You're the little one who lived down the street with Elsie. Tamara, right?"

She considered running, but the way the woman said her name sounded like Granny Nan. "Yes," she breathed.

"Well come on, then. I was about to start the sandwiches."

Tamara picked up the flowers, *In Loving Memory*, and carried them to the stairs. It was the least she could do before clarifying that there had been a mistake. Dottie held open the front door. A door she had seen before in a photograph of a boy's smiling face.

"By the step's good. What are you standing there for? The sandwiches aren't going to make themselves and the day's not waiting on you."

Tamara caught the screen door before it slammed. She followed Dottie into the house. The chairs in the living room had been pushed back to ring a plush pink rocker. Metal folding chairs filled the gaps. Two electric fans oscillated on stands. Both were pointed at the pink chair. She thought this was an especially kind touch.

Propped against a wall was a poster board of photographs. Pictures of him. Pictures of the woman she had seen in the church, her bare arms free of tattoos. In every photo, mother and son were smiling. There wasn't a piano in the house.

Dottie reached down and picked up a pair of white sneakers forgotten in the entryway, boy's sneakers, and tucked them into the closet. Her bra strap slipped down her ample arm. Her elbows were ashen. She sighed when she stood up.

"People will be arriving soon." She slid the closet door shut. Her handprint lingered on the mirror. "You can help."

She followed Dottie down the narrow hall to the kitchen. Pots crowded the stovetop, and the counters were lined with rice casseroles, macaroni, and salads. Tamara could smell cornbread baking in the oven. The propped-open window and back door did nothing to relieve the heat.

"You use the table. Start buttering the bread for the little ones. Cut them in fours. Peanut butter's here and there's homemade jam in the fridge." Dottie peered into the oven window. "Oh Lord, these are done."

She grabbed the oven mitts and slid the pans of golden bread onto the stovetop. "Thank you, Jesus."

Carefully, Tamara spread the soft butter to the edges of the store-bought white bread. The table was cheap, the chairs were mismatched, the appliances avocado green, and the grey countertop was marred with ancient cuts and scorch marks. But the walls had been painted butter yellow and colourful bottles adorned the windowsill. She unscrewed the peanut butter top. The food smelled like Granny Nan's.

"What took you away?" Dottie asked, covering the chicken with tin foil.

"Work." But that felt like a lie. Dottie looked at her as though waiting for the truth. *There was nobody left*, she wanted to say.

"Hmm," Dottie said, and turned back to the job at hand.

Tamara slipped her feet from her shoes and touched her toes to the cool, soothing floor.

"When you're done, you can start carrying things out to the tables. Won't be long now." Dottie retrieved a jar of homemade jam from the fridge and plonked it beside the peanut butter. "And don't skimp on the jam. Everybody's going to need some extra good today."

Tamara set the butter knife down. "I'm not—" she said. "I'm not—" She searched for what she was not. One of her braids was longer than the others and her hands were dark against the white bread.

"This is your home, child. No matter how long you've been away." Dottie swept crumbs into the palm of her hand. "Cut them into triangles. They'll look prettier standing up."

36

When Hassan stepped into his upstairs flat above the pizza shop, it smelled stale and yeasty despite the windows being open. A perpetual air of emptiness. If he were to guess who lived there, he would choose *a transient man. A man who didn't receive guests. A poor man who dreamed of more.*

The walls were bare. One room served as both kitchen and living room. Beside one drafty window were a small table and chair salvaged from the curb, a typewriter, radio, mug, and bowl. And near the other, a worn reading chair, lamp, and stacks of books piled on the floor. He would not guess he was the man who lived there.

He could afford furniture and even a better flat now, but this had been his first apartment in this country and it was all that he felt he deserved. He went to the kitchen sink and checked under the cabinet. To his relief, the mousetrap was empty.

On the street below, two young boys raced down the sidewalk. The older child reached the curb first and raised his arms in victory. In this country, even the children played differently. He never saw them on their knees surrendering, or shooting each other with pretend automatic weapons or firing imaginary bullets into the backs of heads to finish the job. Here, there weren't bullet-pocked walls to kick soccer balls against, or bodies to stare at, or gutters running red to float sticks in.

He filled the kettle and set it on the stove. He looked around the sparse room and added *a childless man* to the list. He took off his suit jacket and headed to the bedroom with its single bed and more books. *A lonely man*. He sighed.

When he dropped his trousers, his body slumped, grateful for its release. A red welt ringed his waist from the constriction. He rubbed the trouser knees to loosen the dirt and dust, but the marks remained. He examined the wrinkled jacket. The lapels were too wide for today's fashion, the buttons cheap, the fabric's weave loose, and the collar still ringed yellow. *A lowly man.*

He flipped the limp collar over. The fabric had frayed where it had been split open at the false seam. Two pages, rolled tighter than cigarettes, had been its starch. He turned the pant legs inside out and ran his fingers along the plucked stitches, remembering the needle's pierce between mangled, swollen fingers. Seven poems per leg. Five per arm. Three in the collar. He would have swallowed a dozen more if he could have carried them five thousand miles. He would have stitched them under his skin. He had sacrificed everything for words. Even her.

His parents feared him getting married. He was too young. She was Sunni and he was not, and they were in love. She was unafraid and righteous in her beliefs of right and wrong. When she spoke, she lit her audiences' eyes. Men adored her, women respected her, and everyone jostled to be in her light. And she had picked him. Together, they were invincible. Students against injustice. A revolution for and by the people.

His gentle mother and thoughtful father raised him and his younger brothers to value knowledge, art, and poetry as humanity's most enduring and important narratives. They believed differences could be solved sitting around the table with good food and drink. Strangers would become friends, and friends could not kill each other.

But they were wrong. His parents didn't survive. His brothers didn't survive. But by then he was already gone. "Run," they had said.

That was the last thing she had said to him, too. "Run." But he stayed and waited through the day and into the night before stealing back to carry her body away, stiff and heavy where she had fallen. He couldn't carry the others. He had loved her, maybe. He had loved her mind. Loved her conviction. He was the student. She was the leader.

He had wanted a proper burial for her. She deserved more than being tossed into the same pits as the culled wild dogs or those carried from the football stadium fields. A game he could no longer watch. A game he once loved that had united Sunnis, Shi'ites, and Christians in one rallying cry: "Iraq!"

But that was before lessons from the Qur'an were broadcast over loudspeakers while hawkers sold green tea and sweet biscuits during the pre-game show and the guilty were ushered in on pickup trucks and taken to the goalposts. Their crimes bleated over the speakers, as justice was meted out with Kalashnikovs amidst cheers of *Allahu Akbar!* God is great! As a child, he had cheered. At first because it was expected of him and he didn't understand the crowd's eyes that shone with such fervour. Later because there wasn't a choice and his own eyes shone with the fear of being found out. *Allahu Akbar!* A revolutionary cry.

Hassan's crooked fingers carefully aligned the creases of the pants. He draped the trousers over the wire hanger, smoothing the linen.

He had wanted to give her a proper mourning ceremony. But there weren't any women he could ask to remove their shoes and drink bitter coffee and recount her acts of goodness. No *addadas* to weep professional tears for hours on end. No *mordeh shoor* to wash her body or wrap her in a white shroud. All he could do was apply dust to her eyes and lay her on her right side facing Mecca and say her name out loud. His wife of four months. "Run," his parents had said, as his mother stuffed his pockets with food.

He unbuttoned his dress shirt. He could smell coconut oil. He slid the fabric from his shoulders and paused as he always did when he saw his own skin. Thick scars mapped his chest, abdomen, and arms. He had only shown them once, to those who had let him into this country. Behind their table, they had stared at the blank wall above his head while one took photographs of the lash marks, burns, dog bites, and lacerations. The camera's flash had seared his eyes with black spots. He blinked every time. "Please, you may put your shirt back on," one said as the others looked away.

He hung the shirt on the coat hanger, straightened the shoulders, and dressed the jacket over it. He folded down the collar and pulled a loose strand from the seam. He twirled the thread of his former life between his fingertips. When they had picked him up, he had poems in his possession. Fifty typed copies. They wanted the poet's name whose words were being passed underground, found in rebels' pockets, and spoken in the streets. They confiscated his typewriter and unspooled the ribbon to show him the jumbled evidence. He swore *he* was the poet, but they knew he was only the typist. They wanted the man responsible for the poems. They wanted his name.

He had tried to resist. He had. But every question was another wound. Eventually, everyone talked, especially the innocent. He tried to warn her and the others. He begged her to leave and them to stop. Instead, she held his broken body up to her followers and said, "This is why we fight." Amidst the cheers pledging allegiance to her and country, he finally understood their marriage was a political action. He was a line in a poem by the poet whose words made hearts beat and sang with a lifeblood that was prepared to die. They had wanted *her* name. "Run," she had said, not knowing he already had.

He carried her words five thousand miles stitched in the seams of what remained of him as a man. He carried them out alive. Time couldn't grant him the mercy to live again. In this country, *shame* wasn't the same word. Here, it was light and disposable, barely a word. There, shame branded him, his mother, his father, his brothers, and if he had children, his sons, and theirs, and theirs, for eternity. His life for hers. It was just. *Allahu Akbar.*

The kettle whistle keened. He understood why Tamara had run from him. Here lived a cowardly man.

He was not a poet.

He slipped the suit back in the closet between his cardigans and long-sleeved shirts.

37

The alarm jarred Mike awake. He was on his back, in his own bed, in his own bedroom. The light bleeding around the blackout blinds told him it was day. He looked at the clock: 4:00 p.m. Time to get ready. One more night. He just had to get through one more night and he'd have three days to recover.

He breathed in deep and exhaled slow. He lay still, working up the courage to move. Maybe it was gone. Maybe life had returned to normal. He felt the choke of relief and hope, and blinked it back. The week had been hell, thankfully it was almost over.

He watched a spider traverse the whiteness of the ceiling. Lori had said he could sleep in the bedroom. She offered him his own bed like it was a gift. He hadn't taken the bait. He was tired of fighting. He had nodded and listened, as best he could through the dull ache shuddering up his spine. She took the boys swimming, insisting the water would be good for Caleb's tender muscle and a friend of hers had free passes. When he asked where they were going, she said the north end and he had said, No.

This ignited another razor-eyed argument with smiles on their faces for the children's benefit.

No, he couldn't tell her why.

No, she didn't have the right to know.

No, she couldn't tell her friend.

Yes, his family's safety was more important than anyone else's.

Because he said so and that should be enough.

That's when Connor fell backward, and the shock of his bum meeting the floor triggered an ear-splitting wail. Lori swore, Caleb repeated the word, and Lori yelled at him to get ready.

They were going OUT.

It was ENOUGH worrying about HIM every time he walked out the door or didn't pick up the phone or came home LATE.

Don't LIE! She had called the station.

SOMEONE ELSE could have done it!

She refused to be AFRAID ALL THE TIME.

When Lori charged out, she forgot the towels and he didn't bother chasing after her. Instead, he hollered, "Make sure the kids are in before you shut the door!"

He knew it was an accident. But she had been distracted and that caused the injury and that made it her fault. Someone was always at fault if you walked it back far enough. Someone always had a moment to make a different choice. Christ, what had happened to his promise to do better? She didn't understand how much he was hurting, even though she had seen him on his knees. She agreed with the docs who wanted him to take time off. But it would take weeks for compensation to kick in. How would they pay the bills? How much did a four-year-old's birthday party cost? He breathed in. Just get through one more night.

The house was still. Maybe Lori wasn't back yet, but it was almost suppertime. Careful not to jostle his body, he switched on the police radio charging on the side table. Catastrophic emergencies weren't jamming the airwaves, nor reports of retribution for a twelve-year-old boy. Of course, it wouldn't occur in daylight hours. These sorts of things belonged to the night. Lori *should* be scared. She had no idea what the world was really like, which proved how hard he worked to shield them and keep them safe. His pain was making him feel sorry for himself. Lori was right. It wasn't her fault. He should have kept his friggin' mouth shut.

He switched off the radio and wished he had a few more hours in bed to gather his strength. He sucked at his dry cheeks and scratched idly at his chest. His arms and legs were itchy, too, and his muscles twitchy. He needed another pill. The spider was making good progress crossing the ceiling, oblivious to the reality that there was no way out. He looked over at the dresser. His gear was laid out in its proper place, safe and ordered. He had made sure of that. On the back of the door, his uniform hung crisply, and on the chair were fresh socks and underwear. She did still love him.

It was just an accident. He should have been home to help her. He should have told her it was okay. He had to apologize. Again. He understood why she was sick of his apologies. He was, too.

The door creaked open a crack. Small fingers poked through, then a nose and a cheek. Mike shut his eyes and snored loudly. The door inched wider. He forced himself to count to ten before roaring his best dragon roar.

Caleb jumped, a small boy's fright, before grinning that goofy kid grin. He was still in his swim trunks. Barefoot, knobby kneed, bronze skinned—he was a golden child. He had that damn stuffed toy in hand.

"Daddy's wake!" He charged.

Mike raised his hand to stop him. "Caleb, no, no . . ."

But Caleb had already leapt, a flying superhero with his sidekick crocodile. He landed with a whomp on Mike's chest. Heaving in agony, tears pricked his eyes.

Caleb rolled off. "I sorry I hurts you like Mommy hurt me."

"No." Mike sucked the pain between his teeth. "Daddy's okay. Daddy's just not awake yet. You were flying so high, I thought I couldn't catch you."

Clutching Snappy tight to his chest, Caleb watched his father's eyes for lies.

Mike resorted to Distraction 101 for four-year-olds. "Where's Mommy and Connor?"

"Connor's nappy with Mommy on the couch." He chewed his bottom lip. "She said be quiet 'cause Daddy's sleep."

"Did you go swimming with Mommy?"

"Uh-huh." Caleb propelled the crocodile's stubby arms. "Snappy swimmed, too. Mommy hung him in the sun upside down to dry, but Snappy didn't like it. He said, Rrrrarrhh."

"Snappy has a lot to say, doesn't he?" The toy looked cleaner and smelled better, too. The chlorine had done wonders. Two dark bruises marked Caleb's bicep. The placebo bandage the nurse had applied was waterlogged and lifting. She'd been good to his son, he had to give her that. You could never tell looking at someone who they really were.

Caleb's eyes brightened. "Wanna see how we dived?" He stood up and belly-flopped on the mattress. Mike groaned as his back ratcheted. Caleb scooted to the foot of the bed with Snappy keeping guard between them. His bottom lip quivered. "Is your back broke 'cause Mommy stepped on a crack?"

Mike exhaled the pain. "Papa just needs his vitamins." He searched the ceiling, but couldn't find the spider. "I have a job for you, Caleb. A big-boy job. Do you think you can help Daddy?"

Caleb nodded.

"I need you to get Daddy his vitamins in his pant pocket. They're in a special pocket that only little fingers can reach."

"A magic pocket?"

"Yes, a *secret* magic pocket."

Caleb scrambled off the bed.

"Reach in the right side. No, the other right side. The other pocket. That's it. Do you feel anything?"

"Uh-huh." Caleb reached inside. The coat hanger rocked.

"Can you get it out?"

Caleb tippy-toed. The pants tugged against the metal hanger and went slack.

"Do you have it?"

"Taa-daa!" He held the pills aloft.

"Now bring it to Daddy. Gently . . ."

Caleb took care not to rock the bed and handed over the pill bottle.

"Good job, little man." Mike uncapped it and took one. He was going through them fast. He wanted two, but Lori would see it in his eyes.

Caleb leaned into his father's legs. "I have an owwie," he said, rubbing his bandage. "And I like vinamims." He watched his father's eyes.

"These are Daddy's vitamins. Only for daddies. Do you understand?"

His son's eyes didn't blink. Mike's voice dropped deeper, "Caleb, do you understand? These are never to be touched by Caleb or Connor. These are like the stove and matches and Daddy's police things—they're only for Daddy. Not you. Never. Do you understand?"

"Yes."

"Pinkie swear." Mike held up his baby finger.

Caleb gripped his father's finger and kissed his hand three times. "I love you, I love you, I love you." He leaned back, cross-legged with Snappy on his lap. The soles of his feet were grass-stained and streaked with dirt. The jiggling bed made Mike wince.

Caleb stroked Mike's whiskered cheek. "Snappy says you're bad."

Mike held his son's probing stare. Caleb slapped his cheek. A soft tap. Punishment or warning, Mike couldn't tell.

"Don't do that." The words growled in his chest. His son had to do better.

Caleb lowered his eyes. His small fingers caressed Mike's cheek. "I said he's a liar." He snuggled in, laying Snappy over Mike's heart. "I told you," he said, stroking its fuzzy green snout.

Mike's chest rose and fell.

38

The shower's spray beat against Tamara's chest, cascaded down her belly, between her thighs, and pooled around her feet. Its lukewarm salve stung the back of her blistered heels, even as it soothed her aching feet.

She bowed her head. Her long braids flowed waterfalls over her shoulders, releasing coconut and musk. Her entire life she had shielded her hair under shower caps, umbrellas, and plastic hoods, never lifting her face to the rain. Hard drops pelted her eyelids and the bridge of her nose. Parting her lips, she tasted chlorine and salt. The grime, sweat, and lies of the day swirled down the drain.

Lathering the soap, she breathed in cucumber and mowed grass. Her hands traced her face, eyes, mouth, the back of her neck, and followed her body's curves. She washed away the funeral, Dottie, and the house filled with mourners in floral dresses and wrinkled Sunday suits.

The water murmured like the boy's house had murmured. She leaned back and the shower whispered the hush that had accompanied the mother's arrival. She held her white, lathered arms under the spray and rinsed herself brown, washing her hands clean of refilled paper plates, pots scrubbed, and scraps discarded.

She had stayed in the kitchen with Dottie assisting in sating the deluge of hunger. Life was voracious in close proximity to death.

The mother's meal had been specially prepared and presented on bone white china. Fat was cut away, a scorched bun replaced, and bruised lettuce rejected. Tamara had wiped the edge of the plate with a linen napkin, and Dottie added an unblemished cherry tomato. *She won't eat any of it*, she said, *but she'll know we care.*

Tamara turned off the hot water and braced for the numbing cold. Ice rain pricked her fevered skin.

Unable to carry both the plate and iced tea, Dottie insisted she accompany her to the living room despite her protests. With the food cooling in hand, she lost her patience, *This day's about the woman in the other room. Whatever else, you set yourself aside.* Tamara followed her through the press of sorrowful faces and questioning eyes. Ice tinkling in the glass. She tried to count the number of dresses, the number of tissues, the number of chairs. Dottie's dress fluttered in the fans' breeze as she set the plate on the folding tray beside the pink chair. The boy's mother stared at the food, but didn't reach for it. *Thank you*, she said and looked up to Dottie, *Have you eaten, yet?*

Tamara bowed into the pounding water. It slammed against her back. Her skin and muscles contracted, arching from the shock. Water roared past her ears, but she could still hear the breath that caught in Dottie's throat, a cello's moan. She could see the shudder of her body trying to gulp it down.

The woman in the pink chair stood and wrapped her thin arms around Dottie's broad shoulders supporting the weight of unhinging, arthritic knees. Their dresses billowed in the cross-breeze of fans. Purple and blue. Tamara left the glass of iced tea melting on the front steps.

She turned off the tap. Water gurgled down the drain, churning with long, snaking strands of hair. As she stepped out of the shower, her skin goosebumped as the heat of the room rushed in.

She wiped the condensation from the mirror. Ragged lengths of braids roped her chest. Edie would be upset with her. She ran her fingertips down the sodden hair, feeling for the woven bridge of hers and someone else's. She trailed her fingers a few inches past, picked up the scissors, and cut. She laid the stranger's hair in the sink. Unbraiding the short tail, she inserted her comb's pick into the plait and gently tugged. The remaining hair slipped free. She brushed it from her hands. She picked up the scissors and cut another and another. Her face and eyes emerged. Patiently, she unwound the strands until she was done.

Her head felt lighter and her neck longer. She raised her chin and her cheekbones sharpened. She ran her hands over the short crop of her hair. Water trickled over her shoulders. She didn't feel the slightest urge to avert her eyes from the woman in the mirror. She was simply curious about who this woman was. She smiled, and the woman smiled back.

Dripping wet footprints across the gleaming hardwood floor, she went and sat at the piano and lifted the fallboard. Black and white. She touched the smooth keys with damp fingertips. Water droplets ran down her cheeks, neck, breasts, and spattered her thighs. She straightened her wrists, barely pressed her toes to the cold brass pedal, and rooted her bare sole to the wooden floor. She closed her eyes and breathed in lemon polish and cucumber skin.

The first notes announced themselves: Sonata No. 14 in C-sharp Minor, the "Moonlight" Sonata. She played the rolling triplet slowly, delicately, as Beethoven had noted, *Adagio sostenuto*. She swam into the formal harmonies washing together.

The current of deep overtones strengthened into each other. The sympathetic vibration of low bass strings churned in resonance. Her right hand lifted pure notes from her heartwood. She breathed in the empty bars of its measured, funereal march. Her right ear cocked to the clear, articulated notes falling into her chest. Driving deeper under her skin. The sombre notes drawing her sightless into its creator's grief. A lament awakened throughout the centuries to mourn the unspoken losses of Wilhelm Kempff's liquid blue eyes and Vladimir Horowitz's sixty years of exile. Bowed heads. Inward stares. Music that refused to cry. She wrapped herself in its grey textures, holding its exquisite hurt until the last dark notes of the first movement tolled. Black on white.

She sat in the space between. Eyes closed. Her tongue flicked against her lips. There was no hallelujah in this music. No coming home. She spread her long fingers and opened the chords, widening the piano's voices. She walked the keyboard, shifting the rhythm to a 6/8 shuffle, into the blues, into gospel. Her left hand strutted the rhythm. Her right hand balled into a syncopated fist pounding the roll. She pressed the pedal to the floor, her free foot stomping time. She was groaning and muttering, a song without words. Ancient sounds before time, before her.

She slapped at the keys, her wrists elastic. She laughed at the boogie roll barrelling up through the floorboards. Her nipples brushed against her forearms. Her wet bottom slid across the polished bench. Her hands flew as she hammered the rhythms of Reverend James Cleveland, Pinetop Perkins, Willie "the Lion" Smith, Margaret Allison, and Granny Nan. She boogied and she rolled.

The music led her back into the blues. Into the blues. Her hands slammed the keys and the gospel triad chord sang out. She played. Grunting and puffing. She played until her arms and fingers were stumbling. Pedal foot stuttering. Breasts clammy. The small of her back and forehead slick. The final notes coursed through her body and she laid her hands on the piano and held on as the vibration emptied the room.

She opened her eyes, saw her breasts, and instinctively covered herself with her arm. She checked the window, but the blinds were closed. Lowering her arm, she examined her body—dark areolas, nipples erect, small pudge belly, dark pubic hair, strong thighs, water pooling at her bare feet. This was her skin.

Gently, she lowered the fallboard. She didn't bother to wipe away the fingerprints. She padded across the floor. She picked up the phone.

Tender fingertips pressed the numbers. Black on white. She listened to the ring. Sweat evaporating on her hot skin.

"Bluebird Taxi, how can I help you?"

Between heartbeats, she hung up.

39

Zeus tugged Kate down the corridor. The evening shift change was under way on the eighth floor. At reception, nurses were huddled in their paperwork. In shaded rooms, suppertime news trickled from rented televisions relaying hurricane warnings.

She had managed a nap after shift, only to wake a few hours later panicked that there was somewhere she had to be. But she wasn't on duty until tomorrow night during the storm and had already prepped all she could at her place. Her fridge was stocked with beer, ice, and barbecue meat. She had candles, dog food, and chips. The propane tank was full. Her SAR and emergency kits were replenished. She had even managed a load of laundry. She was prepared, like she always was. Beyond that, it was her landlord's problem. She had called, but he hadn't trimmed the limbs or cleared the gutters. She'd never understand people who didn't worry, didn't act, and were truly shocked when their worlds caught fire, even though flames had been licking the walls for years.

Zeus strained on the leash and she slowed to bring him back in check. She should be sleeping or watching mindless TV. But if the hurricane hit, she'd be too busy in the ER to check on her mother and she still had to swing by her house to secure what she could. And if her brother was there? She would have to try again. Wouldn't she.

Or she could pretend she didn't see the flames. Walk away and wait for the collapse. His body would eventually fail without food and someone to enable him. Then he could be admitted as a medical emergency, something easier to understand. It was unlikely she was listed as next of kin. She didn't even know if Matthew had ID, or if he would ask for her. If it happened, she hoped she wouldn't be working that shift. Maybe the landlord was right. Let it burn and worry later. The thought curled her stomach.

Years ago, a social worker, who tried to help before moving on to someone who wanted help, said she'd seen Matthew at a Christmas dinner for the homeless. He used an assumed name. Ruth had called her, appalled that he had come home with new socks, mitts, and a bag of leftovers. *Why would he do that when he had a home? People would think she didn't feed him.* Flush with shame, she proceeded to inventory all she had done for him. It was a long list that culminated in the preparation of a second Christmas dinner replete with all the fixings. Ruth said he ate two helpings. It wasn't his fault, Kate reminded herself. It wasn't his fault. Though it felt like it was.

She dropped the lead and Zeus ran into Ruth's room. Country music was crooning. Her mother's favourite. Someone had brought in a radio. On the nightstand, the angel was facing the room again. There was a white carnation in a paper cup and a get-well-soon card signed "Mr. Poranek (Joe)." There were X's and O's.

The nasal prongs had been removed. She was breathing on her own. Kate checked the vitals monitor. Stats were holding in the normal range. Her mom's colour was good and her skin looked moisturizer-smooth. She smelled faintly of roses and jasmine.

She should have brought in one of her mother's steamy romances to read to her. She could replace the Aidens, Raifs, Luciens, and Coles with "Joe Poranek." Maybe that would get a rise. Zeus nudged Ruth's hand and his tongue flicked against her fingers. He studied her face and deemed her still sleeping. He squirrelled past Kate and out the door.

"Zeus!"

His ears shot back and he paused at the threshold of the room across the hall. He looked back and his head lowered. He knew what she wanted, but chose to disobey. He disappeared into the room of the One-Legged Man.

She ground back her anger. She would have to give him a hard correction and haul him out by the scruff. She despised cowing a dog. She hated the wounded look of hurt and betrayal, and the uncertainty and timidity right after. He could tear her throat open before she could raise a hand, but he wouldn't. He would submit and make her the punisher. She hated that most of all.

She stopped short at the door. The man, who had patted her arm while she was scrubbing gravel from his skin and told her not to worry, it didn't hurt, was sitting in the corner chair, and Zeus was standing before him. The man with one leg now had two. A prosthetic extended from the soft, bare flesh of his thigh. He was staring at the sneakers cladding his feet. One was laced tightly around a titanium rod. Zeus rested his chin on the man's stump. His eyes were patient and his ears relaxed. He had assumed his most supplicant posture. *See me.*

She was about to intervene, but couldn't think how, when the man's hand lifted and gently rested on Zeus's head. He looked into her dog's eyes and Zeus licked his chin with one flick. The man lowered his forehead to Zeus's soft brow and his body racked and sobbed. Smothered in flesh and steel, her dog didn't pull away from the constricting arms and fingers clutching his silken coat. He braced against the man's collapsing weight and allowed himself to be held too tight. He glanced to Kate, as though conveying that this was where he had to be, and it had to be okay for him to stay.

She backed out of the room and braced herself against the wall. The man's low moans shivered under her skin. It was a sound she had heard before in the aftermath of stunned, shattered silence. A sound only the heartbroken could vocalize. Once spent, the body even rationed tears more sparingly.

The hall was empty and darkening. The sun had fallen behind the buildings. She should wait until Zeus came back for her. She should stay in one place and wait to be found. But she was certain nobody was looking for her. No one knew she was lost. She bolted for her mother's room.

Ruth's eyes were closed and her lips parted. She was breathing in and out without a care in the world.

"Mom. Wake up." Kate nudged her shoulder. Ruth slept on peacefully. Kate rocked her harder. "Wake up." Ruth's shoulders jostled and her head bobbed. She knew her mother could hear her. She hissed, "You don't get to sleep through this." She dropped her closed fist hard on her mother's chest and rubbed her knuckles over her sternum. "Wake up!"

She wanted to see pain. She wanted her to cry out, or open her eyes in shock, or slap her daughter's face. She wanted her to scream and yell. She wanted to see tears ravage her face. She wanted her to apologize for leaving her alone. She wanted her to say "I'm sorry for forgetting you. I'm sorry, I thought you could find your own way back." She wanted her to beg forgiveness: "I'm sorry, I'm sorry, but he needed me more."

Her lungs heaved. She wanted to join in the One-Legged Man's ragged chorus. But her eyes were dry. And her vocal chords silent.

Ruth breathed in and out. Kate took her mother's hand in hers. It was warm and unresponsive. Her fingers were the same length as hers. She placed it against her cheek to feel its touch. She straightened the puckered nightgown, then lingered over her rising-falling chest and the soothing beat of her unperturbed heart. She laid her mother's hand on her chest, palm to heart, so she could feel it, too.

"It's okay, Mom," she said, her voice raw. She brushed Ruth's bangs over her forehead the way she liked them. "You don't have to say anything."

40

Mike leaned back in his seat. He felt good. He felt friggin' awesome. Every muscle was cocooned in liquid warmth. Cars and taxis streaked past, tailing light, and the street lamps radiated glowing haloes diamonded white with moths. The police radio sputtered and chirped. He loved his job, he loved his wife, he loved his baby boys—he loved his life. He breathed in deep. There wasn't any pain. All life's despair and hurt had dissolved, its frenzy reduced to millisecond frames. He could see it all.

He understood how everything fit together: the lumbering moon, the street's lights, the mosquitoes caught in their beam, the garbage bags in the street, the graffitied walls, the kids, good kids, hanging out on a summer night, the white cat slinking across the road, the reflections shining in the hood of his car, the scar on his ring finger where the screwdriver slipped, and his wedding ring, golden, the bottle of pills in his hand, small and round, glowing redemption-bright . . .

There hadn't been any calls since eleven. The city was dreaming itself whole again and he was part of the dream. Before long, he'd be home in his own bed beside his wife. Lori. Her name shone. Lori who slept with her hand on his heart to feel it beat. He placed his hand over his vest and felt the surge of heat emanating from within. The pulse in his fingertips thrummed. This, he thought, is love.

The car radio squawked. Car 322. Check.

A voice. Watching over him. Watching over all of them. It wasn't Tamara's voice, but he knew she was working tonight. She was part of all this. He didn't know Tamara's last name. But he loved her, too. He hated when they installed GPS on the cars to monitor every time he took a piss. But now he was grateful not to be alone. So, so thankful that someone was keeping watch over him to bring him home. Home . . .

Car 322. Check.

He reached for his mic but grabbed air, which made him laugh. His finger groped for the Talk button. He pressed his lips to the handset. "Car 322. Ten-two. Good check."

He waited for more. It would be nice to talk. Leaning back in the seat, he miscalculated the distance of his hand to the mic's cradle. The handset plopped to the floor. The twist and spin of coiled cord unravelled in slowing, perfect orbits. The window, open a crack, spilled the sweet fragrance of night bloom and warm asphalt.

He, too, was part of all this good. Absently, he rubbed the itch under his vest and the pill bottle dropped from his hand.

41

"911. What is your emergency?"

Tamara glanced over her monitors to Greg, who had snagged the only call in over an hour. His head was bent low and his hands were cupped to his earpiece. She and the other call-takers watched a partial address scroll across their monitors. The entry stalled and deleted. It was a non-emerg. The room relaxed back into their books, snacks, and crossword puzzles.

It was almost midnight. By shift's end, she would have been up for over thirty hours. If her supervisor knew, she'd be reprimanded, maybe even suspended, rightfully so. She had broken the codes of conduct and risked her career to follow a call to the end of its story. But she already knew all tragedies ended the same.

From here on, she was satisfied knowing only the beginnings. That was her job. Stop mid-chapter. Maybe not even that far. A paragraph. Or perhaps nothing more than a single line of a life. That would have to be enough. They weren't her stories.

It was one mistake in her entire career. She wouldn't let it happen again. Only Hassan knew the truth, and she had walked out on him mid-sentence. The end. Her hand trembled slightly and she steadied it on her console.

She fought a yawn and sipped her energy-inducing drink. In a few seconds, the caffeine would tremor her heart to stay alert. Waiting for its surge, she practised Mozart's "Rondo alla Turca" in her head, but kept tripping over the prancing notes. She was so tired. Just a few more hours and this week would be over. She focused on the map and the locations of squad cars standing by. Most were parked in their hiding nooks.

Her fingertips brushed the short, tight crop of curl at the nape of her neck. The entire room had turned when she arrived for shift. Their sharp eyes had assessed her as an intruder before softening to surprised recognition and widening smiles. Greg gave her the thumbs-up. Colleen said she looked powerful. During breaks, everyone stopped by her station for a better look. Beautiful, they said. She adjusted her headset, noticing it didn't snag and tug. Her family of co-workers said *she* was beautiful. Her heart jittered and she braced for the caffeine's quickening. Her fingertips tingled.

She had used another cab company to get to work. It was an old car and an old driver, who talked on his phone the entire trip. He took left turns and didn't slow crossing the bridge. She kept her eyes open the entire way. That was her penance. White-knuckling the safety grip, she thought her heart might stop, but to her surprise she survived and arrived at work twenty minutes early. En route, she saw several Bluebird taxis, but none were his.

The police car icons pulsed. She zeroed in on car 322's location. She would like to tell Mike about her day. He would understand. Maybe it would help him, too. But that would be another breach of boundaries. Her job was here. His job was there. All the life between had to remain unspoken.

"Car 245. Check." She looked over her cubicle to Colleen, manning dispatch, calling in routine checks to her officers every forty-five minutes. She recognized the car number and imagined Constable Wade putting down her coffee and reaching for the handset. She located car 245 on her monitor. It was parked at the point overlooking the harbour. Her preferred waiting spot.

Constable Wade had a puppy now. A rescue. She had brought it into IES for a socialization visit. Tucked inside her protective vest, it was a fluff of brown fur, pink tongue, black nose and eyes. More teddy bear than dog, its body still growing into its tail. For fifteen minutes, the call-takers had tittered and cooed over the skittering fluff bumping into feet, careening willy-nilly. The pup had made Tamara nervous in its wild abandon. When it chewed on her braids, she had swiftly handed it back. But she didn't have expensive braids to ruin now. If Raylene brought the pup by again, she'd ask to hold it. This time, she'd let it lick her ears and marvel at its squirm and pulse between her palms.

Colleen had returned to reading her novel. Tamara gazed at the constellation of pulsing lights dotting the city map. She would like to call them all just to hear their chorus. *Good check, good check, good check.* Constable Wade would be leaning back now, maybe stretching her legs. Her feet would be hot in heavy boots and her coffee cold. She would be worrying about her pup being left too long in its overnight crate. This was Tamara's family and it was enough.

"911. What is your emergency?" Wendy had caught the call. Karl, who was manning fire dispatch, sat up straighter. These were the hours of smouldering cigarettes, forgotten cooking oil and candles.

"Hello, Robert," Wendy said.

Her colleagues high-fived the air. Tamara hoisted her cup, counting herself among the winners. Robert wasn't her concern. From here on in, she would keep the phone between her and them. She had a good job and a good, ordered life. For the first time in days, she was hungry. She thought about Dottie's homemade strawberry jam and wished she had licked the knife. She'd like to see her again. Maybe that would be okay if it was a chance meeting at Edie's. Or if she happened to be strolling through the Square, Dottie might wave and invite her in and they could sit at the kitchen table and wait for the kettle to boil. She'd like her to see her new hair.

Taking another sip of her sickly-sweet drink, she wondered if Hassan was working tonight.

42

Hassan circled back for another run past Liquor Corner. He should go home. He didn't need the fares or someone throwing up in the back seat. And he certainly didn't want to see strangers groping each other, or worse, but he turned left for one more pass.

He knew cabbies afraid to work nights and understood their fear. There had been robberies, stabbings, beatings, and last winter, a cabbie was murdered for twenty-five dollars. He had been working double shifts to send money home to his wife and two children. The judge asked, Why? But, there wasn't an answer.

He'd had his own share of skipped fares—young men and women bolting at red lights, tales of lost or forgotten wallets, offers of services in lieu of cash, both male and female—but mostly, he was invisible to his passengers. A silent ferryman hired to carry them through the darkness, no questions asked.

He preferred the anonymity of night, when the passengers became greater than their ordinary reality. Bigger spenders. Bigger talkers. Beautiful people preening, dancing, seducing. Laughing away their crappy jobs, bills, and relationships in drug- and alcohol-induced hazes. Chasing one shining moment to sustain them through the dull, grinding week. He admired their recklessness, denial, and optimism. But they tipped poorly and when they left he had to drive several blocks with the windows down to dispel the sour, sweet smell of alcohol and hope.

Sometimes, he picked up angry, hateful fares. Men whose courage increased in groups of three, who talked bitingly about immigrants and stared at the back of his head. He pretended he didn't understand and took extra-sharp turns, and braked abruptly, until their nausea silenced them.

Once, he'd had a knife held to his throat, but refused to hand over the forty-three dollars in his pocket. *No*, he had said. Simply *no*. He said it quietly and untroubled, as if declining a free sample at the grocery store. He wasn't afraid. He was ready. Maybe even hopeful. But the young man lost his nerve and ran.

One more pass and he'd head away from the downtown core to the residential streets and look for stragglers. If he passed a house with lights on, he'd slow to admire the art and paint choices on the walls. Sometimes he glimpsed young mothers pacing, or heads silhouetted in a television's pulsing blue, or the red burn of a cigarette end illuminating a face on the porch. Others like him, unable to sleep, who knew the heavy waiting of night.

Up ahead the light turned red and he coasted to a stop on the empty street. Some nights if he was lucky, he'd see the flash of a cat's eyes reflecting golden-green or a streak of fur and tail blazing his headlights. He loved the unexpected wild. Raccoons, skunks, even rats—he'd pull over to watch. He'd seen deer grazing on manicured lawns. Their heads lifting in unison, ears stiff and necks regal, gauging whether they had been detected. An imperceptible flick deciding for all it was time to leap. Gone, in a white-tail flash. And once, returning from an airport run, he saw a coyote dragging the hind leg of a deer clamped in its jaws. In all his travels, he had only seen the speed bumps of porcupines' crumpled remains. He would like to see one alive.

The light turned green and he eased through the intersection. He swung past Liquor Corner. The buses had stopped running and the bars were shutting down. The lucky or unlucky had paired up. He should pull over to save fuel or get out to stretch his legs. He should go home. He looked down the hill to the shimmering harbour and sharp-edged moon and made another left up the hill for one more pass. These were the hardest, loneliest hours.

These hours led to the bridge. He knew the best spot. He knew where the cameras were, and how long it would take bridge security to notice a cab parked mid-span and a man at the rails. For the past few months, he had been calculating the rate at which the prevention barriers were being erected. In another few weeks, he would lose his chance to atone. Twenty years of crossings, and he hadn't yet found the courage to jump. It was his punishment to want to live.

He had considered stopping during supper rush hour, when traffic was gnarled. He'd casually step out of the cab, shut the door, and leave the cab running so it could be easily moved. He'd walk without hesitation to the railing. He was much braver in his fictional guise. Cars would veer around his abandoned vehicle, assuming it had stalled. Horns would honk. A woman in a minivan would adjust her radio. A child would yawn. An old man would blink. And he, the man at the railing, would be gone.

He didn't imagine the moment after that, or the moment after that. His thoughts always stayed on the bridge. He worried about the commuters trying to get home to their families, cats, and dogs. Good people thinking about supper, a cold beer, a glass of wine, or checking their lottery tickets. Because of him, they would be delayed for hours. And what if someone tried to stop him? What then? No, he would never chance the daytime for fear of someone saying something kind to him. That would be the end of his resolve.

Night was best. But still, someone would eventually see. The police or coast guard or paramedics or some poor soul looking out their office window or walking their dog . . . No, he couldn't give someone else his sorrow. Instead, he spent his tips on tolls, waiting for an attendant to look up and wish him a good night so he could go home.

Lately, he'd stopped making those crossings. Ever since he started driving Tamara. Tamara of no left turns who was afraid of bridges and smelled of coconut oil and spoke his name like a whisper. Tamara who gave him a book, and asked him to accompany her to hair appointments and funerals, and relied on him to pick her up and drop her off at work. But tonight, she hadn't called.

He was prepared for that likelihood. Nonetheless, he had shaved and donned a new white shirt. He changed the water, put fresh flowers in the dashboard vase, and vacuumed the back seat. Three times he checked with dispatch to confirm he hadn't missed her call. Beside him, on the passenger seat, was a book of poetry he wanted her to have, even if it meant goodbye. It wouldn't take her long to read.

It was a small, thin book with a dust-red jacket and bone-white letters. His name in small print under hers, *Translation by . . .* , the letters thick with guilt. It took five years to coax the English from the Arabic. Another four years to save the money to self-publish it. He agonized for months whether or not to format it back to front in Arabic or front to back in English, and finally arranged the poems to work from either approach. He placed his confession in the foreword and waited for the police to arrive. But they never came.

Hassan signalled left again and headed down the hill for one more pass. Here, nobody cared about poems. The local bookstore sold a single copy. A one-paragraph review surfaced in an obscure journal extolling its "raw fire and language as delicate and exquisite as a sparrow's bones." The reviewer misspelled her name and his wasn't mentioned. He left the books at bus stops, coffee shops, and in grocery carts hoping they would be found. In the glove compartment was the last copy. If Tamara had called, he would have given it to her. She might have understood what he was trying to say.

On the sidewalk were two young men. They were wearing varsity T-shirts and had the physiques of athletes. Holding each other upright, they staggeringly hailed his cab. One man stumbled and was caught by his friend. Regaining his feet, he kissed him sloppily on the lips. His friend gently disengaged, guided him into the back seat. Hassan's nose crinkled at the stench of cheap cologne and beer. The address was outside the city. His friend passed Hassan too much money but refused the change. "Just get him home safe."

"I love you," the man in the back seat slurred.

"Yeah, yeah," his friend said. "Love you too, man. Fasten your seatbelt." He proceeded to buckle him in, checking that the strap wasn't too tight. He tapped the cab roof to send them off. The passenger rested his temple against the cool window.

"I love him," he mumbled.

In his side mirror, Hassan saw his friend wipe his mouth. He looked in the rear-view. His passenger's eyes were already closed. He took the right turn gently so the man's head hardly bobbed.

He rolled down his window and the hot night rushed in. In the dashboard vase, the wisp of wisteria nodded. Its dreamtime scent lightly blanketed the cab.

She could still call.

43

Kate had only intended to lash down the trash cans and make sure the windows were closed. But when she checked the perimeter of her mother's house she found rotting garbage that hadn't been put to the curb in months. Tomorrow morning was the last pickup before the storm. She looked up at Matthew's window. The house was dark. She hoped he wasn't there. Maybe she could empty the fridge, check the trash cans, and head straight home.

She approached with caution. She didn't reach for the light, feeling safer in the cover of darkness. She waited at the threshold while Zeus searched the lower level. Her eyes slowly adjusted. The outline of wings appeared first, followed by the hulking grey-blue-blacks of furniture carved from moonlit shadows. She traced the deep ink of Zeus's body by the clatter of his nails and huffs of breath at the cubbyhole, into the kitchen, and around. She was relieved when his soft snout nuzzled her hand.

She followed him up the stairs and waited on the landing while his nostrils flared at Matthew's open door. All clear. "Good boy." Her voice sounded husky and pricked from the effort and her body sagged from the day's weight. Moonlight raked the sour, soiled mattress. On the floor were his sneakers, broken-backed and abandoned. Their aloneness made the bruise over her heart ache.

Down the hall, Zeus scratched furiously at her childhood bedroom door. Dread tensed her body and her hands curled into fists. But Zeus wasn't barking. He wasn't indicating "live" or "danger." He was spinning and prancing, "happy" and "play."

The Stay Out sign had long been removed, but layers of yellowed cellophane tape remained. She looked down to the glimmer of Zeus's eyes. He was watching her. She could hear the swish of his tail. She opened the door that she had kept closed most of her life. With the flick of the light switch, she was seventeen again.

Zeus bounded in, following his nose over the shag rug, bookcase, books, and back to the floor. He gave a cursory swipe of the desk, breezed past the dresser to the single neatly made bed with its lime-green comforter, and leapt up. He burrowed his head into the pillow, flipped his snout under the sheets, and rummaged the covers, before rolling upright. Tail waving, he barked loud and deep. He had found *her*.

When she moved out, she didn't take anything with her, and Ruth wouldn't let her discard it. She insisted it was worth good money at the flea market and would sell it all. But there was the second-hand dresser she had painted purple with yellow polka dots and its cloudy, tarnished mirror. Tucked in the frame were the curled photographs of long-gone dogs, concert stubs, and photo-booth strips of a boy she thought she loved.

She pulled open the dresser drawer and Zeus's nose poked up over the edge. Rainbow-hued cotton panties and a training bra were neatly folded. She nudged aside the underwear and lavender satchel still blooming a faint perfume and exposed a single cherry-scented condom. She shut the drawer and slid open the closet. The roller mechanism stuttered. Zeus squirrelled his head between the jean jackets, ripped jeans, and grungy shirts. The clothes smelled freshly laundered. Zeus sneezed. She noticed the bookcase was dusted, the table polished, and the floor vacuumed.

"Come," she said. Her stride said *now*. His tail drooped.

She didn't check the back of the door to see if the chalkboard was still there where Matthew wrote the opening lines of books he thought she should read. She switched off the light and shut the door.

She groped for the hallway light and blinked back the bare bulb's glare. Zeus stared up at her, but she didn't look at him. From the landing, she could see the blinding white of satin gowns, synthetic curls, and praying hands. She wanted one, just one, to move its wings.

When she realized she wasn't rooted there in exhaustion, but was truly waiting, truly wishing, a voice in her head said, *Enough.*

Zeus trailed close behind as she made another trip from the house to the street. She paused to swipe a mosquito from her arm, and hot blood smeared. The wheelbarrow tilted and she wrestled it level, but not before several angels toppled to the ground. Zeus shot forward to herd them back.

This was the last load. When she reached down to pick up the fallen angels, her legs throbbed. Eighteen loads, not including the regular garbage, and another hour securing the yard's lawn chairs, buckets, and debris. She grabbed the angels by their useless wings and tossed them back on the wheelbarrow. She would have burned the lot if not for the fire ban.

If her mother ever came back, maybe she'd be grateful for the space. Maybe she'd thank her for doing what she couldn't do herself because she didn't know how to start. Or maybe she wouldn't even remember that she had ever needed angels. She'd benignly walk in the house and the sun would be shining and she would just feel like she was home. Kate almost laughed at the ridiculousness of her hope. Even now, she wanted a happy ending. Or at least an ending that was merciful, no matter how tragic.

Zeus raced ahead to the end of the driveway, circling and sniffing the splayed wings, hooped skirts, and indignant eyes heaped at the curb. She looked down the street at the sleeping houses and their tidy garbage piles. In the morning, the neighbours would wake to the debris of her family's lives. So be it. She would take the wrath. She dumped the final load.

A tumble of plastic, polyester, porcelain, and chicken feathers sprawled at her feet. Some landed face down. A few clutched each other in awkward embrace. Others were on their backs and levitating on the tips of gosling wings, their rigid arms raised to the moon. Even fallen, their angel smiles were beatific and forgiving. She hadn't asked for their forgiveness. *They* should be begging for *hers*. Her mother's angels hadn't kept anyone safe.

She kicked at one and it flipped over. Zeus gingerly stepped into the pile and nosed the angel's cheek. It rocked on its back. He whined and looked up at Kate.

"Leave it," she said.

He nudged it again and licked its eyes. He slapped his paws against its hooped gown and play-bowed, huffing a low woof.

"They're not real." She nudged another with her toe as proof. Zeus scrambled over the pile, stepping on wings and gossamer chests, and squirmed between her and the angel. He didn't want her to hurt it. Barking sharply, he burrowed his nose under its dress.

"No," she said.

He woofed again. She had trained him to insist. He pawed the silken gown. His claws caught the stand and the angel lifted a few inches before flopping down. He jumped back, barking wildly. It was a game.

She crouched down and tried to see what he saw. Miniature people, eyes open, reaching for him. Zeus stared intently at her, shifting his gaze slightly to the dolls and back to her, willing her to do something. She pressed on a stand and an angel rose upright. Its feathered wings glowed in the moon's light. Zeus's ears lifted and he spun in circles. He pawed another.

"They're not alive," she whispered. He licked her cheek.

Play, he barked forcefully in her face. *Play*. He bowed, luring her back to him and now.

"Okay," she said. "I understand." Her eyes glistened, but her smile was true. "This one?"

Zeus backed up, anticipating another miracle.

44

Mike woke to a rap on the window and the hiss and cackle of the radio. His head lurched and his neck cricked. The stark street light bored into the back of his eyes. He was in his squad car. He turned to the tapping and saw a police officer's vest. Knuckles rapped again. The badge said Wade. The officer leaned in, a woman. He searched the gauze of his brain for her name. *Raylene.* He rolled down the window.

"Hey," she said, studying his face.

"Hey," croaked Mike. His tongue and lips were sticky with dried saliva.

"You didn't respond to checks."

He looked to the dash: 1:14 a.m. A thin, mechanical voice broadcast from his radio. Car 322. Ten-one, copy.

"Shit." He scratched the palm of his hand, which made his legs and the nape of his neck itch more. He glanced down at his lap. The pill bottle wasn't there. Pain knifed his back and he gripped the steering wheel.

"You okay?"

"It's my back. I got banged up on a call." They both knew that wasn't what was asked. The pill bottle was near the brake pedal. He nudged it under the seat with the heel of his boot. His skin was crawling.

"Jeezus." He wiped the sleep and grogginess from his face. *Why was she still standing there?*

"You should check in."

"Yeah." He fumbled for the dangling handset. "Car 322. Ten-two, good check."

Ten-four, copy that. The dispatcher's voice sounded unconcerned. It was no big deal. But Raylene didn't take a step back.

"I hate the sit-and-wait shifts," she said. "I'd rather be moving."

He heard she had aced high-speed driving. She leaned against his roof and casually took in the view of the street. "You think there's going to be payback?"

Her naivety irritated him. "There always is."

"Maybe this time could be different." She sounded wistful and adjusted her hat, revealing the welt of her hatband. He took inventory. She was young, but the corners of her eyes and forehead were creased. Her hair was shorn short and she held her mouth tight. Her vest seemed a size too large for her small frame. She wasn't wearing a ring.

"How's your night been?" He didn't really care, but wanted her on his side. Using the steering wheel to cover the strain, he leveraged himself straighter. *Go away.*

"Same old shit," she said. "Couple of traffic stops."

"I saw a photo on your locker. New dog?" He hoped his voice sounded engaged. Her face lit up. She was quite beautiful when she smiled.

"Yeah, a rescue. Four months. A real sweetie. Wants to be snuggled all the time."

Mike tried but failed to muster any interest in his eyes. He wanted to scratch his thighs.

Raylene's face cloaked back to neutral. "She's a dog, what can I say."

He searched for something to win her back. "Lucky it found you." The words sounded poorly rehearsed. He tried a smile.

She stiffened in her uniform. "I should get back. Paperwork." But she didn't leave. She rested her hand on the roof of his car. "You know, if they ask, you can tell them you were stretching your legs and the volume was down, or you were having a dump and left your radio in the car." Her voice dropped lower, adopting the vernacular of one of the boys. "I didn't see anything."

He avoided her eyes. "Thanks." He might have read her wrong. She was a decent cop, his sister in blue. His radio sputtered. Raylene turned up her walkie.

Ten—thirty. Proceed with caution. Reports of male Caucasian on the road. Six foot, thin, possible mentally unstable. Last seen vicinity of . . .

Raylene hitched up her pants and tilted her chin to the handset clipped to her collar. "Ten-four. Car 245 responding." Still, she didn't leave.

Mike's back quivered from the upright strain. His cheek twitched.

She glanced down to the floorboard and then looked directly at him. "Take it easy on the meds." *Consider this your warning* was understood.

He watched her walk to her cruiser. From behind she looked

like a small man. Too small for anyone to take seriously. She U-turned, squealing tires, her lights already flashing. Mike waved his best *Good seeing ya, bud*, as she coasted past.

Bitch. He was ten years her senior, who the hell was she to reprimand him. He clawed at his thighs until skin scraped under the fabric. The radio fired again.

Ten—sixty—nine. Report of suspicious behaviour. Cutting through backyards. Lone male, race unknown, dark hoodie. Approach with caution. Last seen corner of . . .

Mike looked to the end of the road. He was two blocks away. He knew this call would come. Earlier in the night, he'd seen packs of kids roaming the streets. When he drove by, they watched his car with hard, defiant stares and thrust their hands deep in their pockets. When he asked them what they were doing and where they were going, the alphas growled back, *Nothin'* and *Nowhere*. Lies.

Something big was coming. The entire city was on edge. Overtime had been authorized, extra cars were on the streets, journalists were rabid, politicians were covering their asses. There had been an anti-violence/antipoverty/anti-racism "Take Back the Street" march and a "Justice for Devon" vigil. Homemade signs and uplifting songs demanded peace, love, and equality. The only casualties had been from sunburn and heatstroke. But if the scorching weather continued, it was only a matter of time before the city lit itself on fire.

Mike radioed back. "Ten-seventeen. Car 322 en route." He revved the engine and a shock of hurt shuddered up his spine. He fished the pills out from under his seat. One more and this damn shift would be over. His head was throbbing. He wished the storm's rains would hurry up and wash away the suffocating heat. Criminals didn't like getting wet. The pill passed his lips, bitter and gagging.

He dropped the car into gear. He didn't switch on his red-and-blues. Only a newbie would give up the element of surprise. Easing forward, he plotted his grid search. He just had to get through the next few hours and then he'd have three days off.

They could kill each other then.

45

Kate was too exhausted to drive. She needed a few hours' sleep so she could get turned around for night shift. Zeus brushed past, leading the way down the hallway, past her brother's room. There was nothing wrong with her old bed. A few hours, that's all she needed. She switched on the bedside lamp. The shade illuminated blue-and-purple butterflies.

She sat heavily on the low single mattress with *Katie* written in marker on the headboard. Her fingers trailed over the nubs of the lime-green chenille bedspread. It was a good bed. It'd be fine. Zeus jostled in beside her. The sheets smelled of sunshine and fabric softener. She smelled sweaty and sour and her arms were streaked with grime. She kicked off her boots and socks. She was the dirtiest thing in the room.

She reached between the headboard rails and hoisted the wood-framed window. It jammed halfway. The night's warmth blanketed her. She could see stars. Affixed to the back of the door, the chalkboard was swirled white with dust. Her shoulders relaxed and she tugged the ponytail elastic from her oily hair. Her scalp hurt.

The side table's drawer was crammed with teenage treasures: stir sticks, beer labels peeled off whole, bottle caps, chipped lighters, special rocks, crumbles of dried roses, and a cheap heart-shaped necklace from a boy whose name she couldn't remember.

She extracted a brittle photograph tucked in the back. It had been returned along with her father's personal belongings: a watch, an empty wallet, and a winning harness-racing stub with a payout of twenty-to-one. Fifteen years after he left them and three thousand miles away, he had a heart attack. Upon hearing the news, her mother fell to her knees and wept. Being listed as next of kin was some kind of proof for her. Kate ran her finger along the photograph's worn edge.

He was young and she was diaper-clad in his arms. A paper crease crackled between them. His shirt was off and he had a tattoo of her mother on his bicep that Ruth said didn't look like her. Too manly and the eyes were crossed. The station wagon's hood was up and there was a stubby beer on the fender. He was smiling at the photographer, presumably her mother. She, baby Katie, was looking at his face. Her infant hand on his cheek. She looked like she loved him.

She slipped the photo back in the drawer's hiding spot and retrieved a tin cigarette box. Inside was a decent roach. Some things were worth saving. Dry weed flared and she inhaled deep. Lying back into the snug of the bed, she held her breath until her lungs burned.

Zeus laid his head across her belly as the sweet, sweet smell of forgetting enveloped her.

46

"911. What is your emergency?"

The IES monitors were lighting up. Tamara scanned the incident summaries scrolling down her screen. Greg was in the midst of an MVA on a secondary highway. Single vehicle, three occupants, multiple injuries. Medevac en route, three cars dispatched. She glanced over at Karl manning fire. There was a two-alarm in the industrial park. His fingers blurred the keyboard. Chemicals on-site. A list of hazardous materials stuttered across her screen.

She checked her main monitor and sourced car 322. Mike was grid-searching his area for the third time. She located car 245. Constable Wade had gone as far as the highway leading out of the city. Almost an hour had passed without further sightings for either call. They wouldn't find them now.

Despite her resolve to not get personally involved, she couldn't shake her irritation with Mike. He had missed checks and was twenty minutes overdue when Colleen began relaying his car number every five minutes. After three attempts, she switched to a secure channel to request a personal check. Another four and a half minutes passed before they heard `Good check.` Tamara had asked, "What did he say?"

"Nothing."

There could be numerous reasons why he hadn't responded: his radio was turned down, he'd stepped out of the vehicle to talk to someone, or maybe he was on a 10-100 break. He didn't owe them an explanation, but it was a courtesy to acknowledge their worry and vigilance. It was the decent thing to do.

She knew he was going through rough times. There were rumours he was going to be reviewed because of the domestic call, and a civilian had filed a complaint about him Tasering her son. Other officers said it was clean, but they were his family—the thin blue line. Mike had to get his act together. If he could crack, anybody could.

"911. What is your emergency?"

She focused on the voice. Male. Caucasian. A strained voice, but he was trying to sound calm. Middle-aged. Sirens could be heard in the distance. A female hollered in the background, *I see a fire truck.*

The male circled around the whos, whats, whens. He had heard a bang and could see emergency lights down the road. The female interjected, *Ask what's going on!*

Tamara checked her screen. The call was originating a half-mile from the crash site.

"We are aware of the situation. Emergency personnel are on the scene." The man relayed the information to the woman. The female said, *Give me the phone.*

Tamara pushed back her earpiece. The woman's voice was managerial. A woman who expected answers. She spoke rapidly, swallowing her consonants. "This is the fourth accident in the past three months. I've called about this road and nobody does a damn thing."

"What's your name, ma'am?" Distract and divert.

"Why do you want my name?"

She scanned the screen—with the click of a key she had the address and residents' names. There were multiple complaint calls from this number. Excessive speeding, tires squealing, littering . . . She could hear the thrum of the life chopper disrupting the line.

The woman was shouting over the helicopter. "They tear up and down all hours of the day and night . . ."

Tamara read the first responders' reports streaming across her screen. One female ejected, multiple fractures. One male, amputation. One male, head injuries. Ages estimated fifteen to eighteen. Distance to nearest ER, twenty-three miles. Pagers would be going off and ORs prepped. ETA of air medevac, one minute. She didn't allow herself to imagine the crash site.

"Emergency personnel have the situation under control, ma'am." She binned the call to non-emerg. "Thank you for your call."

The woman's voice garbled. Tamara caught the gist of "screw you" before the line went dead. She took a sip of her energy drink and laid her hand on her thigh to still its jittering bounce. Four hours, two minutes to shift end. She had her day planned:

1. Sleep and wake without alarms
2. Cancel grocery delivery
3. Walk to the market
4. Buy book
5. Bath

She was most excited about the bath. Now that she didn't have to worry about her hair, she could dunk her head and allow herself to float. Maybe she'd pour a glass of wine, light a candle, and read her new book. That would be a good day. Though she wasn't sure how she would keep the pages dry.

She visualized herself in each scenario, confident and unafraid, though she had to keep adjusting the image to reflect her short hair: Tamara with Short Hair selecting the ripest tomatoes and basil; Tamara with Short Hair laughing with cashiers and bookstore clerks; Tamara with Short Hair in her most flattering summer dress. Tamara with Short Hair bringing Dottie a loaf of bakery bread and being invited in for homemade jam. Tamara with Short Hair strolling up to Hassan's taxi and Hassan looking up from his book and seeing her, and the delight of recognition in his eyes, and her—

Car 245. Ten-sixteen. No sighting of a male fitting the description in this vicinity.

Tamara positioned her mic closer to her lips. "Ten-four, copy that. There have been no further reports."

Ten-four.

Soon Constable Wade would be home. She said she was worried the high winds might frighten the pup, so she was taking the night off to be with it.

Tamara re-evaluated her list. She had forgotten about the storm. Not a storm, a hurricane. She should pick up earplugs and another bottle of wine to help her sleep.

She enlarged the north quadrant of the map. Car 322 was repeating a fourth grid check of the area.

Let it go, she wanted to tell him. Some things aren't meant to be.

47

Mike's spotlight spilled long shadows over the dumpsters and up the walls. It was his fourth pass of this quadrant. The suspect was likely long gone. He pulled up alongside the school and shut off the engine. He shifted in his seat, and a dull ache clenched his side. One pill hadn't cut it, but he couldn't risk taking another. Lori would be awake when he got home.

On the off chance the storm made landfall, his morning would be lost storing lawn furniture, tying down garbage cans, and picking up kids' toys. Caleb would be underfoot wanting to help, and then he'd have to take Lori for groceries, bottled water, batteries, candles, and non-perishable food. And the propane tank would need filling, and gas in the van, and cash from the bank, and he should probably clean out the gutters—up to a hundred millimetres of rain were expected. The thought of putting away the barbecue, chairs, and table, let alone climbing the ladder, made his back flinch. He might get a few hours to sleep late afternoon.

But by nightfall he'd have to chat about hurricanes and safety procedures, and Caleb would want to crawl in bed with them. Which would be fine, except for his incessant questions: What if the roof tears off? Or the windows blow in? Or trees fall on the house? Which would lead to worries about where do the birds go and what if a dog was outside and do trees hurt if their branches break. Three bedtime stories later would come the nightmares and bedwetting. Tomorrow was going to be another hell day. Or was tomorrow technically already today?

He flicked on the interior light and checked the pills. There were enough to get him through another day. It wouldn't be enough. He leaned back and scanned the deserted street leading to the Square. He noted the black sash cords tied around the poles. He didn't know what it signified and made a mental note to inquire. Gazing absently at the school's graffiti-smeared walls, he could only decipher the tag *Nothing is OK*. You got that right, he thought.

Beyond the school, welding flashes sparked on the bridge. The night crews were working. The barriers couldn't go up fast enough for him. He checked his watch: 2:35 a.m. The Waiting Hours were under way. He could go back to base but didn't have any paperwork and he wasn't up to faking the required small talk. He yawned. He should have grabbed a coffee earlier. He reached for the handset clipped to his vest.

"Ten-two. Car 322 checking in." He bowed his forehead to the steering wheel and gingerly stretched his shoulders.

A voice responded immediately. Ten–one. Good check.

The voice was neutral. Impersonal. He should apologize for missing checks earlier, but it would mean another lie and he was tired of lying. His back muscles jerked. Groaning, he pushed himself upright. Thirty-eight years old. What would his body be like in another ten years?

At the corner of the school, he saw movement. A male. Hoodie. Hands in pockets. Hugging the wall to avoid the lights. Age unknown.

The suspect's head was down. He hadn't seen the cruiser. The suspect looked over his shoulder. He was jumpy.

Mike exhaled and reached for his flashlight. His other hand was on the door handle. His timing had to be perfect. Fifty feet. Forty. Thirty. Twenty. Mike flashed the red-and-blues and stepped out of the car.

"Police. Don't move." His voice was crimped with pain and sounded more aggressive than he intended. The blinding glare of his flashlight pinned the suspect in the night. The male didn't look up. Mike braced himself against the doorframe.

"We've had a report of suspicious behaviour, someone cutting through backyards. Would that be you?" The male had nothing on him to indicate a B&E. He shone the light on his face, but the hoodie cast dark shadows. He estimated the male to be 100-110 lbs, 5'5". He was wearing long shorts, white lace-less sneakers. Black legs.

"Take your hands slowly from your pockets and remove your hoodie from your face." The male didn't respond.

Mike wondered if the suspect was high. "Take your hands slowly from your pockets." It wasn't a debate. He ran the light down the man's chest to the pouch pocket. There was a lump. He unlatched his holster, frighteningly aware of how exposed he was and that he hadn't called for backup.

"Remove your hands from your pockets!"

The male didn't budge. Mike leaned into his handset. He was sweating. "Car 322. Ten-seventy-six, requesting assistance. Eyes on possible suspect. Uncooperative."

The male's arms moved. He was sliding his hands from his pockets. Mike's hand went to his weapon.

"Slowly!" He didn't sound in control. "Bring your hands out, away from your sides, palms up."

As the hands slipped from the pouch pocket, his flashlight caught the metallic glint of silver-grey. Mike drew his weapon and aimed his light on the perp's hidden face.

"Place your hands on the back of your head." The perp placed his hands on the back of his head.

"Now turn around and kneel down." The perp turned, but did not kneel. Mike stepped away from the shield of his door, his flashlight crossed over his gun hand.

"Do *not* make any sudden moves. Kneel. *Now!*" The flashlight beam jittered across the perp's shoulders. Mike was aware he was driving it too hard, escalating the situation, but he couldn't stop. With each step his back went into spasm. The perp was shaking his head in refusal.

"Don't shoot me," he said.

"Get down on your knees!" Mike roared. In the house across the street, an upper-storey light came on. He could hear the faint whine of sirens. His jaw was clenching. He was breathing heavily and his neck was pulsing. The perp's calf muscle twitched. *Do not make me run, you little shit*. "ON YOUR KNEES!"

The perp bolted. Mike's finger stiffened on the trigger. He had a clean shot dead centre of the man's back. He could stop it here. *Fuck!* He took off running, his utility belt slapping against his hips. He panted into the walkie, "In foot pursuit. Suspect armed. Heading north on Maitland . . ."

The perp was running scared, deking left and right. Mike clomped heavily behind, each stride jolting his back. The perp sprinted across the street, lurched over the curb, and slipped on the grass. One white sneaker came off. Off balance, his head thrust forward, arms and legs windmilling, he regained his footing.

Mike was bearing down on him. The perp's hoodie had fallen back and he could see his scrawny neck. For twenty paces they were lockstep. He could hear his prey's frenzied breath and his own laboured grunts. Five more paces and he was closing ground. Ten more paces and he reached out, grabbed the hoodie, and yanked back, clothes-lining him to the ground. He flipped him face down and pinned his arms hard behind him.

The perp was gasping for air, sucking deep from his diaphragm. Mike ground his knee into his spine and snapped the cuffs around his thin wrists. The perp was smaller than he had thought. He wrenched him onto his side, twisting his wrists up towards his bony shoulders, and reached into the pouch pocket. He felt cold metal. *Son of a bitch.* He jammed the perp's head to the ground with his elbow and from the pocket extracted a metallic grey spray-paint can.

He looked at the face of the perp and saw a boy. The boy's cheeks were wet and he was huffing for breath; his lips and nose were plowed into the grass; blood smeared his front teeth. It was the kid in the park, his hands plugging a hole in his best friend's neck. Mike's stomach heaved. He pushed himself off the boy, grabbed him by the shoulders, and hoisted him to his feet.

"For Chrissakes, why did you run?" He brushed the dried grass from the front of the kid's sweatshirt. He followed the kid's furtive glance to the back of the school and the freshly painted mural of a gun-grey skull—its open bone jaw spilling musical notes. A misdemeanour. A mischief charge at most. He could have shot the kid. He had wanted to shoot the kid.

He fumbled for the keys to unlock the cuffs. He was already making excuses in his head. The boy's knobby knees were scuffed and grass-stained. One foot was bare. Sirens ricocheted around them. ETA one minute.

"Get out of here," he said. It was an apology. An offering. Absolution.

Antoine looked up at him with white-hot eyes. "Fuck you, pig." The boy staggered away and disappeared into the cover of the Square.

Mike hurled the paint can as far as he could. He couldn't stifle the whimper that doubled him over. He thought he might black out. Unfolding the accordion of his back, he limped to the curb.

Wade was first to arrive on scene with lights and sirens baying. Her cruiser fishtailed around the corner. Mike waved his flashlight, directing her south towards the city. Away from him.

48

Hassan followed the winding highway, skirting the Basin back to the city. His reaction time was impaired and his eyes had hypersensitized to the stark light of street lamps searing the night. He gripped the steering wheel tighter and overcompensated for the slight curve ahead. He drifted over the centre line and tugged back into his lane.

Soon there would be delivery trucks, street cleaners, buses, and cars shuttling bleary-eyed occupants with deep frowns and bucket-sized coffees. Kitchen lights were already on in a few houses. He stared at the yellow line slipping past his tires and jerked his eyes back to the road ahead. The waterside view flickered stuttering trees, bush, cheap motels, cheaper restaurants, power poles, railway tracks, guardrails, bush . . . a glimpse of ink-black water holding the city's shimmering light.

A domed roof emerged from the jagged cut-out of trees on the water's edge. He had always admired the Rotunda. It reminded him of Baghdad's shrines. It had been a music room built by a prince, perhaps for his mistress. It was all that remained of an estate that once contained gardens, grottoes, and pathways that spelled her name. The heart-shaped pond was still there, but her name had been erased by the bramble of a mere two hundred years. "Nothing lasts here," he said. He glanced down at the book. He knew she wasn't there. But sometimes he told her his stories anyway. It seemed less crazy than talking to himself.

Trees gave way to guardrail and for several miles he had an unobstructed view of the harbour's reflections and the second bridge's lights stringing the sky. The one they called the new bridge, though it was thirty years old. This land was so young it couldn't imagine its own death. Baghdad must have once believed that, too. Believed Muhammad's words that the scholar's ink would outweigh the blood of martyrs and the Golden Age of Islam would stand forever. They couldn't have imagined the House of Wisdom razed. Or the grandson of Genghis Khan riding his Mongol horses across the Tigris over a bridge of a hundred thousand drowned manuscripts inking the river black with dying words. "Nothing lasts forever," he said. He had read that somewhere, maybe on a bumper sticker. He half expected her to challenge him. It would be so easy to lose one's mind.

A cat streaked across the road. He hit the brakes too hard and the book plopped to the floor. His heart pumped from the startle of a near miss. He slowed to a crawl and strained to reach the book. His fingertips clawed it back up onto the passenger seat, as his eyes dipped below the steering wheel and the front wheel rumbled gravel. The cab fishtailed back to pavement. He wasn't safe to drive. He took a breath and eased up to the speed limit.

"Home," he ordered. *Bed*, his mind countered.

He turned the radio on loud, music that hurt his ears. A girl partying in the U.S.A. He didn't slow for the next curve. The wilted wisteria in the dash vase bobbed and swayed. As he accelerated out of the bend, his mind registered something on the road. Something moving. *Stop*, his mind said. *STOP!*

A man was in his lane. Shirtless and shoeless. He jammed on the brakes and the cab slid to a screeching halt, too late. He veered hard left and clipped the man. The man slammed over the hood against the windshield before slumping out of view. The radio's bass thumped-thumped against Hassan's chest. He shut it off, switched on his four-way flashers, and ran around the car despite his terror at what he might see.

A man, skisn and bones, was leaning against the fender. His left arm hung loose at his side and his breathing was laboured.

"Are you okay?"

The man looked up but didn't respond. Hassan looked for another vehicle on the road to tell him what to do. "I'll call an ambulance."

"No!" The man stood up with the lurch of someone who had traversed a desert. His eyes wild and lost. On his feet were only socks.

"Okay." Hassan raised his hands to show he meant no harm. "No ambulance." But he could see the man was in pain. "I can take you." He cautiously opened the passenger door. "I can drive you." The man sagged as though he might faint. Hassan reached to guide him in and the man staggered back.

"Please, sit." Hassan stepped aside to give him space. "Please." Unsteadily, the man lowered his lanky body into the front seat. The sour stench of fear and sweat overwhelmed the cab. Before Hassan could retrieve the book, it was in the man's hand. He held it gently on his lap. His dirt-caked fingers traced the letters of her name.

"Is this the ending?" the man asked. His voice was dust and sand.

Hassan took in the man's sallow cheeks and the dark circles and deep lines around his eyes. His blue-grey irises were almost lost in the black pools of his pupils. This is what madness looked like. The man's eyes met his. *So this is how it ends*, Hassan thought. *Al-Hamdu Lillah*. As Allah has willed; praise be to Allah.

The man stared at him intently and he realized he had said the words out loud. Behind them, tires hummed. The whir of rubber on asphalt oscillated to an unnatural pitch and a bus appeared around the curve. The man laid his hands, palms down, on the book and his arms stiffened. He looked sickly yellow in the cab's wan light. He was going to die in his cab. "Don't," Hassan said. "Don't."

He ran towards the bus. "Help!" he hollered, flagging it down. "Help!"

The off-duty bus roared past, blinding him in a vortex of dust. When he turned around, the man was gone. He wasn't on the road. He wasn't in the ditch. He looked to the heart-shaped pond's impenetrable pitch-black woods. The open passenger door chimed.

The book nowhere to be found.

49

"911. What is your emergency?"

4:36 a.m. Her colleagues' heads lifted expectantly. They were blaming the approaching storm for the rash of calls. Tamara checked her monitor. Mike's car was parked back in the same spot, but this time he was responding to checks. Maybe he was cooling down after losing his suspect, or catching up on paperwork.

"911. What is your emergency?"

She pressed her ear to the headset and heard a gurgle. Male or female, she didn't know.

"Can you hear me? If you hear me, can you tap the phone?"

The phone scraped something hard. Maybe wood. The floor.

"That's good," Tamara said. "Can you speak?"

A moan. Female. Tamara's fingers flew across the keyboard, searching for a phone number and location. "Can you hold the phone closer to your mouth?" She closed her eyes and listened. She could hear breathing now. Slow and shallow. Medical distress.

"Tell me where you are." She heard a swallow and the smack of dry, sticky lips.

"I thought I could do it," the voice murmured.

"What's your name?" She pulled up the phone's information. It was a cell phone with an unlisted number. "Tell me your name."

"Keira." Her voice was an ocean.

"I need you to tell me where you are, Keira."

The woman took a long, deep inhale. "I don't want you to come." The words exhaled slow and thick.

Her fingers flew over the keyboard, activating the location tracking program. "Are you in medical distress, Keira?"

"No." Weary and slurred. A younger woman's voice.

"Did you take something?" The computer searched for coordinates, bouncing radio signals from tower to tower calculating life or death.

"Yes," the voice breathed.

"What did you take?"

"Hmm . . ." She was drifting.

"Did you take pills?" The pauses between question and response were lengthening. "Keira." The name was sharp and brittle in her mouth. "I need you to answer." She rolled her chair closer to the console. "Tell me what you took." Her words were hard, non-negotiable.

The voice sighed, "Doesn't matter . . ."

A map zoomed up on her screen. Half a city block was lit up with three hundred metres of variance overlapping an apartment building and a dozen row houses.

"Keira, I need you to talk to me." She typed simultaneously. 10-30. Suicidal. Female. Suspected overdose.

"You have a nice voice," the woman said.

"Keira, tell me what you took."

"Everything," she said.

Over the cubicle, Colleen caught her eye. She was standing by for dispatch. Tamara shook her head. She didn't have the address yet. She glanced to car 322 flashing on the screen. Mike was within the zone.

"Are you in your home?"

". . . yes . . ."

"Is it a house?" Her voice was strong and unbending.

". . . yes . . ." The *s* was barely shaped.

She eliminated the apartment building from the map and softened her tone to sweet and caring. "What's your last name, Keira?"

The woman laughed softly. "I can't tell you that."

"Are the lights on in the house?"

". . . there's nothing to see . . ."

Her fingers paused over the keyboard, searching for the questions she hadn't yet asked.

The voice trembled, "Are you still there?"

"I'm here." She didn't have enough information. She couldn't narrow the search.

The voice balled up small and afraid. "I'm sorry, I don't want to be alone . . ."

"Keira, tell me where you are." She stared at the screen. Her words blinked back. *Highest priority.* Incomplete. Useless. She swung her chair around, turning her back to the monitors. As she spun, she glimpsed her supervisor. His eyes questioned if she could handle this. Again.

She shut her eyes and pressed her headphones tight to her ears, "Let me help you." There wasn't a sound clue in the background. She couldn't see in the dark.

"It's too late . . . he's gone."

"Who's gone? Was there someone there with you?"

The woman's breath faltered.

"Who lives with you, Keira?" She glimpsed her shape on the floor, cell phone in hand. "Who's gone?" Keep her talking. She had called them. She doesn't want to die.

"It all looks the same." The woman gagged down the words. "It shouldn't look the same."

"Who did you lose, Keira?" She counted the seconds between breaths. They could start knocking on doors. They *should* start knocking on doors.

"Keira, please talk to me."

She heard the words as soft as a heartbeat. "Hallelujah, by and by . . ."

She swung around in her chair. The highlighted block, the Square. She typed furiously. 10-18 urgent, 10-30/59 Sierra in progress. Drug overdose. She tapped the screen, zooming in tighter for the address. She said, "I'll fly away . . ."

"What did you say?" The voice crumbled.

She made her wait. Dispatch EMT. The house number and street address blazed across her screen. Colleen waved, confirming she had the logistics. Her neutral voice called the action: "Ten-thirty in progress. Female, drug overdose, conscious. Police en route, ETA one minute. Ambulance en route, ETA eight minutes. Fire en route, four minutes. Forced entry may be required."

Car 322 was on the move.

Tamara said, "I heard him play the piano." In her mind, she was walking up the stairs past the white rose bouquets, past the palm streak on the mirrored closet, the pink chair, two fans, smiling photographs, and up the stairs to the boy's bedroom and the woman lying on his floor in the dark with an empty pill bottle. Medically prescribed sleeping pills and antidepressants. Her arm outstretched. His name tattooed on her skin.

"I was there," Tamara said.

The woman's breath caught in her throat. One second, two seconds, three seconds—grief moaned from her lungs.

"I was with him." And they both knew what she meant. Car 322 slid across her screen. ETA thirty seconds.

"Stay with me, Keira." Her words were as soft as a final sustain.

"By and by . . . ," Devon's mother exhaled.

Tamara looked to the tinted glass wall reflecting nothing.

50

"Police! Open the door!"

Mike pounded again. A light was on upstairs. Other lights were turning on in houses next door and across the street. The Square was awash in red and blue. He kicked the hollow-core wood door and his boot broke through the shoddy material. Pain flared up his back. He kicked again and the frame splintered. One more kick and the door flung open. The paperwork to explain this entry would take hours.

"Police! Is anybody here?"

He followed the light up the narrow staircase. The house smelled of a home-cooked meal. He crashed up the stairs two at a time, tripping over the narrow treads. His walkie scraped the wall. The woman was in a child's bedroom, sprawled face down at the edge of the bed, nested on a pile of boy's clothing. Vomit puddled the floor. On the night table were two pill bottles, one empty, the other full. He squinted at the fine print. Codeine and sedatives. He searched for a pulse on her neck. The woman retched. The mattress smothered her nose and mouth. An ambulance screamed closer.

Mike gently cupped the woman's chin and lifted her head to clear her airway. A spew of vomit splashed his boots. In the deepest pages of his mind, he wrote down the name tattooed on her arm and marked three lines so he would never look there again. The boy's mother gripped his trousers and her body heaved.

He rubbed her back just like he had done so many times before to comfort his own children, wishing he could say something that wouldn't be a lie.

51

The police officer at the front desk made Hassan repeat his story twice, and then he waited in the lobby another half an hour before a different officer escorted him to an interview room. Her handshake felt like she wanted to be elsewhere. The windowless cement-block room was smaller than a cell. It was crammed with a narrow table and three mismatched chairs. The air was stale and the fluorescents flickered. It reminded him of Before.

He sat in the uncomfortable metal chair across from her and told her about hitting the man and gave a description. The officer took notes and watched his face closely. She sat very still. She seemed tired, perhaps even bored. She asked if he would describe the man as unstable. Yes, he said, yes, I would. She took his phone number, ID, and cab credentials, verified the location, and said a car would be sent to the area and hospitals would be contacted. Twice she asked him how to pronounce his name and then had him write it down. She thanked him for coming in to report the incident and gathered up her papers.

"There's more," he said.

Sighing, she settled back in the stiff wooden chair, but didn't pick up her pencil. He told her about the book and Her. His wife. The poet. He told her everything about then and there.

First, he said the little words that were easy to say and he tried not to rush. He tried to tell the whole story without blackened-out words. Sometimes the words of there and here tangled and he had to unknot them. He tried to name the long, open vowels of grief and the hard, sheared consonants of destruction. When his voice cracked, he leaned in closer and spoke all the true words he hadn't yet said. Across from him, her face unreadable, the police officer stared back.

He filled the room with his words. Some words had to be touched. Callused and scarred. Or gently lifted up to be seen. Words motionless and staring. Bruised words. Broken words. Hushed words that spoke her name. Words that seared and punished. Word that knelt. Words that begged forgiveness.

He breathed the words nuzzled between heartbeats. Soft and shy, cooing remembrances nearly forgotten. Words touching soft as lips and fingers entwining. Late-night words cuddled close. Firefly words. Sun words. Barefoot words. Ocean words larger than any life ever lived, salting tongues with promises of forever. Words of before that folded hearts inside out and said, Here, here, here. A poet's words. Her words. He rolled up his sleeves and lifted his shirt and showed the officer his scars. She didn't flinch. The words became invisible and their presence throbbed incandescent, until they dissolved seeping into pores, coursing through veins, tattooing dreams.

He never reached *The End*. There wasn't a resolve or release. There wasn't even a period. Simply an exhale.

The officer didn't take notes. Her eyes gave no indication that she had heard. Her stare was controlled and hard. She collected her papers and when she stood the chair legs scraped the floor.

"You're free to go, sir."

"I'm guilty," he said.

The police officer swallowed. "That's not for me to judge."

52

Zeus woofed and pawed at her ribs. Kate inhaled sun-dried sheets and morning glories, and stretched luxuriantly. She opened her eyes to blue-grey twilight, green chenille, and her childhood room. Had she dreamed herself old?

Nestled beside her, Zeus wagged *Good morning.* Ah, she thought, this is me. And her life rushed back in. Her neck was stiff from the sagging springs and her tongue was thick with sour. But she had slept, a deep, uninterrupted sleep, and she thought, *This is a good day.* Zeus was panting. "Okay," she said. "Out." And he leapt from the bed.

Her mother's house was quiet in the dim twilight. Padding barefoot down the hall, she glanced into Matthew's room, but didn't look beyond his abandoned sneakers. From the landing, she could see etched in the living room's bare floors the ghost trail of claw marks left behind by raucous, joyous dogs that had chased her around and around the house playing Find Me. She followed their scratches down the stairs, conjuring their names step by step. She could feel the brush of them against her legs. Zeus scrambled past her. His every wakening a wondrous new day.

Freed of angels, the living room looked larger. She moved from window to window opening the drapes. Night blue was giving way to sailors take warning. With the room cleared out, she could see the rich patina of the original wood trim and the exposed fieldstone hearth that hadn't been lit since she was a child. It was a strong, honest house that had been hiding for too long.

Zeus whined at the kitchen side door. She opened it to green and birdsong. The morning smelled of grass and honeysuckle. His head bopped into the screen door, which confused him and made her smile. The mesh was snagged and the bottom rail gnawed by puppy teeth. She pushed it open with her toes and he bolted outside. The step was missing and the earth was scuffed bare where her mother stood to hang laundry. Zeus huffed the ground for the best spot, then lifted his leg on a scraggly rose bush.

She put on the kettle and waited for the water to boil. The floor was cool beneath her feet. She filled a mug with instant coffee and powdered creamer. Matthew would return before the storm hit. Even birds and animals knew to seek shelter. She retrieved a box of macaroni and cheese and set it on the counter. She would prepare a pot and leave it on the stove. There was nothing more she could do right now.

She stared out the window above the sink at her mom's view of a hydrangea tree laden with fading pink blossoms. The base of its trunk was laced purple and white with delphiniums. Raspberry canes hung rich with swollen fruit. A faerie garden. Beautiful, she thought. Zeus barked.

She peered out but couldn't see him. He barked again. Loud and clear. The water gurgled a low boil. She shut off the stove and picked up his ball. She only hesitated a moment before stepping outside.

The grass was dewy. Night blooms perfumed the blueing sky, greening trees, and fading moon. The stars were gone and the highest crowns of heavy leaves were gilding gold. Zeus barrelled around the corner. His eyes were bright and his tail high. He swung around, waiting for her. Birds were exalting and crows complaining. "Remember this," she said. Zeus's head swung around, but the words were for her.

"Show me," she said.

Before rounding the back of the house, she softened her shoulders, made her muscles loose and her posture non-threatening. She stepped into the tall wildflowered grass certain that there had once been a path. Zeus raced ahead to the rotting woodpile at the edge of the property. He bowed and barked. Loud and sure.

"Good boy," she said.

He ran back, nudged her hand, and she tossed his ball towards the house. Orange and blue, it disappeared in the high grass. He pounced, flattening it in his jaws, and the ball squealed. His ears pricked forward and he dropped it. Plopping down, he gently picked it up again and squeezed out soft, joyous peeps.

Kate stepped around the woodpile. She saw his feet first. His stiff, tattered socks and bloodied heels. Matthew was sitting with his back to her, leaning into the stack of wood. He was shirtless and his left arm was loose at his side. One scapula was higher and dislocated slightly back and his jutting shoulder blades seemed plucked of wings. He was wheezing in and out.

"Hello, Matthew," she said in her softest, safest voice. The one she hoped he would remember. Clutched hard against his rib cage was a page torn from a book. In his other hand was a ragged strip of paper. His eyes darted across her and over to Zeus, back to her feet, up her legs, along her torso, before he found her eyes. Strewn around him were shredded pages. Keeping her distance, she crouched down and trained her eyes on the ground so as not to startle him.

"You're hurt," she said, making herself small and still. "Can I look at your arm?" She inched closer. "Are you having trouble breathing?"

She suspected a punctured lung or internal bleeding. His ribs were bruised and she wondered if someone had beaten him up. He tucked his lame limb closer. "Is that where it hurts?" She leaned in for a better look and he retreated, wincing. She pulled back.

"I won't come closer." Squatting, she rested her arms on her knees so he could see the calm of her hands. She looked at his tender, battered feet. "Can you get up?"

His hollowed chest rose and fell.

"There's a bad storm coming. You can't stay here, Matthew." He watched her mouth say his name. "You're hurt. We should go to the hospital."

He exhaled a ragged "No."

She looked at his starved, broken body and searched for her brother in his blue-grey eyes. "Please," she said.

"I found it, Katie." His pupils consumed his eyes. She looked at the scrap of paper in his trembling hand. It looked like Arabic. An ant wandered over his wrist.

"That's good," she said.

"I know how it ends." He was smiling at her. She thought it was a smile.

"Okay." She smiled back. "I won't worry, then."

She called Zeus. He bounded to her side and followed her to the jeep. He looked back twice to the place where they had left the person behind. She opened the tailgate.

"Up," she said.

Dropping his ball, he settled in the crate.

"Good boy." She pressed her forehead to his and kissed his brow. He looked at her with soft, searching eyes. She closed the hatch and rolled down the windows. When she returned to the house, she took care not to let the screen door slam.

She made her coffee and drank it down, bitter and lukewarm. She rinsed her cup, tidied the counter, and put away the macaroni. The kitchen looked cheery in the brightening light.

She slid back her T-shirt sleeve. Her shoulder was mottled purple and greenish yellow from ramming his door, and her forearms were thorned with scratches from the search. She picked at the scabs until they bled.

"911. What is your emergency?"

The words choked. Her knuckles rapped her welted cheek.

"911. What is your emergency?"

"My brother . . ." She pressed her hand to her chest to keep her heart from falling out. "My brother attacked me."

53

Mike one-finger-typed the last of his notes. His on-board computer was positioned high and too far right, twisting his back with each tap. Attempted suicide transferred to hospital custody 5:10 a.m. He double-checked the logbook splayed on his lap. Tonight had filled the last pages. He drew a hard, diagonal line through the entries. Soon it would be locked in the closet safe and that would be that.

Ten minutes to shift end. It was that odd time when the street lamps were on but the world had already emerged from night. He had returned to the street where so much had gone wrong and some had gone right. He wanted to see it again in the light. Across the harbour, the sun crested, burnishing the horizon gold. He considered retrieving his sunglasses, but they were in the glove compartment and he couldn't bend that far. On the bridge, vehicles with their headlights still on spanned the sky heading towards the city to start another day. Sun skimmed the Square's rooftops, glinting windows, burnishing bricks copper and treetops emerald. *Remember it this way*, he thought. The overhead street lamp shut off.

In the dry grass, he could make out Antoine's white sneaker. He wouldn't have to search far to find the paint can. "Suspect eluded capture. Identity unknown." That was his official report.

A dull knot wrenched his side. He looked down at the passenger's seat, at the full bottle of painkillers with her name on the label. He hadn't lied. He'd told the paramedics what drugs he had found and gave them the empty bottle. He got there in time, that's what mattered. His stomach churned. He closed his logbook and tucked it beside the seat.

Soon he would be home. Lori and the boys would be waiting for him at the window. When he had called, he told her he was taking sick leave and heard her breathe out. She said she thought that was a good idea and asked if he wanted eggs and bacon for breakfast. In the background, Connor cooed and Caleb sang I love yous. Lori said she would have a bath waiting, clean sheets, and today he was to do nothing but sleep. She had forgotten about the storm.

Caleb insisted on talking to him. He said Snappy had been bad and was in the corner, but *he'd* been good 'cause he didn't pee the bed last night, but Connor pooed his and Mommy said a bad word f—

Lori took the phone away and told Mike not to worry. She had put the garbage out last night. Just come home, she said. He was a lucky man.

He opened the window a crack and morning washed over him. It had been a hell night. He leaned back in his seat and curled his toes. He couldn't wait to get his tight boots off. He tried not to think about the nurse's brother's feet he'd seen at emerg. She had made another call. The officers on scene said it was bad. The guy put up a fight even though he could barely stand. It took three of them to strap him to the gurney, but once they got him in the ambulance he just gave up. They said the sister was beat up pretty bad. Bruised upper arm, bleeding from scratches on her forearms, and her cheek looked like she'd been punched. She was tough, they said. She let them do what had to be done. It was sad, they said. Real sad.

Mike didn't tell them he'd seen the mark on her cheek and the same bruise at the edge of her sleeve days ago, or that her scratched arms were scabbing over when she treated his son. He kept his head low, mouth shut, and got out of there. It wasn't his call. Sometimes it was best to look away.

"Car 322 to Dispatch."

The radio squelched. Dispatch.

"Car 322 signing off."

Copy that. Ten—four.

It wasn't Tamara. He wished it was. She would have wished him good days off. The sun was shining and the world was oh so beautiful. He tucked the pill bottle in his inside pocket. The bitter taste of just one more dissolving on his tongue. One more, so he could get out of the car and stand upright. One more, so he could twirl his hat for his sons. He started the engine and noticed a kid coming down the hill. It was Sean.

For a moment, he wondered if he was already dreaming. He had never seen him in daylight before. His head was down, huddled in his hoodie, and his long straggle of red bangs obscured his face. He had on khaki shorts and his thin white legs in red canvas sneakers made Mike smile. They reminded him of a cartoon, what was that rooster's name? Poor kid. He'd be okay, though. Mike would make sure of that. Second, third, and fourth chances. Whatever it took. Everybody made mistakes. The kid still hadn't looked up. He never learned. Mike wondered if he was really worth the effort. Of course he was.

Sean looked up and in the morning's rose glow he appeared even younger. He had freckles, a sunburned nose, and the soft curved cheeks of a child, but his tired ice-green eyes looked like a man's.

Mike was about to roll down the window and wave good morning, *We're good here*, when the kid raised his hand and glass exploded.

54

The intercom squawked, Gun trauma, ETA one minute. The trauma team was suited up. Police were already arriving. One officer, easily sixty pounds overweight, was sobbing, crumpled in the arms of another officer who could barely hold him up. Kate thought, *Get a grip.*

She was seated outside her brother's locked-down room. Her fogged mind cleared with the pulse of incoming. The nurses' station was brittle with preparation. Standing off to the side, the young security guard knew better than to interfere with the blue line clogging the trauma bay entrance.

A chair had been set up for Kate on the nurse's side, apart from the civilians. A gift of privacy for one of their own while she waited for the psych consult. Amy had apologized that it could take hours. There was an Attempted ahead of them. The woman's name was on the board next to Matthew's. *Keira* and *Matthew* apart from the others. She looked down at the towel rolled up against Matthew's door to filter out light and sound. It was meant to be calming, but served more as a warning to enter with caution.

Amy said Matthew was sedated and sleeping. She relayed this to the polished floor, because it was easier that way. It was the same reason Kate was asked to wait outside. Three cracked ribs and a dislocated shoulder, but he wouldn't let them set it. He didn't like to be touched, but she had already told them that. It was surprising how shiny the floor was. She had refused medical attention for herself. She was fine. Amy gave her a handful of antiseptic wipes to swab her arms, offered tea, and then did the most humane thing she could do. She, and the other nurses, pretended she wasn't there.

Sirens wailed closer. Kate stood, and the warm sheet draped around her shoulders slipped to the floor. She moved towards the bay, her body assuming the calm gait of an ER nurse. She was grateful for the rhythm of a trauma that she understood.

Dr. Savoy was team lead. He was rocking gently side to side. Rhonda was primary, with Amy, Jenn, and Donna rounding out the team. Her team. She tucked into the corner beside Trauma Room 1 away from the congestion and behind the action. The ambulance was in the bay. Outnumbering medical personnel, officers crowded in, craning to see. The nurses looked small penned in by their wide backs and towering shoulders. She wanted someone to tell them to back off.

Dr. Savoy said, "We need more space."

The wall of blue retreated and the bay doors swung open. The wounded officer was on his side on a blood-smeared gurney. The lead paramedic was holding the oxygen mask in place. Tethered to her, another EMT cradled the tank. A third held a fluid bag aloft while applying pressure to the wound, and a fourth wheeled them in. Their gloves and arms were red.

"Single gunshot wound, one entrance, left side under arm. Couldn't find the exit." Her words were brisk and her eyes sharp. "BP 156 over 109. One unit of blood on scene. Lung collapse."

Curled in a fetal position, the cop was writhing, gasping for air he couldn't get. It was bad.

The crying officer with the bloodshot eyes of a drinker tried to reach for him. "Mike, Mike, I'm here!" Two of his colleagues held him back.

Dr. Savoy asked, "Has his family been notified?" A car was en route.

The team moved as one towards the ER. Automatically, Kate swiped her ID card and the trauma room doors slid open. She pressed herself small against the wall to allow the EMT at the head to pass. Blood trailed on the floor. The gurney rolled by and the officer's fear-filled eyes met hers. It was the same cop, the one she didn't like. He grabbed her hand. Something jabbed her palm. He wouldn't let go. The paramedic at the rear swept towards her and she was dragged into the trauma room. Rhonda shot her a sharp look.

"I know him," but that was an unacceptable excuse. She tried to extricate her hand, but he was crushing her fingers and she had to squeeze back. "One, two, three—lift." She crouched to get out of their way and was caught in a web of snaking lines and monitor feeds. Paramedics' stained gloves pulled away and the fresh blue gloves of nurses laid hands. The doors opened and the on-call surgeon entered. Outside the trauma room, police officers, tight-jawed and rigid, glared back. The doors shut on them again. Stats were being relayed, IVs run, there was a call for two more units of O neg. A chest tube was readied.

Donna pushed on the man's back, trying to ascertain the path of the bullet. "Mike, can you feel this?" He thrashed. Jenn held his legs. "Mike you have to stay still." But he couldn't hear them. He was fighting the IVs. "Mike, we need to roll you over. One, two, three—"

They tipped him forward. He screamed. They couldn't find an exit wound and rolled him back. Monitors alarmed. His head tossed and Rhonda readjusted the mask he had shaken off. They considered restraints.

Kate leaned in closer. "Mike. Mike, listen to me." The cop's panicked eyes found hers. "You have to lie still. They're going to help you breathe. You have to help them." His body quieted and he gulped broken air.

"That's good," she said. "You're doing really good. Just look at me." She glanced up at Rhonda, who nodded okay. She could stay. Morphine was ordered. The surgeon slid his hand along the heaving ribs, probing for the incision point. The chest tube was standing by. Mike was trying to say something, but all that came were gasps.

"Don't talk," she said. His chest spasmed and his hand flashed open. In her palm was a pill bottle with a woman's name on it. Yellow pills. Codeine. He clamped her hand shut again. His eyes were pleading. He needed her to understand something. His eyes shifted to their hands and back to her eyes.

"He takes codeine," she said. The team paused. "I've seen him before. There's something wrong with his back."

Dr. Savoy came around to look his patient in the eyes. "Mike, can you hear me?"

But the cop's eyes were fixed on hers. She bowed her head, so he would have to look at the doctor.

"Mike, can you hear me?"

He nodded.

"Have you had any in the last two hours?"

He nodded again.

"How many?"

Mike sucked air. Spittle clogged the mask.

"One?"

He nodded.

"Two?"

He nodded again.

"Three?"

He held his head still. The effort trembled down his arm to Kate's crimped hand. His hand was huge and the nails clipped short. There was a scar on his knuckle.

"Cancel morphine. Local anaesthetic. Fifteen mils."

Kate looked up. "You did good, Mike. They're going to give you a needle. Just a little sting." She knew a local wouldn't be enough. Amy prepared the syringe. Jenn suctioned. Rhonda swabbed, sterilizing his side. His skin stained orange-brown. Mike whimpered as the needle was inserted into muscle. She thought, *That will bruise.* He pulled her closer. Nose to nose. The mask was fogged. "Tell Lori," he gasped. "Tell . . ."

"I will," she said. She had heard all the words before. The surgeon's fingers marked the spot between the ribs. The team looked to her and she braced her hand. Heart rate rising, BP dropping.

"It's just one bad day," she said. "Hold on." But his eyes weren't listening. "I remember your little boy." She searched for his name. "Caleb."

By the twitch of his hand she knew she was right. "He was so brave when he was here." The man's deep blue eyes held hers. Tears streaked his cheeks. She made her eyes calm to hide the pain he was about to feel. The surgeon made a small incision and inserted his finger to determine the tube's path. Mike flinched. "He told me his alligator's name was Snappy, right? He said it wasn't an alligator, it was a crocodile."

Outside the trauma room, voices skirmished. The doors opened and two more units of blood arrived. Skin was snipped and scissors inserted. The blades opened, tearing a wider entry. The man's wife tried to claw her way past the scrawny security guard. A scrum of officers shoved him aside and a spider of blue arms held her back. She screamed, "I love you! I love you! I love you!" And the doors shut again.

"Hang on," Kate said. His pupils were pinpoints in a constellation of blues. Her eyes promised-promised she wouldn't let go. His eyes begged, trusting her with his life. The tube pushed through skin and muscle between the ribs and into the chest wall. The man's face screamed ten on the pain scale. Her hand screamed eight. She dropped to both knees, pressing down on his wrist to ease his crushing grip. Blood flushed into the tube. Mike's eyes rolled back and his hand went limp.

Rhonda knocked against her. Spent needles and sterile packs rained to the floor. She staggered back, freeing herself from the flurry of arms and legs, and him. Mike's face was lost in the huddle.

He was naked. She couldn't remember his clothes being cut off. The floor was slick with blood. Tatters of his uniform were balled in the corner and his utility belt and holster were coiled on a surgical tray. There was an old bruise on his back, scrapes on his elbows and knees, and his heels were callused and cracked. He needed better boots. She had never stood in this spot before.

She wondered who was watching his boys and why he had the

pills of the woman in the room two doors down. She looked at the jutting tubes and wires barbing his body. It was going to be a long, hard recovery. Her throat flushed hot and she almost cried.

Get a grip.

The doors opened and a portable x-ray machine was rolled in. She emptied her eyes for the long walk back to her chair. His family would be searching for tells.

She dropped the pill bottle into the hazardous waste bag.

55

It was morning. Not a cloud in the sky. It was hard to believe a hurricane was coming. Tamara shut her eyes and breathed in dew, tinged with warming tar and asphalt. A bird warbled in the bushes. Traffic droned from the road below, and nearby a back-up signal beeped-beeped. She blinked away the overexposed world. She and the rest of the team had stayed beyond their shift, awaiting word.

Her feet were swollen and tight in her sandals. She cut across the parking lot to the strip of grass littered with cigarette butts and sat at the picnic table. Beyond the warehouse rooftops, tugs were guiding a cruise ship out of the harbour. Heading to a safer port ahead of the storm. Its wake rippled becalmed waters, rocking the sun. She picked at a flake of peeling red paint.

Long ago, someone had carved a line down the middle of the table and scored an *L* and *S* in the top board. *Lost* and *Saved*. Lines crooked and straight, thick and thin, light and heavy kept count. Some had the sharp edge of a penknife, others the shallow dent of a fingernail, the wobble of a stone, or the scratch of a quarter.

She picked up a small rock. A sharp, thin line appeared under *Lost*. She carved it deeper. The *Saved* section was crammed full. Soon the gouges would drop over the edge. A few had already been chiselled on the seat. She added her week's tally, making the notches small and close. She carved her last nick under *S* deeper to match the first. Mother and son. She trailed her fingertips over the pocked sheet music spanning between them. Mike's mark wasn't hers to make.

Sitting up straighter, she lifted her hands to the table's edge and played the random notes in her head, Tamara's Opus Under Blue Sky. She sped it up and slowed it down. She held the deep cuts, long and full. The softer ones, she barely brushed their slivered edges. She used both hands to draw out the deep chords, rolling them together in a tumbling wave, ebbing and flowing, building repeats, until it soared, flourishing highs and lows. It sounded like birdsong and sideways rain and laughter and hallelujahs and turning pages . . .

A steering belt squealed and a car pulled into the parking lot. She laid her palms flat against the warm heartwood. The cab followed the curb to the picnic table and kept the engine running. Tamara with Short Hair stood and straightened her dress. The sun shone on the nape of her neck. Hassan stepped out. He wasn't wearing his cardigan. He looked at her and smiled, just as she had imagined he would.

"Good morning, Tamara."

"Good morning, Hassan."

He walked around to the passenger side to open the door and waited for her to choose front or back. In the vase were freshly pulled dandelions. Her favourite flower.

"It's a beautiful day," she said.

"Yes," he said. "Another beautiful day."

The dashboard gleamed lemon-polished.

Navigating the labyrinth of streets, Kate scanned the taut, grey faces of caffeine-deprived drivers heading to work and wondered if her own face was as steeled with resignation. Go home, they had said. We'll take good care of him. It'll be easier, they said. They didn't say Matthew didn't want to see her, but it was understood. She should have gone straight home and washed away the lies, but she'd forgotten to lock up her mother's house. In truth, she wanted one more good sleep in her old bed before the storm. She wanted to wake and hear the sound of birds.

She looked at Zeus asleep in his crate. He hadn't barked when the police and paramedics took Matthew away. He had lain across her lap trying to quell her shaking and licked her hands, coaxing her to pat him. Poor boy. Later, she'd take him for a walk and let him wander wherever he wanted to sniff. She hoped he would forget.

She eased onto her mother's street and thought about the police officer who wouldn't be going home today. She had heard they left the bullet in. The lung would heal. The nurses all agreed it was a good day for him. There were thousands of people walking around with bullets lodged in their chests.

She geared down to second. Up ahead, a crowd was milling in the street, strobing in and out of the sun. She hoped it wasn't an accident, but sat up straighter, preparing to respond. Zeus stood. Slowing, she proceeded past the trash bins, discarded lawn chairs, broken toys, and garbage bags piled at the ends of driveways. Light flared and shimmered along the curb. She lowered her visor. Wing to wing, her mother's angels blazed in the morning light. She pulled over. The bruise over her heart throbbed.

A woman wearing fluffy blue slippers and pink sweatpants strolled by with an angel cradled under each arm. "Morning," she said. She looked Kate directly in the eye, confident that she had finders-keepers rights. At the curb, a small boy lifted an angel's dress to see what was underneath. Kate looked back at Zeus.

His tail wagged and his eyes said, *Play?*

"Later," she said.

She shifted into first and cautiously drove past a beer-bellied man sheepishly towing a child's wagon. His wife added another angel to a tottering pile and he shrugged an *if-it-makes-her-happy* grin. An older lady hid her loot behind her back and waved. Burlesque feathers fanned her ample hips. She could hear her mother's laughter. "Told you," she would have crowed. "Told you they were worth something!"

Two small girls in sundresses chased each other through the weave of wings. Their arms were flapping and the older girl was singing, "I'm flying higher!" And the little one sang back, "No, I'm flying higher!" And by the arch of her neck, Kate thought maybe she was.

Zeus pranced in his crate. *Play?*

"Soon," she said.

He pawed her seat and warbled his happiest sing-song groan.

She shut off her buzzing pager and said yes.

"Yes," she said.

Far out at sea, a hurricane was churning, and inside the eye, a thousand birds—terns and petrels, chimney swifts and tanagers, a dozen white-tailed tropic birds, five godwits, and one brown pelican—were circling the spinning wall calling each other's names.

Ahead of the blackening cloud, propelled by the tailwind's outermost shears, laughing gulls and frigate birds were hurling north shouting warning-warnings.

And flying south, following its ancient rightful path from the tundra to the mangrove mudflats, a lone whimbrel tucked its head, spread its wings, and flew headlong into the roar.

WORKS CITED

QUOTED WORKS ON PAGE 235

> But in the world according to Garp we are all terminal cases.\ You must go on, I can't go on, I'll go on. / "Like a dog!" he said; it was as if the shame of it must outlive him.\ It was a fine cry—loud and long—but it had no bottom and it had no top, just circles and circles of sorrow./ He never sleeps, the judge. He is dancing, dancing. He says that he will never die.\ That may be, Nora said, but it's all pretty unsatisfactory./ One bird said to Billy Pilgrim, "Poo-tee-weet?" | Yes, she thought, laying down her brush in extreme fatigue, I have had my vision.| Then there are more and more endings: the sixth, the 53rd, the 131st, the 9,435th ending, endings going faster and faster, more and more endings, faster and faster until this book is having 186,000 endings per second./ Yes, I said. Isn't it pretty to think so? \

Irving, John. *The World According to Garp*. New York: E.P. Dutton, 1978.

"But in the world according to Garp we are all terminal cases."

Beckett, Samuel. *The Unnamable*. Paris: Les Editions de Minuit, 1953.

"You must go on, I can't go on, I'll go on."

Kafka, Franz. *The Trial*. New York: Knopf, 1937. Translation Willa and Edwin Muir.

"Like a dog!" he said; it was as if the shame of it must outlive him."

Morrison, Toni. *Sula*. New York: Knopf, 1973.

"It was a fine cry—loud and long—but it had no bottom and it had no top, just circles and circles of sorrow."

McCarthy, Cormac. *Blood Meridian*. New York: Random House, Inc., 1985.

"He never sleeps, the judge. He is dancing, dancing. He says that he will never die./"

Hammett, Dashiell. *The Thin Man*. New York: Alfred A. Knopf, Inc., 1934.

"That may be, Nora said, but it's all pretty unsatisfactory."

Vonnegut, Kurt. *Slaughterhouse-Five*. New York: Random House, Inc., 1969.

"One bird said to Billy Pilgrim, 'Poo-tee-weet?'"

Woolf, Virginia. *To the Lighthouse*. London: Harcourt Inc., 1927.

"Yes, she thought, laying down her brush in extreme fatigue, I have had my vision."

Brautigan, Richard. *A Confederate General from Big Sur.* New York: Grove Press, 1965.

"Then there are more and more endings: the sixth, the 53rd, the 131st, the 9,435th ending, endings going faster and faster, more and more endings, faster and faster until this book is having 186,000 endings per second."

Hemingway, Ernest. *The Sun Also Rises*. New York: Scribner, 1926.

"Yes, I said. Isn't it pretty to think so?"

QUOTED WORKS ON PAGE 258

You must go on\ Yes, I said. \ the shame of it / —loud and long—/ the judge. He is dancing, dancing | But in the world \ That may be/ One bird said / I have had my vision / there are more and more endings

Beckett, Samuel. *The Unnamable*. Paris: Les Editions de Minuit, 1953.

"You must go on."

Hemingway, Ernest. *The Sun Also Rises*. New York: Scribner, 1926.

"Yes, I said."

Kafka, Franz. *The Trial.* New York: Knopf, 1937. Translation Willa and Edwin Muir.

"the shame of it"

Morrison, Toni. *Sula*. New York: Knopf, 1973.

"—loud and long—"

McCarthy, Cormac. *Blood Meridian.* New York: Random House, Inc., 1985.

"the judge. He is dancing, dancing"

Irving, John. *The World According to Garp*. New York: E.P. Dutton, 1978.

"But in the world"

Hammett, Dashiell. *The Thin Man.* New York: Alfred A. Knopf, Inc., 1934.

"That may be"

Vonnegut, Kurt. *Slaughterhouse-Five*. New York: Random House, Inc., 1969.

"One bird said"

Woolf, Virginia. *To the Lighthouse*. London: Harcourt Inc., 1927.

"I have had my vision"

Brautigan, Richard. *A Confederate General from Big Sur.* New York: Grove Press, 1965.

"there are more and more endings"

POEM ON PAGE 154-5

Anonymous. *Where Shall I Write Your Name?* Iraq: appeared in Al-Yanbou Literary Journal, date unknown, Translator unknown. Published as *Ayna Aktib Ismiki*.

MUSIC REFERENCES

"Happy Birthday to You," Patti and Mildred J. Hill, *Song Stories for the Kindergarten*, Clayton F. Summy Company, 1896.

"I'll Fly Away," Albert Brumley, *Wonderful Message*, Hartford Music, 1932.

"Party in the USA," Miley Cyrus, *The Time of Our Lives*, Hollywood Records, 2009.

"Piano Sonata No. 11 in A major; Turkish March," Wolfgang Amadeus Mozart, 1783.

"Piano Sonata No. 14 in C minor; Moonlight Sonata," Beethoven, 1801.

"Stayin' Alive," Bee Gees, *Saturday Night Fever*, RSO, 1977.

"Suite Bergamasque, L. 30 No. 3; Clair de Lune," Claude Debussy, 1905.

“Sunday Mornin’ Comin’ Down,” Kris Kristofferson, *Kristofferson*, Monument, 1970.

“Take My Hand, Precious Lord,” Rev. Thomas A. Dorsey, 1932. First recording Heavenly Gospel Singers, Bluebird, 1937.

“Touch Me Lord Jesus,” Lucie Campbell, (Margaret Alison and) The Angelic Gospel Singers, *Touch Me Lord Jesus/When My Saviour Calls Me Home*, Single 78-Gotham, 1949.

“Twinkle, Twinkle, Little Star,” Jane Taylor, *Rhymes for the Nursery,* D. Appleton & Co., 1849.

ACKNOWLEDGMENTS

My thanks to all those who guided me to find my characters, allowed me access to worlds that weren't mine, and challenged my perceptions. All errors are mine alone.

Those who walked me through their worlds: Halifax Regional Integrated Emergency Services (IES): Sandy Gillis, Mickey Zinck, John Webber, Linda, Wendy, Gillian Foran, Donna McNeil. Halifax Regional Police: Sergeant Publicover, Constable Don Jenkins, Constable Raylene Waye, Constable Tara Doiron. Emergency Room Nurses: Donna Haverstock, Jennifer Lightfoot, Jackie Atwood Cody. Halifax Regional Search and Rescue (SAR): Janet Cooper. Agility Trainer, Brenda Juskow. Pianist, Paul Benoit.

Those who helped in big and small ways. Joanne Matheson-Søvik, Sue Goyette and the Bears—Penelope, Kathleen, and Stephanie. Elvera Ross, Grant Curtis, Medric 'Cous' Cousineau and his therapy dog, Thai, Ashley Antle, Wendy Coffen, James Fraser, Stephens Gerard Malone, Joëlle Désy, James Nicholson, and Lori Forbes.

Those who held the early pages and asked the hard questions. Thank you for shining your light on the words and for your guidance, patience, and generosity. El Jones, Juanita Peters, Penelope Jackson,

Kathleen Martin, Taleb Abidali, Tony Elamyoony, Paul MacLeod, Barb Luxton, and Shauna Hatt.

Those who said yes and held me through the hurricanes and coaxed me towards more—my editor and touchstone Nicole Winstanley, editor Helen Smith, copy editor Shaun Oakey, editorial assistant Alanna McMullen, and all those behind the scenes at Penguin Canada, CookeMcDermid, Cooke International, and my agent and friend Suzanne Brandreth—you held my heart.

The Canada Council for the Arts and Arts Nova Scotia for the time to write when the page was still blank.

The Writers' Trust Woodcock Fund for giving me time when all seemed lost.

All those who wrote their stories on me.

And Annie dog who tried to teach me.